Praise for the
Home Repair Is Homicide
mysteries of
SARAH GRAVES

WRECK THE HALLS

"This book has it all. . . . Fun and gripping."
—*The San Diego Union-Tribune*

"[*Wreck the Halls*] entertains. . . . Graves's characters
are very human creations, warts and all, with Jake in
particular making fine company." —*Publishers Weekly*

**"What distinguishes the novel are its likable,
no-nonsense protagonist-narrator, her references to
home repair that the author cleverly fits tongue-and-
groove into the story and, especially, the detailed
descriptions of the town."** —*Los Angeles Times*

"Eloquently depicts the beauties and hardships of life on
an island in Maine . . . Filled with believable and engaging
characters, exquisite scenery and extravagant action."
—*News and Record,* Greensboro, NC

"One cool caper." —*MLB 2001 Gift Guide*

**"A witty, wicked and to-die-for winter read . . . a
holiday homicide that will make your yuletide season."**
—*Old Book Barn Gazette*

"The town of Eastport and its warmly wondrous
citizens continue to enchant!"
—*Booknews* from The Poisoned Pen

WRECK
THE
HALLS

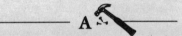

Home Repair Is Homicide
Mystery

SARAH GRAVES

BANTAM BOOKS

This edition contains the complete text
of the original hardcover edition.
NOT ONE WORD HAS BEEN OMITTED.

WRECK THE HALLS

A Bantam Book

PUBLISHING HISTORY

Bantam hardcover edition published December 2001
Bantam mass market edition / November 2002

ISBN: 0-553-58226-7

Published simultaneously in the United States and Canada

Bantam Books are published by Bantam Books, a division of Random
House, Inc. Its trademark, consisting of the words "Bantam Books" and
the portrayal of a rooster, is Registered in U.S. Patent and Trademark
Office and in other countries. Marca Registrada. Bantam Books,
1540 Broadway, New York, New York 10036.

PRINTED IN THE UNITED STATES OF AMERICA

OPM 10 9 8 7 6 5 4 3 2

For John Squibb

WRECK
THE
HALLS

Chapter 1

Blood was everywhere, so much of it that at first
Ellie and I didn't realize what it was or understand
what we'd walked into.

Before us lay Faye Anne Carmody's familiar Eastport
kitchen, the woodstove at one end faced by a bentwood
rocker and a small cushioned footstool, the table at the center with four painted wooden chairs pulled squarely up to it,
and at the other end the sink with a few clean glasses up-
ended on the drainboard. Tucked into one corner was a
white, ornately framed metal daybed with a heap of quilts
on it, a common item of furniture in an old Maine island
home.

A door led to the butcher shop that Faye Anne's husband, Merle Carmody, owned and operated in the ell of
the house. The door was secured with a slide bolt near the
doorknob and with two big hook and eyes screwed into the
door frame.

"Jake," Ellie said, nearly whispering it.

"I know." So *much* blood . . . "Go next door, Ellie, will
you? And call Bob Arnold and tell him—"

Bob was the police chief in Eastport, Maine, and the man

to call when you happened unexpectedly on a thing like this.

Whatever *this* was. "Faye Anne? Merle?"

No reply. The blood had begun to dry, darkening in sludgy droplets like paint. The smell of it hung in the air along with something else I did not yet want to identify.

It was just past nine on a Monday morning in early December. Ellie and I had knocked and walked in; in Eastport—three hours from Bangor and light-years from anywhere else—you locked your house up only if you went to Florida for the winter.

But now . . . "Tell Bob something bad has happened and we need him right away," I said, but by then she had gone; when something bad does happen, Ellie is generally on her way to take care of it long before I've even absorbed it.

So I was alone. "Faye Anne?" I said again, not expecting anyone to answer. A sad, drowning sensation of comprehension was beginning to replace the shock I'd felt when we first entered; Faye Anne was dead and her husband, Merle, must have killed her. Everyone always said he would and now it had happened.

Said it, I mean, the way people do say such things: shaking their heads. Sympathizing with Faye Anne. Wishing she would leave Merle, even making offers designed to save her pride while ending the chronic parade of black eyes, split lips, bruised arms, and other injuries that Faye Anne blamed, utterly unconvincingly, on her own clumsiness.

I myself had pressed the card of the local women's shelter, printed with the 800 number and their slogan, "Domestic Violence Is Everyone's Business," into her unwilling hand. But none of us had ever really expected to walk into a kitchen painted in her blood. No one ever does, I guess.

Faye Anne, I thought—damn it, I should have just gotten her out of there when I had the chance—Faye Anne was probably the only one who had really expected it.

Ellie's voice came from the hall. "He's coming. I called Bob from Kenty Dalrymple's."

Kenty lived next door to Merle and Faye Anne, and I had not much doubt that Kenty was on the phone right now, telling all and sundry of the excitement going on over at the Carmody house. If a pin dropped in Eastport, Kenty heard it.

And reported on it. But pretty soon the whole state of Maine would know what had gone on here; Kenty, whose own life offered little in the way of excitement, might as well have the ghoulish thrill.

Ellie came up behind me. "He says stay right here, don't do anything or touch anything," she said, and I heard the irony in her voice, mingled with grief over Faye Anne.

"You mean we're not supposed to barge in, put our hand-prints into all that . . . that . . ."

"Or make footprints," Ellie agreed. Bob sometimes tended to state the obvious. "Poor Faye Anne. We should have done more."

The smell was of meat cooking, mingled with the sour reek of scorched fabric. The last of the previous evening's fire still sulked in the woodstove and the room was warm. I opened the stove door; there was an old pot holder tied to the iron handle so it wouldn't have held fingerprints, any-way.

Not that I thought anyone would be checking for any. Inside: rags, partially burned. There was enough fabric left to see what they were stained with. Sickened, I turned away. Winter sunshine slanted mercilessly between the white eyelet lace panels Faye Anne had hung at the kitchen windows.

Or they'd been white when she hung them there. A few small clay pots of herbs stood on the windowsill; cuttings, I supposed, out of Faye Anne's herb collection, from her homemade greenhouse. The first time I'd seen it, I'd made fun of the slammed-together two-by-fours, bent nails, and flappingly overlapping plastic sheets that formed the slanting side. Not to her face, of course, but still . . .

Later I learned better; inside that slapdash structure Faye Anne had grown a paradise of exotic plant varieties, heirloom flowers, and antique pharmaceutical herbs. A shy, softly passive woman with moist brown eyes; pale, often bruised skin; and a breathy little voice that rarely rose above a tentative murmur, she'd been a self-taught expert in a kind of horticulture most people don't even know exists: the indoor growing of useful, not merely ornamental, botanical specimens.

What would happen to Faye Anne's collection of greenery now? With the thought and as a distant siren came from outside I realized how perilously close to weeping I was, and gritted my teeth.

"Jacobia," Ellie began steadyingly.

For our visit to Faye Anne's that morning Ellie had put on a bright purple turtleneck and an orange cardigan sweater she had knitted herself. And because Ellie's knitting is long on creative charm but short on the precise measurements needed to make hems end where they ought to, she was wearing it as a tunic. With it she had on magenta ribbed leggings, thick wool socks, and hiking boots tied with green-and-purple plaid laces; a yellow ribbon of some sparkly, gauzy stuff held back her red hair.

All of which should have made her look like an explosion at the thrift store's used-clothing bin, but Ellie is so tall and slender that she could wear the bin itself and look ready for a stroll down a fashion runway. Now her pale green eyes assessed me gravely through her new glasses, their lenses magnifying the tiny flecks of amber in her eye color.

"How are they?" I asked irrelevantly.

The glasses, I meant. Anything to stop looking at what was all over the walls and floor. To stop conjuring with such hideous precision, complete with sound effects, of where it had come from and how.

Ellie touched the frames, heavy tortoiseshell that set off her hair. Below them, the freckles across her nose were like a sprinkling of gold dust. "All right, I guess. I'm still getting used to them."

Ellie was so farsighted that she could spot the nostril in a sparrow's beak at two hundred yards, but without her glasses anything much nearer was just a blob to her. "What I want to know is, how are . . ."

You, she would have finished; Ellie had been my friend since nearly the moment I'd arrived in Eastport, four years earlier. But just then we heard it, through the howl of Bob Arnold's approaching squad-car siren: the sound, like a muffled half-sob, of a person waking in pain.

The heap of quilts on the daybed shifted and sat up.

It was Faye Anne Carmody. Frowning and blinking in the bright, warm sunlight of her own blood-splattered kitchen, she peered fretfully at us. Her eyes seemed to focus partway; an uncertain smile twitched her slackened mouth.

"Oh," she breathed, swaying a little.

Then the quilt fell, exposing the apron she wore, a bibbed canvas butcher's apron, and her hands encased in yellow rubber gloves. The front of the apron was entirely painted in red, the gloves' palms and fingertips clotted with rusty material.

She'd been burning the rags, I thought, in the woodstove. But before she could finish she'd collapsed onto the daybed. A gust of frigid air came in from the hall, the front door fell shut with a rifle-shot bang, and footsteps approached the kitchen.

"Didn't occur to you," Bob Arnold said admonishingly, "he might still be here? Lurkin' around in a drunken fug, one o' them big sharp cleavers o' his, still in his hand?"

Merle Carmody, he meant, because if anything had

happened to Faye Anne then Merle had done it. Bob knew it as well as anyone and better than most; Faye Anne wasn't the only local woman whose husband thought a smack in the head was the ultimate—or indeed the only—useful method of domestic communication.

Bob's face was pink with cold, his reddened hands rubbing together. He wore an open denim jacket over a plaid flannel shirt and blue jeans, the earflaps of his fleece-lined cap snapped over the top of his head; no native Eastporter ever buttoned a jacket or pulled a pair of earflaps down until the red on the thermometer sank convincingly below the zero mark and stayed there.

From where he stood behind us he couldn't see Faye Anne, and neither of us had yet really begun believing that we were seeing her, so we said nothing. And Faye Anne still seemed stunned.

So there was a moment of silence. Then:

"Holy moley," Bob said. The place looked like an abattoir. "That son of a bitch really went to town on her, didn't he?"

"Um, I don't think so," I said. Over in the corner, Faye Anne was still having trouble focusing. But she was getting there.

"Bob?" Ellie looked at me and I could see she was beginning to suspect the same thing I was: that our old buddy Merle wasn't lurking around here with a cleaver in his hand, in a drunken fug.

Or in any kind of fug whatsoever. Noticing again the door with its slide bolt and hooks and eyes fastened, imagining the butcher shop beyond with its cutting block, slicing machine, and rack of sharp knives arrayed by the cooler and the walk-in freezer, I had a sudden, very clear and detailed notion of exactly where that wife-beating bastard Merle Carmody was at that moment.

And may heaven forgive me but what I wanted to do was

stand there and cheer. But then it hit me, what that meant to Faye Anne.

If I was right. If . . .

"Well," Bob began, "I'd better secure this scene. State boys'll want in on this one, you can be sure, God forbid I don't set it up right. Poor girl has got to be here somewhere, too, I imagine, might as well get an ambulance, tell them they're going to have an awful job."

He sighed heavily. "And I can get on the horn, tell Timmy to grab Merle up from wherever he's prob'ly still lying drunk."

Tim Rutherford was Bob Arnold's second-in-command in the Eastport Police Department. Bob eyed the open stove door without comment, then said: "Neither one of you went in any further than right here? Or did more'n that?" He waved at the stove.

"No, Bob," Ellie said patiently. We both knew better than to try interrupting him when he was confronting a situation. It got him irritated, and he was already plenty irritated.

"You know," he went on, "there are people, I hate to say it, but there are people who if this happened to 'em, you wouldn't mind so much."

Over in the corner Faye Anne was peering around, a frown creasing her forehead. A bit of brown blood above her eyebrow flaked away; she blinked, tried brushing at it, then noticed with a look of intense puzzlement that she was wearing the gloves.

She hadn't yet looked down at the apron and suddenly I didn't want her to. I didn't want to ask her what had happened, comfort her, or find out for sure that she was—as she appeared to be—whole and unharmed.

Instead I wanted these dazed, muzzy moments of confusion to go on, for Faye Anne Carmody at any rate if not for the rest of us. Because it was clear that whatever had occurred here—fueled by the contents of a trio of empty wine bottles on the floor by the foot of that daybed, perhaps—she didn't remember it.

Yet. But she was going to. And when she did . . .

Quietly, I backed away from Ellie and Bob. Not thinking too clearly myself, maybe. Not reckoning the cost of my actions any more than Faye Anne had been, the night before.

No, I just wanted to know.

Winter in Eastport came early that year. Starlings massed in the treetops in August and frost clamped down on the gardens overnight in mid-September. Lawn mowers were stored away, the children's Hallowe'en costumes peeped from beneath heavy scarves and jackets, and we ate our Thanksgiving dinners to the wheep-and-jingle of the snowplows massively to-ing and fro-ing outside, pushing up white mountains and spraying fountains of brown sand so we would not be killed in collisions, going home.

Now I let myself out of the Carmody house into the picture-postcard brilliance of a Maine island winter. It had snowed three days earlier and the air felt crystalline, smelling of iced saltwater, fresh-cut pine, and the sweet smoke of parlor stoves cozily burning all over town.

In the side yard my boots creaked in the frozen white stuff, plowed and shoveled from streets and sidewalks but lying pristine everywhere else. It blanketed the roofs of two-hundred-year-old clapboard houses and surrounded brick chimneys, drew thick white lines on slats of green shutters and atop picket fences, capped red fire hydrants and clung like white moss to the north sides of the fir trees.

I let it all dazzle me, feeling cleansed by the whiteness and cold. A few blocks downhill—past Town Hall, the old grammar school, and the soaring white clock spire of the Congregational Church—the blue, unbelievably cold water of Passamaquoddy Bay showed glitteringly between the red-brick commercial buildings on Water Street.

An evergreen wreath with a fat red bow hung on the Carmodys' front door; two weeks till Christmas. I stood looking at it, taking deep breaths and thinking about how murder divides everything into *before* and *after*. Then I followed the shoveled path along the side of the house out to the shop Merle ran in the ell and found the key under the doormat.

Everyone in Eastport, if they bought their holiday hams or turkeys from Merle Carmody, knew about that key, because on most holidays Merle started drinking two days beforehand. So if you wanted a suckling pig—or your venison, which you'd shot in the autumn and Merle would have butchered and kept frozen for you, for a fee—you had to get into the shop and retrieve it without his help. And Faye Anne of course would be busy with holiday cooking, herself, since heaven forbid Merle shouldn't get a good dinner to wash down with his bourbon.

Thus Faye Anne had taken to leaving the key. The meat, wrapped in butcher paper, would have your name on it along with the price; you left your money in the cash box, made change if you needed to, and tucked the key back under the mat when you were finished.

The locked door being only a signal, in other words, that Merle was absent, not a way of preventing entry. I let myself in.

Everything was clean and as silent as death in the shop, the knives and cleavers gleaming in their racks and the air smelling faintly of Clorox. Nervously, I glanced around in case Merle really was lurking here somewhere, waiting wild-eyed with one of his butcher tools, ready to strike.

But I knew he wasn't. I took a slow step toward the walk-in freezer but stopped when I noticed something unusual in the glass-fronted display counter. After the shop closed each evening, Merle cleaned the display case thoroughly. Anything left over he ground into sausage meat, or if it was fish he chopped it into chowder pieces and sold it cheaply. You never saw anything left sitting in that display case overnight.

Except this time. I took another step. There were a dozen or so biggish packages wrapped in butcher paper in there now, each sealed with a strip of tape upon which ordinarily a price would have been marked in Merle's black grease pencil.

Not on these. From the case I removed the largest one and—holding my breath, my hands shaking—forced myself to open it.

Whereupon its contents, even only half-unwrapped because that was where I had to stop, told me what must be in the remaining ones:

Merle Carmody, there in his own butcher shop, resting in pieces.

Chapter 2

When I first came to Maine I was familiar with one kind of tool: the capitalist tool. At the time, I was a New York financial manager specializing in the blue-chip portfolios and slick tax-shelters of the fabulously wealthy. And at caretaking the fortunes of the fortunate I was the cat's silk pajamas: when they came to me with dot-coms they wanted to invest in I raised the gypsy hex sign, uttered imprecations, and shooed them into underwriting the dot-com companies' big initial public offerings, which was the real moneymaker.

But I was helpless in any other department. If I happened upon a TV program meant to explain how to repair a loose doorknob, I thought it was the Sci-Fi Channel. I owned a small screwdriver for prying the battery out of my cell phone; otherwise I went through life secure in the belief that if something got broken, somebody else would fix it.

The idea was reasonable for a person like me, with a neu-rosurgeon husband who couldn't change a lightbulb and an infant son, Sam, who obviously couldn't change one either, living in a luxury Manhattan co-op with a doorman, a porter, a housekeeper, and a maintenance specialist whose number was on my speed dialer. And it might have gone on being reasonable if over the course of the next dozen years my husband hadn't turned into a philanderer so promiscuous, the nurses at the hospital where he worked took to calling him Vlad the Impaler.

And if partly as a result I hadn't just chucked it all and moved to a Maine island. The house in Eastport was a white, 1823 Federal clapboard with three full floors, eight fireplaces, forty-eight heavy old double-hung windows with green wooden shutters, and a two-story ell that was dangerously close to tumbling into the cellar. I loved the house on sight, but I no more comprehended the demands of old-house maintenance than I understood chaos theory—which, by the way, I have since found that old-house fix-up work strongly resembles.

For instance, the first night I slept in the house I was awakened by pitter-pattering. Mice, I decided. I would buy mousetraps. But the next morning I discovered that the sound was of plaster crumbs raining down onto the sheets. The ceiling was collapsing.

Which was how I found out that plastering is a pain, but it isn't difficult. You just stand on a ladder, trowel in the patching compound, and sand the result until little drops of blood begin popping out of your forehead.

Or until the new plaster is smooth, whichever comes first.

Anyway, soon after Sam and I moved here (he was fourteen by then, in a period of his life involving rage, hormones, and a laundry list of illicit substances; also his father and I had divorced, in a period of my life involving rage, hormones, and a laundry list of expensive lawyers), I set up an account at Wadsworth's hardware store on Water Street in Eastport.

The owners of the store have assured me repeatedly that when they saw me coming they did not go out immediately and buy a boat. But they got a dinghy and I'm sure I'll see it any day now, trailing behind a yacht. The amount of stuff I bought just in that first week must have financed the teak deck chairs, none of which I'm going to be reclining in any time soon; four years later, I'm on the mailing list of every tool catalog printed in English, meanwhile struggling to maintain the land-locked equivalent of the *Titanic*.

Because the patter of falling ceiling pieces turned out to be a signal from the house: SOS! Just try imagining one of those many-armed Hindu goddesses, each graceful hand firmly grasping a hammer, a saw, or a forty-pound sack of plaster mix, and you will get an idea of what my life has become nowadays, pretty much on a daily basis.

Which brings me to what was waiting on my back porch that morning when I returned from discovering Merle Carmody's disassembled remains:

A package.

Well, as you can imagine, I was in no mood for a package. For me any pleasure I might feel about opening any packages whatsoever had gone *kaput* about forty-seven minutes earlier. This one, however, did not appear to contain body parts, bearing as it did the return address of one of those tool catalogs.

So after I got inside and scrubbed my hands twice, I did open it, and what I found in it instantly wiped all Merle Carmody's parceled-out anatomy portions from my consciousness.

It was a Fein "Multimaster" combination spot-sander, polisher, and cutter complete with sanding fingers (single- and double-sided), two scraper attachments (rigid and flexible), grit pads in every possible grade from gravel to diamond dust, and more sharp cutting accessories than Jack the Ripper.

I'd wanted one badly, since besides falling plaster my old

house came equipped with door frames, moldings, window trim, sashes, chimney pieces, balusters, bannisters, mantels, chair rails, pillars, posts, pilasters, and numerous other intricately hand-carved wooden geegaws, all thickly encrusted in old paint.

So after experimenting with a variety of chemical paint-stripping substances—I especially liked the one whose instructions listed a number of indoor applications, then warned me to USE ONLY OUTDOORS or to TURN OFF ALL POWER WHEN APPLYING because the stuff was EXPLOSIVE!—I'd ordered the Multimaster as an early Christmas present to myself. Now I began examining it, laying it with the box's other contents on the table in my big old barnlike kitchen.

Winter sunlight slanted in through the high, bare windows, making the maple wainscoting glow with the dark-orange leaf color it had captured over decades of Maine autumns. This winter I was planning to rehabilitate all those windows, a project that meant taking off the side trim and pulling out the sashes.

Thus I'd also purchased a hollow screw extractor, since taking off the side trim otherwise would mean prying it, which was guaranteed to break it. But with the hollow screw extractor you can core out a fastener—a nail, say, or a stubborn wood screw—along with the wood around it. Then you simply coat the hole with white glue, tap in the right-sized, similarly glue-coated wooden dowel, and voilà!

Or *viola,* as my son Sam insists on pronouncing it; he's dyslexic and has decided to believe that letter-transposition is hilarious. Also as used here the term *simply* is subject to interpretation; depending upon how deeply and inextricably I have gotten myself into a project, muffled shrieking might actually translate it rather nicely.

The last thing out of the box was a shavehook, which is a handle to which you can attach a variety of odd-shaped blades. I won't go into the whole hideous process of window repair, now; suffice it to say that even with new tools, by the time I finished I'd be looking around hopefully for a blade shaped like my wrists.

What with the price of heating oil, though, it was fix the windows or just start burning the furniture in the fireplace. And the tools did make me feel very cheerful and optimistic, as they always do right up until the moment when I begin using them.

As a test run I meant to redo the cellar steps with them; chilly as it was, the kitchen had a spare, New England-ish charm I didn't want to ruin. But I couldn't make the cellar steps look worse. Or the hall, now littered with packing material and the box the tools had come in.

While I dealt with that, my black Labrador, Monday, wandered in and began nosing the stuff unhappily; lately she'd been acting as if anything new in the house was worrisome. "Hey, what's the matter, girl?"

I bent to smooth her ears and she leaned against me, sighing gustily and letting her glossy head rest in my hands as if the weight of the world lay on her shoulders. "Poor baby. Sam's coming home."

Sam was due any minute, in fact, for winter break from his first year in college. Hearing this, Monday brightened and followed me back to the kitchen where to welcome him home I began fixing Sam's favorite meal: New England boiled dinner.

As I worked, I tried erasing Merle Carmody from my mind, though the sight of a whole head of cabbage was unhelpful in this regard. And as for the big, red chunk of brine-dripping corned beef, I would as soon not discuss it. But I'd gotten it simmering—slipping tidbits to a still-oddly subdued Monday while averting my eyes from the awful spectacle of a pile of beet peelings, trickling red—by around noon.

Which was when I heard my ex-husband's footsteps on the porch. This as an omen was like Typhoid Mary phoning to say she'd be stopping by for a cup of tea, only instead of a disease he usually brought junk he'd decided he wanted to get rid of, then dumped on me. Moments later he came in without even a courtesy knock, carrying an old blanket, a tea kettle (no spout), and some ancient venetian blinds.

Well, Monday could use the blanket. Quickly I put away the last piece of broccoli quiche, which I had taken out of the refrigerator for my own lunch. My ex-husband (his name, appropriately enough, is Victor) believes I am barely capable of constructing peanut-butter sandwiches, and anytime a culinary creation of mine suggests otherwise he wants to eat the evidence. Once he has done so he pretends it was never there in the first place, confirming his original impression.

This—confirming his original impressions, I mean—is Victor's design for living.

"What's all this I hear about you finding a body?" he demanded as he opened my refrigerator, located the quiche, and devoured it in a few bites. Next he looked hopefully around for coffee, apparently in the belief that his eager hand-rubbing was somehow attractive.

I filled the coffeemaker, since although I am perfectly capable of having (and winning) a knock-down, drag-out fight with Victor anytime you care to name, I like to pick my moments.

"Why were you visiting a murderess, anyway?" he wanted to know as he accepted a fresh cup minutes later.

I'd given him the short version, leaving out the inflammatory parts such as my decision to investigate the meat-counter contents. Victor likes to think he controls my behavior as if I were a sock puppet: anything he wouldn't do, I shouldn't, either. But when I got to the part about visiting the wife of a known wife beater, he went all huffy on me anyway.

"Why, that could be extremely unsafe, Jacobia. Don't you know that?"

He frowned, wagging an admonishing finger at me, and of course I did not chop the offending digit off with the shavehook. Back when he was married to me, worrying about my safety was not exactly a daily point on Victor's to-do list. But now that it had become absolutely no business of his, he was rabid about it.

"Not that I'd expect you to realize the danger," he continued. "You have to admit, Jacobia, that you don't always use very good judgment."

Which was a valid criticism. Proof positive: I'd married him. "First of all, the term *murderess* is *so* last century, Victor. Murder is getting to be a gender-neutral activity these days. Or hadn't you noticed?"

I edged back into the hallway where my tools were; handling them, knowing that I was able to use them, felt calming to me. "Anyway, what did you want?"

Crouching, I began scraping paint off the top cellar step, since keeping my hands busy stopped them from moving toward Victor's throat. Next I would sand the risers down to the bare wood, a tedious chore. But next spring that cellar would be damp again due to its nifty, nineteenth-century flood-preventing feature: French drains.

"Oh, nothing," Victor said unconvincingly.

Don't get me started on French drains, which are constantly open to let any possible flooding *out* of the cellar but are also effective at letting humidity back *in*, and have I mentioned that Eastport is on an island? So if I didn't sand now to get the damp-rotted wood right down to a new surface, the paint job I had planned would start peeling off like dime-store fingernail polish twenty minutes after I applied it.

"I don't see the point of your doing that yourself," Victor commented as I rubbed at the step. "Why not get a man?"

Nobly, I refrained from pointing out to him that there was a man sitting just about three feet from me, right that very minute. Instead I muttered something about him walking east until his hat floated, but he didn't hear me.

Actually, I enjoy painting. It's the prep work I can do without, but the house can't. Old Maine houses suck up prep work almost as fast as the other thing they most like consuming, which is money.

"We visited Faye Anne," I said—if I didn't talk, Victor was going to, which could lead to another murder—"because it's Christmastime."

"So?" He sipped coffee, giving me a view of his jawline; over the past few years it had been getting just the tiniest bit less taut. His dark, curly hair had a few threads of grey in it, too, and he wore glasses, peering owlishly through them with thick-lashed hazel eyes. He was, it occurred to me suddenly, nearly forty years old.

"So," I replied, buoyed by the surge of mean glee this realization produced, "people visit each other around this time. Eat cookies, sing carols, exchange little gifts. You know—holiday cheer."

"Oh." He looked puzzled. Victor's idea of holiday cheer is the French Riviera. But to be fair, his job as a neurosurgeon probably accounts for this; people's brain ailments occur with so little regard for the calendar that for years, the only way he knew it was Christmas was by the slices of processed turkey floating in yellow gravy in the hospital cafeteria.

Now he had abandoned his big-city medical career and followed me to Eastport, where he had started a trauma clinic. He claimed it was to be near Sam but I was sure what he really wanted was to drive me crazy, so crazy that in the end my own brain would become damaged and I would develop one of those ailments.

"There was another reason we visited Faye Anne," I added. "A few days ago, she told Ellie she thought someone was stalking her."

I hesitated saying this, not wanting to provoke more critical comment. Still, it troubled me: such an unlikely coincidence. And Victor, although I hated admitting it, could be perceptive; years of picking legitimate symptoms from masses of trivial, poorly organized complaints had made him uncannily sensitive to the alarm bells in people's stories.

And to the false notes. I dug the shavehook into a paint blob and was rewarded by the removal of half a dozen more old paint molecules. This wasn't working the way I'd hoped.

"Which was silly," I went on. "Who'd stalk Faye Anne? Especially here, where just about everyone knows where you are and what you're doing."

In Eastport the back-fence telegraph is so effective that if you cut your finger at one end of town, someone will get out the Band-Aids and Mercurochrome for you at the other. "I mean, why follow someone if you already know where they're going?"

No answer. I scraped some more. From his expression I half expected Victor to begin scolding again. But then as I'd hoped he clicked into diagnostic mode, instead.

"People don't usually think they're being stalked when they're not," he pronounced. "Unless it's a symptom of something. A paranoid delusion, maybe."

And there it was, the connection I'd been groping for, the thing that made Faye Anne's funny feeling of being watched and Merle's murder seem like parts of a single event. I was about to ask Victor if paranoia could get worse so suddenly that a person could become violent, possibly without warning, and attack someone. But before I could, something else I'd said reminded him of something about *him*.

"You know, Jacobia, there *was* something I meant to ask you. I want . . ."

Well, of course he did. When he doesn't want something it's time to put the paddles to his chest, give his heart a little electrical wake-up call. Because if his heart is beating, Victor wants something, and the person he wants it from almost always turns out to be me.

"What?" I put the scraper down. At this rate I would be finished with the cellar steps and ready to start on the kitchen windows in fifty years.

Victor started to ask whatever favor he'd come angling for; this, I saw now, was why he had paid his visit in the first place. But just then my actual, current husband came in: Wade Sorenson.

"Hey, Victor," Wade said genially, stomping snow from his boots. Tugging his wool cap off, he brushed a big hand over his wiry, blond hair. Only a faint darkening around his pale-grey eyes betrayed that Victor at that moment was about as welcome as a case of eczema.

But that was Wade: so decent, I wondered sometimes what planet the man had come from. Broad at the shoulder and narrow at the hip, he looked like a cross between a stunt pilot and a rocket scientist, with maybe a dash of rodeo cowboy thrown in for good measure: square jaw, leathered skin. Dropping his jacket, he drew me into his arms and kissed me thoroughly.

"Looks like whiskey, tastes like wine," he remarked appreciatively. Whereupon I tottered to a kitchen chair and sat; he has this effect on me.

"Heard you and Ellie ran into some trouble," he said, pulling a bottle of Sea Dog ale from the refrigerator. He'd been out for three days on a freighter that was having navigation problems off the coast of Nova Scotia. "In," he added, tipping the bottle up, "Merle's shop?"

As Eastport's harbor pilot, Wade guided big vessels in through the tricky tides, ledges, and currents of Passamaquoddy Bay. People in town swore Wade could dock a battleship in a child's wading pool. But his skill at troubleshooting the delicate equipment was becoming known, too, up and down the Maine coast.

"Yeah," I answered. "It was a mess."

More repair jobs spelled more paying work for Wade but they also meant he was away more nights. Now the clean smell of him—fresh air, lanolin hand balm for the cold weather, lime shaving soap—was making my knees weak.

Well, that and the kissing business. "They grabbed Faye Anne up?"

So the story was already spreading. "She's at the hospital," I said, "getting checked out. After that I guess they'll put her in a cell at the Machias courthouse while they get the lynching party together."

Not that anyone was likely to get lynched for killing Merle. But black humor was all I could muster at the memory of Faye Anne being led brokenly out of her kitchen. Mercifully, they had put a coat over her shoulders and shoes on her feet.

"I've never seen anybody look so scared in my life," I said.

"You all right?" Wade set his ale down and went to the cabinet where we kept the frequently used tools. His question about my welfare was seriously meant, but he wasn't going to make a big deal of it in front of Victor. Also, like most Eastport men Wade tended to focus first on problems he could do something about. And he hadn't missed my glance of despair at those cellar steps.

"I guess I'm okay," I said. "Compared to Merle, anyway." I got up and began washing my hands again, not quite knowing why.

Victor snorted as he peered past Wade into the crowded tool cabinet, jammed with items that were of no obvious immediate use: proof, to his mind, of my woefully deficient housekeeping habits. Never mind that if he'd quit dumping junk on me, they wouldn't have been so woeful.

Besides, in an old house you never know when the only thing standing between you and disaster will be a ten-pound mallet, a massive pipe wrench, and a roll of duct tape. And in a real emergency—one having anything to do with any hot-water radiators, for example—mostly you will want that duct tape.

"I told her," Victor piped up virtuously now. "I said she shouldn't socialize with people who get themselves into bad situations, and . . ."

Wade turned slowly and fixed Victor in his mild, pale-grey gaze, at which Victor's mouth snapped shut so fast, it was a wonder all his fillings didn't crack.

"You know, Victor, I think I hear your mother calling you," Wade said evenly. Because tolerating Victor was one thing—he was, after all, Sam's father—but putting up with his bushwa was entirely another, in Wade's opinion.

Victor thumped his coffee cup down on the table, from which I would pick it up later and wash it, and put it away. The first thing he did when he moved here to Eastport was hire a cleaning woman, and when he found out she didn't wear housedresses and aprons to work he went out and bought some for her.

"So long, then," he said, readying to vamoose.

"Wait a minute." I stopped him at the door.

Wade had already gotten out an electric sander and gone down to the cellar with it, bringing along an extension cord. "What did you want from me?" I asked Victor.

Because when it comes to knowing what it is that Victor's little heart pines for, later isn't better. Over the years I have found to my sorrow that if no one is helping it, tending it and encouraging it and just sort of generally paving its way, Victor's little heart goes after whatever it wants regardless, with disastrous results.

"Spill it, Victor."

In the cellar, the sander went on. I grabbed a dust mask

from the cabinet and tossed it down. If the paint dates from before 1978, it's lead-based, and this paint met the criteria by a century or so.

"Thanks," Wade's muffled voice came from the shadows at the bottom of the stairwell.

My ex-husband shifted uncomfortably. "Well. Actually, I was hoping you'd invite me over for dinner tonight. With a guest of mine. Joy Abrams."

The light dawned: news around town was that Victor had acquired a new girlfriend. And while this for Victor was like saying he habitually breathed oxygen—during our marriage he'd kept *two* little black books, one local and one long-distance—I hadn't known who she was.

Until now. "I see. Giving you trouble, is she? And you think that a dinner here might just possibly open her eyes to the pleasures of domestic life?"

Right; in his dreams. Joy was a buxom beauty whose wild youth was the stuff of local legend; lately she'd returned home to run a beauty parlor out of a mobile home in nearby Quoddy Village. That neighborhood was the closest thing Eastport had to anything like a suburb.

And Joy, whose lush curves made the Maine coastline look straight as a boardwalk, was the closest it had to a bombshell. With her gold ankle bracelet, complicated hairdo, and the fouled anchor prominently tattooed on her left shoulder, Joy was not the sweet, pliantly adoring type Victor usually went for.

"That was the idea," Victor admitted. "So, can I? Come for dinner?"

I didn't know Joy, but on her reputation alone I figured that when she got through with Victor there'd be nothing left of him but a little pile of bones and hair.

Which to tell you the truth I thought was not a half-bad idea; while I considered it, Wade returned from the cellar.

"If you hit them with the sander first—real coarse

sandpaper, not the fine stuff—you'll jolt the old paint up out of the cracks so it scrapes easier."

He came into the hall, saw Victor still there but didn't comment. "It's backwards, but it'll speed the job, you want to do it that way," he added. "Why not just pour a coat of chemical stripper on them?"

"Because the fumes have the charming habit of flowing downhill. Toward," I added, "the electric starter on the furnace. So, ka-boom."

"Right. Ka-boom," he repeated pleasantly to Victor, who seemed to feel opening the back door in some haste was a prudent move, all of a sudden.

Wade went on out to the parlor where, before his freighter job, he'd been finishing up his plans for decorating the harbor tugboat for tonight's winter holiday festival. During the event, tubby fishing vessels and barges would tootle around Passamaquoddy Bay, twinkling and hooting, their crews taking a break from the hard, dangerous work they'd be out doing again tomorrow morning.

"Fine, you can come," I told Victor. "Bring Joy, too, if you want."

I took no pleasure in his childlike faith that I wouldn't queer his pitch: by, for instance, telling Joy about the little black books. He was right, though; I wouldn't. After a divorce you think it's all going to be so clear and simple. But it isn't.

It just isn't. "Sam will be home, too."

"Oh," he said, wincing as the outdoor cold hit him. Despite the sunshine bouncing whitely from every snowy surface, the air was bone-frigid and the sky was the dangerous pale blue of thin ice.

In the yard, chickadees quarreled around the bird feeder. A single cardinal perched silently on a branch above, bright as a drop of blood. "Okay, thanks," Victor said.

And then he *did* vamoose, probably convinced that if I had time to think it over, I might change my mind.

But part of Joy's legend was that when she'd been away from here attending beautician school, she had supported herself with a strip club act featuring a live snake: perfect training, I thought, for any woman who dated Victor.

I wouldn't have missed meeting her for the world.

Besides, I hadn't told him whom else I'd invited.

The poor sap.

Chapter 3

H is *head*?" my son Sam repeated happily, his eyes shining.

It was five-thirty in the evening, a perfect night for Eastport's winter festival: the stars glittering like ice chips in the clear black sky, snowflakes condensing from the humidity rising from the harbor into the frigid air. Barrel-fires along the breakwater sent up orange flares around which people huddled, stomping booted feet and cupping paper containers of hot spiced cider in mittened hands.

"You," Sam said again, "found his . . ."

Sam's the kind of kid who likes the goriest parts of the scariest movies, which I'd always thought was strange because in real life he is the gentlest creature. So a few years earlier, I'd sat him down and asked him why.

Gravely he'd explained that he knew what he was supposed to be feeling, and was able to, at such spectacles. He was twelve, then, and his father and I had been fighting forever; the next day I'd gone out and hired an attorney.

"Sssh," I told him now. People were turning curiously. Everyone knew what had happened at Faye Anne's. But no one had approached to ask me for the details yet, and I hoped they wouldn't. "I'll tell you all about it at home."

"Okay, but . . ." For the festival, the storefronts on Water Street were garlanded in strings of colored bulbs. In the park behind the library, kids from the middle school were having a snowball skirmish, taking turns firing down on one another from the bandstand.

". . . but I want to hear *all* about it."

Four men in tailcoats and top hats strolled the sidewalk, singing "Silent Night." Which this wasn't: we were waiting for the boat parade but one of the vessels had blown her electrical system, and the crowd was getting restive. Running the bilge pump and lighting a Christmas tree at the same time hadn't been on the agenda, apparently, and now a deck seam was spurting.

At last a loud cheer went up as a thirty-foot wooden Eastporter, the classic little fishing boat so emblematic of Maine lobster, popped on bright as a flashbulb in the dark waters off the far end of the dock. Buddy Teachout had papered the abovedecks of his vessel in aluminum foil, tied a red ribbon around the operator's shack, and aimed floodlights at it.

"Wow," Sam said, looking handsome in his red quilted vest and a stocking cap. Taller than me, with dark hair and hazel eyes like his father, he was fit and muscular from scuba diving in Passamaquoddy Bay—when he wasn't at school he had a small business finding antique bottles underwater and selling them on eBay—and from working out in the college weight room. And he carried himself well; living away, I saw somewhat reluctantly—but with relief, too—had been good for him.

The rest of the boats lit up all at once, their colored lights spreading out on the waves like spilled paint. A sigh of pleasure went through the crowd as the parade left the dock in a rumble of diesel engines, each boat doing its jauntily nautical bit for Christmas tradition: there was a sled with eight lobsters pulling it, a Nativity scene with actors costumed to resemble sardines, and a Christmoose with buoys, mackerel jigs, and safety reflectors dangling from its antlers.

Sam looked around, scanning the gathering, probably hoping to see old high school buddies. "Hey, who're those guys?"

A pair of strangers in dark overcoats, polished wingtips, and fresh haircuts stood at the edge of the crowd by one of the bonfire barrels, now dying down. I spotted Ellie across the street; she'd seen them, too.

"Two of our dinner guests," I told Sam, more lightly than I felt. Out on the fish pier, an impromptu local band—fiddles, guitar, two accordions, and a banjo—swung into a rousing rendition of "Foggy Mountain Breakdown," which was not particularly Christmasy but got a lot of toes tapping on the breakwater, nonetheless.

So between the candy canes tossed to the children from the town fire truck, the raffle for the battery-operated tabletop tree that played one of half a dozen tinny-sounding Christmas carols when you pressed a button, and the small brown bottles whose contents vastly augmented the firepower of those hot cider drinks, it was another successful Eastport winter festival.

Finally the boat with the iffy bilge pump snapped its lights out and reversed course; the guys at the dock got the lines ready and a generator fired up, its gas engine roaring. This signaled the end of the festivities; the other boats puttered cheerily a bit longer, then came around, too, toward the finger piers inside the boat basin.

Leaving Sam, I made my way through a crowd headed eagerly for the Waco Diner, its neon Coors sign reflected in the thick tinsel garland around its windows. Ellie's cheeks were pink with cold and with the pleasure of the event; she'd been on the decorating committee, helped make the cider, and gone to school with many of the men who were out on the boats.

But her gaze was still following the two overcoats. They'd reached their car, a late-model GM product with official state plates.

"Ellie. Are you sure this is a good idea?" The car pulled slowly away from the curb in front of the Eastport Gallery, whose big gold-sprayed wreath of pomegranates and bay leaves gleamed under a garland of balsam tied with maroon ribbon.

It had been Ellie's idea to get the pomegranates and spray them. "I don't care if it's a good idea or not," she told me. "Faye Anne is my friend and I'm going to do whatever I need to do to help her. And I don't care what Victor has to say about it, either," she added firmly.

Which would be plenty, because the second thing Victor did on arriving in Eastport (after hiring the housekeeper and putting her in an apron, I mean) was to get involved in a fairly nasty case of murder, himself. Now just the sight of a pair of state guys was guaranteed to send his blood pressure rocketing and his rhetoric sputtering.

But Ellie had put her idea to Bob Arnold that morning before we'd even left the Carmody house, reminding him that with the festival going on tonight, the few eating places in town would be jammed. The next thing I knew it was decided: the state guys here to wrap up the paperwork on Merle's murder would be dining at my table.

It was, Ellie maintained, the only possible hospitable arrangement, her own house being under repair. The recent snowstorm had brought down an old fir tree and part of her kitchen with it. But I knew the real reason behind her plan, and it wasn't hospitality.

"I just want to know," she said now, "which tack they'll follow. Are they going to be reasonable, or not?"

Not, was my best take on the matter. Back in the city I had met a few law-enforcement investigators. People with money (i.e., my clients) drew them like flies. And none of those investigators had been looking to complicate his or her life with anything like reasonableness.

Not by a long shot. "Because look: there were wine bottles," Ellie insisted. "Someone drank that wine. But the dishes were all done. And maybe Faye Anne was not a complete teetotaller, but I can tell you right now she's never swigged wine out of a bottle in her life. *So who washed the glasses?*"

We walked uphill past the dime store, the Quoddy Crafts shop, and Bay Books with its window full of lusciously attractive new hardcovers, toward the police station recently relocated to the old red-brick Frontier Bank building, solid as a bunker with its massive grey granite window lintels and door frame.

"Then," she went on—obviously, she'd been thinking about this—"her canvas apron. Stuff soaks through those, you know. It's not as if they're made of rubber like the aprons they wear at the fish plant."

Just offshore, thousands and thousands of farm-raised salmon swam in underwater pens, eating nutritious meals upon which their pink flesh fattened marvelously. Later at the fish plant people made steaks and fillets of them; fish farming, along with lobstering, clamming, and the more traditional variety of open-water fishing, was a mainstay of the local economy.

"But that sweatshirt she had on underneath," Ellie continued, "looked absolutely clean."

She brushed snowflakes from her glasses with her mittens, green-and-white ones knitted in the traditional downeast Maine fox-and-geese pattern. Working at lightspeed Ellie can toss off a pair in an evening—somehow with these she seems to have no trouble knowing when to stop—but when I try, I always end up with that other traditional pattern: snarls and tangles.

"And what's up with that locked door?" Ellie added decisively.

The one between Faye Anne's kitchen and Merle's butcher shop, she meant. "Right. It bothered me, too," I admitted.

Because if Faye Anne had locked it, why hadn't she also taken the key from beneath the doormat and locked the front door? We reached Peavey Library, its reading-lamps amber behind the tall leaded-glass panes set into its red-brick facade. A framed placard inside the front door instructed All Gentlemen to Remove Hats.

"But my biggest question is," Ellie said as we turned the corner, "who cleaned the tools? Not just the wineglasses, but—"

"Right," I whispered, pausing by Millie Hildreth's snow-covered formal perennial garden, where stalks of her purple "Autumn Joy" sedum poked up through the humped drifts. "Ellie, look."

Just ahead, a fox poked its pointed nose from between the little white clapboard houses set cheek by jowl along the lower portion of Key Street. Spotting us, he veered off, his defiant cry half domestic dog's bark, half rusty hinge screeching.

Eastport is a real city, with sidewalks and streetlights. But it is also located on an island perched at the windswept, granite-cliffed edge of the back of beyond. The fox vanished into the snowy darkness.

"The blood on the gloves was dry," I told Ellie, glancing over my shoulder as I paused to catch my breath. Across the bay, house lights on the Canadian island of Campobello twinkled whitely: half a mile, an international boundary, and a time zone away.

"Flaking, not all smeary as if they'd been in water," I added, continuing uphill. "I doubt you could wash anything, wearing them, and have them look that way afterwards."

"And if she did it with the gloves off," Ellie agreed, "why put them on again? There must've been a lot of washing up to do, too. You saw the things in the shop."

The cutting tools, she meant, because it would have taken more than that one knife we'd seen falling from the daybed, to do the job. Such work had to take serious blades, I thought, heavy and sharp; not the usual kind you simply pulled from the nearest kitchen drawer. Yet Merle's butchering implements had all been spotlessly clean.

I thought of what Victor had said: If you believe you are being stalked there is probably a reason. Not necessarily a *reasonable* reason.

"Ellie, once you've done a thing like that, who knows what you'll be thinking or doing afterwards? Maybe she changed clothes, wore three aprons, and guzzled out of those bottles like a sailor on shore leave. We don't know what happened in that house. Maybe she'd meant to finish cleaning up, and passed out before she could."

"I don't think so," Ellie maintained stubbornly. "But . . ."

"What?"

"Her whole plant collection," Ellie said. "Jake, we have *got* to try to keep that quiet. Or at least tone it down some, if those state guys are good and pick up on it at all."

I gazed longingly at the crest of the hill. Key Street ascended the last slope of the island before the water's edge, so steep it got your heart racing even in summer; in the winter you practically needed Sherpas. My chest was heaving and my breath came in quick, visible puffs.

"That's the other reason I want a look at these state guys," she said, her own breathing unhurried and her step effortless. I swear, the woman was like a mountain goat. "See how smart they are."

"Ellie," I managed at the top, leaning forward to rest my

hands on my knees. My house was in sight, its windows warmly aglow and its chimneys dark cutouts against the stars. I had a mental flash of what it must have looked like decades earlier, illuminated by firelight and gas lamps; in those days a one-horse open sleigh was an ordinary winter vehicle, the late-nineteenth-century equivalent of four-wheel drive.

Which was exactly what I needed, if the wheels were attached to a nice, warm ambulance. My heart valves were hammering and my lungs felt like someone was pushing screwdrivers into them.

"I don't see (gasp) how a collection of exotic plants (gasp) can influence a (gasp) case against her, one way (gasp) or another."

Gasp. "You don't, huh?" We climbed the porch steps. Above, a thick, sparkling row of widow-maker icicles dangled from the frozen gutter; the attic was going to need even more insulation before winter was over, I thought, adding the reinforcement of this to my already lengthy hurry-up-and-fix-it list.

"Let me ask you, then," Ellie persisted. "What if she was accused of killing him with a shotgun, and *besides* that, she had a collection of knives, crossbows, and those little blow-guns they use in tropical places, to shoot poisoned darts?"

"Oh. I get it." Inside, the standard thermostat setting of sixty-three—because the rich *do* get richer, but not on *my* back, thanks—felt like a heat wave from one of those tropical climes, after the cold outside. Steam from the simmering New England boiled dinner dripped on the inside panes of the windows, increasing the rain-forest atmosphere in the house while also encouraging quick peeling of all its wall-paper.

Wallpaper glue, I thought; a seam roller, and a new razor knife. I used to have an available short-term memory but now all I have is a mental hardware-store list.

"A lot of the plants she grows are pharmaceuticals," Ellie told me. "And medicine's just poison in little doses, you know, no matter whether it comes from a pharmacy or out of somebody's greenhouse." She pulled her mittens, hat, scarf, and fleece-lined jacket off. "Faye Anne doesn't need anyone thinking that if she hadn't killed him *this* way, she had *other* methods all ready to use."

"You've got a point," I admitted, a shiver hitting me abruptly as I stood washing my hands at the sink.

An icy draft strong enough to fly a kite on was coming in at the windows despite the caulk I'd stuffed in around them, and the floor felt like Arctic tundra. Suddenly the obvious hit me: those window sashes I'd been planning to pull out and repair, even inefficient and leaky as they were now, weren't coming off until spring.

Not unless I wanted the kitchen floor to develop permafrost. Plastic sheeting, I thought sadly, to cover the windows in hopes of insulating them better until May. Or June. And more duct tape.

"I want to know if they're going to figure it out," Ellie said, putting on a pot of coffee. "I mean that there's lots more ammunition for a case against her, in that greenhouse."

I laid a fire in the dining-room fireplace and stole woolen socks from Sam's clean laundry in the basket by the washer. "But Ellie," I objected when I could feel my toes again. "Wouldn't an obscure poison have been a *better* method?"

Monday padded in morosely and sank into her dog bed by the radiator without even bothering to turn in circles. "You poor thing," I said, patting her, then went on:

"Why kill someone *that* way—messy, ugly, labor-intensive—when you've got a substance? Possibly an *undetectable* substance?" For all I knew, Faye Anne could have been growing obscure neurological toxins in that little greenhouse.

"I agree." Ellie got the good plates out from the butler's pantry and began setting the table. "But I know what *they'll* say if they find out she had plants she might've used to kill him: that she snapped. She planned it one way, but push came to shove so it happened another."

I reached past her for the paper sack of tomatoes on the pantry floor. People say you can't grow tomatoes in Eastport but what they mean is, you can't ripen them outdoors because frost gets them first. Back in September I'd picked green tomatoes as big and hard as baseballs, and piled them into grocery bags from the IGA to sit in the darkness of the butler's pantry.

Now they were red. "Then why get dressed up for it?" I asked. "The apron and the gloves. If you *didn't* plan it . . ."

"Right. That's the thing. You don't put on a protective costume for something you do on the spur of the moment. On the other hand if you really have planned it, you don't take off the protective costume until you've finished, do you? So none of it makes sense. Meanwhile . . ."

She counted on her fingers: "Digitalis. Jerusalem cherry. Castor bean. Aconitum and false parsley. To name but a few."

"Wow." Even I knew that stuff was poison. They'd have done the trick, all right, alone or in concert, especially if the victim was so drunk he might not even feel the symptoms, so he wouldn't call for medical help. "And Merle drank so much, if he'd been found dead in his bed one morning no one would've even wondered about it."

"Uh-huh," she said. "But these guys who'll be feeding facts to a prosecutor: will they see it that way?"

"Hmm. Probably not." Because Ellie was right: having a variety of weapons to choose from rarely tended to exonerate a person. To the contrary, actually. I put the corned beef on a platter and began surrounding it with vegetables—

cabbage, parsnips, and beets—and set it all in the oven to keep warm.

"You're right, Faye Anne's in it up to her neck," I went on. "But Ellie, we still don't have to . . ."

Ellie put condiments on a tray. "Get involved? Of course not. But let me tell you a little story about Faye Anne."

Creamed horseradish, spiced grape, and homemade cranberry chutney, all in little cut-glass dishes with silver spoons in them. "Remember my mother's funeral?" she asked.

"Yes," I ventured, unsure how sensitive Ellie still was on the topic; her mother had not been the most beloved woman in town. People came to the service, all right, partly because they adored Ellie, but mostly to assure themselves that rumors of the older woman's demise weren't exaggerated. In the little chapel, you could almost hear them humming her funeral march: *ding-dong, the witch is dead.*

"Well . . ." Ellie began. But just then Sam burst in and with him was Tommy Pockets, an Eastport boy who had been Sam's best chum practically forever, so of course I had to invite Tommy to stay for supper.

Next Wade arrived, having prevented the boat with the bad bilge pump from sinking in the boat basin, and headed upstairs for a shower. Ellie's husband, George Valentine, came in wincing stalwartly; he'd smashed his thumb doing something or another while working out at the town's generator the evening before, but George's upper lip is so stiff that you could use it to open clams so I wasn't sure how badly he was really injured.

And the two state guys showed up, looking shocked with the cold and even more freshly barbered than they had from a distance.

And more like bad news. I'm not going to name them, here; possibly they are perfectly nice men with wives and children, under other circumstances. But even though I put drinks in their hands right away so they wouldn't feel so awkward, strangers among us, both still kept glancing around as if they thought we Eastport folk might set the dogs on them.

They didn't know that the only dog available for the purpose was in the coat closet, shivering. Which was also worrisome; Monday ordinarily seems to think it is her job to wriggle and slobber over every single person who enters the house, even if the person is wearing a burglar's mask and carrying a swag bag. Now a glum thump came from the closet as she settled; I made another mental note to take her to the vet in the morning.

Finally, when the state guys were on their second drink, Victor arrived with *two* women in tow: one on his arm and another clumping along behind like a dragging anchor.

"This," he began nervously, "is . . ."

But I knew: Joy Abrams was a big, gorgeous woman who looked capable of crunching Victor up in her strong white teeth. She had dark violet eyes fringed by thick false eyelashes, hair the color of a sun-bleached apricot, beautifully curled and elaborately piled atop her head, and smooth hands with almond-shaped nails manicured to perfection.

"Hello." Warmth and street smarts mingled in her smile; I liked her at once.

Standing behind her was a grim little imp of a woman with short white-blond hair, a pug nose, and nails nibbled to the quicks of her small, childish fingertips. She looked like a thirteen-year-old pressed unwillingly into joining the adults' party.

"This is my sister Willetta," Joy added, her tone changing to one of apology over the unexpected extra dinner guest.

"H'lo," Willetta mumbled, sticking a small hand out. She was actually twenty or so, I thought, and Joy a few years older, though her hair and makeup made her look more mature.

Victor set a rusty pair of pliers, a near-empty roll of packing tape, and a handful of bent nails on the hall shelf where I suppose he thought I might not notice them right away.

"Come along," he intoned. "Drinks in the dining room."

Despite his air of command he appeared terrified, like a kid with a new toy he is sure all the others will try to take from him. Even Tommy Pockets, the boy most likely to be voted a dead ringer for Howdy Doody, earned a glare when he said hello to Joy, his voice cracking and his big ears reddening. Tommy was a fine young man, a friend through thick and thin to Sam; unfortunately, though, his ears stuck straight out from his head like teacup handles.

"Sorry they've sprung me on you," Willetta told me diffidently. Her costume of blue chambray shirt, black jeans, and white canvas sneakers contrasted sharply with Joy's glamorous getup: low, white lace peasant blouse, long velvet skirt, soft suede slippers. "Victor insisted."

Somehow I didn't think so. And despite her appearance, Willetta was not a child: she could have refused. But never mind; at this point I had so many guests in the house, it wouldn't have mattered if the Rose Bowl Parade had filed in behind her, seeking refreshments.

Besides, the more, the merrier: What with trying to make a party out of folks who had no more in common than the contents of a box marked "nuts & bolts assorted," at least I would be spared further talk of murder and mayhem, for a couple of hours.

Or so I believed.

Eastport, Maine (pop. 2000) is not only the easternmost city in the United States; it is also the smallest. But this was not always true:

In the 1800s, its port rivaled New York City's in annual shipping tonnage. Eastport boasted hotels, saloons and theatres, a hospital, two newspapers, furniture and millinery shops, public stables, grocery and dry goods emporia, and every service and supply that was required by a prosperous coastal center of commerce and manufacture.

The manufacture being mostly shipbuilding: in those days, great wooden sailing vessels slid down the ways from every inlet and cove on the island. Even now, the notion that for a lad of good family the road to manhood lies over a tilting wooden deck on a cold, rolling sea, under a good, stiff set of wind-filled canvas sheets, is within living memory.

But as the sailing ships faded inexorably from service to be replaced by steam, their owners and builders turned their black-coated backs on the huge, ornate houses they had erected on the elm-canopied streets, decamping en masse with their wives and children to guard the capital they had created, preferably in warmer climates.

Still Eastport thrived, bolstered by Prohibition—for a while, Canadian whiskey and the molasses to make it were both liquid gold if you happened to have a boat and a little gumption—and enough good fat codfish to match the miraculous loaves a thousand times. But then came the fishing collapse.

It was bad enough that the herring got fished out, or if you accept the other tale, just decided to go elsewhere in the collective belief that those big, air-breathing creatures upstairs were bad for their health. Worse, suddenly enormous factory boats were vacuuming cod by the metric ton out from under the smaller vessels, processing and freezing them aboard, too, faster than even a species that produces its offspring by spawning could match.

When the fish were gone, the factory boats departed, leaving behind wreckage which consisted principally of the absence of codfish. That was twenty years ago and today the fishing industry is regulated by the same geniuses who couldn't (or wouldn't; this being the commonest theory, in Maine) prevent it from being ruined in the first place.

And I mention this here because it is a part of the reason why:

(a) in Eastport, money is so scarce that as a motive for murder, love has actually managed to replace it in almost all cases, and

(b) with few exceptions any government representative not born and bred right here in Eastport is in danger of receiving a welcome about as warm and penetrable as dry ice.

Both of which facts lurked at the back of my mind that evening as I served a corned beef dinner with baking-powder biscuits, a fresh endive salad with butler's-pantry tomatoes, and a white pear wine from the local winery, Bartlett's, to a group including two thoroughly non-Eastport-born-nor-bred government representatives.

Although on account of their manner I was having trouble believing they were born at all. From the cold-fish attitude they'd both exhibited since they got here, I'd just about come to the conclusion that they'd been spawned, like those cod. But suddenly the pear wine kicked in as I'd been praying it would, and things took a turn for the better.

Sort of. "So," Cold Fish Number One said with a smile that looked as if he'd practiced it that morning in a mirror, not very skillfully. "Tell us about Merle Carmody."

Big, blond, and blockily built, with squarish blue eyes like two miniature ice cubes set in his chunky face, he was an investigator for the Maine State District Attorney's office. His lip curling with distaste, he'd already described his drive here from Augusta; through Ellsworth and Dennysville, Cherryfield and Pembroke, past the little houses with their nonstandard windows, jutting stovepipes, and massive woodpiles. I'd done the drive myself, many times:

Out on the porches of those houses in winter would be hung the day's laundry, frozen-stiff sheets, towels, and underwear on a sagging line strung upwind, if possible, from those stovepipes. Two cars—one up on blocks, one still operable, plus maybe a pickup truck—would be in the driveways. And in the side yards would be parked one or more brand-new snowmobiles, blue-tarp-tented.

It wasn't the only kind of house he'd have passed on his way here, but it was the kind he'd have noticed. And I could just hear Mr. Cold Fish thinking what he wasn't quite saying: that people with nonstandard windows and bent stovepipes didn't deserve new snowmobiles. As if someday on their deathbeds, after a life of hard work, regular church-going, and good citizenship, people should be saying: Well, I might not have had much fun but I sure did balance the living hell out of that checkbook, didn't I?

So I didn't like him. But I tried not to show this. "Merle wasn't a nice man," I began slowly. I didn't want to say anything ill-considered or get anywhere near the topic of Faye Anne's own character, either. The object of the evening was to learn if there was a chance of getting Faye Anne off the hook.

Manslaughter, say, instead of murder. And although Merle Carmody had been a brute who couldn't find a civilized thought with both hands and a road map, from there it was only a hop, skip, and a jump to the fact that Faye Anne had married him, hadn't she, so what did that make *her*?

Someone who could be made to look bad in front of a jury, that's what. A person who had, as Victor would probably say, bad judgment. It was the first dark color a prosecutor could use to start painting a damning portrait.

Of, as Victor would say, a murderess.

"That doesn't mean he deserved it," said Cold Fish Number Two. "Getting"—he cut a chunk of corned beef—"dismembered."

I take it back about those wives and children: spawners, definitely. This one was the primary investigator's assistant and compared to his boss he was Fish On Ice: dark, wavy hair, pitted skin, and very dark eyes without any discernable pupil, like a shark's.

I poured more wine, tried gathering my thoughts before replying. But before I could complete this ambitious—some say hopeless—task, a voice from the end of the table spoke up:

"Truth is, anybody here would've been right tickled to wrap old Merle Carmody's head up in butcher paper. Difference is, we'd of stuck it on a pike, first, set it outside of Town Hall for a week or three, let the seagulls fight over it."

It was this sort of pronouncement—swift, accurate, and bloody-minded in the good-old-fashioned, scram-if-you-don't-like-it downeast Maine way—that made me proud to have married the man who was sitting there making it. Wade had proposed six months earlier, but we'd gotten around to tying the knot (or, as he so nautically put it, lowering the boom) only the previous week.

Still, it wasn't the way I wanted the table-talk heading. "This old house," I began, trying to change the subject, "was built in 1823, the very same year that the poem 'Twas the Night Before Christmas' first appeared in a small-town newspaper in upstate New York."

"Isn't that fascinating?" Ellie commented brightly, catching my drift.

But too late: George had interrupted his stolid chewing to agree with Wade. "Fella was bad business. Faye Anne used to come down where I was working, back when we were putting the furnace in the medical clinic. Beg me to steal them butterfly bandages from the storeroom down cellar. The ones they use to close cuts, instead of stitches."

"Because she couldn't afford to get medical care?" This, I could see, fit right in with the DA man's idea of local household economics: all those snowmobiles.

George had dark hair and the pale, milky complexion

that runs in some downeast Maine families, and a bluish five o'clock shadow on his small, stubborn jaw. His knuckles were permanently grease-stained; in Eastport, George was the man you called if you couldn't get hold of that duct tape fast enough.

Now he looked patiently at his questioner. "No. She was ashamed. Old man hit her, she didn't want folks to know about it. So I got the bandages for her."

Then he returned to eating his dinner, while the DA's fellows pondered what they'd heard. "So somebody might say she was justified? Even that it was self-defense, or could have been?" the assistant asked.

"Absolutely," I began enthusiastically, trying again to get the conversation back on track. But this time, Sam interrupted.

"That's not what she's saying. She's saying she didn't do it. Or doesn't remember it. Anyway, what happened to presumed innocent?"

I shot him a glance. We wanted them to feel sorry for Faye Anne, not angry at what they might perceive as deceptiveness, or defiance; not only the facts but the tone these guys presented them in would be important. But the damage was done:

"She is, isn't she?" Cold Fish Number One said complacently. "First statement was that she couldn't imagine where all the blood had come from."

"And she did have a boyfriend," Gill-Boy Number Two put in. "This guy she was seeing," he added with a glance at his colleague, "Peter Christie."

He spoke as if women possessing boyfriends also had the number "666" tattooed in hidden places on their bodies. Or at least that juries could be brought around to believing that they did. Peter Christie was just about the last person I'd have wanted these two to run into.

But: "Wait a minute," Sam protested. "Peter isn't a

boyfriend. Not what *you* mean by a boyfriend. Besides, Faye Anne is—"

Married, he'd been about to say, stopping only when he realized that was the point in the first place: marrying a bum like Merle was blameworthy enough, in some eyes. But *cheating* on a bum . . .

Well, that was a hanging offense, or it could be if you presented it to that jury properly. Because when you came right down to it, this was all about perceptions. And about winning and losing.

Mostly the latter. "Peter Christie is a computer repair guy," Sam said, trying to end what he'd started and becoming indignant in the process. "He's not hooking up with any married women. Why should he? He's from *California.*" Which to my son was like being the Dalai Lama, but with *sun!* And *fun!*

"Sam," I said, and at my tone the temperature in the room dropped ten degrees. A boyfriend was bad; a promiscuous one could be even more damaging. But as they explained over coffee and baked apples with maple syrup and cream, our guests already knew all about Peter Christie.

A recent Silicon Valley transplant who'd moved here to Eastport and set up, just as Sam had said, in computer repair—as a sideline he also fixed copiers, fax machines, and mobile phones—Peter hadn't waited for the DA's men to find him and ask their questions. Instead I gathered that he'd sought them out and insisted on spilling his guts, incriminating Faye Anne more than ever, so as to clear himself of any possible suspicion.

Not, of course, that Peter had put it quite that way. But due to his forthcomingness the DA's men now knew things we might have preferred that Peter had kept under his hat.

Such as, for instance, that Faye Anne didn't believe in divorce. And that despite Sam's opinion, Peter had been in love with her, or so he'd maintained; that he had begged her to leave Merle and marry him. But she'd refused, and in the end he'd told her that they would have to stop seeing each other. With Merle in the picture, Peter said he'd told Faye Anne, further contact between them would only go on hurting them both.

"So," Ellie summed up unhappily. "The way Peter tells it, the only way she could be with him would be if Merle were to leave. Or die."

Sam shot a contrite glance at me. But, I realized now, it didn't matter; the government guys had known all that Sam or any of the rest of us might've clued them to, and more. Not that picking up personal facts was all they had accomplished:

They'd already taken photographs, bagged up the apron and gloves Faye Anne had been wearing, and sent Merle's remains down to the medical examiner in Augusta. They'd talked to the neighbors and taken all the cutting tools out of Merle's shop, too, they indicated, and they would go over Faye Anne's house one last time in the morning.

And that would be that. "Wrapping it up" was a perfect phrase for their day's activity; not information, but confirmation, was all these two wanted.

Of the obvious: that she had done it. "What a guy," George said, meaning Peter Christie. "Real bail-out artist."

My thought exactly. What I didn't know was how come these fellows were telling us all this? It didn't seem usual, so I asked them about it.

"It's not, I suppose. But it's no big secret, either. Christie's not bound to keep quiet about anything he told us. And *if* it came to trial, the defense attorneys get it all anyway. We have to tell what we've got," the DA's primary investigator said.

"But you think there *won't* be a trial because of . . ."

He gestured with his dessert spoon. "The battered-woman aspect. Juries don't like chronic abusers, and everyone in the county knew the victim was one, just from what we've heard already. So she's probably going to get offered some kind of a deal."

"She'll plead to a lesser charge and accept a sentence, no matter what she says now," his second-in-command declared, scraping up the last morsel of baked apple.

But Ellie was shaking her head: *no, she won't.* And these two guys worked well together, but to my ears that last comment had sounded rehearsed; I decided we were being played.

Then Joy Abrams spoke up unexpectedly. "Peter Christie might not exactly be the right one to believe, where Faye Anne Carmody is concerned."

"Joy," Victor said, "are you sure you want to discuss this? It's really not the sort of thing . . ."

Victor liked his women to confine their conversation to suitable topics: cooking, sewing, flower arranging. The evening wasn't going as he'd planned, either, although the government men had given no sign of recognizing his name—contrary to his belief, people the world over didn't spend *all* their time thinking about *him*—so he'd relaxed a little.

Joy touched his hand lightly, silencing him. Under other circumstances this alone would have been worth the whole evening; silencing Victor ordinarily requires a brickbat.

"Peter's a stone liar," she said. "And a flatterer, sort of a . . . a serial romancer, but with a twist. He likes women, all right. Just not in a nice way."

She swallowed some wine. "Don't ask me how I know. I'm not going to tell you. It was told to me in confidence. But I will say, if Faye Anne turned Peter down she's smarter than I thought. He's trouble. You be careful of what *he* says, is all." Then, to me:

"Dear . . ." *Dee-yah:* the downeast Maine pronunciation.

"I just can't thank you enough for the truly wonderful dinner." *Dinnah*.

Victor's little pinch-purse mouth kept opening and closing as Joy went on: "I keep telling him he was a fool to lose you, Jacobia." She laid the accent firmly and properly on the second syllable; I do so enjoy people who know the difference between a woman's name and the seventeenth-century English historical period.

Although strictly speaking it is a man's: James, in Latin, though my mother wouldn't have realized. She spent her girlhood in a Kentucky hill town, never learned much history except maybe for Russian history. But that was later and another story.

Joy looked around at the dining room's tiled hearth-apron behind which glowed a fire of cedar logs, at the red candles nested in balsam in the table's centerpiece, at the old brocade curtains gleaming richly before the windows. Mistletoe hung on the door to the butler's pantry, and she smiled a little at that.

"Everything's lovely. I just adore boiled dinner and nobody makes it, anymore. Baked apples, too. And real cream, wasn't it? You whipped it for us from scratch?"

By then I'd have told her that the moon was made of green cheese, if she'd wanted me to. Because the thing about Joy, I was starting to think, was that she was *real*. Not faking anything; genuinely herself. It was that more than anything else that made her so beautiful, I thought.

Willetta got up as if linked to Joy by an invisible cord. "Thank you," she said colorlessly, and followed her sister.

Accompanying them to the hall, I glanced into the front parlor where Monday was circling the best chair nervously, her ears flat and the hairs on her neck-ruff prickling defensively. Seeing me emboldened her to put a paw up onto it— Monday is allowed on any furniture that will hold her, except for the guest beds—but at the last minute she lost courage again and turned tail, whining.

"Oh, Monday," I said sadly, and she skulked out to the kitchen as if embarrassed by her own cowardice.

Meanwhile George had retreated to the back parlor for football on TV, carrying a cup of ice to soak his sore thumb in. Tomorrow he would get plenty of cold on it; scalloping season had opened and with the church pipes thawed, the generator repaired, and the materials for his own house repairs undelivered, he was going out on one of the boats.

George worked, Ellie said, the way other people breathed; now the rest of the men got up to join him, hungry for scores.

"Joy," I began slowly while Victor was in the hall retrieving their coats; it was none of my business. But I already liked her a great deal.

"Don't," I heard Victor say distinctly to Willetta from down the hall, "be such a baby."

"Victor has a way of making you feel . . ." I hesitated.

"Special," she finished my sentence accurately. Her cologne was L'Air du Temps. "Like you're the one, after all the others, that he's been looking for."

"Exactly," I said. "And I don't want to be the one who . . ."

"Puts a hitch in his git-along?" Her laugh made me like her more.

"Yes," I admitted, "exactly that."

She patted my arm. "Don't worry, dear. I've been paddling my own canoe for a good while, now."

I'd been right about her age, I saw; much younger than her hair and elaborate makeup made her appear. But her eyes were intelligent and there was a kind of seasoned hardness in them, so I believed her when she went on:

"It's going to take lots more than Victor Tiptree to capsize me." She glanced down the hall. "Listen, about those state guys—"

"What about them?"

Joy looked uncomfortable. "A friend of mine was having a few drinks in Duddy's Bar out on Route 214 last night. You know the place halfway to Meddybemps?"

I knew. Duddy's was a dive; thick smoke, loud music, a pool table full of cigarette burns in the back room. A place for people who were banned from other bars; bikers, hookers, and drug dealers: oxycontin, methamphetamines.

Thinking of it reminded me that my view of downeast Maine was a privileged one: that of a person safe inside a warm house after a good dinner. But not everyone around here was so lucky and the unluckiest salved their wounds with booze or pills.

I also knew that Victor had been tied up in surgery the night before, working on a logger who'd been hit with a whole tree over at the lumber mill's debarking machine, on the mainland.

So Joy had been on her own. "Your, um, friend," I prodded gently. "What's she got to do with those state guys?"

"She saw them there. Both of them. Stuck out like sore thumbs, even though they weren't wearing suits at the time."

I could imagine. The dress code at Duddy's ran to jeans so greasy you couldn't see what color they were, boots that looked as if they'd been used to stomp rival gang members, and T-shirts bearing slogans so foul, you wouldn't clean the bathroom with them. People said it wasn't a matter of *if* Duddy's would get raided, but *when*.

"I don't think," Joy added carefully, "they saw her."

"Wait a minute," Ellie said, coming up behind us. "We didn't find Merle till this morning. And it's six hours to get here from Augusta. I did think they made it pretty fast. But what were those two doing around here *last* night?"

"Who?" Victor wanted to know, appearing with the

coats. Willetta came along with him, sulkily. I had a flash of just what a burr under his saddle she must be, grumpy and seemingly ever-present.

"No one you know, dear," Joy told him sweetly. "Why don't you go out and get the car started, warm it up a little?"

"All right," he agreed, and went.

"What kind of drugs are you feeding *him*?" I asked. "The change is miraculous."

"We'll see," Joy responded, which was when I knew she understood what I'd been saying earlier: that Victor in the first, fine flush of infatuation was one thing. Long term, though, he was something else.

"Anyway, they're sure not telling you everything," she finished, meaning the state guys. "Better watch out for them."

Which I'd already figured out, too. Still: last *night*?

". . . *incredible* stuff people are selling," Sam was saying to Tommy. "You can buy the right to perform a hit song in public, or a snow globe with Charles Manson's face glowing inside, or cancer drugs."

On the Internet, he meant, from which I gathered that his semester-break independent study project was moving along okay. Entitled "Weird or Wired? E-commerce in the 21st Century," it was an examination of exactly what he was saying to Tommy: the stuff people bought and sold on-line. Only secondarily and perhaps subconsciously was it a joke on his own dyslexia. I wasn't even sure he'd noticed the ana-gram—yet.

Then in a final flurry of thanks and farewells, Joy and Victor were gone, along with Willetta. The investigators left soon after, proffering chilly handshakes. So I was free for postdinner analysis in the kitchen with Ellie.

"How can they be done already?" she complained. "Aren't they going to dust for fingerprints, or look for hair samples, or . . ."

"Why should they? It's not like on TV, where every crime scene gets gone over with tweezers and a microscope. They've already got a suspect, so it's a matter of resources. And of confidence, which they've got, too."

"I guess so," she conceded reluctantly. "But . . ."

"And 'no trial,' my aunt Fanny," I said, drying a relish dish. "Expert testimony gets bought and paid for like anything else, along with the expenses of the expert: travel, lodging, and anything else they can think of, to fatten the expense sheet. You get it if you can pay for it, and you don't if you can't. And Faye Anne isn't going to be able to afford anything remotely like that, and I'm sure they know it."

And nothing else, I felt sure, would induce the offer of a deal. "They just thought if they told us a lot of stuff that didn't matter," I said, "or that probably wasn't so; like that business of her maybe pleading to lesser charges, we might say something that *did* matter. Make her look worse, and make their lives even easier than they already are."

"It's true. I don't think they start out by offering deals to people who chop people up and put the pieces in a butcher shop counter," Ellie agreed disconsolately. "Besides, I know her. She'll never say she did it if she didn't."

I'd been thinking more that Faye Anne didn't remember. But:

"Never, ever," Ellie finished, soaping a coffee cup. "So what did you think of Joy Abrams? To look at her now, you'd never know she was the same girl who left Eastport. Her hair is so fancy, you can't even see where it's connected to her head."

"I thought," I began, meaning to say that this time Victor's reach might possibly have exceeded his greedy little grasp. But I never got the chance to finish:

Outside, holiday carolers were fa-la-la-ing from the back of a pickup truck, up and down Eastport streets. The season was in high gear, though by the sound of it the pickup was struggling mightily to get out of low. A series of loud back-fires exploded in the night like a string of cherry bombs.

"Mom." Sam put his head around the corner. "Sorry about my big mouth in the dining room."

"That's okay," I said. Outside, the truck backfired again. "No harm, no foul." But then I focused on him; back in the city he'd been in a little trouble, but now he was healthy. Clear-eyed and energetic.

And he had good friends, here. Tommy was upstairs waiting for him; I gathered they were going to be a team on the Internet project. "Hey. I'm glad you're home."

"Me, too. Anything in the fridge?" Without waiting for an answer he bounded past me to forage for nutrition; it had, after all, been half an hour since we'd finished dinner.

Then: "Mom, do you think Tommy should have his ears fixed?"

I turned in surprise. "Is he thinking about it?"

Sam shrugged. "Sort of. He says they're freaky looking, and there's a clinic in Bangor that sent out some sort of bulk-mail brochure, gave him the idea."

I'd seen the brochure, too, tossed it out without reading it. "I think Tommy's ears are fine," I said, only crossing my fingers a little bit. Tommy worked the fish pens for an hourly wage and few benefits, and was helping to support his mother. "I'm sure your father would be happy to talk to him about it, if he wanted. But that surgery is expensive."

Sam grinned. "Yeah. I hope he doesn't do it. I told him they make him lots easier to find in a crowd."

Which I wasn't sure was quite the variety of reassurance Tommy had wanted, but before I could say so Sam had taken his supplies—sodas, a box of cookies, apples, and a bag of potato chips—back upstairs to share with his friend.

When he was gone, Ellie got out two of Wade's bottles of ale and sank into a kitchen chair. "I let her down, Jake. I should never have let Faye Anne stay with Merle. I should have gotten her out of there."

"So should we all have. But it's too late to do anything about it, now."

Ellie is ordinarily a sweet, kind person, but every so often she gives me a look that would etch glass. "No, it's not."

"Okay, okay," I said, backpedaling. "Maybe it isn't. Maybe if we spend all our free time on it, we can work up some kind of convincing argument for extenuating circumstances, enough to make even what's happened seem like— well, not so much what it is. But Ellie . . ." I tried a last time to escape doom. "I've got a son home from college, a house that needs attention, a dog acting spooky, a new husband . . ."

After marrying Victor, I spent most of what was supposed to have been our honeymoon in the waiting room of the neurosurgery suite at NYU Medical Center. Our nuptials were apparently the signal for every fool who thought he could drive a Harley to find out otherwise, with predictable results.

". . . and besides, it's nearly Christmas. I wanted to get the tree, buy presents and wrap them, do some baking, and . . ."

Ellie just fixed me with that penetrating gaze of hers, so unfoolable that you could set her up at the CIA and use her to detect spies.

I gave in to her scrutiny. "And I need time to figure out how I can get a wedding ring and an engagement ring," I finished. "Diamonds, in platinum settings."

Ellie looked at me as if I'd admitted that I wanted one inserted through my nose. "Jacobia, I had no idea you were such a traditionalist."

Charitably, she didn't snicker. Usually, I'm more the type who would want a new tool belt. "Yeah, well. Make fun if you want to, but I notice you're wearing one."

She glanced at the plain gold circlet on her left hand. "But this is different. It was George's grandmother's, and his mother wore it, too, so it has . . ."

Then she looked at me, her gaze softening behind her thick glasses. "History," she finished. "Oh, I see."

After she died, my mother's wedding ring went to her family in Kentucky, where one of my uncles traded it for a winter's worth of firewood and kerosene. Well, they'd needed to keep warm; I'd put it out of my mind.

Mostly. "Anyway, I want them and I've been trying to figure where Wade and I can get the money for them. Because buying your own rings all by yourself isn't a bit traditional, is it?"

Also, much of the money I'd had when I got to Eastport was spoken for now: Sam's college fund, an investment in Victor's trauma clinic, an emergency fund for the house, all untouchable. With what was left I could just about rub two nickels together. "Besides, Wade wouldn't hear of it. So I wanted to think about rings, not about murder."

"I do believe," Ellie said thoughtfully, "that to make Wade feel less manly you'd have to hit him pretty strategically with one of those whole trees, over at the debarking machine."

True. "You know he'd still want to be in on it, though. And I'd want that, too. But even if shipping stays strong so there's plenty of harbor piloting, *and* navigation repairs start bringing in more cash . . ."

In Eastport, the phrase *spare money* is an oxymoron for almost everyone, Wade included. Besides harbor piloting and equipment fixing, he also had a gun-repair shop in the ell of the house. But even the three jobs together just about kept him solvent.

"I thought I'd have time to come up with a plan," I finished inadequately.

Ellie nodded and was probably about to say something

useful, as a knock came at the back door. Those carolers, I thought, looking around for something to offer them, because when people are out riding in the bed of a pickup truck, freezing their posteriors off to spread a little holiday cheer, I figure they deserve substantial refreshment.

But when I opened the door, I found no carolers standing there. In fact, it wasn't anyone spreading any sort of cheer at all, Christmas or otherwise.

It was Peter Christie.

Chapter **4**

I f you don't get a warm spell you can't keep the
streets clear in Eastport, if by "clear" you mean a dry,
snow-free surface of the kind people in other cities are ac-
customed to enjoying. Because frozen condensed humidity
(augmented by sleet, freezing rain, freezing fog, freezing
drizzle, and the many other Maine meteorological delights
whose common denominator is "freezing") tends to accu-
mulate.

Thus what you get here soon after the plows pass is a
smooth, deceptively sand-streaked surface that offers about
as much traction as a toboggan slide. But minutes after Peter
Christie showed up on my porch I was careening along
those icy surfaces in his old Ford Falcon, hanging on for
dear life while remembering what George had once said
about Peter and women: that the man had more spares than
a bowling alley.

More balls, too, from the way he was driving. "What's
your hurry?" I groused, slamming both feet onto the imagi-
nary brakes as he sped to a stop sign and tromped his own
brake pedal at the very last instant.

"Sorry," he said, and took off more sedately, spinning his
wheels no more than we all did when snow had been recent.

"Now that you've got us out here, maybe you'd like to tell us a little more about what we're doing," Ellie suggested.

Peter was slim, dark-haired, personable, and equipped with the loveliest confidential smile you ever saw in your life: in its glow, one felt both adored and adorable. The trouble was, the smile had more miles on it than the Ford, and everyone in Eastport knew it.

"To get Faye Anne's diary," he told us. "At her house."

Oh, great. All he would tell us at my place was that it was "an emergency," something to do with Faye Anne's "predicament."

So I'd been against coming out with him, but Ellie had been bound and determined. And I couldn't very well let her do it alone. If I needed help, Ellie might not quite walk on water, but she would try.

"I'm sorry I couldn't tell you before, but I didn't know who all was still at your house and I certainly didn't want anyone else overhearing," Peter said. "It'd be disastrous for her if anyone found out about it."

"What makes you so sure it won't be disastrous if *we* do?"

Now that he'd saved himself by throwing Faye Anne to the wolves, I didn't have much faith in his opinion of what might help her. But at least he'd slowed down, so the holiday decorations on the elaborate old houses we passed were more than colored smears:

Eight plywood reindeer pulling a sleigh up the steeply pitched roof of a carpenter Gothic. Ribbons circling the pillars of an old Greek Revival. A Queen Anne mansion with stars on its far-flung gables, looking vast as an ocean liner in the darkness. In its heyday, Eastport's well-to-do citizens had built whatever sort of dwellings they might fancy, and bigger was better.

But he hadn't answered my question. "What makes you so sure," I persisted as he pulled into the alley behind the

Carmodys' house and shut off the engine, "that *we'll* keep it a secret?"

He turned the ignition key enough to put the dashboard lights back on. In their glow, his features were as classically modeled as the old architecture all around us. But his eyes were shadowy pools as he paused to compose his unhelpful reply and I thought again of what Joy Abrams had said of him: that he was a liar.

"Look, Faye Anne's in trouble. And I think I've helped put her there."

Wow, as Sam would have said; brilliant deduction. But before I could reply aloud Peter picked up on my mental skewering of him.

"They were going to come and ask me, you know." The state guys, he meant. "It's not like they were going to ignore me, or not find out about me. Hell, in this town you can't even go for coffee with a woman without people talking."

He frowned. "Especially a married one. Just because I was seeing her, it got so I couldn't walk down the street without people *looking* at me. Going to the post office was an ordeal, even before this. And now it's going to be worse," he complained.

Right. And it *was* all about him, wasn't it? Inconvenience *he* had to suffer, embarrassment *he* might be required to endure. Never mind that *he* wasn't in a jail cell, right before Christmas.

I controlled my impatience. "But there was more than coffee? The talk was accurate—you two were an item?"

He looked sulkily at his hands: long, tapering fingers and neatly clipped nails. "Yes. I'd never felt that way about anyone before."

Mm-hmm. I glanced back at Ellie. Word was, Peter always had at least two women on the string, so when he got done with one there was another all lined up, ready for action. But he was speaking again:

"It wasn't any of their business, people who talked about us." He slammed his fists onto the steering wheel, in the sort of spoiled, ladies'-man frustration I recognized from living with Victor. "It wasn't *fair*."

Sam used to say *that* a lot, too. But I understood. When you first come to Eastport, it's easy to believe that its active gossip mill is an amusing but ultimately inconsequential feature of local life. After a while, though, some of the gossip inevitably starts being about you.

And that, as they say around here, is what separates the culls from the keepers. "So, what's in this diary?"

We were still sitting in the car because for one thing, this was a dumb idea; I'd come this far but I'd already decided that I wasn't getting out. For another, I could see Kenty Dalrymple's windows from where the car was parked, which meant Faye Anne's neighbor could also look out one of them and see us. "Back the car up about fifteen feet," I told Peter.

"What?" He frowned, but did as I asked.

"Good," I said. "Now, you tell me what's in the diary that you're so worried about, or I'm going to reach over there and lean on the horn until the cops come or your ears start bleeding, whichever happens first."

He flinched, and I noticed with pleasure that my "do it" voice still worked. But he still didn't answer directly.

"Anything seem funny to you about the method?" he mused. "I mean, cutting him up like that?"

"Poetic justice," I snapped. Something about Peter Christie had really begun getting on my nerves. Maybe it was the "I'm such a sweet guy" crap he was exuding from every pore.

Or the way he kept evading my questions. Also the dash-lights were still on but the heater wasn't.

"Hey, buddy. My feet are cold. Get on with your story and make it a concise one, please. Or take us home."

Ellie still sat in the backseat: no comment. But I knew she was listening. This wasn't the first time we'd found ourselves in, shall we say, unusual circumstances.

By which I mean murder. People do it, here, and try to get away with it, too, just like anywhere else. And in the snooping department, Ellie and I had our division-of-labor routine pretty well written up and initialed. Maybe Peter believed we wouldn't be blabbermouths because, in all the strange stuff Ellie and I had been involved in, we were always so far on the side of the underdog that we practically had fleas.

Still, what Faye Anne really needed was a lawyer, not a pair of sympathetic but officially powerless Eastport women, teamed up with the dubiously motivated town Lothario, on a goofy mission. It all made me almost decide to insist on going home immediately.

Almost; instead, I glanced down at my ringless left hand, illuminated in the dashboard glow.

"I don't want to say anything. I want you to look at it, and tell me what you think," Peter said stubbornly. "I want *your* opinion."

I want, I want. Now he *sounded* like Victor. "Well, isn't that special?" I began sarcastically, but just then a blue-and-white Eastport squad car went by in the street behind us, tires squeaking on snow.

It gave no sign that its driver had seen us, though, not slowing. And with any luck, Kenty Dalrymple hadn't noticed that we'd backed up, but hadn't driven away.

That she might not have seen us at all was way too much to hope for; Kenty was famed as a combination surveillance-and-public-address system.

The squad car didn't come back.

"And you have to see it here," Peter went on, ignoring my remark. "We certainly can't take it with us."

But we could break into the house and rifle through the

diary's contents, maybe muck up evidence . . . "Yeah," I retorted, "let's not do that. It would be *wrong*." Oh, this guy was a hoot.

Still, I was curious about that diary. And Ellie *was* sitting there, waiting patiently for me to decide. But neither of those things were what really turned the trick for me in the end. It was Faye Anne, herself. Alone and in trouble she reminded me of someone I barely remembered, someone I *hadn't* been able to help.

Because when that help had been needed, I'd been only three years old.

"And let's not get too comfortable with the first person plural, either," I told Peter irritably, getting out. "We are *not* a team."

He slammed his car door. In the snow-covered neighborhood it sounded like a bomb going off. "Oh, for criminy's sake," I protested.

"Sorry, sorry. I forgot. I'm not used to this kind of thing."

"Sure, everything else in *your* life is *so* well ordered," I shot back.

"Ssh," Ellie interjected quietly. A porch light had gone on two houses away. We stood rooted. The only sound was the breeze clickety-clicking in the frozen branches of the mountain ash tree in Faye Anne's yard.

When the light went out we hurried to the butcher shop door. The key was still under the mat where I'd replaced it; the state guys hadn't found it. I let us in and closed the door hurriedly behind us. If the door to the kitchen was still hooked, this errand was over.

The door opened, the three of us tiptoeing in like cartoon burglars. "Okay, where is it?" Of course we couldn't switch on any lights, but the streetlight shone in enough to show the shapes of the furniture, so we wouldn't break our necks.

The stove fire had gone out and the central heating had

been left on only enough to keep the pipes from freezing; it was cold as a tomb in here, the air faintly metallic smelling.

Rank, actually; like meat that has begun spoiling, then gone into a cooler too late to keep it from being ruined. Suddenly I wished I were home where I could wash; my hands felt sticky again and my stomach did a slow, warning roll.

"I don't know," Peter confessed. "Somewhere in the house. She's showed it to me, I've even read parts, but I don't know where she keeps it."

"Oh, terrific. Anybody ever tell you you're not one of the great minds of the century, Peter?" The sticky feeling faded. Right about then if I'd had a cleaver I'd have put *him* in that cooler.

"Well, I'm sorry," he said huffily, "but I thought you could help find it. You two are supposed to be good at that kind of thing. And if you don't want to, why did you agree to come?"

"Never mind," I told him. My motives were none of his business. Simultaneously it occurred to me that Faye Anne hadn't been the only one with a reason to kill Merle. If Peter really loved Faye Anne, or thought he did, he had one, too.

"I didn't know it was going to be a goose chase," I said. In the windows, the dark outlines of leaves on Faye Anne's houseplants stretched like small groping hands. White frost traceries unfurled on the panes behind them. Ellie had gone to the front of the house where the streetlight was brighter.

"Anyway, what were you saying about the method being funny?" I started opening cabinet drawers at random, looking for one that maybe Merle wouldn't have gone into, so it would be safe for Faye Anne to tuck a diary in it.

The room hadn't been cleaned, but the carnage had occurred at the other end, mostly. And as my eyes adjusted to the gloom the large shapes and smaller items around me began clarifying, like a black-and-white photo negative coming up in developing solution. In the drawers: silverware, napkins, larger utensils. One held flashlights; I lingered over these but rejected the temptation. Someone going by outside would be bound to glimpse a light.

"Let's say your hobby was indoor gardening," Peter said. "And one of your specialties was pharmaceutical herbs. You know, like Saint-John's-wort, or echinacea."

I turned. Against the streetlit window he was a dark hulk, faceless. "Or digitalis," I said. "Or wolfsbane. Or . . ."

"Right." He'd been thinking along the same lines we were. "Now let's say you'd decided to kill someone—"

"Why use a knife?" I finished his question for him.

The dark shape nodded. "Ugly, messy, and hard work. Also, likely to leave inconvenient evidence. You can wipe up blood, but there's some kind of special spray the police can use so it shows again, isn't there? Makes it glow? I saw it," he added somewhat unconvincingly, "on a TV cop show."

Not that I didn't think he watched cop shows. It was just such an interestingly convenient piece of information for him to have retained, that's all.

And anyway, the blood hadn't gotten wiped up. "Luminol," I said. I'd already given up on the diary. To find it we'd have to make a detailed search, which we couldn't do in the dark.

"Also benzidine, malachite green, and phenolphthalein, among others. Depends on the situation," I added.

Back on Wall Street I'd gotten into the habit of doing my homework. And murder, whatever else it was, was a topic I could research.

Even in the half-dark I saw him start looking a little more respectful, as if he hadn't really expected me to know anything at all. Another idea at the back of my mind was developing, too, like that photo negative.

"So tell me the rest of it," I said, opening another drawer: sets of placemats, some tablecloths, linen towels.

"What rest of it?" Defensively.

"The rest of why Faye Anne didn't do it."

Thinking: if by some chance he had really loved her, he'd have wanted Merle gone. And one way to make that happen would be to kill Merle, get Faye Anne accused of it, and then show somehow that she could not have committed the crime, so the two of them could end up together.

And since getting falsely accused persons cleared is not a common habit of actual murderers, in doing that Peter would also be diverting suspicion from himself.

Complicated, dangerous. But it could work if both of them were in on it. If Faye Anne had been desperate enough to go along with such a risky plan, or if perhaps he'd never informed her of her part in it, at all.

At least, not in advance. And if my own suspicion was correct, Peter was starting to think I might be a tad too quick on the uptake for his comfort.

"Come on, Peter," I coaxed mildly. "You can tell me."

It also occurred to me that if by some chance I was right, I was standing in the middle of a darkened murder scene—with the murderer.

Peter began speaking again, nervously. "Let's just say you planned to use poison but then something happened. Maybe you'd been drinking a little. Or maybe you were under a lot of different pressures and you went crazy or whatever, and the next thing you knew you'd hit him with a hammer, cut him, something. Snapped and did it a different way."

No sound from Ellie, somewhere in the dark house. I turned, wanting to call out to her, but Peter was still talking. "And I don't know, if you had a . . . a psychotic break, or something, maybe you'd do more things."

Like, for instance, dissecting your victim. A chill touched me, only partly to do with the cold draft now coming from

the front of the house. Such a neat theory, and so very like
what Victor's comment had suggested: insanity.

Almost as if it were planned to seem that way. And the silence . . . "Ellie?"

No answer. Had she gone out? Then it hit me: that greenhouse of Faye Anne's. If I were a hidden diary that was definitely one place where I might be, and Ellie had no doubt
realized it.

But now she hadn't returned. Meanwhile I didn't like the
sound of Peter's recitation one little bit. Either he had a very
vivid imagination or he wasn't just theorizing.

"Faye Anne was almost as experienced a meat cutter as
Merle was," he went on. "Because sometimes he was just too
drunk to be allowed near the knives, but it was their living
so she'd had to learn."

"Ellie?" I called again.

"The thing is," Peter hurried on, "if you broke down, if
you just went *crazy* . . ."

"*Ellie!* You there?"

The front door slammed. The icy draft cut off abruptly.
Footsteps approached. It struck me suddenly that it was also
possible for Merle's killer, whoever it was, to have had another accomplice.

And for that accomplice to be coming down the hall at
me, this very minute.

". . . what I want to *know* is, why put on the apron? Or
the gloves? Why dress up in protective clothes," Peter demanded of the silence in the dark kitchen, "if you don't
know you're going to do it?"

"Interesting questions," said Eastport police chief Bob
Arnold from the doorway.

I put down the iron skillet I'd snatched from the stove
top. "Criminy, Bob! I just about brained you."

"We'll talk about brains, later," Bob said. From his tone I
didn't think he intended to tell me I had a lot.

"First, though, I've got a question of my own for Mr. Peter Christie."

Uh-oh. Bob was pretty hot about us being here. Worse, Ellie was now standing behind him and she looked ill, the way she had the previous summer when she'd accidentally eaten a bad clam.

So something else was wrong, too. "How'd you know Faye Anne was wearing the apron and gloves?" Bob asked Peter Christie.

"Well, I . . ." His hands dropped to his sides and for a moment I thought Faye Anne was rescued, somehow. But:

"I was watching the house when they brought her out," Peter blurted. "From my car. I had a view of the front door. With," he admitted, "binoculars."

"*You* were the stalker, then, I'll bet," Ellie said accusingly. "You followed her and watched her, you probably even peeked in her windows, you *terrified* her . . ."

"I didn't *mean* to," he burst out. "I never meant to scare her, but I was worried about her, I was out of my *mind* with worry about her. But she wouldn't let me near her, wouldn't talk to me, and you *know* what that bastard was like, he might have *killed* her and I knew I had to *do* something . . ."

He stopped, hearing what he'd said. Because somebody had, hadn't they? Done something.

About that bastard.

"It was in the greenhouse," Ellie said. "The book you're worried about," she added, turning to Peter. "I found it."

And then of course Bob Arnold had found Ellie. Bob didn't look all that sharp when you first met him: round face, thinning hair, a little belly pooching out over his shiny Maine Police Association belt buckle.

But Bob was plenty smart enough so that when he noticed people looking for something, he didn't interrupt them until they'd finished. Now he had a little green spiral-bound book in his hand.

"Faye Anne's diary?" I asked, and he nodded. "Did you read any of it?"

He'd seen us, of course. Since the squad car went by when we were still out in the alley, he'd known we were here.

"Ayuh. With my trusty flashlight." He tapped it where it hung on his belt with his other cop gear.

"Seems Faye Anne had a plan all worked out, get rid of her old man and take off with our friend Peter, here. Kill old Merle with one o' them exotic bow-tannicals she grew. Poison plants." He practically spat the words. "Hellebore. Foxglove. Plenty more just like 'em."

"Fast reader," I remarked.

"When I want to be," he replied. "Found the good parts quick. But you're the ones who found the diary itself, where she wrote it all down, which if you hadn't found it maybe none of it ever would've been known."

Suddenly I knew *why* he was so angry. He didn't think Faye Anne had killed Merle, either. Or more likely, if he did think so, he considered it rough justice.

"Only now," he went on, "it *will* be known." He turned and stalked to the front of the house. His whole posture radiated disgust at what we had been up to.

"Maybe we had manslaughter," he said. "Or a half decent shot at diminished capacity." He opened the front door.

"But now, with the Miss Marple Society on the case—"

Mah-ple.

"Now what we've got, damn it all, is capital murder."

The following morning I sat in a lawyer's office, thinking about how people who *do* remember history are doomed to repeat it, too:

The idea of a little knowledge being a dangerous thing was never so fully proved as in the person of my father, who killed himself with a combination of haste, arrogance, and criminal carelessness in 1969.

A self-styled sixties anarchist, he thought putting a bomb under a Brinks truck was the best, most direct way to attack the evil capitalist-industrialist state, and maybe to grab up a bit of cash in the ensuing confusion, besides.

Instead he touched the wrong wires together and took out a Greenwich Village town house, his accomplices, and my mother. The firemen found me sitting in my bed in the backyard where the explosion had blown me. A section of the roof had come down over me at an angle like a lean-to, sheltering me from flying bricks.

So I've been told. That was a long time ago. But now in a poorly planned attempt to help someone who reminded me of my own past—

If only someone had told my mother that the sky wouldn't fall if she walked out on him, or that if it did, at least she wouldn't be at ground zero when the pieces came down.

—I'd done the same damn-fool thing that my father had done: I'd made everything worse.

The voice droned on at me: "Unlawful entry. Tampering with evidence. Conspiracy to obstruct justice. Shall I go on?"

Clarissa Arnold looked severely over her gold-rimmed half-glasses at me, from behind the big oak desk in her law office over the old candy store on Water Street, in downtown Eastport. Clarissa was Bob Arnold's wife, and at the moment she was also my attorney.

But only at the moment. She'd already made it clear she was up to her eyes in work, way too much to take on any more, and the folders piled on her desk underlined this.

"Bob gave the state fellows the diary you and Ellie found at Faye Anne's house last night," she said. "He had to hand it over to them, of course."

Of course. "*And* he had to tell them who found it and how," she added.

People in Eastport hadn't taken kindly at first to the idea of a lawyer "from away" setting up in town. Four years earlier when Clarissa had come here from Portland, about the only work she could get was representing drivers who'd failed their field sobriety tests. And there's not much you can say in court for a drunk driver other than "Yes, Your Honor."

Pretty soon, though, people cottoned on to the idea of a lawyer who didn't know their whole life histories and those of their families. They appreciated having an attorney whose great-grandfather hadn't been cheated in a card game, snookered in a land swap, or had a mule stolen by one of their ancestors, thus tainting the family name for lo these many generations unto the present. They felt Clarissa's newness to the area allowed her to view their own characters from a novel perspective.

Rightly or wrongly. "So how much trouble am I in?"

Personally I thought there was not very much novel about Clarissa's perspective. Rather it was biblical, with special emphasis on the story of Cain and Abel. Most of the time, she said, her job was just to make sure Cain didn't get screwed.

"None, if no one presses charges against you."

My spirits rose minimally.

"And since your meddling has turned up a nifty piece of evidence the prosecution might not otherwise have gotten," she added pointedly, "they probably won't."

Clarissa's big windows looked out over Passamaquoddy Bay: blue, cold, and dotted with scallop boats. It was low tide, the tree-trunk pilings of the fish pier rising thirty feet or more over the water's surface near the shore.

But out in the middle I saw a nice, deep spot I could sink myself in.

Clarissa tipped her head, upon which every short, dark

strand was in place. Tiny diamonds sparkled in her earlobes and her short, neat fingernails gleamed with clear polish.

"On the other hand, Jake, if you had something else they wanted, they could threaten to prosecute unless you gave it to them."

She looked like a million bucks, smelled like Camay, and was, if you can believe it, the mother of an almost-two-year-old. When Sam was almost two years old you couldn't even see if I had fingernails at all, because he was driving me so nuts, my hands were too busy pulling my hair out.

"Whether or not you really had it," she added meaningfully. "Whatever."

In other words they could squeeze me for something I could not possibly give them because I didn't have it, then prosecute me on account of my failure to cooperate, either because they thought I really *did* have it or for pure revenge: Our finding the diary when they hadn't made them look dumb.

"So I'd better not give them an idea that I do. Have something, I mean." By, for instance, snooping around anymore.

She nodded, as I remembered something else. "Clarissa, did they say anything to Bob about why they were here *before* Merle died?"

In the one creased snapshot I still have of my father you can see how handsome he was, the smile that attracted my mother. And the hint of danger in his eyes, the suggestion that if you dared hitch your star to his bright star, you might go far.

Or fall far. But this, to a girl who was barefoot and skinny-legged in Kentucky hill country, would not have seemed much of a risk. One of Clarissa's dark, wing-shaped eyebrows rose minutely.

"No, they didn't say why they were here before Merle died," she said, "and I wouldn't tell you if I knew." She looked hard at me: if she *did* know, it was confidential.

"I swear, Jacobia, you're just like one of those dogs an old uncle of mine used to have, to hunt rabbits. Not geniuses, but when it comes to rabbits you can't—"

"Beagle," I interrupted; my uncles had had them, too. And I recalled what they had said of the breed: stubborn as a mule and twice as smart. But the part about me not being a genius had been proven too recently for me to argue it.

"Anyway," I went on, "Joy Abrams said she saw them out at Duddy's in Meddybemps the night before last. I suppose she could be wrong, but she *was* very definite about it."

Victor had already called me that morning to complain about Willetta. As I'd suspected, Joy's kid sister was quite the little splash of cold water in my ex's love life; he hadn't even managed to be alone with Joy yet, he'd reported indignantly.

"And can you believe the nerve of that kid?" he'd demanded, "inviting herself along and then cross-examining me about who-all would be there? She *always*," he'd fumed indignantly, "does that."

And, he added, Willetta worked at the hospital in Calais where he had medical privileges, so he had to see her there, too. But Victor's romantic trouble was the least of my concerns now.

"Joy also said that Peter Christie's a . . ."

Liar, I'd been about to finish. And I was starting to think that might not be even the half of it. Once again Peter couldn't have gotten Faye Anne in more deeply if he'd been trying.

Maybe he had been. The difference was, this time I'd helped him. But the half hour I'd begged from Clarissa was up.

"Hearsay," she pronounced crisply, and got to her feet.

White silk blouse and slim black skirt, wool tartan jacket with a holiday pattern of red and dark green; motherhood agreed with her. So did getting back to her law practice full time. Furthermore she was that most fortunate of women, the one with the utterly lovely and lovable, baby-adoring local mother-in-law to take care of Thomas.

"Thanks, Clarissa," I said at the doorway leading downstairs. "I guess there's no hope you'll take on Faye Anne's case, either, then?"

"Not unless one of my other clients decides to plead out."

In the end, the thing that had really turned the trick for Clarissa in Eastport was one of those routine DUIs: the guy was staggering and slurring his words when the cop asked him out of the car, couldn't walk the line if his life had depended on it, and when he was asked to point at his nose he poked himself in the eye.

Meanwhile there had been a big fire that night in St. Stephen, just over the border in Canada, and the hospital in Calais had taken the overflow of firemen with exhaustion, smoke inhalation, and chest pains. So there'd been a delay on the blood alcohol test the guy insisted on.

And it came back under the limit. The cops, who had not been equipped with Breathalyzers that night, argued that the low result was on account of the delay, that the guy had metabolized some of the booze he'd guzzled, while waiting. Must have, they said; he was obviously loaded when they stopped him. And except for wanting the blood test, the guy's behavior *had* seemed to support that idea.

At least it did until Clarissa sent him to Bangor for some *other* tests. Comes time for the guy's trial, who does she call to the stand? A neurologist, who testified that the defendant had an undiagnosed seizure disorder. And what the defendant had done to make all this happen was, he'd sworn to Clarissa: only two beers. On his mother's grave, he'd said.

And she had believed him, paying for the medical expert herself. Because, as she liked to say, you could usually bet the farm on Eve tempting Adam, Cain killing Abel, and the Sabine women running into some very bad dudes.

But then there was the story of Job: occasionally, bad stuff just poured down on someone who didn't deserve it. That, Clarissa also liked to say, was when her job got interesting.

"Hey," she said. I turned on the stairs. She stood at the top of them. "Call her lawyer."

And at my puzzled look: "They'll appoint Faye Anne an attorney if they haven't already. I'll find out who it is and tell him—or her, if it's a her—to expect to hear from you."

"Clarissa, thanks. But I thought *you* thought . . ."

"I do. You should stay out of it. And yes, I do know about the door, the wine bottles, and the rest. Bob told me. And if I were a prosecutor I could knock it all down. House of cards."

"But . . . then, why?"

"Because I used to try to make those dogs of my uncle's into pets. Make them learn tricks. Jake, have you ever tried teaching a beagle to do anything *but* hunt?"

Oh.

The vet says she's fine," Sam called from the passenger seat of Tommy Pockets' old jalopy—raccoon tails, a jury-rigged muffler, and a thrillingly penetrating oo-*ooh*-gah! horn—as they pulled rumblingly up alongside me on Key Street.

Monday, he meant; he'd taken the dog for her checkup so I could go see Clarissa. Now the animal lolled happily in Tommy's backseat: head out the window, eyes bright and ears alert. Not a care in the world.

"Woof," I said to her, reassured; the vet on the mainland worked out of an old blue sheet-metal quonset building whose appearance didn't inspire confidence. But the vet did.

"Come on, dog," I said, snapping her leash on. Tommy's

car horn oo-*ooh!*-gahed as they pulled away with a bang of backfire and a burst of tailpipe smoke.

The rest of the way up Key Street was two steps forward and one step back, the sky brilliant blue and the ice on the sidewalk watery-slick. But for the moment I hardly minded; with Monday judged healthy and me not in immediate danger of prosecution, the cold fresh air tasted sweet as spring water.

Monday frisked along beside me, past the red-brick library flaunting its green cupola against the sky, its brass weathervane glinting. Behind it in Library Park the bandstand rose from the snow, white on white, its latticework crisply perfect.

At the top of the hill I turned to gaze down at the harbor where the boat slips had been empty since dawn; scalloping is daylight work, and with the fishing regulations so picky and the winter day so short, the men took advantage of every minute.

George was out there helping to haul the shellfish, which meant we'd be able to have a nice casserole of them soon: butter and breadcrumbs, white wine, and presto! instant ambrosia. The notion cheered me further, as did the scarlet-ribboned wreaths and garlands and the pinecone-studded swags at every door and window on Key Street. Even Victor's place on the corner, its iron scrollwork fence a black ink-sketch on the snow and its oil-fired furnace chimney puffing a spiral of pale smoke like a genie being let out of a bottle, gleamed in the chilly, salt water-scented winter sun.

But inside my house, Monday sank once more with a glum *oomph* into her dog bed, her face a mask of canine tragedy and her eyes accusing. You haven't killed the enemy that's scaring my wits out, her look said. And although for now she accepted the substitute I offered—a dog biscuit—I knew sooner or later I was going to have to do battle. But against what?

On the other hand, I did have a fresh supply of plastic sheeting. And putting some on the windows might help lower the heat bill while working on the cellar steps would not, unless we all decided to live down there huddled next to the furnace.

So after washing my hands I got out the roll of plastic, which I'd used only for true cold emergencies in previous years: ugly, thick, and milky-opaque. The first step, caulking the spaces between the sashes and the sill, went quickly. Next came what I once thought was the tricky part: getting the plastic up.

Tricky, that is, until I learned about double-sided tape. Around the window: top, sides, and bottom, making sure first to pull a corner tab of the tape's backing material; it's a hint I learned while teetering at the top of a tall stepladder, trying to separate the backing material from the sticky part. Once the tape was mounted, I pulled the backing off: zip, zop.

Then, struggling a little but getting it up there finally, I hung the plastic sheet. Suddenly the view through the window was grey and blurry as if through an out-of-focus camera. You can get clear plastic for about the same price as the heating fuel you'll save on, which pretty much moots the whole operation, it seems to me. Sighing, I resigned myself to seeing my own backyard again sometime in summer, and I added copper weatherstripping to the list in my head, too. It was expensive, but judging by the windchill in here, it was also essential.

Monday whimpered, gazing at the back door. "Oh, okay," I said, and she leapt up, so eager to get back outside again that I thought if she had one of those tramp's bundles and could sling it over her shoulder, she'd run away from home.

Which was a little like what I felt like doing, too, now that I'd had time to think. No one knew yet about the disaster over at Faye Anne's the night before. But Kenty

Dalrymple had almost surely observed major components of it.

And would talk about it. Once a noted gardening writer who'd had her own program on public TV, Kenty was now a frail semi-invalid, living alone with her books and plants. So it was hard to begrudge her the gossipy conversations that gave her such pleasure.

Still, right now I wished she enjoyed them a little less avidly. By this evening my name—linked with Peter's, curse the luck—would be featuring prominently in them, I felt certain.

As if to underline this, the moment I got outside, Peter's old Ford turned onto Key Street. My efforts to blend invisibly with the snowbanks were fruitless; the car slowed. Behind the wheel, Peter wore a tan leather jacket and cream scarf and looked as usual like the man most likely to be depicted on the cover of a romance novel. And there was—surprise—a woman with him.

"Jacobia, what a ghastly experience, finding Merle. It must have been an awful shock," Melinda Devine gushed, leaning over to search me avidly for hoped-for signs of psychological trauma. "Was it *very* terrible?"

If it had been, Melinda would simply have loved it to bits. A tiny, wiry woman of thirty or so, she wore a black cashmere turtleneck sweater and black slacks, her hair swept up and sprayed into a gleaming brunette helmet. No coat; she always said if your personality was warm enough, you didn't need one.

"Hi, Melinda," I said. "I'm fine, thanks. Peter, what can I do for you?"

I made my tone so businesslike that Monday glanced up, thinking I'd uttered an obedience command. But I had a reason: After Bob Arnold had discovered us in Faye Anne's kitchen, Peter had promptly decided the whole thing was *our* idea: Ellie's and mine.

"Listen, about last night," he said uncomfortably. "I don't want to be involved in any of that, anymore. I want you to drop it."

"Really." I kept looking at him, thinking about how nice it must be to run the world. Or to believe you did.

"You're just going to make things worse," he told me. Melinda appeared fascinated. "I want you to stop."

"*Such* a loss," she mourned transparently. "Faye Anne was a great asset to the garden club."

By which she meant the one *she* ran: there were two garden clubs in Eastport. The official one held its meetings in the gloriously restored Gerrold Bannister house, now home to popular children's book author Sylvia Harrington, on Boynton Street. Sylvia had put in formal gardens, espaliered fruit trees, and a topiary menagerie, to create the perfect setting for the official club's officers, agenda, regular educational speakers, garden-tour program, and hybridizing projects.

The *other* club, its membership consisting mostly of people whom the official one had jettisoned, was Melinda's.

"Why, just the other night we were saying at the meeting how much we missed Faye Anne," Melinda said. "Although we missed you, too, of course, Peter," she added with a sly glance at him. She wasn't even shivering, although it was so cold I felt that if I breathed in too fast my teeth might shatter.

The garden club schism began when Melinda announced she didn't like being pushed around by the first club's leadership. Translation: she wanted to do the pushing around herself. Only Ellie belonged to both clubs. But then, Ellie could bring peace to the Gaza Strip.

"I even called her right from the meeting," Melinda said, "in case she needed a ride. But of course Merle answered. He said Faye Anne wasn't home. And I feel *awful* about it now, of course."

She pulled down the windshield visor, applied clear lip

gloss in its little mirror, and adjusted the long, gold-fringed paisley scarf she always wore. All to demonstrate, I supposed, just how awful she felt.

Peter said to me: "You leave me out of it. I mean it, I'd better not hear my name mentioned in this anymore. I can get a lawyer, too, you know."

Interesting, since I'd left Clarissa's office so recently. Either Peter was psychic or Faye Anne wasn't the only one he was keeping tabs on. Also, what did he think he needed a lawyer *for*?

Then the light dawned: I knew what Melinda had meant by her sly remark. "Maybe you should get a lawyer anyway," I said, and noted his anxious flinch.

Beside him, Melinda simpered prettily. "Peter's helping me set up my new computer," she said, as usual turning the conversation back to her own concerns. "We're going to do it now, and I'm going to address all my holiday cards electronically."

We were saying at the meeting how much we missed Faye Anne. . . . and you too, Peter. Melinda meant that Peter and Faye Anne had been *together,* on the night of Merle's death. Her comment, light as the flick of a whip, had been aimed at him. And knowing Melinda—her motto was, why bother having it if you can't flaunt it?—I came to a simple-arithmetic conclusion:

Melinda was Peter's *other* current girlfriend, the second-stringer everyone knew he always had. Now she'd moved up to first place without wasting a bit of time, and to show how secure she felt in her new position, she'd delivered her little jab. Not realizing, perhaps, just how sharply pointed it was.

Or maybe she had. Melinda could be as reckless as a child, and as heedless of the mischief she created. I considered telling her that before her computer would spit *out* holiday greetings, she would have to type the recipients' names and addresses *in.*

But let Melinda learn that, I decided, for herself. Besides, who wants a computer-printed holiday card?

"Anyway, Peter," I said, "if you do end up wanting a lawyer don't bother asking Clarissa Arnold. She's already too busy. I just saw her, and—oh, but you already know that, don't you?" I tipped my head in pretended thought. "Funny, I didn't see you. But I guess you're pretty good at spying on people without their knowing it, huh? Following them around, maybe watching them with binoculars. The way you told Ellie and me that you'd been watching Faye Anne."

Peter's mouth moved but no sound came out.

"Why, Peter," Melinda breathed, "you naughty boy." She looked at me, a bright note of query in her eyes.

But I wasn't giving her anything. " 'Bye, Melinda," I said as they drove away down the ice-packed street: good riddance.

Still, I didn't like seeing her going off with him. Melinda was shallow and manipulative, and she took a greedy, unseemly interest in the misfortunes of others. Cheap, too: the previous summer she'd gotten a town librarian fired on account of a quiet romance with a Bangor book salesman. "Conflict of interest," Melinda had trumpeted, when in fact her campaign was retaliation for the librarian's not voiding her sky-high overdue fines.

She wasn't all bad, though. She could work like a horse; Ellie said refreshments at the splinter-group garden club meetings were like champagne suppers. When Melinda said she would do something, she did it come hell or hibiscus, as Sam used to say.

And she was vulnerable in the way the truly oversized ego can be: the notion that *she* might ever come to harm never crossed Melinda's mind, I felt confident.

So I made a mental note to call her later; a word to the

wise. Or unwise. Then I turned, meaning to head indoors; the wind had shifted and a breeze knifing in off the water made the sunshine little more than window dressing. But Monday yanked the leash, sniffing the air as if any minute she might meet up with a passel of cats. And Peter Christie had gotten my dander up with his impertinent *I wants*.

I wanted something, too: to be shut of this whole business. Even Ellie, surely, must know now that it was useless.

But before I could put Faye Anne Carmody's troubles out of mind altogether, there was a final question I needed to ask. And Kenty Dalrymple, bless her nosy heart, might have the answer.

A few cold blocks later I reached Kenty's cottage on High Street and knocked. She opened the door instantly as if she'd been waiting for me, hoping I would arrive.

Or that someone would.

Chapter 5

"I don't want to talk about it. It's none of my business," Kenty Dalrymple declared, closing the door behind me.

But Kenty had something she wanted to talk about, all right; it was in her expression and the way she seized my jacket, hanging it hurriedly on the hall coat tree as if she feared that I might go away again before she could unburden herself.

Outside, a white Channel 7 van sporting the logo of the Bangor station and the familiar peacock of the national network had slowed in front of the Carmody house as I climbed Kenty's front steps. Her lips tightening, Kenty peeked past the curtains at the parlor window. "Good, they've moved on," she said with a frown.

Which I thought was odd. I'd have thought she might like getting attention from newspeople, especially since she had been in the television business herself, once. But her reaction to the news van wasn't as odd as what came next.

It started out straightforwardly enough: "Good doggy," she said to Monday, whose worried look faded as she determined that no enemies lurked in Kenty's furniture as they apparently did in mine.

Then: "I won't gossip," Kenty repeated determinedly, pouring tea from a china pot with a tremulous, freckled hand. "I'm not going to *talk*."

Au contraire. But Kenty, I'd heard, wasn't the sort of gossip who came on too strong, right off the bat. First I would have to make a show of persuading her, so she could tell herself she hadn't volunteered anything; that instead I had inveigled it from her.

The hot, strong tea worked its magic swiftly, and the room's temperature was a good ten degrees above what I was used to at home; I began thawing as Kenty put her hands in her lap like a child awaiting a scolding. I got the message: I was to persuade, but not waste time doing it.

"Kenty," I began in the stern, loving tone I'd once used on Sam. It hadn't worked, but at the time he hadn't so much wanted it to.

She began to cry. "Oh, it was *horrible*," she gasped, wiping her eyes with an embroidered linen handkerchief from her skirt pocket. "It went on and on, every other day, practically. The shouting, the cursing. Him screaming and threatening her. I told her, I said, Faye Anne, next time I'm going to call the police."

"But you never did." There had not, to my knowledge, ever been an official complaint about Merle Carmody.

"She begged me not to. Said it would go much worse for her later, if I did."

It was the excuse we'd all given ourselves, the one Faye Anne had pressed upon us. Kenty peered at me in appeal through her glasses, their lenses' lower halves thick as Coke-bottle bottoms. So heavy they made Ellie's heavy-duty prescription seem like clear glass, they were the kind worn by people who have had old-fashioned cataract surgery. Behind them her watery grey eyes had a wobbly, gelatinlike appearance.

"So I didn't. I never called."

The room smelled of sweet tea and furniture polish tinctured with a hint of liniment, and the furnishings themselves were the sort of New England heirlooms you see in museums: a slant-topped secretary, a brass-handled highboy, a sideboard with bird's-eye-maple drawer fronts. At one end of the tea table were a clutch of small, often-used items: a box of tisssues, the TV remote wand, a needlepointed eyeglass case, prescription eye drops, and three orange plastic pharmacy bottles.

"But I should have," she added wretchedly.

A wonderful old Persian rug spread a rich, red pattern over the floor. These were things from another time in her life, when she had been busy, important, and social. In the bookcases stood rows of books on horticulture, several of them written by Kenty herself, and on the sideboard stood a silver tray with glasses and a decanter, empty now.

The only exception to the elegant theme was a Laz-E-Boy recliner looming like an elephant among the gazelles, where in the evenings she probably watched TV instead of appearing on it as she once had. I saw the word *nitroglycerine* on one pill bottle, *digitalis* on another.

I couldn't make out the third label. "What I should have done," she said with sudden venom, "was kill him, myself. I'm an old woman, what can they do to me?"

Her change of mood startled me.

"They can't scare me. Old age," she grinned, "is scary enough."

Which made me begin thinking that maybe Kenty was a little scary, herself. Oh, she was sharp enough, and her costume, a pink plaid housedress, thick stockings, and soft shoes, was clean and neat, properly belted and buttoned. Her hairdo was a perfect blue-white clip-job with a fresh permanent wave set into it, above pearl earrings.

But I had doubts, now, about what she could have seen:

glasses. And about how accurately she might re-
too.

er grey eyes filled with tears magnified by the cataract
lenses. "That poor child," she mourned quaveringly.

So *emotional* . . . "Kenty, the night it happened. When's
the last time you saw Merle alive? Someone must've already
asked you that, right?"

She nodded grimly. "Those men. Tweedledum and
Tweedledee."

The state guys, she meant; they'd mentioned interview-
ing the neighbors. I repressed a smile as she went on: "I told
them. I saw Merle that afternoon. Saw him go out, come
back. Maybe," she went on, sounding confused, "Faye
Anne was right in there *waiting* for him, right that minute."

But then she looked calculating. "No. That couldn't be."

"Why not?" She was bewilderingly changeable; as if she
weren't sure, herself, what she might say or do in the next
moment. But her answering words were certain, not at all
confused.

"Because I went over there that evening. I didn't see him,
but I heard him. He was alive. Be sure and say that, dear,
will you?"

My turn to be confused: say it to whom?

Then: "Dear, would you like to see my new babies?"

An inward sigh. Sure, Kenty; and after that let's just the
two of us hop down the rabbit hole, pay a call on the
Cheshire Cat. If we're lucky we'll find something to drink
that will make us very small. Or large.

I didn't know Kenty very well; her social circle, such as it
was, consisted of women and a few men who would have
been my parents' age. But this was so disappointing. She
crossed the room in halting steps.

"Come and see them. I've been nursing them along."

What I wanted to know was whether Kenty had seen
anyone going in or out of the Carmody house, other than

Merle or Faye Anne. But now I wasn't sure if there was any point to asking her anything.

She gestured impatiently at me, her expression eager; humoring her, I obeyed. She was a sweet person but the sad truth was that she'd gotten a little batty.

In the next few minutes, however, my impression of her was turned upside down yet again. "Here they are," she announced proudly. Under a fluorescent light fixture stood a tray of a dozen two-inch plastic pots. In each, a plant so small it looked embryonic put up leaves no bigger than the nail on my little finger. A plastic stick bore each plant's varietal name: Victorian Velvet. Rodeo Clown. Coral Sunset.

"Oh," I breathed, amazed. The tray was a collection of tiny miracles.

"People say African violets don't root well in water, but mine always do," Kenty said. "I use little pimento jars to get them started in, and they do fine. Of course, it *is* quite a trick to manage to eat up all those pimentos."

Her chuckle sounded thoroughly sane, now; this was eerie, like a Jekyll-and-Hyde act. "But about the other night," she recounted briskly. "I went over there to borrow some sugar for some cookies I was baking. Only it was a garden club night, so Faye Anne was out. The *other* garden club, I mean."

Everyone called it that, even its own members. All except Melinda, of course. Meanwhile as Kenty spoke, I began getting the uncomfortable feeling that she was telling me this for some reason.

Other than to get it off her chest, I mean. But that was silly; especially given her general frailty, what reason could there be?

"I don't know why Melinda insisted on moving the meeting night to Sunday. She's a foolish girl anyway. Do you know she never wears a coat?"

I did. I also thought I knew why she'd moved the day of

the club meetings: Monday night was football night, and talk around town was that Melinda's brother, a guy no one knew well at all, had come to live with her a few months earlier.

And Melinda was the kind of snob who didn't want you to know she even owned a television, much less that football was ever displayed on it. More to the point, though, Melinda had said that Faye Anne *wasn't* at the meeting. Or Peter Christie, either. "What happened then?" I asked Kenty.

"I knocked, got no answer, walked in and called for Faye Anne," she replied. In the bluish winter light from the parlor window you could see how lovely she had been, once: high forehead and swanlike throat that even now was only a little crepey, and her cheekbones were still to die for.

She preened a little under my admiring glance. "Then I remembered where she must be," she went on. "But I knew where the sugar was, so I got it, and called out once more. That time, he did answer me."

Kenty's lips tightened. "He sounded grumpy, as usual, and also a little drunk, of course. So I didn't go out to the shop to say hello, as I might have otherwise."

I glanced questioningly at her; greeting Merle wasn't the high point of anyone's day or evening. "I tried to keep on civil terms with him," she explained. "For Faye Anne's sake."

"And that was the last time you saw him. Heard him, I mean. And you did not see Faye Anne at all."

Something else was wrong about all this, too, but at that moment I couldn't quite figure out what.

Kenty turned from fiddling with one of the plantlets. "Oh, no. I saw them both later that evening. After I'd done my baking I went back with the sugar and a plate of cookies. Faye Anne was home, by then, and everything seemed fine. Nothing amiss."

She drew back from the plants. "Nothing was wrong, for once. And *that* was the last I saw them."

"What about Peter Christie? Ever see him hanging around when he shouldn't be? Faye Anne mentioned she had the feeling someone was watching her. And *he* said he was keeping an eye on her, because he was worried about her. So I'm assuming it *was* him, but . . ."

Her gaze darkened. The glasses made her eyes huge, as if they were the eyes of some other kind of creature entirely: strange and intensely vulnerable.

"If it was him, he was doing more than watching," she said. "Faye Anne told *me* she was getting phone calls. Somebody just waited until she answered, then hung up. She even asked the phone company to put some sort of a tracer on the calls, but it turned out they couldn't."

Out in the parlor, Monday sighed contentedly. I hated to make her go, but Kenty was moving me expertly toward the hall, having accomplished, apparently, whatever she had intended. "Because it seems . . ." she began.

By now she sounded fully in command of her wits, her emotions, and anything else that could possibly have needed commanding; it was as if a magic wand had somehow been waved over Kenty Dalrymple. Witnessing this transformation, I found myself wondering if maybe something out of that third pill bottle had kicked in, suddenly and beneficially.

". . . it seems," she concluded, serene and in control, "that it's still very difficult, even nowadays, to trace a cell-phone call."

On the way home I thought over the rest of what Kenty said, as she'd ushered me out: that to her knowledge no one else had entered the Carmody house the whole day and evening before Merle was found dead in it. She'd sounded certain, not a bit quavery.

Or batty. "But *would* she have seen them?" Ellie wanted to know when I found her back at my house, working in the kitchen.

Monday started shivering as we went up the porch steps. I had to lure her in with a biscuit, after which she wormed her way under the kitchen table and curled up with the chair legs.

Ellie was cutting candied fruit. A dozen empty coffee cans stood on the drainboard with a bottle of brandy, a roll of waxed paper, baking ingredients, and a mixing bowl big enough to mix a load of concrete in.

"Kenty says she would have. What she wanted me to know, though, was that she didn't. And she seemed particularly intent on making sure that I would tell other people so, too."

Once upon a time this kitchen had held a woodstove, an icebox, and a soapstone sink, and it was not much more modern now. But the preheating oven, the board-and-batten wainscoting, and Ellie's calm competence made it feel cozier, if a bit less convenient, than any up-to-date kitchen I'd ever been in, much less owned.

I peered at the things Ellie had assembled.

"Fruitcake," I said. "Oh, good." I think fruitcake makes an excellent doorstop. "But isn't it a little late to be baking them? I thought you had to leave them in the brandy a long time. Months, even. To mummify, or whatever they do."

Ellie turned from cutting an orchard's worth of candied cherries. Pouring me a mug of hot coffee, she opened the brandy bottle and added a generous dollop. "Here. It'll make you feel better."

Just breathing the fumes made me feel better. I swallowed some. That made me feel better, too.

A lot better. "You know what? Something's rotten in Denmark." On the kitchen table with more coffee cans and

Ellie's handbag lay an old photo album; she must have brought it.

"These cakes are for next year," she said, returning to her work.

"Did you hear what I said?" I opened the album.

"Rotten. Yes. I agree." In another bowl she'd already beaten what looked like a dozen eggs. The microwave beeped; she removed the butter she'd been softening and added white and brown sugar. Next came the eggs, flour, and a tree-load of chopped walnuts, plus raisins and the candied fruit: pineapple, citron, cherries, and some green things that I didn't know what they were, exactly, only that they were the color of something left over from St. Patrick's Day.

Looking down, I glanced at the album photos, then gazed at them. Some were of Faye Anne Carmody, only not the Faye Anne I'd known. In one photograph—a class picnic, I thought, or a party—she wore a long skirt, slim knit shirt, and strappy sandals, her long hair flying behind her as Ellie pushed her high on a swing. They were both about seventeen, then, it looked to me, laughing and long-limbed.

Next photo: Faye Anne perched on a high rock overlooking the water, one graceful foot outstretched as if daring gravity to take her. Not believing, though, that it ever could. Her blithe confidence, wide grin, and upturned face, nearly arrogant in its happiness, were all new to me; the Faye Anne I'd known was a cautious, hunched creature, scuttling and shy, with an anxious giggle in place of a laugh and shoulders habitually tensed as if readied for the inevitable next blow.

In the final shot of her, Merle stood beside her, she gazing up at him as if he'd just recently descended from heaven, he in the act of crushing a beer can in one fist, the other ropy, muscular arm looped possessively around her and his grin leering, already smeary with drink.

She didn't see that part, though. Not yet; to her, Merle Carmody would have seemed merely a walk on the wild

side, one she could return from without lasting harm whenever she liked. In her wide, innocent eyes I could read all
that Faye Anne had hoped for, all she'd expected on that
sunny, long-ago day.

But it wasn't what she'd gotten and if no one did anything about it, it never would be; nothing would be salvaged
of that smile or that bright hope, nothing at all. Even
chopped in pieces and wrapped up in butcher paper, Merle
would've won.

Forever. I closed the album, not commenting on it. Ellie,
either; we both knew why she'd brought it.

By the time I'd poured more coffee—without brandy, this
time; I wanted to be relaxed, not comatose—Ellie was fun-
neling batter into the coffee cans lined with buttered waxed
paper. She'd already checked the oven temperature as carefully as if it were a vital science experiment.

"There," she said finally, dusting her hands together.

The aroma of fruit, nuts, and spices in a batter rich with
butter and brown sugar filled the room, covering the faintly
rank smell I had noticed when I first walked in. I got up and
washed my hands.

"*Now* you can tell me all about it," she added. So I did,
omitting the smell I kept smelling and a few other things,
such as the way my hands still felt: sticky. As if they couldn't
get clean of something.

"I'm getting the feeling that maybe Peter and Faye Anne's
breakup was one-sided," Ellie said. "But not one-sided the
way Peter told it. It sounds more to me as if *she* broke up
with *him,* but . . ."

"Right. Peter didn't accept it. Following her. Hang-up
calls, too, according to Kenty. And who knows what else?"

"Melinda said *neither* of them were at the meeting?"

"Uh-huh." A mental picture of her popped up. "Criminy,
Ellie, you should have seen her, dressed in just a sweater.
Melinda must have antifreeze in her veins. But anyway,

that's right: *Kenty* says Faye Anne wasn't home. But Melinda made a big thing of how she called in case Faye Anne needed a ride. Zinged Peter about being absent, too."

"Which means they were together," Ellie concluded, as I had. "Peter and Faye Anne. And she'd told Merle she was going to the meeting. That's how she got out of the house. But if Melinda talked to Merle, then . . ."

That part, I hadn't thought of. "Until Melinda called Merle, he must've thought Faye Anne *was* at the club. Melinda spilled the beans, that Faye Anne wasn't where she'd said she was going."

Just then Sam came in the back door and began rummaging in the hall closet, but he didn't sound as if he needed my help creating even more chaos than was already in there, so I left him to it.

"Kenty said she went over there," I went on, "to give them some of the cookies she'd baked, after Faye Anne got home. Everything was hunky-dory at the Carmody house at . . . what, maybe eleven or so?"

Ellie nodded. "That's another thing Melinda didn't like about the original garden club, you know. Too much business, not enough partying. With this group you've got to fight off the dry martinis. And the meetings go so *late,* I can't get up at a decent hour the next morning."

By which she meant five-thirty or so, at the latest; in Eastport, early rising is a moral imperative. "It's why I don't attend a lot of them," she finished.

". . . gloves?" Sam muttered. His work gloves, he meant. Tommy had decided to save up for ear surgery, after all, so they were working on Tommy's car instead of paying someone to try getting the backfire out of it.

"*Here* they are," I heard Sam say, then rummage some more.

"Kenty was strange," I mused. "One minute sort of . . . loosey-goosey and emotional. Couldn't stick to a subject.

Then suddenly as clear as could be, very focused. You couldn't believe she'd been an author and a TV personality, until she . . . switched herself on, or something."

Sam paused in the doorway with the gloves in his hands. "Sounds like some of the guys in my class who take Ritalin," he said. "You want to talk about before-and-after. It's like a magic wand, that stuff."

"I thought only little children had to take that," Ellie objected.

"Nuh-uh. Anyone can." He'd been tested, back when we were trying to find out why he had such a hard time in school, for just about every learning disorder human beings could have.

A light went on in my head. "You know, I remember thinking when I was there with her that it was as if a drug of some kind had just kicked in. One of her medicines, maybe."

With a wave Sam went out again, as Ellie checked the oven. "You know, these cakes have to bake for hours. Which gives us time."

Uh-oh. But she was already pulling on her coat, a silvery quilted one that would've made anyone else look as big as the Goodyear blimp.

She looked smashing in it. "After last night, don't you think we had better keep hands off?" I asked. "We're in enough trouble with the law-enforcement establishment already. And besides . . ."

There's an old sailor's phrase, rude but accurate, about doing something into the wind. I quoted it to her.

Ellie sighed patiently. "Jacobia. Remember the story I started to tell you? About my mother's funeral?"

"I do. So what?"

Stubbornly, I remained seated at the table. The brandy bottle was looking good to me, again. And the smell was back, coppery sweet.

"And do you remember the Shasta daisies, enormous vases of them, along the altar that day?"

Resignedly, I got up. "I remember them, too. But what does that have to do with . . ." And then I got it. "Faye Anne. From her garden."

"Correct." She pulled her boots on, short brown furry ones that should have thickened her ankles and made her calves appear clumpy.

They didn't. "Shasta daisies look simple to grow: those big white flowers with yellow centers. Nothing to it, right?"

Wrong. It's the little white chamomile daisies that are simple. Those big, luscious Shastas are the devil to winter over; right then, a dozen new plants were in my garden border, bedded down so carefully and lovingly that you'd have thought they were newborn infants.

Probably they were already dead. Ellie went on: "After Mom passed away, Faye Anne didn't say anything to me about those flowers. She just went out the morning of the service with a pair of garden shears, and cut down her whole border of them."

"Oh," I said inadequately, wiping my hands dry.

"When I saw them in the chapel, I started to cry," Ellie said, "and it was the *only* time I was *ever* able to do that about my mother."

She paused. "Funny, isn't it? Not being able to, I mean."

"Uh-huh." Ellie knew all about my own mother; all I knew, anyway.

Sam stuck his head back in, looking puzzled. "Hey."

"What?" I snapped at him, looking for the hand cream. Between the cold weather and all this washing, I was getting raw.

"Did I hear you two say Kenty Dalrymple was over at the Carmodys' delivering cookies at eleven o'clock at night?"

A little silence fell. "Well, yes," I began doubtfully as my son went out again. The unlikeliness of that part of Kenty's tale hadn't occurred to me. But now it did.

"So anyway, don't tell me we aren't helping Faye Anne." Ellie's tone rose heatedly again as she pulled on a wool knit hat. The purple yarn tassels poking out of the top were particularly fetching. With a sigh I began hauling my own boots back on.

"Because I'm not having it. Stay here if you want, but darn it, I'm *not* giving up yet, and . . ."

Jacket, mittens, scarf. "Fine," I said, grabbing Monday's leash.

All around me, urgent household tasks loomed: painting steps, renewing radiators, caulking more windows, insulating attic rooms. But even higher now loomed a fascinating question: why had Kenty Dalrymple looked me in the face and lied?

And then there was Ellie. "What?" she said, blinking back tears of angry determination as we got outside. To the east in the already-waning winter daylight, a huge, peach-colored moon peeked over the watery horizon.

"I said, fine." My eyelashes prickled with the brutal cold and the hairs in my nose froze instantly. "You've got a plan. I don't know what it is, but I'm out here, aren't I? So let's go do it."

"Oh." Her answering smile was beatific, as if she'd caught sight of that moon floating up into the sky.

Or something.

Ellie's plan turned out to include more hot coffee, which by the time we got downtown I'd have preferred having pumped into my veins. A wind like a knife's edge was rising off the water as daylight faded. The moon was higher now so that each wave-top shone, laced with a silvery glitter.

Inside the Waco Diner, I stamped my feet which felt

leaden with cold and sent Monday to lie down by a radiator, which she did happily, the weather outside being too frigid even for a Labrador retriever. Then we settled ourselves: me shivering, Ellie pulling layers off, as in her native-Eastporter opinion the day was a little nippy but nothing to exclaim over.

"Sorry, my aunt Fanny!" Dimity Wilson replied to Ellie's report of my running into Melinda that morning. I didn't know why Ellie wanted to start that way, but it was her party.

Dimity smacked two coffee mugs down in front of us. A tall, raw-boned woman with glossy black hair and a big, square jaw, she wore yellow stretch pants and an oversized red sweatshirt with the slogan *I ♥ Eastport* in white letters on it.

"Melinda Devine's never been sorry about anything in her whole life," Dimity pronounced, "other than the fibs she's been caught out in, and the mean tricks she's pulled, like on that poor woman at the library."

We were in the old section of the Waco: worn yellow linoleum between the long Formica counter's red leather stools and a battered row of comfortable booths, a chalkboard listing the day's specials. In summer, Dimity opened the new back room where sliding glass doors looked out onto the deck's Cinzano umbrellas.

Now snowdrifts pressed against the glass. "Damn fool woman, walking around in shirtsleeves in the middle of December. And so *superior* about it, as if being a freak of nature was something to brag about, too. If Melinda called Faye Anne the night of that club meeting, and I have no doubt she did, it would be exactly like her, it was to tip Merle off on purpose and nothing else," Dimity said.

"Why would she do that?" Ellie sipped the ferocious coffee brewed for men who worked outdoors in cold weather:

on the snowplows, at the cargo docks where the big ships loaded, or at the aquaculture plants.

"Two reasons." Dimity slapped a plate of eggs in front of one of the salmon-pen workers beside us at the counter, and pancakes before another. They'd been out since five A.M., their faces chapped and hands reddened despite the enormous amount of clothing they'd shed as they came in.

"Same reasons why Melinda does everything," Dimity answered. "Jealousy and spite. I went to a few of those *new* club meetings," she went on. "Thought I'd see what it was all about. And I saw, all right."

The fellows down the counter ate their meals with the grim purposefulness of men shoveling coal into a furnace. Dimity set a full pot of coffee and a bowl of sugar packets between them, and they nodded without speaking.

"First," Dimity ticked off on her blunt fingers, "she was jealous about Faye Anne and Peter Christie. It just about killed Melinda, handsome fellow like that payin' his main court to Faye Anne, 'stead of to *her.*"

That jibed with what I had seen earlier; Melinda didn't seem to have wasted any time filling the vacancy created by Faye Anne's arrest.

Dimity plunged used coffee mugs into a plastic tub of hot, soapy water, swishing them around. *Clean,* I thought longingly. And everywhere I went, it seemed, had that coppery smell to it, now, like the taste of an old penny.

"Saw Melinda going by a little while ago, matter o' fact," Dimity said, "no coat as usual, and with that foolish string shopping bag she carries so everyone can see all the fine stuff she buys. Endive," she snorted. "Wild rice and cooking sherry, and probably sirloin tips."

"Sounds good to me," I joked, but Dimity wasn't having any humor on the subject of Melinda.

"For fixing Peter Christie what she calls one of those 'delicious little suppers' of hers, probably," Dimity snorted.

"Way she was all fluttery around him at one o' those foolish meetings I went to, that won't be all she's feedin' him, 'fore long."

Some men from the road crew stomped in: orange jackets, high boots, and thick wool sweaters. They nodded familiarly at Ellie whom they'd all known since she was in kindergarten, a little less so at me, and ordered pie and coffee.

"But Melinda hates Faye Anne anyway," Dimity went on as she cut big wedges of lemon meringue. "Faye Anne grows better roses, her compost heats up without her having to put chemicals into it, *and* she's friends with Kenty Dalrymple, who won't give Melinda the time of day. And that's not all," she added, going away with the pie and coffee.

"What's not all?" I asked Ellie, under my breath. "She's already told us everything but Melinda's blood type and Social Security number. What more could there be?"

"Everyone comes in here," Ellie answered. "And they talk. That's why *we're* here. I guess Dimity's heard something."

"The girls from Town Hall were in the other day," Dimity confirmed when she returned. By which she meant the clerks and secretaries who actually did the day-to-day town business.

"And you know," she went on, "they're careful about not hashing over anything confidential when they're out in public. Who has a tax lien, who's not paying their sewer bill, so on and so forth."

We waited as she started a new pot of coffee. "But what they *did* say was, Merle Carmody and Melinda had a great big shouting match the other day in the town office."

She turned, hands flat on the counter. "You know that strip of property there at the edge of Melinda's side yard?"

Melinda lived in one of the last houses on Water Street, at the north end of the island looking out toward New

Brunswick; between her house and the next was a half-acre strip of brush and trees, with one enormous old maple at the center of it.

"Well," Dimity declared importantly. "A couple of months ago, that next house went to auction on a foreclosure. No one paid much attention; some people from away owned it, and talk was they'd worked a deal with the bank to buy it back at the last minute, 'stead of the bank getting stuck with it. But the talk was wrong, and do you know who wound up getting that property?"

She paused for effect. "Merle Carmody is who. All on the quiet-like. Bid on it at auction, walked away with it clean as a whistle."

Ellie looked taken aback. This, apparently, was news even to her. "Where'd Merle get the money?"

Which was my first question, too. Merle didn't do much more than butcher a few deer carcasses for people, maybe a moose now and then, order in the holiday meats, and sell a few lamb chops. And Faye Anne didn't earn any money that anyone knew of.

"All I know," Dimity answered, "it included a bit o' land that Melinda always thought was hers. But Merle spied out that it wasn't, after the property survey was printed in the foreclosure ad. And I guess he took advantage of the fact, quick as he could."

"You know," Ellie said slowly, "a few months ago he bought all new storm windows, too. And he had his driveway paved."

In Eastport, having your driveway paved is like announcing you've won the Irish Sweepstakes. After all, once all the frost is out of the ground—say, by the end of June or so—that mud will probably dry up by itself.

"Yes," Dimity agreed. She began filling the paper napkin holders with practiced motions: flip-snap. "He did start in to spending, didn't he? Anyway, that land deal got Melinda all het up. Worst thing, though, was what Merle wanted to do next, what the shouting was about. What the girls from Town Hall said, he was planning to *cut that tree.*"

"Ayuh," put in one of the men from down the counter. "He said it was bird's-eye, sure as shootin'. Fortune in hardwood just a-sittin' on that propitty, a-goin' to waste."

The other man spoke up. "Bird's-eye maple's big business, I hear. Up around Princeton last year a couple of poachers got into a sugar maple stand, 'bout wrecked the whole place. They'll cut into the trees one after t'other, looking for the bird's-eye marks in the wood," he explained.

Turning to Ellie and me: "But ol' Merle said he could tell about this here tree 'thout cuttin' it," the man finished.

"I don't think he gave a damn about the land or house," Dimity said. "He just saw a way to make a quick buck, sell off that wood. It was funny, though, how he came up with the money for that land so promptlike."

There was a time in my life when if I could get hold of your IRS filings, and a few other items of information like your date of birth, your mother's maiden name, and your Social Security number, I could get any other information about you that I wanted.

But not anymore. Or not on my own, anyway. And with my move out of New York, the list of people I could pull favors from had shrunk pretty dramatically, too. What have you done for me lately is the big question, back in the city, and as time went by I had fewer answers to it.

"I don't know where he got the cash, either," one of the town crew said as he finished his coffee and got up. "Far as I know, nobody does. Tell you one thing, though." He pulled his jacket on. "Merle Carmody kickin' the bucket's about the best thing could've happened to that poor little Faye Anne. Even if she goes to jail, she's not gonna be beat half to death."

The other men nodded grimly, getting their gear on, also.

But Dimity slammed the coffeepot back onto the warmer and said, "Maybe so. But it seems to me Melinda's who gets the brass ring. Merle gone, Peter Christie up for grabs, and Faye Anne gets the blame. Couldn't have worked out any better for Melinda if she'd planned it."

Outside the Waco, long blue shadows stretched across the sidewalks and the few cars moving in the streets had already turned their headlights on. The two tugboats regularly berthed at the fish pier chuffed diesel smoke, their engines grumbling and their yellow deck lamps illuminating the bulky figures of the men casting off lines, readying to depart.

Wade was on one of the tugboats right now, preparing to be ferried out to whatever vessel was arriving. Once on board, he would oversee the piloting of the large craft into the harbor as regulations required, since in these fast-changing waters it wasn't enough to go by the charts; you had to know the territory.

It must be a freighter, I decided as I peered through the murk, hoping to see Wade; otherwise Federated Marine wouldn't be sending both tugs. And this was good news: more work for the truckers and stevedores.

"So," Ellie said. "What do you think now?"

Far up the bay on Deer Island, a Christmas tree winked on like a special lighthouse set up for Santa Claus. From the way the wind felt now, though, he wouldn't need it; if the plummeting temperature was any indication, the North Pole was just out of sight, over the horizon.

Wade, I guessed, was already belowdecks on the tug. "It's no big news that so many people hated Merle," I said.

"No," she agreed, "but . . ."

Suddenly all the downtown Eastport Christmas lights came on, twinkling red and green. In the storefronts, holiday scenes were set up: a toy train ran in circles in the dime store. At the art gallery, a star made of hundreds of pieces of colored beach-glass shone softly. The pizza parlor had hung a wreath of green peppers, sun-dried tomatoes, purple onions, and heads of garlic.

"No," Ellie conceded. "Not news." She sighed.

In the window of Wadsworth's hardware store every possible kind of nail, screw, nut, bolt, pin, washer, tack, or heavy-duty staple had been fastened to a background of red-foil-covered plywood, in a holiday mosaic. It spelled out "Noel" at its center; around it, dozens of brightly colored pushpins formed the words "Happy Hanukkah" and "Happy Kwanza."

"And I don't suppose Melinda really did plan the murder."

"I don't see how," I said. Monday sniffed along the sidewalk in case the pizza-parlor wreath had shed any treats. "For one thing, I doubt she would know how to cut a person up. Her specialty is the cutting remark."

Ellie nodded. "Melinda *is* the dirtiest fighter in town. But I don't see how she could have made Faye Anne forget committing a bloody murder, either."

Or how anyone could have done it but Faye Anne, herself, I thought, but I didn't say it.

We headed up Water Street past the big old granite-block Customs building. To our right lay the vast L-shaped concrete dock, stretching out to form the boat basin. In the dusk the running lights of the scallop boats were approaching, their engines a faint hum at first, deepening as they came in.

"There are messages on your phone machine," Ellie said.

Oh, great. So many newspeople had left their cell-phone or pager numbers on my machine, I'd stopped listening to the messages. Monday snorted, smelling raw shellfish. "Reporters?" As Ellie nodded, I told her about the TV van that had been outside Kenty's. There'd been a few others cruising, too.

Not, I suspected, very productively. No one in town would want much publicity for a thing like this. "Funny

Kenty wanted to avoid them, though," I added. "You'd think she'd be eager for the spotlight again, even if no one else is."

"Uh-huh. Maybe." Her eyes searched the incoming boats just as mine had scanned the tugboats. "I didn't think you wanted to talk, either, so I didn't pick up the phone."

"Good." Reliving what we'd seen at Faye Anne's was the last thing I felt like doing. All I wanted was this cold fresh air, salt-tasting and clean.

Although actually I could have used it a little warmer. "Is George down there yet?"

In the basin on the boats that had already come in, bright white work lights illuminated gangs of orange-suited men, six or eight of them to a boat. Crowded around work tables on the decks they were shucking the scallops, shoveling shells overboard into nets and tossing the meats into buckets.

Ellie squinted. "Not yet."

A welder's arc flared, throwing pink sparks. A half-dozen small refrigerated trucks, engines idling to run the cooler compressors, clustered along the dock's edge. Out on the water, boat lights bobbed, white hulls ghostly in the moonlight.

We walked on in silence, leaving the harbor area to pass old wooden-framed houses, trimmed Christmas trees twinkling nostalgically from their front parlor windows. At the ferry landing, snow heaped the ramp, blue-shadowed runner marks showing where the town kids had been sledding down the steep incline.

Now they had all gone home for supper. "Faye Anne," I said, "could be lying."

From the top of the hill you could see all the way up the bay to Canada. The freighter the tugboats were readying for sat out there waiting for the tide to rise and the tugs to arrive, its lights making it look like a small city adrift in the night.

"I mean," I said, "she could be lying, but still not guilty. . . ."

Ellie looked sharply at me as I explained the suspicion I'd had the evening before: that Peter and Faye Anne could've planned the whole thing together.

"Maybe Peter was the one who did the . . . you know. And maybe he didn't tell Faye Anne until afterwards what the plan *was*."

It was still hard to imagine, even though I'd seen the awful result of it myself. But somebody had done it. And that meant someone *could* do such things; maybe someone still among us.

"But she wouldn't have let Peter—"

I stopped her. "Ellie. What I mean is, what if Peter killed Merle and *then* told Faye Anne what she had to do, to keep him from being caught for it. And we didn't live in that place with Merle. We don't know what-all went on there, how desperate she was or what she'd have agreed to do to escape."

Headlights gleamed briefly from behind us; Ellie glanced back as a car slowed, then took the plowed turnaround on the bluffs above the old gas-plant ruins. We'd reached North End. Here the bustle of town drained away to land, sea, and sky: long fields blanketed in snow, clumps of fir trees, a few houses widely spaced with sumac and raspberry bramble making wildernesses between them.

"If the idea really was for Peter to get Faye Anne out of trouble after he got her into it," Ellie declared, "he's doing a darned poor job of it."

"Right. The thing is, what if that was the original plan, only now . . ."

Just ahead, Melinda's house was a shingled cottage set back from the road and half hidden by landscaped shrubbery. A pair of old spruce trees loomed like dark sentries at either side of her drive, huge and forbidding.

It was where we'd been heading all the while, I realized. But I didn't know why. "Only now," Ellie said slowly, "what if Peter has changed his mind?"

"Got scared, maybe," I agreed. "The planning was okay, but the reality part of the program turned out to be more than he'd bargained for? And . . . speak of the devil."

His car was by the gate. Beyond it, at the end of a long, dark driveway, a lamp gleamed ochre yellow.

A terrace walled by a row of fruit trees, their branches resembling spider legs clambering a wire trellis, divided the drive from the front of Melinda Devine's house. We walked in silently from the road, turning once when a car slowed at the end of the driveway but then moved on. Then Ellie spoke again.

"How *did* those fellows from Augusta know to come a day before anything happened?" She answered herself. "Because someone told them, that's how. Someone wanted Faye Anne to be found the way she was. Only we happened to walk in on her, first."

Well, that was one theory. But: "What could you say to get them here a day early?" *Hi, I'm planning a murder for tomorrow. Want to come?*

Another theory, more likely, was still that Joy Abrams had gotten it wrong, had seen some other two men out at Duddy's Bar in Meddybemps. "Also," Ellie said, "Peter said he loved Faye Anne. But now . . ."

She gestured back at his car which had been sitting out there long enough for a thick frost to form on the windshield. "Maybe Melinda needed more computer advice than he expected," I said.

Ellie rolled her eyes. From where we stood you could just glimpse the top of the big tree Merle Carmody had meant to cut down, its bare branches towering vastly over a low roofline dimly visible beyond: the house Dimity Wilson had mentioned, that had gone to a foreclosure auction. "Or maybe it's been Peter Christie and Melinda all along," Ellie mused aloud.

"Oh, come on. Just for *that*?" I waved at the venerable old maple. It was impressive, all right, a gigantic specimen that in summer would be a green paradise, in autumn a ball of flame. It had probably been planted around the time Washington crossed the Delaware. But it was hardly, I thought, a motive for murder.

"We don't know what killing Merle was for," Ellie said. But as we reached Melinda's door she said, "I just wanted to talk to her."

By now it was full dark although my watch said the time was just four-thirty. Monday frisked in the snow, rolling in it to make doggy snow-angels.

"But I'm not so sure that surprising them together is a good idea," Ellie went on, frowning at the house.

Going in somewhere, though, was essential. Walking had kept my blood moving but now the cold was seeping through the soles of my boots, turning my toes to ice cubes.

"Look, I'm freezing. Let's go in and call, see if Sam's home, and ask him to come get us." Otherwise, the trip back to my house was going to be a survival trek.

"Maybe they *won't* be delighted to see us," I went on, "but if things get ugly we'll walk out again, wait outside for Sam, and go home as if nothing happened. It'll be fine," I said.

Which may have set the record for the largest number of complete inaccuracies uttered by me in a single breath. Because we did go in, and things did get ugly.

But we didn't walk out again as if nothing had happened.

Not by a long shot.

"**What are you** doing here?" Peter scowled up from the red velvet settee that formed the centerpiece of Melinda's lavish sitting room.

Simple decor would have been the natural choice in a Maine island cottage overlooking Passamaquoddy Bay. Instead she'd filled the spaces with enough gilt mirrors, brocade wallpaper, fringed draperies, and figured lampshades to furnish a bordello.

Peter held a glass of wine in one hand and a complicated-looking hors d'oeuvre of some sort in the other. A fire burned in the state-of-the-art propane fireplace Melinda had put in, preferring it of course to the labor and mess of wood. The stereo was playing "Bolero." An upholstered wing chair was draped with Melinda's signature paisley scarf; no doubt she'd looked fetching by the firelight, toying with its fringes. But now at the sight of us she'd jumped to her feet, and what she looked, primarily, was livid.

Thin, gorgeous, and furious with us: black slacks that made her look slim as a switchblade, cashmere sweater, angry pouting mouth below cheeks made even pinker than usual by her emotion. "Peter," she said, not trying to hide her annoyance, "please pour our unexpected guests a—"

"Shut up, Melinda," he snapped. "They don't want a drink."

Or if we did, I gathered we weren't getting it. I glanced around: no sign here of Melinda's rumored brother-in-residence. Suddenly I wondered how accurate a story *that* was, too.

"Haven't you two made things bad enough already?" Peter demanded, glaring at Ellie and me. "For God's sake, I've had *reporters* calling."

I wondered as well why Melinda let him talk to her that way; it wasn't like her. I'd seen her split a fellow's lip once at a dinner party after he got tipsy and said—not realizing she was standing right behind him—that he didn't care how warm-blooded she was, she was still too skinny to make a man a decent mouthful.

Thinking of that reminded me that she was capable of violence. But: beyond the sitting room, china and crystal gleamed on the dining table. Tall red candles were lit, the cloth was a festive green-and-gold, and delicious aromas drifted from beyond the swinging doors of her designer kitchen. She wanted something, all right, enough to let Peter Christie sass her.

Or feared something. And not for Melinda the direct approach when devious would do.

"Listen," I said, "I'm not trying to get you in trouble. But I've got a decision to make about what I tell Bob Arnold," I continued to Peter. "I know you weren't here the night Merle died. And I know Faye Anne wasn't, either. If you were together, and you don't want that getting out, I understand. But if not, if you were doing something else . . ."

Such as getting ready to knock off Merle Carmody and make it look as if Faye Anne had done it, I added silently. ". . . well, that would be another matter. Wouldn't it?"

Melinda's eyes narrowed. "Peter, dear, I think you should confide in Jacobia, don't you? Because it *might* look—"

Oh, what the heck; we were here, and the two of them were already mad at us. So I interrupted:

"Yeah, it sure might. And here's how: you, Melinda, *and* Faye Anne all get together in a plan. Peter kills Merle, and Faye Anne takes the blame with her cockamamie story about not remembering what happened, counting on you, Peter, to get her out afterwards. Melinda's part in it is, she gets rid of an enemy in return for helping you."

Precisely how that part would work, especially since she didn't seem to be helping him much right now, I hadn't figured out yet. But maybe if I rattled them enough, *they'd* tell *me*.

"Maybe Faye Anne goes to jail for a while," I added firmly as Melinda gasped and Peter looked as if I might be his next victim any minute. "Maybe not. Merle's habit of hitting her could play a part in how that turns out." In the other room, Ellie spoke quietly on the telephone, calling Sam.

"But what Faye Anne doesn't know," I continued, "is that Merle's bad habit is the *only* thing she's got going for her. Because whatever you promised her, Peter, it could be that you weren't planning to deliver it. Or," I added, glancing around at the romantic setting, "you aren't, anymore."

I was just fishing, hoping he'd bite if he got angry enough, and start talking. To my complete astonishment, he did.

"All right, all right, we were together, Faye Anne and me. Is that such a *crime*? I needed to talk with her," he added to Melinda, who despite her earlier joking on the topic now looked seriously unhappy at his admission. So either she was a marvelous actress or she really hadn't known where he was, on Sunday night.

"The thing is, Melinda and I were becoming . . . involved," he told me. "And it was over between me and Faye Anne. She'd made that clear. But it wasn't like I didn't care about her at all."

Melinda was watching him carefully, waiting for more.

Me, too. Meanwhile, Ellie had wandered into the dining room, to the long row of windows that looked out over the back garden. Four balsam wreaths made matched, ribboned bull's-eye centers on the windowpanes.

"So I got her to agree to see me, when Merle would think she was at the meeting," Peter said, with a frown at Melinda.

"Peter," she protested, "I *told* you why I called Merle. If you'd just let me *know* that you were with her instead of keeping it a deep, dark *secret*, why then of course I'd never have . . ."

I had a feeling there were plenty of things Peter didn't tell Melinda. Such as, for instance, that as his current romantic interest, she was little more than a bead on a very long string. Not that she wouldn't have heard the talk about him, but she was just the type to believe she could change his womanizing habits.

"Anyway, you saw Faye Anne that night," I interrupted. "I guess you drove around, talking?"

Because they couldn't have stopped anywhere or someone would have seen them together, maybe pass it along to her husband. Peter nodded. "Right. We drove around. And I got a little emotional with her, I guess. I was angry with her for staying with Merle."

"So you argued about it. Drank a little, maybe?" I wasn't sure why that mattered. The three wine bottles made me ask, that was all. He nodded again.

"Yes. She wasn't drunk when I took her home, though. Faye Anne never drank much. Just a sip. She said Merle drank enough for both of them. And I don't know what she did after she went inside. I parked around the corner so he wouldn't spot me, but I made sure I was where I could still see her opening the door, going in. So I'd know that she was all right."

Yeah, he was a real Boy Scout. He frowned, remembering. "The house was mostly dark. A light in the kitchen, I think, but that was all. It was around eleven. The meetings went later but that's the latest he let her stay out."

"And that's the last you saw of her."

"Yes, the last I—"

"But wait, that's not right. You saw her come out of the house the next morning, didn't you? That's how you knew she was wearing the apron and gloves, you saw them when the police were bringing her out."

He flushed in the waning glow of the fire; I'd led him right into another lie, deliberately, then snatched him out of it.

"Because," I added, not looking at Melinda, "you'd been watching Faye Anne again. Following her. Calling her, too, maybe, and hanging up?"

I watched him hesitate, then decide to try working out

some way of putting a good face on that part of it. Because how could a lot of hang-up calls be construed as benevolent attention? He managed it, though.

Defensively, to Melinda: "I worried about Faye Anne, that's all. I wanted to hear her voice, be sure she was okay. But I couldn't speak to her, let her know it was me, in case Merle might have been listening in."

"Peter is always so concerned about his friends," Melinda commented acidly, and stalked away from us.

Ellie returned as the door between the dining area and kitchen swung angrily; moments later I heard ice cubes clinking. Something stronger than wine, apparently, was needed to wash down the information that Peter had been tracking Faye Anne around Eastport as if he were a bloodhound *and* harassing her with phone calls.

"Nice dinner cooking," Ellie said to him. Her face looked strange, as if she'd had bad news, and her voice was subdued. "I guess you and Melinda are a pair."

"I told you, it was over between Faye Anne and me," Peter insisted. Melinda returned with a tall glass full of ice and amber liquid, her eyes still blazing.

"Right," Ellie said, "and I'll bet it's *really* over, now. After all, she's in trouble, and what fun is a woman in trouble?"

That riled him again. "She's the one they found covered in blood. You want to know if my feelings about her have changed? Big surprise: yes, they have. At first I thought she *couldn't* have done it, but now that I've had time to think it over, I can't figure out any other explanation. Other than that she killed him. And finding out that she could do *that*—"

Melinda broke in. "The very idea of us all making up some big plot to kill Merle is nonsense. For one thing, *I* wouldn't have any reason to go along with such a—"

"I guess that property dispute is all settled, too, then," I interjected mildly.

She reddened. "How did you know about that?"

"Merle didn't by any chance try to double-cross you on the land, did he? Or . . . maybe *you* lent him the money to buy it?"

"Why would I do *that*? Why, that's the silliest—"

"Because anyone else would want the house *and* the adjoining land. But you wanted the specific piece of land *between* your house and that other one, nothing more. You don't want a second house, or another tax bill."

She shuddered involuntarily: Melinda the penny-pincher. "But the property wasn't for sale in two pieces," I said. "Bank foreclosures don't work that way. So you needed someone to buy it for you. Someone you could control, who would agree to pass the tree part to you and sell the house part to someone else, maybe."

"Wait a minute," Peter objected. "First of all, why not just buy the whole place herself and sell off the house? Second, what makes you think Merle would've cooperated in all this? And if he would cooperate, why change his mind?"

He swallowed some wine. "Seems like he'd come out of the whole thing with a house free and clear. You think she'd buy a house for him just to get one silly maple tree for herself?"

He sat up looking proud of himself and from the glance she gave him, I could see that with this argument he'd gone a long way toward getting himself back into Melinda's good graces. I said: "I think she'd buy a house for Merle if she knew she was going to get the money back, once *he* sold it. Which he would, but meanwhile he would hold the title *and* more to the point, pay the property taxes and transaction expenses."

"And how exactly would I know to do all that?" she asked thinly. "I guess you think I've got know-how in the real estate area?"

"I think it ain't brain surgery. And I think you know how to manipulate guys like Merle. Ones who are greedy, stupid, and—here's the important part of it—usually drunk. So maybe he didn't read the contract real carefully? A contract between the two of you? Or even read it at all?"

Her face told me my wild guess was also a lucky one. I decided to push my luck. "A contract, say, that included your holding a *lien* on the entire property? And made sure you got the lion's share—or maybe even all—of any profit on the house?"

Like I say, once upon a time I was the cat's pajamas in the money department. An ugly red began climbing Melinda's throat.

"This is foolish speculation! Believe me, if Merle Carmody had made any deal with me, he'd have kept it, contract or no contract."

"That is the big question," I agreed. "Once Merle made the deal, why *did* he go back on it?" Her confident answer had already told me there was nothing in writing that I could research, or anyway nothing among public documents. By now she'd have disposed of any private paperwork that he might have signed.

And it was too much to hope for that he'd have taken a copy for himself. If he had, she wouldn't be looking indignant; she'd be looking scared.

"One possible answer: he figured out that he was getting screwed," I said. "So he decided to do what you most wanted to prevent: cut the tree, or threaten to, anyway, to force you to forgive the lien."

But Peter was shaking his head. "Merle wouldn't have gone for it. He was stupid, but sly. If a deal looked too good, he'd have smelled a rat to begin with."

And that stopped me, as Melinda looked warmly at him again. Raw cunning was indeed one quality Merle Carmody had possessed in abundance. Yet the money for the property and his recent home improvements had come from somewhere.

A car pulled up outside: Sam. Peter followed us to the door.

"You're wrong about all this."

"You wanted Faye Anne's diary found." I untied Monday's leash. "You knew what was in it, knew it could be read as premeditation."

"No," Peter insisted. "I wanted to help. You're giving me way too much credit."

I wouldn't have called it credit. And anyway, I didn't believe him. I wasn't convinced that he'd murdered Merle Carmody *or* that Faye Anne hadn't. But there was something so cravenly opportunistic about Peter Christie, so anxious to spy out his own best chance to come out of this all right—and as comfortably as possible—that I didn't trust him.

He was hiding something; I felt certain of it. But what? Ellie still looked troubled, too, as we made our way to the car where Sam waited, just outside.

"Jake. While you all were talking I was looking around in the house, and at them."

Her voice sounded strained. At the end of the drive another car slowed, moved on. "I noticed," I said. "And?"

"Melinda was wearing fancy cloth slippers with metallic embroidery. Peter wore loafers, expensive ones. And they were dry."

"So?" The air was coldly crystalline, the stars overhead as sharp as splinters.

"There were footprints out back. Fresh ones, boots in the snow. Right up to those back windows. And another thing. Her phone has the buttons you program. For frequently dialed numbers? So I pressed the first one."

"And?" Across the bay, the holiday lights on Campobello Island twinkled distantly. The Roosevelts used to summer there: FDR had been stricken with polio there. No boats were in sight. The freighter had passed through the channel by now and the fishing boats were home for the night.

"Well, *if* you were part of a plot to kill Merle Carmody—"

"And," I added, "you want to lay the blame on Faye Anne—"

"Right," she said. I opened the car's back door; Monday leapt in gratefully. Sam was behind the wheel, alone.

"Why," Ellie went on, still sounding distracted, "would you have Bob Arnold's number on your speed dialer?"

"Huh," I said. "That is interesting."

But it wasn't all. When I opened the front door, the inside light went on and I saw her face.

She'd learned something else. And she hadn't wanted to say it, not until we were away from Melinda and Peter. "What?" I demanded.

It was Sam who answered grimly. "The scallop boats are all back. All of them but George's," he said.

Eastport women have been sending their men to sea for hundreds of years; no one makes much fuss over it. But by six that evening all the wives of the *Etta*'s crew were in my kitchen, white-faced and silent.

Ellie took the fruitcakes out of the oven, burning herself in the process. One of the women wrapped ice in a towel and another got some butter.

"Don't care what they say," she muttered, dabbing a bit on the spot. "The old remedies ease you best."

But there was no easing what we felt. Wade came in at around seven, dressed in winter storm gear, and we all looked at him.

"Coast Guard's out," he reported. "Search helicopter's coming. I'm going, too. Had a position on them from the EPIRB, out past Crow Island."

The electronic position indicator radio beacon, he meant;

an essential piece of safety equipment on a fishing vessel. But there was no actual guarantee that the beacon was still with the boat. In a catastrophe it could be sent drifting. The tides and currents could carry it for miles.

"When?" one of the younger women cried, then pressed her fingers tight to her lips. Anything you said, now, could be the wrong thing. Around us the old house seemed to hold its breath: none of its usual creakings and sighings as it settled. As if like us it could only wait, hoping, to find out what would happen.

"Little while ago," Wade answered tersely. Which could mean anything from a couple of minutes to a couple of hours; he was in no mood to talk about it. He went out again.

In the summer the men had contests to see who could scramble into the survival suits fastest, and onto the life rafts. Always a lot of laughter and good-natured joshing, the idea of night and disaster the farthest thing from anyone's mind. Now we tried hard not to imagine them out there, doing it in earnest.

Hard but unsuccessfully; at seven-thirty, Victor called to whine some more about his love life, and I felt so beaten and hopelessly hollowed out that I let him, although I made him call back on Wade's line so mine would be open.

Victor hadn't heard yet what was going on, and I didn't tell him, in case he said something inappropriate about it and I would have to begin hating him. What he did say was, "Jacobia, I am at my wit's end."

This being, I thought, only a few millimeters from its beginning, but never mind; as I'd suspected, Willetta was still driving him crazy. The chip on his girlfriend's sister's shoulder was Vermont-sized, he complained, and she was always around. The way he told it, she had broken up with some local guy recently and was taking it out on Victor.

From the karmic standpoint, I thought taking it out on

Victor was fully justified. But I didn't say so, just sat there listening to him, making a few noises now and then so he'd know that I was still on the line. Agreeing with him, which was all he wanted; eventually he got tired and we hung up.

It was eight o'clock. A little later, Sam came downstairs and made sandwiches without being asked to. Nobody was hungry, but we all picked at them as the minutes ticked by. The women had stowed their children across the street at the church hall with the ladies from the Altar Guild, and bedtimes were imminent.

But no one wanted to fetch them. It was as if we were all in suspended animation, or a nightmare from which we were collectively unable to wake. I got up to wash my hands again.

"Mom." Sam took me aside. He'd been with Tommy most of the day, working on the old car, then on the computer and doing errands for his Internet project. "There were messages for you when I got home." Ellie had said so, too. But everything about the earlier part of the day now felt as if it had happened on the moon.

I shook my head. "I don't want to talk to anybody." Outside, the helicopter from the air station at Cape Cod whapped heavily overhead. Each deep thud-thud cut into my heart like a dull blade.

"I figured that," he said. "But there was a weird one."

This was torture. All I kept remembering was that survival time in the water was about fifteen minutes, if they hadn't got the gear on.

I looked at Sam, trying to focus on him. "What do you mean, weird?" The girl who'd asked Wade the question earlier sat at my kitchen table now, crying.

"Just . . . Here, I wrote it down." He went to the phone alcove.

"Stop that," I heard Ellie tell the girl evenly, as Sam came back with the paper he'd written the message on.

It must have seemed important to him or he wouldn't have tried writing it at all; Sam is so dyslexic, he records classroom notes on a cassette player, and he pays other students to tape reading assignments.

Now he frowned at the note, laboriously printed. "Whoever it was didn't leave a name, and I didn't recognize the voice." He handed the slip of paper to me. "But they said . . ."

I stared at it. The words were clear enough, but . . .

The weeping grew louder. "It's only nine o'clock," Ellie said over it, her own voice rising. "What're you going to do, start praying the rosary and giving his clothes away?"

But the girl was inconsolable, and no one dared say any of the words that would comfort her. No one but Ellie, cold rage lighting her face. "Listen to me. They. Will. Come. *Back.*"

Sam closed his eyes a moment. Ellie was tempting fate.

Defying it, even. Sam continued: "Whoever it was, Mom, they were whispering. I couldn't even tell if it was a man or a woman. And they said, 'Check out Ben Devine, Melinda's brother.' Then . . . click."

"What?" I crumpled the notepaper. It was as if I were listening—thinking, feeling—through a thick, sense-blocking layer of cotton batting.

A protective layer. I dreaded the moment when it would be pulled away. The sound of the search helicopter faded out into the distance over the water.

Ellie went on angrily: "They'll come back and they'll be fine. Do you hear me? Every single one of them will come . . ."

She spoke with such certainty that I almost believed her: that the laws of cold water might really be suspended, just this one time.

". . . *home,*" she pronounced savagely.

And then I did believe.

"That's the whole message," Sam said, but I wasn't listening anymore. While Ellie was talking, the back door had opened and I turned to see who it was. The man who had entered the house now stood silently, witnessing her faith.

Her furious faith.

It was her husband, George Valentine.

Later, upstairs with Wade in the dark: "How close was it?"

"Pretty close. Lost engine. Battery, too, so no comms."

Radio, he meant. "The EPIRB had drifted," he went on, "and they were taking on water."

Which was the mariner's way of saying the boat had been sinking. "Safety equipment was maintained, though, and the guys out of Jonesport found 'em quick, or it'd be a different story."

Different from this drained, almost disembodied sense of relief: the boat was history, but the men were all safe.

I put my head on his shoulder. "It all happened so *fast*." Or so it felt, now: as if the dark wings of disaster had brushed us, swooping past. Sparing us. Wade settled against me.

"Yeah, well, one minute you're the dog and the next minute you're the fire hydrant, out there on the water."

Monday looked up from where she nested between us, hearing the word "dog." She wouldn't sleep downstairs, anymore; not by herself.

"But you try not to take chances, and you trust people to help you," Wade said. "That's all"–he yawned hugely–"anyone can do. When push comes to shove we are in each other's hands, is the long and short of it."

Then: "Jake, I didn't get the freighter repair job."

To fix equipment on the big boats on a regular basis. "Wade, I'm so sorry."

" 'Sokay. Guy who got it, he's got some degrees and so on. All the qualifications. So they took him. I met him, he's an okay guy. And there's still plenty of harbor pilot work."

He sounded all right with it but I was still glad I hadn't said anything about diamonds.

"Wade," I began again after a while.

I was thinking of Ellie, the message Sam took, and what Wade had said: *in each other's hands.*

And about something else: that no matter how I washed them, my own hands still felt sticky and I kept smelling blood.

But he was asleep.

Chapter 6

The next morning dawned blisteringly cold. The sun over the bay was like a lemon slice hovering over an iced drink. By then I'd decided not to say anything to anyone about how I was feeling; I decided it would pass.

The anonymous call looked less significant in daylight, too: "The story's been in the papers and on TV. And even though you and I so far have managed to avoid being interviewed, by now everyone around here knows we found the body."

Ellie nodded silently. George's narrow escape was still hideously present to her.

"Or it could have been Peter, I guess, but from the look of it he'd been out there with Melinda for a while." Sam hadn't been sure, exactly, when the call came in.

I was pressing rope caulk between a dining-room windowsill and its sash. The glass in the sash seemed to suck the warmth right out of my fingers.

"Just a mischief-maker, then." Ellie tried out the idea. "Not anyone who's really involved at all."

"Calling us just to try stirring up trouble for Melinda," I agreed.

Well, it could happen. Eastport's not immune to that sort

of idle mischief. And plenty of people didn't like Melinda: her unspoken assumption that she was much better than you, and that you should do what she wanted the instant she decided she wanted it, rubbed people the wrong way.

And that business of her never wearing a coat. "I didn't see any evidence of the brother at her house, though, did you? Does she," I asked, pressing in the last bit of rope caulk, "even *have* a brother? Someone named Ben?"

As a person from away I was not expected to have the names, ages, and occupations of all the members of local families in my head. But Ellie did.

"Oh, yes. Ben got drafted to Vietnam, and his and Melinda's parents went to Bangor for a few years, around that time. Their dad worked at the Air Force base, and their mom taught school. They came back after they'd retired, Melinda along with them, and they left her that house. But . . ."

Give Ellie enough time and she could trace every family tree in Eastport right back to the original acorn.

". . . but Ben was out of the service, through college, and was teaching, too, by then." She tipped her head in thought. "At some private school. He is—or was, I guess—a math professor. And then I thought I heard he was sick. But maybe that part was wrong because I never heard any more about it. And I think George said something about him being around here again."

The phone rang and I got up grudgingly, thinking it might be another reporter, though the volume of those calls had dropped. I felt lucky to have escaped them all and fortunate, too, that no one in town would tell a stranger where I lived, or where Ellie did. Eastporters know how to circle the wagons around their own.

It was Bob Arnold. "I just got a call from our friend Melinda Devine," he said.

Speak of the devil yet again; my eyebrows went up. Why

call Bob? Ellie and I hadn't sung songs of holiday cheer at
Melinda's. But I didn't think we'd done anything illegal, either.

"*His* boots," Ellie said thoughtfully to herself.

"She says she's been trying to get hold of Kenty
Dalrymple," Bob went on. "Something about a garden club
meeting?"

Melinda was always trying to lure Kenty into her club.
"Only Kenty's not answering her phone," Bob said.

"Yes," I replied slowly, still not understanding what that
might have to do with me.

". . . and I'm tied down here with some state cops trying
to help get a plan together, set up surveillance on a bar in—"
He stopped short, probably not having meant to say that
much.

"I understand, Bob." Duddy's, I supposed. It had been
only a matter of time before its reputation reached Augusta.

"So I can't go," he finished, and waited.

Which was when I got it. This would be another of
Melinda's maneuvers to ingratiate herself with Kenty: fake
concern for the older woman's welfare.

A neighborly gesture, but without, of course, Melinda
having to do anything, herself. "Okay," I said resignedly.
"Ellie and I can take a run over there, make sure Kenty's
okay."

"Hey, thanks, Jacobia." Bob sounded relieved. "Probably
Kenty just turned off her phone. Strangers've been calling
her, those newspeople and all, I guess 'cause she lives right
there next to the Carmodys. But if she's fallen and can't get
up, you know I'll never hear the end of it from Melinda."

"Right." I hung up. Ellie already was pulling her coat on,
having caught the drift, and Monday brightened at the
prospect of going out again; I'd practically had to drag her indoors after her walk that morning.

A few minutes later we were making our way up snowy

Key Street past the Episcopal church hall; through the hall windows we could see the Altar Guild ladies, unfazed by their vigil labors of the night before, making evergreen garlands for the chapel.

"Maybe Kenty's gone out," Ellie said as we knocked and waited.

No sound from within. "We should try to make sure, though," I said, trying the door.

It swung open with a faint creak. Inside, the house was icy cold. Monday sniffed at the still air and didn't want to go any farther.

Me either, suddenly. "I don't like this," I said. "Maybe we should . . ."

"Kenty?" Ellie called, stepping inside. "You around, dear?"

Dee-yah. In the parlor, the three pill bottles stood on the table where I'd seen them before. The fluorescent bulbs set up over her collection of tiny plants glowed bluish in the otherwise darkened room, the draperies drawn.

No fire burned in the parlor stove. Monday trotted to the foot of the hall stairs and whined, pawing the bottom step.

I went up: smells of camphor, age, and loneliness.

"Kenty?" I called.

But she didn't answer and she wasn't going to.

Kenty Dalrymple lay fully clothed in the narrow upstairs hall that led from the bathroom to the bedroom. A fist pressed to her chest, no mark of violence on her; not unless you counted the expression on her face.

I did. "Ellie," I said quietly, and she came up.

"Stand here, please, and look in the direction she'd have been looking as she came out of the bedroom."

Ellie silently obeyed. Kenty was wearing the same print

housedress I'd seen her in the day before. Maybe she'd gone into the bedroom after I'd left her, for a nap.

But then she'd come out again. "The hall closet," Ellie said, looking at its partially open door. "And . . ."

She pointed at the soft chenille belt of a bathrobe on the floor. "But she isn't wearing any bathrobe," Ellie added in the tone of mild interest she uses when her mind is busily putting things together.

I moved to the hall window. From it you could see into the Carmody house; Faye Anne's white lace panels covered only the lower sashes. You could see the garden, its raised beds covered now by a foot of snow, the compost heap in the corner a white, rounded lump, the picket fence broken by a pair of gates: one for the driveway and one for the front walk.

And you could see the street, and the front door. A row of low cedars, neatly trimmed long ago to form a dark-green privacy fence, blocked all other aspects. So that was all you could see from Kenty Dalrymple's windows.

But it had been enough.

"If someone came in while she napped . . ." Ellie said.

I nodded. "And hid in that closet."

"Waiting. With that belt, to strangle her when she came out into the hall. She was so frail, it wouldn't have taken much. And the belt is chenille, soft enough so it might not leave a mark if someone was lucky and quick."

"But they didn't have to be, maybe." I peered into the closet, pulled the string that switched on a bulb.

Its harsh yellow glow showed where items on hangers had been pushed aside. A shelf at the back of the closet had served as a low bench. A few sweaters on it were shoved over untidily. The small enclosure held a mingled fragrance of lavender and scented talc.

"Wouldn't have to be quick, I mean." Visualizing it all in my mind's eye made me back hastily out of the closet. "The shock of seeing someone bursting out here at her unexpectedly . . ."

Ellie looked down at the dead woman, nodding. "Her heart could've just stopped."

We got a bedspread from one of the spare rooms—white sheer curtains, dressers with doilies, neat narrow twin beds no guest had slept in for many years—and put it over her, and I called Bob Arnold, not mentioning what we thought might have happened. To look at her, you would think she had simply suffered a heart attack.

Except for her face, the expression of horror etched deeply into the soft, white flesh, and I already knew what would likely be said about that. Down in the parlor while we waited for Bob, I examined the pill bottles again without touching them.

One was nitroglycerin: "for chest pain." The second vial held tablets of a digitalis compound. Ellie peered at the third one, frowned at the blue-printed pharmacy label.

" 'Methylphenidate,' " she read aloud. " 'Take BID.' That's not very enlightening."

But it was enlightening to me. Once upon a time I'd been a veritable human *Physician's Desk Reference* when it came to the pharmaceutical substances that might be used to assist learning-disabled kids.

"Methylphenidate is the generic name for Ritalin. So Sam was right." I went to the bookshelf, and sure enough, there were two volumes on ADD, attention deficit disorder, both fairly new hardcovers with gold stickers from Bay Books affixed to their bright jackets, slid in among the garden encyclopedias and the how-to plant books.

Ellie looked perplexed. "I don't get how this stuff works, though. If you're already too flighty, too agitated or whatever, and you take a drug like this, sort of an amphetamine-type thing, doesn't it just speed you up more?"

"It speeds you up only if you don't have the disorder it's

prescribed for," I replied, shivering. It was so cold in the house. But there was no sense turning any heat on.

Not anymore. "But look at it this way, Ellie: what if you're *too* active, too impulsive, because you don't have the brain chemical you need to turn *off* the impulses. That's the deficit they mean when they talk about attention deficit, see? So the impulses you have just stay in control, and you have no choice but to go along with them, whatever they are. You can't control your *self*. Like some hyperactive kids."

I remembered Kenty's inability to stick to any topic, her seemingly random veering from one emotional state to another. And then, as if a magic switch had been flipped in her mind, she'd been able to focus.

Because her medication had kicked in. "This," I pointed at the small orange vial, "is the chemical. If you think of the act of quelling an impulse *as* an act, not as the absence of one, you'll get the picture."

Or anyway that was how it had been explained to me, back in the days when I'd have dosed Sam with eye of newt and toe of frog if only it could have helped him. But Sam hadn't had ADD or any other chemical disorder. In addition to his dyslexia, which had not been vulnerable to drug therapy, he'd just been messed up royally, principally by me and his father.

Another memory niggled at me; searching for it, I went to Kenty's kitchen. It was a big, old-fashioned room with a round-shouldered Frigidaire and a gas stove that had a wood-burning section on one side. A basket of newspaper spills stood by the soapstone sink.

I opened the cabinet doors. No baking supplies. "But she said she'd baked cookies, that she went to Faye Anne's house to borrow—"

I opened the refrigerator. Skim milk; no butter, no eggs. In the trash, no egg carton or butter wrapper.

Bob Arnold's car pulled up outside. "She lied about baking," I told Ellie. "And she did it after she'd started seeming sane and in control, as if . . ."

As if it had been deliberate, even planned. Kenty had let me in as if she'd been waiting for me, or for someone she could talk to.

Someone she could *tell.* "Ellie, I think maybe the night of Merle's death Kenty could have seen something she wasn't supposed to see, and someone knew it."

"But if that's true, it means she really was . . ."

Murdered, she would have finished. But she didn't want to. Instead, we went to meet Bob as he came in, and what with waiting for the ambulance so Kenty wouldn't have to get into it alone, and afterwards making sure the house was locked up and the furnace set high enough so the pipes wouldn't freeze, Ellie never did get a chance to make herself draw the conclusion aloud.

But she didn't need to because we both knew what we thought. Walking home with Monday, we kept our eyes peeled; inside, we locked up and checked every room in the house, like kids coming home from a scary movie. Because no matter what the medical examiner said—and he did, too, the very next day, calling it heart failure and explaining her facial expression as involuntary muscular contraction—Ellie and I were convinced another kind of death had been planned for Kenty. Her unstable heart had merely made the planned action unnecessary.

And that to us meant: (a) there'd been two killers running around Eastport this holiday season, which was about as likely as two meteors striking us simultaneously.

Or (b) there was one.

Still running around, I mean. Not in jail.

Ergo: not Faye Anne Carmody.

But when a lady of advanced years drops dead among her pill bottles and her African violets, a bathrobe belt and

an unhappy expression are unlikely to be seen as convincing
evidence of her murder.

So we knew, or thought we did.

But we were the only ones thinking about it that way.

Other, I mean, than the one who'd done it.

"None of your business," Ben Devine told Ellie and me a
little later that morning. We were sitting at a table at the rear
of La Sardina, Eastport's sort-of Mexican restaurant.

Not much on the menu would be recognized as Mexican
food, by a native; the meat in one taco would feed a
Mexican family for a week, and the house specialty—fresh
scallop tortilla, in season—was an especially downeast twist
on the cuisine.

But what the place lacked in culinary authenticity, it
made up in decor; twinkling lights, candle-jammed Kahlúa
bottles, serape curtains, bright checked tablecloths, and
oversized houseplants all combined somehow to give the impression that a large, colorful *piñata* had exploded somewhere nearby.

Ben had pulled up in a standard Eastport work vehicle:
an aged Ford pickup, light blue, lots of Bondo. Now he
glared at us across the table.

"Taught math. Quit. Came here. That's all you need to
know."

He took another drag of a cigarette, crushed it out. You
can still smoke in a bar in Maine, if the bar owner pays a
higher license fee and prohibits unaccompanied youngsters.
Personally I'd rather eat dinner with a chain-smoker than a
health-nazi; at least the smoker isn't pretending to be interested in my welfare, instead of in his own superior political
correctness. But anyway:

"So, you're staying with Melinda?" Ellie inquired
brightly. She thinks there aren't many barriers that can't be

broken by a dose of her own pure, unadulterated friendliness, and usually she is right.

But not this time. "Yeah," Ben Devine said. He was a big man, rawboned and fiftyish, wearing jeans and a flannel shirt, his thick, greying hair tied back with a leather thong. One of his huge boots would've swallowed both my feet, with plenty of room to spare.

Then out of the blue the math thing rang a bell. "You wouldn't happen to be the B. J. Devine who wrote the Devine candlestick formula?" I blurted, not thinking it could be true.

Candlesticking is one of the trickier methods of charting stock market activity; the graphing patterns, with colorful names like Three White Soldiers, Advancing Blocks, and Bearish Counterattack, are used to predict what a stock may do in the future—i.e., go up or down—based on what the patterns have presaged in the past.

Devine's eyes flickered briefly with interest. "Yeah. That was me." But his tone suggested that this had been in some other life, no longer relevant.

In my own money career, I'd gone straight for fundamentals: How much cash? How much debt? What's the burn rate? Do people want the product? And—the most important question, perhaps—is the CEO a solid, smart person or a power-mad looney-tune? A lot of people swore by candlesticking, though, and by the variation on it that B. J. Devine had invented, after I'd left the business.

"But"—he mashed another cigarette—"that's history. You want to know about Merle Carmody."

Interesting segue: two things that were history. "Right. Somebody called me," I said. "Someone who seemed to think you might know something about Merle's death. D'you have any idea who might want to implicate you in it?"

Because while Ellie and I were going around my house

making sure no one lurked in it—Monday following us approvingly as if to say it was about time someone did an actual *search,* for heaven's sake—something occurred to us. If the call about Ben was not mischief, might it have been meant as misdirection?

Devine drank black coffee with his cigarettes, and from the harsh sound of his laugh it was a habit he'd been pursuing for years. "Unfortunate. That's a good one. Like wiping out smallpox. Maybe someone thinks I'd be good to implicate 'cause I'm so glad he's dead."

"Your frankness is refreshing." Also a little worrisome, I thought. "May I ask why you disliked Merle Carmody so intensely?"

"Nope. But I'll tell you how you know I didn't kill him."

He leaned across the table at me, his eyes locking onto mine. "Because I'm a knife man, see? A *meticulous* knife man. And if I'd cut that son of a bitch up there wouldn't have been a head in one of those packages."

Word of that had gotten out, of course. Ben Devine smiled down at his nicotine-stained fingers. "If I'd done it, I'd have started with his tongue. Skinned it, trimmed it, boiled it with an onion. I'd be at home now, having it in a sandwich."

The knife on Devine's belt was a big Randall in a hand-sewn leather scabbard. Not the kind of item you would use to dress out a deer. This was a Vietnam infantry knife; Wade had one, up in his workshop. A killing knife.

"But I didn't," Ben said. "I just mind my own business. And I expect other people to mind theirs. Any more questions?"

Not waiting for an answer he slapped money on the bar and went out; the blue pickup roared to life, its carburetor banging out a couple of smoky backfires like parting shots.

"Well," Ellie said into the silence afterwards. Ben had blitzed in, laid his rap on us, and blitzed out, all in about ten minutes. "Another happy member of Merle Carmody's fan club. Not."

Ted Armstrong, La Sardina's daytime bar man, came over with fresh coffee and we drank it gratefully to get the bitter taste of Ben's remarks from our mouths. "What did he mean, Ted? Do you know *why* Ben hated Merle so much?"

Ted nodded, running a towel on the bar trim, straightening the backgammon and cribbage boards and the boxed chess set, all stacked at the end of the polished surface.

"Ayuh. Don't see Ben a whole lot. Not that I particularly want to. He is way too intense for me."

He was that, all right. You ran into guys like Ben now and then in Eastport: with oversized personalities that had not fit comfortably into whatever mold they'd burst out of. They lived on the mainland, mostly, sometimes in desperately ramshackle little off-road cabins without electricity, plumbing, or central heat, and came to town a few times a year for medicine and supplies.

Mostly, they were perfectly fine people. But a few of them weren't: if you wanted it to be, Eastport was the perfect spot for vanishing right off the face of the earth, out of sight of any pursuing authorities. Even a murder only got the city news crews here for two days.

"I heard where he was some kind of math wizard back at the school he was at," Teddy said, pouring pretzels into a bowl.

"Right. And Michael Jordan was a basketball player."

"Uh-huh. The real deal, huh? But anyway, when he got to Eastport last summer he wasn't like that. Started doing odd jobs. And one of 'em was, when hunting season got here, he cut up deer for people."

"Oh," Ellie said, enlightenment spreading over her face. That was one of the things Merle Carmody had done for money, too. Professional woodsmen did their own butchering but if you only went out once a year, got your deer and that was the end of it, it wasn't the kind of thing you got much practice at.

"And Merle didn't like it," said Teddy, "that someone from away was cuttin' into his customer base. Get it? Cuttin' in? And Merle, he started talkin' about Ben." He smiled at his own joke. "Tales out of school, you might say," he added, chuckling again.

"So Merle started some nasty rumor about Ben?" Could that explain the tongue references?

"Ayuh. Said Ben left bone chips in the meat. And other icky stuff I won't go into." Teddy made a face. "Ended up that nobody wanted Ben Devine handling their edibles anymore."

He wiped his hands on the bar towel, tossed it in the dirty linen hamper. "And Carmody started doing more business after that but it wasn't enough for him. He kept after Ben in the flappin'-his-yap department. Just kept talkin'." He began flicking at the bottles behind the bar with a feather duster. "Hear Merle tell it, Ben was the real killer that O. J. Simpson's been lookin' for."

He flicked a bottle of Galliano, squinted at it, and flicked it again. The Harvey Wallbanger, I gathered, had been out of favor for a while. "Merle kept bad-mouthin' Ben any way he could, and Ben didn't like it."

All of which presented another motive neat as a butcher's package. So far by my count we had love for Peter Christie, money for Melinda, vengeance for Ben, and self-preservation for Faye Anne, herself; if there'd been an Olympic event for racking up mortal enemies, Merle would've won the gold.

"Why did Ben leave the college?" Ellie wanted to know. "Have you heard anything about that?"

"Well," Teddy replied uncertainly, "what I heard was,

folks there thought he killed a fellow. But I don't know how much truth there really is in *that*."

Ellie and I looked at each other. "Is that so?" she said mildly, waiting for more.

"Uh-huh. Some guy at the school he was at was s'posed to've disappeared. But they never found a body, was what I heard, and he never got charged with anything, Ben didn't. Only suspected hard, the story goes."

"I'm surprised we've never heard about that," I said.

Teddy shrugged. "You know how it is. Thing gets to be old news." He waved at the street beyond La Sardina's front window. "And Ben keeps his head down pretty good. Guy's not around much, that's not the guy people're going to be gabbin' about. 'Cept for Merle. And *he's* not going to anymore, either."

Ted began rinsing the glasses: more hot water, then onto the rack for drying. I wanted to plunge my hands into the steaming soapy basin.

"Not," he added, "that *anyone* was too hot on hearin' *Merle* gab. And toward the end, there, I didn't have to, 'cause he was hangin' out more at Duddy's. Glad to lose *that* business." He picked up the rack of glasses, moved it toward a pad of towels he'd prepared for it. "Ben's an okay guy in the bar, here, though, the few times he's come in. Quiet drinker, not a smart-ass, and in my business I like that."

He set the rack down. "Only thing is," he added, "you don't want to bad-mouth that sister of his, Melinda. You know her, lives up to North End? That damn-fool woman, all skin and bones, never wears a jacket?"

We indicated that we did.

"Fella made the mistake once of mentioning her name wrong when Ben was in, I had to order a new bar mirror and a dozen beer glasses."

"That's what I heard from George, too," Ellie said to me, *sotto voce*.

Ted peeked at himself in the replacement mirror, patting a dark hairpiece so perfectly made and well-arranged you'd never have known he had it, but for the betraying gesture. "I guess Ben'd do about anything for that Melinda," he said.

Or unless you'd known him before he got it; three months earlier when he'd first put it on, it had been the talk of the town. "Met her a few times, too, in here, and I didn't notice much pleasant about the woman, myself. But," he let his hand drop self-consciously as he caught my eye in the mirror, "I guess that's true about blood bein' thicker'n water."

"Right," Ellie agreed thoughtfully. "I guess it is, at that. Does he talk about anything when he's here? Ben, I mean?"

Teddy nodded. "His travels, after he got out of the service. 'Specially Africa and Belgium. When he does talk, it's about how he liked those places. But not," Teddy added, "what he did there."

"Africa and Belgium," Ellie repeated. "Where diamonds come from, and where they get bought and sold."

I stared at her in surprise. "You said you wanted some. So I went on-line and read up on them," she told me, as if this were the most natural thing in the world.

Which for her it was; she may be only an Eastport girl—a designation in which she takes justifiable pride—but she is the perfect living example of acting locally, thinking globally. If I wanted a little jar of pure radium, it's a good bet Ellie could find out how to get one for me.

"Yeah, well, he's not flashing a Diamond-Jim-sized bankroll around, that's for sure," Teddy commented. "Two beers, max. Not the fancy stuff, either. Just whatever's on tap." He dumped Ben's ashtray in a metal container he kept for the purpose, as we gathered our things to go.

"Not very productive," Ellie commented as we stepped out the door into the icy wind rushing off the harbor, and she was right:

For all Ben's apparent willingness to meet with us—we'd called Melinda's, and he'd surprised us by being there and coming down to the bar on very short notice—all he'd really given us was a silent warning: that he wanted to be left alone.

And that we'd better, if we knew what was good for us. Other than that, we went out into the cold, bright day no wiser than before.

Which was very unwise indeed.

Ellie and I parted outside La Sardina; she had a load of nails and tar paper coming for her kitchen roof work, and George was out scalloping, again.

Different boat, of course. "He says after a close call like that, if you don't go back out right away, you never will," Ellie said. "He says you'll walk around drowned on dry land, the rest of your life."

Which I thought was better than the alternative, but never mind; George, we both knew, would work till he dropped or until someone poleaxed him. And at least he wasn't feeding whole trees into the debarking machine over on the mainland, which Victor always said was a job so dangerous that any man who worked at it should bank his own blood, as a precaution.

So she went home to take delivery of rebuilding materials and I went back to my own house, which in my absence had begun smelling like a cat-food factory in the middle of July.

Well, it was better than the blood smell.

Still . . . a *lot* like a cat-food factory.

"Hi," Wade said cheerfully as I came in, dropping a bay leaf into an enormous steaming kettle on the stove and replacing the lid. His face was like a six-year-old's on Christmas morning.

"Mmm," I said, sniffing. "Smells . . . interesting."

It was one word for it. I put my arms around him, re-minded again of one of those whole trees; Wade is the sort of man whose muscles don't show on the outside, particu-larly.

"Salt fish dinner," he said, peeking into the pot once more. A wave of ferociously potent aroma steamed up into my face; I reeled back.

"In the old days, people around here used to live on salt fish all winter." He started peeling another potato. On the counter already were a whole quartered cabbage, a jar of pearl onions, and a pound of bacon.

"They used to survive crossing the Rocky Mountains by eating their shoes, too," I commented. "And sometimes by eating each other."

He only grinned. "You'll see," he said, draining the onions and separating the slices of bacon, laying them in the cast-iron skillet. The smell of frying began partly obliterat-ing the aroma of fish.

But only partly. "My uncle," he confided enthusiastically, "used to make this all the time."

Uh-oh. If you want to get me really doubtful about a food item, tell me your uncle used to cook it. "My uncle used to cook things, too," I said, washing my hands at the sink. "Usually they were things that he'd hit with a load of buckshot that could've blown a hole right through the side of the barn."

Also, the things were usually squirrels, these being the only live creatures in the county without the sense to hide when my uncle got out the shotgun. Mothers kept their chil-dren indoors when they heard him blasting away with it, cursing when he missed and rebel-yelling on the few occa-sions when he didn't.

Back then, I'd hated squirrel. I saw it as a symbol of all that I'd lost, along with my parents: eating stuff that I had to pick the buckshot out of before I could chew it. But when I moved back up North and saw the fat, half-tame ones gamboling in the parks, I'll admit I felt comforted, knowing that if worse came to worst at least I would never lack protein.

"Anyway," Wade said, "it has to simmer for a while."

"How long?" I looked around at the house I lived in now: high ceilings, generous rooms, and everywhere that sense of balance and proportion like an elegantly solved equation. Then I glanced into the telephone alcove. The machine was blinking.

"Oh, about fifteen hours," Wade answered, meaning the fish. "You change the water three times," he added matter-of-factly. "To get the salt out and make it nice and tender." He rinsed the jar the onions had come in, and tossed out the fish wrappings.

"Really." I turned my back on the dratted phone, cautiously approaching a bit of salt fish that hadn't made it into the pot. Picking it up, I touched my tongue to it very briefly, whereupon every single cell in my body absorbed approximately twelve times the lethal amount of sodium.

"Gack," I said, grabbing a glass from the cabinet. Also, that salt fish was so hard you could have ground it up and spread it on the roads; it would have given traction while dissolving the ice.

And the pavement beneath. "It will be a lot better," Wade said gently, "after it's cooked."

"I hope so," I gasped between big, salt-diluting gulps of water. The machine was still blinking at me. "Where's Sam? And doesn't anyone answer the phone in this house except me?"

"Down at the post office waiting for a package. Him and Tommy, all excited about something they ordered on-line for Sam's school project, supposed to come yesterday but now they think it's coming today. And I'd have answered it but I wasn't here, and no one ever calls me on that line, anyway, do they?"

He forked the bacon strips out of the pan, blotted them on a pad of paper towels and wrapped them in foil, finally put the drained onions back in the jar and capped it, and put it away. When Wade cooks, it's like someone preparing for a rocket launch.

Which I sincerely hoped our salt fish dinner experience was not going to resemble. "Wouldn't you rather know what you're ignoring?" he added, angling his head at the telephone alcove.

I could've asked him the same. The answer was similar, too: no. But that little red light would keep on winking slyly at me until I found out. So I pressed the play button and the first call was Victor, of course, moaning yet again about his romantic trouble, the subject of which I found as interesting as the smell of that fish.

The second call was from Melinda Devine, who was becoming as unwelcome and seemingly ever-present to me, lately, as Willetta Abrams was to my long-suffering—and long-winded—ex-husband.

The third call was from Faye Anne Carmody's court-appointed lawyer, Geoffrey Claiborn.

Having a defense lawyer who believes you is in my opinion highly overrated. The idea, when it comes to lawyers, is to have one who can get other people to believe you. And in that department, as in so many others, lately, Faye Anne Carmody was apparently out of luck.

"Three hundred thousand," said Claiborn when I called him back. He sounded about fourteen years old. "A chunk in cash, the rest against real property."

As he was speaking it came over me again suddenly, the thing I'd been missing until I'd seen Ellie's photograph album: that Faye Anne was as real, as *physically* real and in trouble as the men who had been on that doomed boat last night.

"I argued for less," Geofrey Claiborn said.

Well, of course he had. I sat down in the phone alcove. Faye Anne was sitting somewhere, now, too; the wings of disaster had not merely brushed her. They enfolded her, holding her in their dark embrace.

". . . lucky to get any bail at all," Geofrey was saying. "But they'll probably revoke it altogether, you know, when the DA gets his ducks in a row, ups the charge, and gets himself a grand jury indictment."

There's no bail, in Maine, for capital murder: the flip side, I guess, to there being no capital punishment, either. But in Eastport, a three-hundred-thousand-dollar bail judgment is equivalent to requiring the accused to put up a lung and a kidney. Any dim thought I might've had about getting Faye Anne out of custody for the duration went right out the window.

"But the part about cutting the guy into pieces hit hard," the young attorney went on. "The judge says it was heinous."

"Yeah, well, no arguing with that."

I sat there struck with the unwanted realization that had come over me. *In each other's hands.* "So what's next?"

"Well, there'll be a bunch more hearings. What that'll be, the judge will send the case along to Superior Court. See, in Maine we have a two-tiered system where . . ."

I knew about the two-tiered system: little crimes, local court. Serious crimes, Superior Court. Maine has a pool of judges who travel around on a regular schedule to the district courts, mostly for the formality of hearing people plead out to nonviolent crimes: DUI, hunting and fishing violations, minor auto stuff, and the ubiquitous "theft by unauthorized taking," which covered all kinds of sticky-fingered activities.

But this was the big time. "Then there'll be the trial, of course. It'll probably take a couple of days, unless she decides to plead guilty. Then . . ."

"Wait a minute." I gathered myself together. "A couple of days? I mean, I know she can't afford all the expensive bells and whistles."

If she could have, the first thing she'd have done would've been to hire an attorney, or Ellie would have gone out and hired one for her, not have waited until the court appointed one.

"What kind of defense are you planning, Geofrey, one built of Tinkertoys?"

There was a brief silence while he digested this, decided not to respond. "We're going to say he beat her up, even though she won't admit it," he said finally. "But that's common, I'm given to understand, among battered women. Being," he added, "ashamed."

"You mean she's *still* not saying Merle hit her? Does she know how serious this is, the situation she's in?"

"Yeah. She's getting there, anyway. But it's a hard thing to get your mind around, you know. For anyone. That something like this has happened to you. *Could* happen. And as I say, Faye Anne's getting there. But what she's absolutely not saying, says *didn't* happen, though, is that he hit her *that night*."

Which would be the best thing: flat-out self-defense. What happened afterwards wouldn't help her argument, but . . .

"And you're right, we're not going to get the top expert people," he went on. "But we'll bring in X rays that'll probably show old fractures, and I've talked to a woman from the battered women's shelter, who'll testify on our side for free—"

Impatience overcame me. "Still, we're talking about a murder charge, aren't we? Not clamming without a license or driving a snowmobile on a public way. What about other medical testimony?"

"I didn't get her case until twenty hours after the arrest," he responded. "She'd had a cursory medical checkup at that point but no lab stuff. And by then, once I was up to speed on the whole thing, any blood work I might've asked for would have been worthless."

A blood alcohol test and screening for other drugs could have assisted in her defense, had they been done immediately. If they showed that she was likely to have been heavily under the influence at the time of Merle's death, Geofrey could argue it hadn't been a calculated crime.

But now it was too late. "As for the bail, I actually had some hope when I heard she had a house. But it turns out there's already so many mortgages on the place you couldn't raise a dime against it. And the cash, that's out of the question, too."

"Yeah." Not surprising about the mortgages. Eastport had a little bump in real estate values fifteen years ago, when the eighties were in full swing and city people thought they had money to burn. Now the second mortgages folks had taken back then were millstones around their necks.

Whatever Merle had spent on his windows and driveway work would've been nothing, by comparison. Probably he and Faye Anne had barely been making their monthly payments, nothing left over. A common situation in a part of the world where—despite a good economy a few hundred miles south of us—people thought little of working three jobs just to get by; it was why Clarissa Arnold had assumed Faye Anne would need court-appointed representation in the first place.

And yet there *had* been the newly surfaced driveway, and the windows . . . I put it aside to consider, later. "You don't suppose they're open to some kind of deal on the charge? The prosecutors, because of the battering thing?"

When the DA's men from Augusta had mentioned this notion I'd mentally pooh-poohed it; now, however, it seemed one of the few straws left to grasp at.

But Geofrey didn't think so. "No. I understand your thinking but the so-called battered woman defense is very difficult and complex. It's not just 'he slugged her, so she's innocent,' the way most people think. It's a syndrome that has to be proven with evidence; specific, technical evidence. We don't have a great shot at it without expert testimony, I'm sorry to say. Or even with it; it's controversial. And they know it, the other side does, so they're not about to deal on a slim-to-none chance that we might win with it."

"Okay." No surprise there, either: that the tag team from Augusta had not exactly been open and forthcoming. Or that we had a chance in some kind of legal David-and-Goliath match. It was what I had thought in the first place: dismal all the way around.

"So I guess all that's left is, when can we visit her?"

But this time, Geofrey did surprise me. Unpleasantly:

"Not anytime soon. She's been hospitalized in Bangor, over at the mental health institute."

"What? What's she doing there?" My dismay was genuine; for one thing, it was a couple of hours' drive each way for Geofrey, which by itself wasn't good. The law says you have to be provided with an attorney but it doesn't say the arrangement has to be convenient for anyone involved, if it's not so inconvenient as to make the conviction reversable on appeal; I'd discovered this to my sorrow back in the city, when a RICOH-indicted client of mine got the bright idea to start faking a mental disability.

"After the hearing, I guess it came over her, all that's happened," Geofrey said. "She started talking about hurting herself and she sounds like she means it."

You think visiting in a jail is difficult, just try the locked forensic ward of a mental health facility. By the time my city client's attorneys managed to confer with him again, the other patients had convinced him he was Frederick the Great.

"What's the matter?" I asked; by now, I was truly unhappy. "Couldn't the fellows down at the jail figure out how to get the shoelaces out of her shoes?"

But Geofrey wasn't having any more snottiness out of me. He didn't sound fourteen anymore, either, suddenly.

"Look, it wasn't their call. I got the order issued after I met her. She's depressed, angry . . . she's much better off in the hospital. And I," he added in tones that said he'd had enough of me, too, "am going to sleep better with her there, okay?"

"Oh. Okay." It was what I'd been waiting for, actually: some sense that he had a spinal cord. My assessment of Geofrey went up a notch.

"So could her temporary commitment do any good in an—"

"Insanity defense? Dream on." He, I realized, was unhappy, too. "That damned diary deep-sixed that idea. Clear as springwater. How she would do it, how to hide it . . . if they decide she did it, she's never going to persuade anybody she didn't know *what* she was doing, or didn't know that it was wrong. She has no psychiatric history, her speech and writing are lucid and well organized, and nothing suggests she was hearing voices or feeling compelled, or anything like that."

Wonderful; maybe Faye Anne could write a book in prison. The silence on the phone lengthened. Then: "So what do you know about the divorce she says she wanted?" he asked, out of the blue.

Worser and worser, as Sam used to say. "Divorce? She's never said anything about a divorce. In fact, she's *opposed* to—"

"Her story, as far as you could even call it a story,"

Geoffrey interrupted, "is that she'd changed her mind about that, and she *didn't* kill him but why *would* she kill him when she was already planning to divorce him?"

Well, maybe she had changed her mind; certainly plenty of people had urged her to. But it wasn't a great argument now, because: "But that's not the way a prosecutor would look at it, is it? From that angle, it would be that they fought over the divorce, and she killed him during the fight."

"Yup," Geoffrey agreed. "And over the infidelity she planned charging him with. So she says."

Oh, brother. I could just hear the prosecutor describing Faye Anne's outrage over Merle's cheating on her. Her murderous fury . . .

Never mind that Faye Anne was just about as murderous as a sand flea. "And you're telling me because she's already talking about this. Not just to you. Volunteered it, while she was being questioned? Waived her right to an . . ."

Geoffrey confirmed this bad news. "They couldn't shut her up. She also says that although they were cash-poor he owned property besides the house. Know anything about that?"

Ye gods. "The property, yes, some land here in town. That's the rumor, anyway." With that tree on it, next to Melinda's. "Infidelity being a circumstance she thought she could bring up in a settlement argument?"

But not being beaten. Pride's a funny thing. At the moment I wasn't laughing.

"Sure. But it didn't sound to me as if she had any good proof. She said he was seeing a woman but she had no photographs, no letters, no tapes. Not that they'd necessarily have held water either; infidelity isn't the bugaboo it used to be, in divorce court. For getting property, or anything else."

I liked him for the word: bugaboo. "Faye Anne," he went on, "is a sweet-seeming woman, but she's also kind of . . ."

"Clueless," I supplied when he hesitated.

It wasn't fair: she'd known enough to do exactly the right thing about those daisies for Ellie's mother's funeral. But that didn't mean she knew how to handle herself in the world beyond Eastport.

Or at a murder trial. "She say who it was?"

"Well, yes," Geofrey Claiborn said. "When I pressed her for the name of the woman, she didn't want to say. But finally—"

"Who?" I demanded impatiently. What the hell, might as well pile up all the bombshells in one place.

"Mickey Jean Bunting," he said. The name wasn't familiar to me. "Anyway, I'll do what I can," he went on. This conversation was ending. "But you know . . ."

I knew: lousy situation. Before hanging up, Geofrey promised to keep me posted on further developments. But we both knew that if Faye Anne didn't change her story— and at this point, maybe even if she did—all that remained was for a jury to pronounce what everyone in Washington County probably already believed: that she was guilty.

Which to me meant that somebody would be enjoying an extra-special holiday gift this year: getting away with murder. Because I'd been thinking about it ever since we'd found Kenty, and I'd come to the conclusion that if Faye Anne Carmody had killed her husband Merle, I would personally shoot Rudolph and serve him for Christmas dinner.

Unfortunately, my certainty wasn't going to cut much ice with a grand jury. If something didn't happen soon to prevent it, by the end of the week Faye Anne would be indicted for just what Eastport Police Chief Bob Arnold had predicted: capital murder.

And after that, the blithe, laughing girl in the photo album would likely be in prison for the rest of her life. Thinking this, I glanced out the dining-room window to where the pale blues of afternoon were darkening to indigo and aquamarine. Against lead-colored clouds mounding high over the Moosehorn Refuge to the west, the white clap-board houses, red-studded barberry bushes, and blackish-green fir trees of town stood etched on the snow, coldly elegant.

Upstairs, music thumped on as Sam and Tommy set to opening the package they had come in with while I was on the phone. A whine from the parlor told me Monday was still afflicted by some private terror. The bandsaw went on in Wade's workshop where he was rejiggering a gun stock for somebody; with boat repair down the tubes, he was depending on harbor piloting and gun work, for the foresee-able future.

At last I returned to the kitchen, hoping to interest myself in some project I could actually finish, noting mournfully how the thick, opaque plastic at the windows blurred the view. I was wondering what Faye Anne could see from her locked hospital ward, and if two layers of clear plastic might be better—even if more expensive—than the milky-looking stuff, when it happened:

A face appeared. Only for an instant, obscured by the plastic to dark eyes, the blob of a briefly pressing nose, and a mouth that stretched to a crescent grin.

Or grimace. Then it was gone. And although I raced out, I saw no one in the yard or on the street. Footprints dotted the snow, too many to distinguish which were new ones.

A truck passed, its tire-chains jingling, and then a second one, backfiring copiously. A purple finch hopped from one bare, thorny rose cane to another. Then nothing moved but blue shadows lengthening on the snow, gathering up what remained of the thin, desolate winter light.

Wade went to a Federated Marine meeting that evening, came in around eleven, and watched the sports wrap-up on TV before coming up to bed.

"Hey," he said comfortably, seeing I was still awake.

I hadn't been, but then I'd had an awful dream. In it I was standing on a hillside looking out over blue water: sun on my arms, the smell of flowers, the whisper of dry grass. But when I turned to gaze down into the valley behind me, everything in it was glittering with a thick, deadly coating of white frost.

"Hey, yourself." I slid over against him. No matter how cold the weather or how long he'd been out, Wade was always warm.

He curved his arm around me. "Bad night?"

"Yeah." I ran the nuts and bolts of it for him quickly.

"I started out just wanting to help Ellie. Faye Anne's her friend. We wanted extenuating circumstances, or something. But now I'm sure she didn't do it." I told him why: all the small, wrong things about it, and Kenty. And the face at the window.

I didn't mention anything about my hands still feeling sticky, or that I was almost grateful for the fish smell in the house. Wade had taken the big kettle off the heat for the night but tomorrow it would simmer again; as I lay there I'd been imagining the fish's stony flesh yielding under the persistent onslaught, like a hard heart softening.

But I didn't say that, either. Just the facts, ma'am.

Monday padded in. "Oh, come on up," I said, and she jumped onto the bed, creeping to settle in the crook of my arm.

"You think Faye Anne's lying about not remembering?" Wade asked me.

"Maybe. If someone threatened her, scared her so badly that . . ."

I stopped, not wanting to say it. But Wade figured it out.

"And now you think someone knows *you* know?"

"I'm not sure what I think. Maybe whoever was at that window was just some neighborhood kid, peering in, and running away when I spotted him. But by now it's all over town that Ellie and I found both bodies. Merle *and* Kenty. That could be enough to be a problem for someone, that we might make a connection."

Monday sighed.

"And in the problem-solving department, seems like somebody's a big fan of the direct approach," I finished.

Down the hall, Sam's stereo went off. He and Tommy had been oddly subdued at the dinner table that evening, as if they'd run into some difficulty they didn't know what to do about. "I called Melinda back," I said. "No answer."

Nor from Victor, either, and now none from Wade. Ellie said George slept that way, too: deeply, innocently.

Later I got up to peer past the shade at the sleet angling sharply through the cones of light under the streetlamps. Cold wind from Canada rattled the storm windows and set the iced tree branches clattering together like frozen bones; tomorrow, people would be hunting for Christmas wreaths that had blown off their front doors.

But inside, everything was warm and secure. Even when I was alone in the house it always felt well-inhabited, as if its very fibers were permeated by the lives that had been lived in it, over the years. As if, in some way I couldn't fathom but which felt both comfortable and comforting, they were all still here. I slid back into bed where Monday snored softly, safe for the moment against whatever had been terrorizing her.

Me, too.

For now.

Chapter 7

O h," said a familiar voice from the back hallway, early the next morning. "I've never been in this house before."

It was Melinda, and if I'd had my way she wouldn't have been in it, now. She came into the kitchen. "This is all so *homey*," she gushed. Which from Melinda was like being informed that your sheet-metal walls and dirt floor were *comfy*, another term she used when what she clearly wanted to say was *oh, dear God.*

Turning, she batted her lashes so hard at Wade that it was a wonder she didn't rise right up off the old hardwood floor. "And I see she's got you smacked into line, doing the cooking. Marriage so civilizes a man, don't you think?" she added to me.

I could think of some smacking I'd have liked to do. Wearing a cream fisherman-knit sweater, ski pants, and shiny black boots, she sniffed exaggeratedly. "Mmm, that smells . . . authentic!"

What it smelled like, actually, was the bottom of a bait bucket. Wade put his thumb-knuckle to his front teeth to keep from laughing. Then, replacing the lid on the fish kettle, he fled the room.

Which was good; he can take Melinda in small doses but if you push him, Wade can come up with the conversational equivalent of a flame-thrower. And for the present, I wanted her uncharred.

Uninvited, she sat down. "Jacobia, we need to clear the air."

As she was wearing one of those perfumes that gets slopped onto the ad cards in glossy magazines, I agreed. For a personal fragrance, low tide might possibly have been a worse choice; on the other hand, it went well with the fish.

She eyed me loftily. "I understand that you and Ellie have been harassing my brother. I called yesterday to say I want you to stop."

For a woman who tipped the scales at ninety pounds soaking wet, she thought her word carried plenty of weight. "I wouldn't call it harassment," I said. "He agreed to meet us."

She sighed impatiently. "Ben has a good heart."

I'd already spoken with Victor that morning, so I'd had my fill of manipulative silliness for the day. "Right. And I've got a spare head. Get to it, Melinda, will you? What's got you so hot and bothered you had to rush straight over here?"

She bridled at my tone. "I think *you* think, and Ellie too, that I really did have something to do with that Carmody business. Or that Peter and I did. Although how you believe *we* could have fixed it to look as if Faye Anne did it, and didn't remember . . ."

"It's not just how *you* could have, it's how anyone could have." Or why. "You'll admit, you had a great motive."

Her lips tightened. "I'll admit that you're right about the land deal part of it. I lent Merle the money, and I did make him sign a note for it, with a lien, and he didn't read it. Now that he's gone I'll end up with that property, sooner or later.

And if I could've gotten away with it I'd also have put a bullet through that man's brain. *Ghastly* creature."

"How much money?"

"Just the bid amount."

"You're sure? No other money, ever?" That driveway paving and the new storm windows hadn't come cheap.

She looked straight at me. "Never. And I didn't kill him, *or* have Ben do it. I'm here to put that foolish notion to rest."

So *that* was her real worry: that we suspected Ben.

"Ben was with me all evening." Her brunette head lifted nobly. "He helped with the garden-club meeting preparations, and stayed for the lecture. It was a talk by a very well-known woman from Bangor, contradicted all Kenty Dalrymple's silly theories about African violet culture."

Sure; Kenty having been only an international authority. Kenty's whole trouble in dealing with Melinda, according to Ellie, was that Kenty had said what she thought: that, for instance, the twisted-leaf habits of Melinda's houseplants were due to spider mite, not the appearance of a new cultivar that Melinda had developed and aspired to have named for herself.

And now here she and Ben were, alibiing one another: cozy. "What about afterwards? When the meeting was over?"

"He was with me until at least four in the morning. To settle down after the meeting, we watched old movies." She smiled: sweetly, triumphantly.

And . . . falsely? Somewhere under all that superficiality there was a real person, I felt sure: hidden by makeup, mannerisms, and quirks of costume. I had no idea what part—if any—of her story was true.

But something sounded wrong about it. "I can even tell you which movies we watched," she finished, rising from her chair in a jangle of bracelets that made Monday jump.

I peered at her: was she being deliberately obtuse? Did

she think being able to read an old *TV Guide* was proof of anything? She barged right on, ignoring my look of skepticism.

"While I'm here, I also want to correct any mistaken idea you may have on the subject of Peter."

"You mean the idea that with Merle dead and Faye Anne locked up for it, things are pretty hunky-dory for you in the Peter department, also?"

She glared at me for an instant, then softened so calculatingly, you'd have thought she was taking directions from stage left. "Kill to get Peter? Oh, please," she drawled, putting on her confidential, one-female-to-another face.

It might have worked if I'd been a female wolverine. "Peter is charming, but let's be realistic. I like puppy dogs, too," she said.

Sure, if someone else fed and walked them. But she had a point: town talk was, a long-term commitment wasn't her style any more than it was Peter's.

"The truth is, I'm going to have to do something about Peter." She sighed. "It happens so often to a woman like me, that the man gets *too* attached." She tossed her silk scarf tragically.

It was the scarf that did it, finally, like the red cloth in a bullring. That and a flash of something in her eyes when she said it: *do something about Peter*. Just for an instant I saw again the face at my kitchen window, a smear of white in the darkness, there and gone. It had frightened me. The way Faye Anne had been frightened, I supposed. She'd told Ellie that she thought someone was stalking her; later, Peter Christie had confessed that he was behind those episodes.

And now Melinda was frightened. It was in her face, in her voice, and even in the urgency of this visit. "Peter's the reason you've got Bob Arnold's phone number on your speed dialer, isn't it?" I guessed.

Bright pink spots appeared on her cheeks; I'd happened upon some tender nerve. "That's my business."

"But if Peter's bothering you, you may need help."

Although of course it depended on *why* he was bothering her. Did he know about something she'd done? Or the other way around?

Or . . . both? "You're humoring Peter. Seeing him socially. Letting him hang around, fiddle with your computer and so on. You wanted him as a trophy when you couldn't have him, but now you're a little scared of him, too. Maybe you're not confronting him for fear of what he'd do? And as for your brother . . ."

My next thought didn't make much sense, but I decided to have a whack at it, anyway, see if it stimulated anything.

"Melinda, what do you know about Mickey Jean Bunting?" Which as it turned out was like seeing if matches would stimulate dynamite.

"Oh! Jacobia, you breathe a word of that to anyone, and I'll . . ."

A word of what? "Too late," I said, improvising madly. If she realized I *didn't* know whatever she thought I *did,* she would clam up.

"Faye Anne knew about Mickey Jean. So does her attorney. I think you'd better tell me the whole story, and I will try to help you with whatever . . ."

Nothing doing. "Leave him alone," she ordered. "Leave them *both* alone. They aren't hurting anyone. They've had enough interference from snoops and busybodies. After what they've been through they deserve some peace."

Now I was really confused. "Melinda, are you sure we're talking about the same people, here?"

But I'd pushed her too far. She was mad, she was scared, and she blamed me, which made no sense but was absolutely typical of Melinda. Also, maybe she wasn't the sharpest hook in the tackle box, but where her own interests were concerned Melinda was perceptive. She knew I'd sussed something screwy in her story about the night of Merle's murder.

As she went out she was actually weeping into a hankie she'd produced theatrically out of her bag, and I felt a little bad about it. For once, Melinda's distress seemed genuine.

Just not bad enough to refrain from calling Ellie and reporting the whole episode, along with the events of the previous afternoon. And although I had no idea what to do next, Ellie seemed to.

Twenty minutes later as I got into Ellie's car and we pulled away from the snow-crusted curb, I wondered what Melinda was going to do now. Throw a party? Redecorate her house? Switch from sweaters to cotton T-shirts whenever it snowed?

Something, I figured, that would allow her to ignore the whole situation for a while; that was her standard operating procedure. But her problems weren't going away, because while I was waiting for Ellie I'd figured out what I knew that Melinda didn't.

"Ellie. Sunday night, when George was out working at the power station. Tell me again what he was doing?"

She glanced at me, puzzled, then returned her attention to the treacherous roadway. We were headed out of town on Route 190, on the long curving stretch past Quoddy Airfield with its newly plowed runway like a black X-marks-the-spot in the snow. Beyond, the water in the bay was mercury-colored.

"The transformer at the powerhouse needed replacing," she recited obediently. "So George and the fellows from Murphy's Electric went over there, met the bunch from Bangor Hydro, and did the work."

Ahead lay the causeway to the mainland, a low, curving concrete ribbon passing over the tidal channel. At nearly high tide, choppy waves were the only sign of the treacherous currents rushing in beneath us; six hours from now, these would be exposed tide flats, but at present the serene-looking water on either side of us was thirty feet deep and fatally cold.

"The powerhouse being the little oil-fired plant that would give us electricity, if the main power went off."

Which can happen. A truck hits a power pole in Cherryfield, we're out of service; in the big ice storm of ninety-seven, the electricity went out for a week and people really were burning furniture in the fireplace.

"Yes. Jake, why are you asking me this?"

We were almost to Route 1, driving between abandoned farms whose gnarled apple trees dropped frozen fruit into mushy drifts, making the air smell cidery and staining the snow red and yellow.

"We were asleep," I said as we pulled up to the intersection. An eighteen-wheeler pulling a load of logs roared past. "It's why they did the work at night; best time to turn the power off."

Ellie crossed the highway, took the first left turn onto South Meadow Road. "Oh," she breathed comprehendingly.

I'd already told her about Melinda's alibi for the time of Merle's death: that she and Ben were at her house, watching movies on TV until at least four A.M. But I hadn't made the connection.

Or, more accurately, the disconnection. "So unless old Melinda's got a TV that runs on batteries, I'd say that movie-watching story's full of beans."

Two minutes off the highway, winter closed in around us. The road surface was packed snow sprinkled with sand, the drifts at either side Swiss-Alp mountainous and frozen solid. Beyond them, long, white pastures dropped abruptly to stony streambeds edged with hardwood, then flattened to salt marshes where cattails poked up from the brackish open water like velvet fingers.

"Which means Melinda lied," I said. A bald eagle sailed overhead, wings outspread, so close you could pick out the shaggy white feathers of his leggings, yellow talon-tipped. "I wonder why?"

Ellie frowned, peering into the winter landscape. "I know it's one of these places," she said of the ruts leading off the paved road into snow-choked thickets.

"*What* is one of these places?" To me, one snowy wilderness looks pretty much like another.

"The old Hardesty camp." In Maine your camp is your summer place: anything from a primitive shack to an architect-designed million-dollar structure of glass and cedar. A few, though, had been updated to year-round dwellings. "I've been hearing that someone from away bought it and was . . ."

She slowed uncertainly, then came to a decision and swung the wheel hard. ". . . living in it," she finished as the car's engine howled.

Alarm pierced me; if we got stuck here either someone was going to come along to help us, or that eagle was going to have himself a larger-than-average lunch.

"Ellie," I began, but it was too late. Tires spun and gears ground as she muscled the car up a rutted snow track past firs and tamaracks, between sagging fence posts whose tops barely cleared the plow-packed drifts, finally onto a straightaway I thought would offer a little relief, but didn't. She hit the accelerator hard.

"Momentum," she explained, gripping the wheel as the car's rear end slewed. "The key to getting through snow like this is sheer momentum."

As the fence posts flew by I thought it was a lot more like sheer madness; any minute I would be impaled on one. If not, we'd end up in one of those salt marshes, miles from help, the car sunk to its wiper blades.

I outlined this last possibility fairly urgently to Ellie while she continued bulling the car along. "And no one could possibly be living here now," I finished, "could they?"

The track became glare ice prettily dusted with just enough fresh snow to make it even more treacherous. "And if anyone does, they're too crazy to say anything useful to us."

"Oops," Ellie said. This was not a syllable I wanted to hear. Nor was the wild-ass maneuver she pulled next anything I had ever yearned to experience, in a car or anywhere else. But by then I was so fear-frozen, I merely whimpered as we shot forward between a pair of firs so huge, either one of them could have compacted us into a cube of scrap metal. One nearly did before we skinned through into a wide, white clearing.

"There," Ellie said, shutting the ignition off. She wasn't even breathing hard. "We've made it."

"Yes, I suppose we have," I said crossly, hauling myself from the Vehicle of Doom with a grateful sigh. "And it only took about twenty years off my life span."

She just smiled brilliantly at me, waving a silent hand. I looked around, still grouchy with remnants of terror. And then I noticed:

We were in a forest clearing in remote, downeast Maine, in the middle of winter. The absence of sound was like a living presence, huge and obscure. Tall trees stood sentinel-like as the silence went on.

And on. "Oh," I said softly. It was wonderful and pure. "Thank you."

"You're welcome." Our voices were loud as gunshots.

Or they were until the *crack!* of an actual rifle was followed by the ker-*whang!* of a metal projectile, ricocheting off granite. A puff of snow exploded glitteringly a few feet away, erasing any possible doubt in my mind: someone was shooting at us.

"Huh," Ellie remarked. Her nerves, I guessed, were made

out of titanium, or some other equally and annoyingly un-flusterable high-tech stuff.

"Mickey Jean Bunting," my friend added, "must know we've arrived."

She had a short, squat body, little suspicious eyes like raisins pressed into raw dough, and no patience whatsoever.

"It stands to reason," Ellie had been saying. "No one's seen whoever lives here. *And* no one's seen . . ."

"Hurry up," Mickey Jean Bunting ordered. "Think I'm going to stand out here, freezing my tail off all day, waiting for you?"

I felt like suggesting that she go back inside and get warm right away, and we would just turn around and struggle back down the ice rut and maybe even freeze to death, no problem.

I'd have said anything, at the moment, to get out of Mickey Jean's line of fire. But Ellie kept moving forward, even when two dogs as big as wild boars and nearly as friendly looking burst out of the brush and came barreling toward us, snarling and slavering.

"Skip! Rascal!" Mickey Jean Bunting bellowed. *"Okay!"*

At her command the dogs halted, lowering their hackles. The blood lust went out of their eyes as if a switch had been flipped; moments later they were just a pair of let-out house dogs, delighted to see us but mostly interested in a romp in the snow.

The house itself, concealed by a cedar windbreak, was a low log structure with a wide front porch and several out-buildings in the rear, one topped by a satellite dish. An old Honda sedan of indeterminate light color was parked by one of the sheds.

Mickey Jean, still gripping the rifle in businesslike fash-ion, ushered us into the cabin and slammed the door brusquely behind us. We just stood there as she wiped the rifle, racked it, and stoked the woodstove before speaking again.

"Coffee in the pot. Whiskey there, too. Suit yourself." She waved at a shelf where a bottle and glasses were ranged neatly.

Ellie took coffee but as far as I'm concerned, when a rifle shot misses me by two feet, cocktail hour has arrived. I poured, meanwhile examining Mickey Jean Bunting and her extraordinary living quarters.

Wearing a red plaid flannel shirt, bib overalls, and leather work boots, she looked like a female version of Paul Bunyan. Cropped greying hair, a hatchet face, and a grimly set jaw completed the picture. By contrast, the cabin interior was a woodsy version of *House Beautiful:*

Thick braided rugs, Mission-style furniture, hunter-green draperies, and fat pottery lamps with huge pleated shades. A pair of bentwood rockers with dark red cushions faced the enameled woodstove; two wicker baskets held split kindling and newspaper spills.

"Yeah, I messed with Merle some," Mickey Jean admitted in answer to my second question.

The first one was how come she'd shot at us, to which she'd had a ready answer: that a woman alone out here in the woods couldn't be too careful. Personally I felt firing a rifle in the direction of persons unknown wasn't particularly careful at all, and the "alone" part didn't strike me right, either. But by then I'd decided that if she wanted to shoot a hole clean through me instead of merely in my vicinity, she'd have done that. So I let it go.

For now. Meanwhile she'd realized what I meant, and backtracked. "Oh, hey, not messin' around *that* way. That whiskery little runt?" Her laugh was a harsh bark. "Lent the son of a bitch some money, is what I did. You think he kept that pretty little wife of his in a rose-covered cottage, on what he made from a butcher shop hardly ever did any business?"

Waving for emphasis, she brushed against a low table; on it, a blueberry-colored iMac computer popped out of the sleep mode when she bumped it, long enough for me to scan what she'd been doing on it when we had arrived.

"How did you meet him in the first place?" I asked.

Stock charts vanished from the computer screen as she touched the keyboard. And the newspaper spills in the stove basket were of *Barron's* and *The Wall Street Journal:* Fascinating.

Something else interested me, too; a business card, its corner tucked under the edge of the computer's keyboard. It read, "Peter Christie, Computer Repair," with a phone number and his address in Eastport, on Prince Street. Criminy, the guy was like a bad penny.

"At a bar," Mickey Jean replied. "Duddy's in Meddybemps. You know it?"

Another place where bad pennies turned up.

"Yeah, well, it's not a regular hangout of mine," she said, as if she'd heard my thought. "Went in with a friend once just to satisfy my curiosity." She shook her head. "Never again. But Merle was there."

I wondered what he could possibly have said to her, to engage her in conversation. Because Mickey Jean was rough around the edges but she had a strong, penetrating intelligence; you could feel it in the energy of her speech, sense it merely by being in the room with her: physical vigor, lively brain.

"That's rich," she went on. "You thinking I wanted old Merle for his body. Faye Anne thought so, too? Hah. When all along it's me who was funding that lovely little garden of hers."

She poured a neat whiskey twice the size of mine,

knocked it back in a gulp. "Nope, I wanted a return on my money."

Two plates and cups on the wiped-clean drainboard, two cast-iron reading lamps, one by each of the bentwood rockers. "Merle was supposed to pay me back when he cut his bird's-eye," Mickey Jean declared.

The iMac had a phone line connection. "But now that he's dead, I guess I'll never get the money," she added.

That caught my attention. "How often did it happen? Your loans to Merle Carmody, I mean. One lump sum, or—"

A bitter laugh. "I wish. No, he got into me pretty regular. Once a week or so, there at the end."

And there was my answer about his house improvements. "If he signed a promissory note," I began, but her laugh cut me off again.

"No note. No nothing. I didn't want my name on anything with that rascal's name on it, too. Handshake deal."

"I see. So you have no record of these loans."

She shrugged, daring me to disbelieve her. "Wouldn't tell you but if I don't that other story'll keep goin' around, the romance version." She shuddered. "Not an idea that I want floatin' in people's heads. Just the mental picture gives me the heebie-jeebies."

Funny, that's exactly what her story was giving me. For one thing, no one in town knew Mickey Jean, so why would she care? "Kept a record of it in my head," she went on, "and he knew I'd come collecting if he didn't pay it eventually, and with interest."

She nodded at the rifle in the gun case. A matching one stood in the slot next to it. Two of everything.

But only one person in evidence. "When that land deal of his was straightened out an' the wood sold, Merle Carmody owed me big-time."

She moved toward the door, opened it. Skip and Rascal barged in exuberantly, two big bundles of doggy energy shedding snow, and headed for their water bowls. "Guess that wraps up the other thing you wanted to ask me, too," Mickey Jean said.

She pulled a towel from a hook by the door and bent to the first dog, lifting his paws to clean ice crystals from between his pads: an oddly humane gesture from a woman who was otherwise taking pains to show us how rough-and-tough she was. "I mean, whether maybe I cut him up. But how would I ever get my money back, if I did that? Which now I won't."

She released the dog. "Yeah, I'd like to find the person killed Merle. Give whoever a real special downeast Maine thanks." She angled her head at the gun case, to indicate the kind of gratitude she wished to express.

Beside the gun case stood a table with a potted living tree on it: a Norfolk island pine, its evergreen fronds decorated with carved wooden Christmas ornaments: angels and stars, candy canes, and little drummer boys. A foil star shone at the top.

It was charming, and again not part of the character she was trying so hard to project to us. Ellie spoke: "You seem comfortable with the rifle."

Mickey Jean released the second dog, who followed the first to a plaid L.L. Bean dog cushion in the corner. Even the animals used classy furniture, around here.

"No sense keeping a gun, you don't know how to use it if you need to," she said.

"Maybe, but you could use a refresher in weapons safety," I retorted. I was still pretty steamed about getting shot at, even though it was obvious now that she'd meant it as a gesture. I gathered she'd brought us inside just to get a good look at us, to size us up in case we actually were some sort of threat.

From where I stood I could see into a pantry area, shelves loaded with supplies: bottled water, economy-sized sacks and boxes of provisions: flour, salt, coffee. Kerosene, too; lamp oil, and batteries. There'd been a feeder line over our heads on the way in for electricity, but out here, I figured, you hoped for the best and prepared for the worst.

"So," I said, trying for a change in the atmosphere, "do you do any shooting at the target range in Charlotte?"

And there you had it, straight out of the Miss Marple Society's official handbook: try to establish a common interest or activity before moving on to the damning questions. Such as: what's your *real* connection to the dead guy whose noggin I found sitting in a meat counter?

Mickey Jean just shook her head impatiently. "You see any holes in you?" she demanded. "No. But if I wanted there to be any, you can bet there would be. So you go on, both of you. Get back to town where you belong." At her tone, Skip and Rascal lifted their heads. Skip bared his teeth in a big white grin.

Rascal merely opened one blue eye. But the look in it said that if his mistress should happen to call upon him or his pal, we were dog chow.

We went. So much for asking any questions, damning or not. It would have been like trying to push thumbtacks through bullet-proof glass. Not that I wanted to contemplate bullets or anything else at all related to them, just at the moment.

In the car: "So what do you think?"

The drive out wasn't as thrillingly perilous as the trip in. Ellie knew the way, now, and gunned it through the treacherously snow-choked parts as before. But I only bit my tongue twice.

"She says she lives alone, but she's got two of everything people use," Ellie replied, swerving to avoid a tree stump that would have creamed us if she hadn't spotted it in time.

"And she's got the reading material and computer

connections you'd expect of a serious money hobbyist," I mused. "But no record of a loan to Merle Carmody."

"Think she made it up?"

I considered this, partly in order to avoid considering the massive snowbank hurtling toward us. I'd forgotten to bring my cell phone; back in the city the thing had been practically grafted to my hip.

But not anymore. "Nope."

Ellie swung the wheel, the car fishtailed, and the front tires caught on about an inch-wide strip of bare, sanded pavement. We shot out onto the road.

"No, I think that part probably was the truth," I told Ellie. "That he had money of hers. And she didn't like it."

The look on Mickey Jean's face when she'd said it convinced me: she was kicking herself hard for some kind of a money deal that involved Merle.

"But why lend money to him at all?" I went on. "She said that she wanted a return. From what I saw, though, she knows other ways of getting that."

We crossed Route 1, headed back to Eastport. It was two in the afternoon, the sun already more than halfway through its short winter arc; in the east a band of frigid darker blue was beginning to fill the sky. Wind buffeted us across the causeway.

"Maybe she's worried that *he* kept a record," Ellie suggested, glancing in the rearview mirror again. "If she thinks she'll have to explain the loans to him, she might be worried that *she* could come under suspicion."

"Maybe," I said doubtfully. Ellie slowed for a pickup loaded with evergreen tips bound for the seasonal factory on Sea Street. This time of year some people worked twenty hours a day, tying Christmas wreaths or harvesting the makings out of the woods. The labor was brutal but it put something under the tree for their own kids, come the big day.

We turned in at my house. "I went to Kenty's funeral," Ellie said suddenly.

The church service, she meant; no burying would happen until the spring, when the earth lost its granitelike winter hardness. "How was it?" With a guilty pang I realized I'd forgotten the service entirely.

"Sad." She shook her head. "Not many there. Kenty basically didn't have any life of her own, anymore, so she gossiped about other people to keep from feeling so alone, I guess."

Then: "Someone was following us back there," Ellie added.

"Really." Her daredevil driving took on a new meaning to me. "Could you see who it was?"

She shook her head. "I noticed them just before we got to Route 1. They fell back whenever I slowed down. Little light-colored car, I didn't see much else about it. So I decided, if I couldn't find out about them, they weren't going to find out about us, either. Where we were headed, I mean. And I guess they didn't. Whoever it was, they weren't waiting when we got back to the main road."

"Nice going," I said lightly, slamming the car door. Snow squeaked frozenly under my feet.

Ellie put the car in reverse. "Just one thing, though."

"What?" As I spoke, a shadow darted from the granite foundation of the house and scuttled across the snowy back lawn. Peering into the gloom where it came from, I saw that a pane in a cellar window was broken. And on the edge of it hung a tuft of long black hair.

Coarse, musky smelling: skunk hair. "Like you said, there aren't lots of people living out there," Ellie said. "Not in winter." With that she backed the car out, drove away.

I stood holding the tuft of hair, feeling like a scientist who has just found a dandy little nest of plague germs, because one skunk exiting did *not* mean no more were inside. Skunks enjoy cuddling up together in a warm place, such as for instance behind the mop bucket or under the paint tarps in my cellar.

Grimly, I went over my indoor-skunk-equipment list: live trap, blanket to put over it, gloves, and a long stick with which to urge a skunk firmly out again, once I'd gotten it far away. Also if possible a gas mask; skunks do not tend to be in good moods while they are being evicted. Maybe once I'd evicted this one, Monday would return to her usual calm self.

All the while, though, I kept thinking about what Ellie had said: that considering how few places we could reasonably have been going on South Meadow Road in winter, maybe whoever was behind us hadn't needed to follow all the way to Mickey Jean's, to learn our destination.

Just far enough to think *suspicions confirmed.*

"Whoever else is or isn't involved," Clarissa Arnold pointed out that evening, "the question remains: how would anyone cause Faye Anne's claimed amnesia for the event?"

We were having corned beef hash, which follows New England boiled dinner as night follows day, and the company was a near-reprise of the one we'd assembled two evenings before, minus the government guys but plus Bob Arnold, his wife, Clarissa, and their toddler son, Thomas.

"That's the trouble," I agreed. "Unless she's lying about it. Remembers, and just won't say, the same way she won't admit that Merle was the hitting type."

In the parlor young Thomas was coaxing Monday from under the coffee table by offering her a teething biscuit. Ordinarily I do not encourage the dog to eat anything except dog food. But she'd been so glum and skittish, I'd have sat her up at the table and fed her corned beef hash if I'd thought it would help.

"Checked out the cellar for that varmint," George Valentine said. I'd piled the skunk equipment in the hall and from it he'd drawn the correct conclusion. "No live ones that I could spot, but there's a little heap of shavings and such in the corner. A start of a nest, seems like. I set the trap just in case."

It was his birthday so we had a cake with candles waiting for him in the kitchen, and Sam had taken all our pictures with his digital camera. But the mood wasn't very celebratory: For one thing, George's injured thumb had turned out to be broken and he was wearing a splint on it. For another, at the end of the table sat Victor, Joy Abrams, and Joy's sister Willetta; suffice it to say they were not a gleesome threesome.

"What reason would Faye Anne have not to say what happened?" Willetta asked sourly. "Going to jail instead of somebody else? It just doesn't make sense."

Victor said Willetta had decided she didn't like staying alone at night, so she'd moved in with Joy. This continued to crimp the progress of his hoped-for romance; what Willetta needed, he had opined to me out in the kitchen—meanwhile depositing a stack of old paperbacks, a broken hammer, and a cracked cream pitcher on the kitchen table—was a new boyfriend, and couldn't I *please* find someone for her?

But looking at Willetta, whose pallid little face reminded me of a glass of buttermilk—splotched with yellowish freckles and made even less delightful by a peevish expression—I thought hooking her up was going to require more matchmaking horsepower than I possessed.

"She makes a point of running into me whenever I'm there at the hospital," Victor had complained. "Like she's got radar. Then she drenches me in her hatred."

"The amnesia *doesn't* make sense," Ellie said quietly to Willetta. "Unless she's frightened of someone. If she thinks telling the truth about what happened could make something *else* happen. To her."

"What could be worse than getting blamed for something that's not your fault?" Willetta snapped now, but no one answered.

Meanwhile Wade sat calmly eating his corned beef hash. I'd told him all that had happened, including Mickey Jean Bunting's unorthodox way of greeting visitors and Ellie's belief that we'd been followed. In response, Wade had gone thoughtfully up to his workroom and opened the lockbox.

Now there was a .38 special police revolver in his bedside table, and another in the kitchen drawer. "Emergency equipment," he'd said. I didn't know if he was carrying any firearm on his person, but if I'd found out he was, I wouldn't have tried talking him out of it. There was a time in the not-too-distant past when I'd have been carrying one, myself: a wonderful old Bisley .45 caliber revolver Wade had given me and taught me to use, a no-kidding weapon with a punch like a prizefighter and a kick like a Kentucky mule.

It did the job, all right. But none of the gun-related incidents of that time had turned out quite the way I'd planned. So in the end I'd decided to leave weapon power to the experts and concentrate instead on brainpower. I shot at clay pigeons and paper targets at the range on the mainland in Charlotte with Wade, who kept his certifications up religiously, but that was all. Instead of a handgun I carried a cell phone—if I remembered to—and so far, that had worked out just fine.

"There's a guy selling real vampire blood on the Internet," Tommy Pockets announced cheerfully, digging into his hash.

Sam looked uncomfortable. I sent a thought-question at him but he avoided my gaze.

"And another one," Tommy went on, "with an actual alien eyeball he found in the desert, from Roswell."

Sam nudged Tommy hard. "Um," Tommy said, his ears reddening, "but we aren't actually *buying* any of those things. Nothing to worry about, that's for sure. Nope, we sure aren't."

Sam looked crucified, as Wade and Victor both glanced queryingly at him. But then George spoke up. "What's Ben Devine's connection to all this, anyway?"

Wade and Sam got up to clear the table, as Ellie replied with a summary of what we'd learned about Devine. "I wish we could find out more about the fellow who disappeared at his college," she finished. "Just because he wasn't charged doesn't mean—"

"Wasn't a fellow," Bob Arnold spoke up. "It was a woman. I don't know the details either, but I heard she was a model. Or had something to do with modeling. Some fool thing."

"And she had money," Joy Abrams put in unexpectedly. "The college was Bates. I lived in Lewiston when all that happened."

Victor frowned, reminded, I supposed, of what else had gone on in Lewiston: the snake act. Though the Abrams sisters had moved back to Eastport only the previous summer, he much preferred pretending his ladies didn't have pasts, or anyway not ones they bothered recalling after they met him.

"So what was the deal?" George asked, turning to Joy.

"Well." She glanced around the table. "She disappeared. Ben was supposed to be a friend of hers. A *close* friend."

She paused, looking at Bob Arnold. "I'm not sure about that part about the modeling, though."

"I thought I heard something about her being connected to the school," Clarissa agreed.

Bob shrugged. "Could be. We got a flyer when it happened. But like I say, I didn't follow it close. Out of my territory. Papers in Portland and so on, they covered the story."

"So then what?" Ellie wanted to know.

"So, of course the police investigated, like Bob says," Joy said. On anyone else her perfect makeup would have been way too much, but she was good at it.

"*And,*" she added significantly, "her money had vanished. The woman who disappeared. A lot of money."

"So the plot thickens," I put in. "They checked to see if Ben had any of it?"

Joy nodded. "Uh-huh. But he didn't. Or if he did, he hid it somewhere that no one could find it. And they couldn't find any way to hook him up with her disappearance, either. So in the end, they had to drop it."

"If people behaved better they wouldn't get into trouble." Willetta's bitter tone produced an uncomfortable silence.

"She's sensitive right now," Joy apologized for her sister. "She's just had a bad time with somebody, herself."

"Oh, a bad time, is that what you call it?" Willetta shot a dark look at Victor, then got up, flung her napkin angrily onto the table, and left the room. Victor gazed after her and I could see in his eyes the desire to follow her, preferably while gripping a sturdy length of piano wire in both hands. And for once I didn't blame him; Willetta, I decided, was a pill.

In the parlor, the dog had come out from under the coffee table and was seated gravely across from little Thomas, offering her paw. I was so glad to see her acting normally, I didn't even mind seeing the bits of stuffing the baby had apparently pulled from the upholstered chair. Maybe, I thought hopefully, there really had only been one skunk.

But the evening was over; George said he was sorry but he didn't want any cake. He thought he'd go home and take one of the pain pills he'd gotten at the health center—which to me meant that sore thumb of his felt like it was being sawed off—and he and Ellie left soon thereafter.

Victor came up to me, carrying coats, while in the parlor Joy bent cooing over the Arnolds' baby. "I'm going to kill her," he fumed.

Willetta, he meant; she'd already gone out to the car. I made sympathetic noises while thinking about the poetic justice of him having somebody around all the time, driving him bonkers. In the old days, Victor could make me so crazy I feared I might swallow my tongue.

"You're so nice to him," Clarissa observed when Victor and Joy had departed.

Sam and Tommy had vanished back upstairs, Bob was out warming the car up, and the dog was under the coffee table, again. Thomas had offered her one of the stuffing bits from the chair and she'd reeled back in doggy horror.

I shrugged. "Path of least resistance," I said.

Clarissa pursed her lips. "Oh, not really. You know Victor's weak spots. I think you could get rid of him anytime you wanted and I think you know it. Just . . . destroy him, psychologically. But you don't."

"Too chicken, maybe?" I said it lightly as Bob came in, stomped snow off his boots, and joined Wade in the kitchen.

Clarissa removed Thomas's grasping fist from her dark hair. He was already bundled into his red snowsuit, bright as a Christmas elf. "I doubt it," she said. "I think it's that you'd have to remember doing it. Like the live trap—you won't kill something helpless when you don't have to."

She wasn't only talking about Victor, I realized. Or the skunk.

"Kenty Dalrymple was a fragile old woman," Clarissa went on. "I can go with the verdict of heart attack. Bob, too."

"But?" Neither Ellie nor I had mentioned anything about our suspicions over Kenty's death. A stray bathrobe belt and a bad feeling just weren't enough to get folks all het up over, as George would've put it.

But Clarissa didn't need anyone to mention it; she had seen more of life than the view from her Water Street office afforded. "But if by some chance it *wasn't* what it looked like . . ."

"Then," I answered slowly, "maybe she saw something that she shouldn't have. Or someone was worried that she had."

Clarissa nodded. "That's what I thought you thought."

By now Thomas was asleep on her shoulder. She hefted him to a more comfortable position. "I'm not convinced," she said. "Faye Anne might have killed Merle, and Kenty might've dropped dead of her own accord. But if that isn't what happened, then someone's out there."

Hearing her say what I'd been thinking sent a chill over me. "And if you're expecting that person to feel any guilt, or have any mercy, or to care at all . . ." Clarissa added.

"I get it." Nervousness made me laugh. "Murderers aren't like you and me."

But she didn't smile. She was—it was easy to forget this, with Thomas around—an experienced criminal attorney. "But that's just it, Jacobia. That's the problem. Murderers *are* like us. On the outside."

The baby awoke and whimpered; Bob came and took him from her, his eyes meeting hers in the sort of glance that always made me glad these two had found one another. "Don't suppose any friends of yours will be hangin' out, out to Meddybemps, tonight," he said.

At Duddy's; the bar with the pool table and rough clientele. "No," I answered. "Not that I know of. Why would you think that?"

"No reason." His eyes met mine and I remembered his comment: that the state police had surveillance on a place.

So I guessed they were doing something there this

evening and Bob was in on it. "Not a good time for girls' night out?" I hazarded. It happened sometimes, a carful of young town women looking for a harmless thrill, a few drinks and some loud music. Something to break the monotony of husbands and kids, make the winter seem not so long.

Bob nodded, laying his cheek against the baby's soft hair while Clarissa pulled her coat on.

"It's the inside," she said, "you need to worry about."

Of killers, she meant. She stepped onto the porch. Overhead a disk of full moon shed light without heat, making the street into a black-and-white photograph.

"Like," she said, "the dark side of the moon."

"That was pretty sobering. What Clarissa said."

Wade nodded, crouching by the wire contraption George had set up in the cellar to trap our skunk. He'd pushed insulation material into the broken window frame, too, and puttied in a new glass pane. It was too cold to do the job right without preparation, since putty and cold weather aren't exactly bosom buddies. Still, it would do for now.

Nothing in the trap, yet. The bait—a peanut-butter-and-cheese lump smeared with grape jelly—didn't look attractive to me. But then I wasn't a skunk intent on setting up housekeeping.

Wade straightened. "S'pose you could put a sign in your car window. I mean, seeing as you think somebody's watching."

I took his point and laughed, but it was weak-sounding even to me. "Yeah. 'No Snooping—Closed for Repairs.' "

"Trouble is," he added ruefully, "it wouldn't work."

I put my cheek against his shoulder. "No. Probably not."

All Kenty'd done was see something accidentally. Ellie and I had actually gone out looking for trouble.

"Sam and Tommy are pretty involved in his project," I commented.

"Uh-huh. I lent Sam a few bucks so they could buy some stuff for this display he's planning."

"Not the Roswell eyeball, I hope."

His weathered face crinkled in amusement. "Make a hell of an item for the show-and-tell portion of the program."

"You don't think he's run into any trouble? At the table, he and Tommy seemed kind of . . . secretive."

Wade looked unworried. "I doubt they can get into real difficulty just buying a couple of things on eBay. Tomorrow, they'll have figured out how to solve whatever it is, you'll see."

I wasn't so sure. Sam had seemed antsy, the way he had after he broke a deck window in the Coast Guard boat with a baseball he had hit on a dare off the fish pier.

"Mmm. Well, I guess it's all right if he pays you the money back. Or gives you the eyeball."

Wade pulled an IOU from his pocket. "Got it covered." Then: "Jacobia. I'm not going to tell you what to do."

Of course not. He never did. "But?"

"But Ben Devine's a loose cannon. He keeps his head down and you don't see him drunk in the bars, any of that sort of nonsense."

Teddy Armstrong had said so, too. "But on the docks, and out on the water," Wade went on, "all the guys know about him. If you say the wrong thing to him . . ."

"He'll go off on you?" Teddy had said that, as well.

"Ayuh. Couple of months ago he put Lonny Altvater in the hospital. Lon told me it was like trying to fight off a wild animal. All he'd said was, Melinda looked hot in her Fourth of July outfit."

"Oh, gosh." The outfit in question had been a red-white-and-blue jumpsuit, cut up to here and down two inches past there, with strategically placed stars. They'd let her ride in it on the parade float but she'd had to sit behind a flag made of geraniums when the float passed the nursing home, for fear of the effect the patriotic costume might have on residents' health.

Wade finished tinkering with the live trap, kissed me hard, and followed me up to the hall where he handed me my jacket, and grabbed a leash.

"You have more questions for Ben?" he asked.

He knew I did. I wasn't sure which piqued my curiosity more, Joy Abrams' dinner-table report about the woman who'd vanished from Ben's life or Melinda's lies about his whereabouts the night of Merle's murder.

"I think maybe he's got some answers, too," I replied. "But as for getting him to tell them," I added, "after the day I've had, I'd rather face the skunk."

Wade grabbed his own coat. As he'd said, he wouldn't dream of telling me what to do. But he's not above adding himself to the mix, when it's appropriate. "Let's go try to find Ben, see if we can talk to him one more time about all this. You think?"

Let's see, now: with or without backup?

"Gangway," I said.

Monday hurled herself ahead of us out the storm door to get away from whatever was still bugging her in the house, and we set off in Wade's pickup with the dog perched on the bench seat between us.

Minutes later we pulled up quietly on the empty road at the north end of the island, not far from Melinda's. Against the moon-bright sky the enormous maple tree stood sentry, its branches stretched up as if to ward off an onslaught of stars.

"Wade, why are you doing this?"

He set the brake. "Don't know. You haven't told me why *you* are, yet."

I looked down at my hands. "Yes, I did. To help Ellie." *And Faye Anne. And because nobody helped my mother.*

A silly reason, that last one. Or not; it depended on how you looked at it.

"And," Wade added, unfooled, "you don't have to tell me. Not now, not ever. If it's important to you, it's good enough for me, Jacobia."

Back in the city, nobody ever just took me on faith. I felt selfish, suddenly, for even thinking about diamonds. We got out, Wade handing me a flashlight from the truck's glove box and taking one, himself.

No lights burned ahead as we made our way in on the shrub-lined avenue toward Melinda's, snow crunching under our boots. Monday romped happily.

"She's okay away from the house," I said. The dog, I meant.

"Uh-huh." Wade peered into the gloom.

No light blue pickup truck in the driveway, or any other vehicles. We went around back where the drapes at the windows were open: no movement within. A propane tank was neatly hidden by a screen of wooden lattice; no mess of a wood fire for Melinda when she could have almost the same thing by pushing a button.

In the garden, straw mulch on perennial beds resembled huge nests blanketed in snow; I flashed momentarily on that bit of chair stuffing at home in the parlor. Then I moved on, admiring Melinda's handiwork in spite of myself.

Big stone urns stood at either side of a flagstone path; in a nice touch, Melinda had filled the urns with evergreens and rose canes, the red rose hips like blood-colored Bing cherries frozen to the foliage. Touches of snow frosted the greens and the urn rims artfully.

"Here," Wade called quietly as Monday nosed beside me.

The footprints Ellie had seen earlier were obliterated now by back-and-forth tracks: Melinda, no doubt, doing little outdoor chores. As Ellie said, the woman could work like a horse when she wanted to.

The dog vanished ahead of us. I switched my flashlight on, followed its beam past a snow-topped grape arbor to the door of a low shed. A scattering of what looked like cigarette ash lay in the snow by the corner of the shed, whose wooden door stood open an inch.

I pushed the shed door wide, aimed the flash at the threshold to keep from tripping over it. Scents of cedar mulch, topsoil, and fertilizer came from within. The light picked out a patch of something dark glistening on the floor.

Blood. "What the hell?" a voice muttered thickly.

I swung the flashlight.

Wincing at the glare, Bob Arnold sat up unsteadily among a heap of broken clay pots. Some bags of potting soil, vermiculite, and peat moss had fallen around him. He put his hand to his head; it came away red.

"Wade!" The overhead lights snapped on, dazzling me. But I could still see the big purple split in Bob's scalp.

A car started smoothly, far down the road. The sound of the engine faded as I just stood there, struggling to understand.

But then I got it. "Sit there," I told Bob. "Just sit there, and we'll get you some help."

"Don't need . . ." He tried to get up, sat down hard again. "Jesus."

"Hey." Wade appeared, crouched briefly. A small hand axe of the type used to split kindling lay by Bob's feet, its sharp edge bloody.

A car pulled up out front; an instant later Melinda appeared, dressed to the nines: black pants suit, sequined bag, impractical shoes. No coat, of course. "What is going on?"

she demanded, flinging her scarf back. "I come home, find you tramping around my . . ."

Then she saw Bob. "I'll call an ambulance," she said.

"Thought I'd drive around once more," Bob muttered, touching his head again. Blood slicked his fingers. "Give it a last once-over for the night, before I . . ."

That was Bob: his town, his duty. "Saw a light back here, moving around. Parked down the road a ways, not to spook someone, burglar or something."

He shook his head to try to clear it. Then he coughed, a thickly bubbling sound that should have alerted me. Melinda came back. "They're coming. I told them to get Victor, too."

Bob coughed again, working at it. Which didn't make sense. The head wound looked ugly, but—

"I'll go wave them in," Wade said. "Hang in there, buddy."

Bob's face was ashen and he couldn't keep still. "Just wait, okay?" I told him. "You need to get checked out before you . . ."

An anxious expression appeared in his eyes as he tried struggling up again. A sudden gout of red appeared on his jacket front. His look went gently thoughtful, as if something interesting had occurred to him and he needed to ponder it.

I ripped his jacket open. The head wound wasn't the problem. Bunching my gloves into a ball I pressed them to the slit pulsing steadily beside his breastbone.

The gloves soaked through. His eyelids fluttered. "How's it going?"

"Fine. It's going fine," I lied. "You're going to be okay, Bob."

But he wasn't fooled. Me either, really. This was the bad thing, right here and now, and it was going so fast.

He was going so fast.

"Bob, listen to me. Do you remember when I first came here? And you all thought I would last about six months?"

The corners of his mouth turned up. "Summer complaint . . ."

It's what downeast Mainers call people who stick around only in fine weather. I spoke hurriedly, as if the rush of my words could do what pressure to the wound had not. "But I made it a lot longer, and that's what you'll do, too."

He regarded me mildly. "You're a good egg," he whispered.

Then his lips moved with no sound at all: "Take care of them."

"Bob?" I pressed harder on his chest. "Oh, please."

A small red bubble appeared in his left nostril. Another. Terror seized me. "Bob, don't. Please, you have to . . ."

Live, I was going to say. Be with us.

Breathe.

Stay.

Chapter 8

When the ambulance had departed, its siren screaming uselessly, I went out behind the shed and vomited, trembling with grief and fury. Wade held my head, wiped my mouth with clean snow, listened to me rage until I was only weeping with simple sorrow.

And then I couldn't even do that anymore. My eyes felt like hot stones, matching the larger one beating painfully in the center of my chest. Across the dark bay, the blur of lights on Campobello condensed into bright sharp points.

Wade held his hand out. After a moment I took it and stood up. Suddenly I remembered Monday, looked around in fright. "Where is she?"

"I put her in the truck. Come on, now. You're soaked through."

"So what?" I asked bitterly, wanting to hurt someone.

But he only drew me against him, preventing me from sinking back down into the snow and just sitting there.

Sitting until I froze.

"I called George. Ellie's going over to Clarissa's," he said as we drove back through town.

The Christmas lights were all still on in the shop windows, full of fake cheer: reindeer with hard, sharp hooves poised ready to batter and smash, Santas with sly, evil grins on their garish plastic faces.

"Right," I said dully. "I'll call Victor later, ask him to let us know when . . ." My throat closed.

". . . when they know something," I finished.

Wade nodded, pulled up in front of the house. "I'm going to drop you off, okay? George and I are going to go back and get Bob's car. And Timmy Rutherford—"

Timmy, the other full-time cop in Eastport. Soon to be the only.

"—Timmy's going to meet us, have a look around. Get the weapon bagged up and so on. Talk to Melinda."

The other houses on the street had their late-night lights on: one upstairs window or the glow of a television from a darkened room, as people got ready for bed. Innocent people who didn't know how a dying man's eyes looked, how his breath felt as it rushed out onto your lips.

Softly. Lips salty with tears and blood. "Jake," Wade said.

I turned. "It's okay, you go." Monday leaned hard against me, her heart beating strongly under her ribs, and I was crying again.

"Jake, what we did back there."

There was blood under his fingernails, dried droplets in pockmarks on his cheek. I brushed at it and it fell away in crumbs.

"What we did, it'll make the difference," Wade told me. "Or not."

It wouldn't. How could it? We had done CPR until the ambulance arrived, then let the EMTs take over.

"But for you, it's one-foot-in-front-of-the-other time."

Monday wriggled against me: alive, alive-o.

"And thinking time."

I shook my head: not at him, because we'd both heard that car starting down the road from Melinda's. That was what Wade meant. But what I was thinking about it—the *other* thing I was thinking, besides that Bob's attacker had almost certainly been in that car—couldn't be true.

"Wade," I began softly, and then it washed over me:

Sitting in a lean-to built by an explosion of my father's greed and foolishness, watching flaming pieces of my life float down out of a clear, blue sky. And knowing, as much as a three-year-old child can know anything: that she was gone.

She was, too. My mother's body was found in the ruins. But: a car starting out in the street just after an explosion so strong it broke windows for blocks around.

Why would anyone, at that moment, be driving away?

I forced my mind back to the here and now. "You got an IOU from Sam for just that little bit of money you lent him."

"Keeps a fellow from having to depend on memory, is all."

"But if a guy came regularly for money, you gave it, never asked for an IOU. Or kept a record. What would you call that?"

His answer was swift: "Blackmail."

Of course.

Of course it had been.

By seven the next morning Bob Arnold had been stabilized in the hospital in Calais, then airlifted to the thoracic trauma center in Portland, where he was still in surgery for a torn pulmonary artery.

"That's the one to his lungs?" Ellie asked.

Her voice on the telephone, taut with artificial calm, made me want to scream and break things. But at the moment everything made me feel that way.

"Yes." Victor had no hands-on chest surgery experience, but as he'd said he had no choice: on a wing and a prayer he had improvised a graft out of plastic tubing, tied it in with a couple of surgical sutures, and kept his fingers on it, Bob's chest still surgically opened, for the helicopter trip. Victor said the surgery in Portland would take about fourteen hours.

Or until Bob died. That, in a nutshell, is Victor with medical information: straight, no chaser.

"Timmy Rutherford says there're lots of footprints all over that field," Ellie went on tightly. "Kids ride snowboards. People walk their dogs. No way of knowing whose are whose."

Like my backyard, and Melinda's. "The axe?"

"Gone to the state lab. But Jake . . ."

"Yeah. No one else thinks this is connected to—"

I did, though. And I'd been up all night thinking: love and money, money and love. And about what Bob Arnold had said.

They covered the story in the Portland papers.

So I'd started calling Portland at six A.M., leaving messages on the newsroom voice mail. At eight-thirty, my own phone had rung. "Somebody was at Melinda's," I told Ellie now. "When Bob showed up, whoever it was grabbed the nearest handy weapon and attacked him. Why?"

"Because he saw—"

"That's what I think, too. To keep Bob from *telling* something he either saw or figured out from what he saw. And Bob said that the woman Ben Devine was suspected of murdering was a model, or had something to do with modeling."

"I don't get the connection between—"

"But Clarissa said *she* thought the woman was connected to the school, somehow. And they were both right."

"I don't see—"

Love *and* money. "Statistical modeling," I interrupted. "The high-powered math they do in college economics departments." And on Wall Street.

"Oh. But what's that got to do with Melinda?"

"Well, it's a little complicated. But the reporter who

covered the story at the *Portland Press Herald* says the woman who vanished from Lewiston *was* a professor at Bates."

I'd asked for a faxed photo and it had come through. But it was a splotched, unrecognizable blob on the fax sheet; luckily I had a backup plan. The rest of the story had arrived clearly enough, though:

"And get this: the woman who vanished had complained to the cops in the weeks before she disappeared. She was being stalked."

"Like Faye Anne."

"Right. And unless I'm mistaken, like Melinda Devine. And what do those two have in common?" I answered myself. "Peter Christie. Whose business card I just happened to notice, by the way, at Mickey Jean Bunting's place."

"But Jacobia, he's from California. He wouldn't have been in Lewiston—"

"Do we know that for sure?"

"No." Ellie thought it over. "This won't be easy."

"Probably not. Not for us to do, anyway. But we could do it if we had Peter Christie's little black book. Phone numbers."

Back in the city when a client got in trouble by doing something he hadn't bothered clearing with me first, I went into research mode. Because for the client, money was always all tied up in feelings: do I look smart? Do I *feel* smart?

But for me it was just the facts, ma'am.

And it had worked. I felt certain that Peter would have one, too: a little black book. Like Victor.

"So we can call . . ." Ellie began.

"Yup. Old girlfriends. Old buddies." Maybe even some old enemies. I didn't have a clue how any of this hooked together yet, but it was a cinch more facts couldn't hurt.

"We'll call them all, get the scoop on him. *And* find out all about just exactly where he was, when."

First Peter; then Mickey Jean, about whom I was beginning to have a very strong suspicion: all that investing stuff, *The Wall Street Journal* and stock screens on the computer. But I didn't want to say anything about that to Ellie, yet; not until I was certain.

Before I was done I planned to know all about both of them. The trouble was, I had no idea how to get hold of Peter's book.

But Ellie did. "You know, I'm the one who put Victor in touch with the woman who cleans for him," she said thoughtfully. "Lucky for him he doesn't have a woodstove; she won't work for anyone who does. Too grimy, she says."

"You're kidding," I said, not meaning the stove. It was too good to be true. But if a sparrow falls in Eastport, Ellie sees it and tries to help it, and a lifetime of that had knitted a lot of strands into her personal one-hand-washes-the-other network.

"Don't tell me she works for Peter, too?" Meaning the woman Victor called a domestic technician, even as he enforced a dress code that smacked of the 1950s.

Hoping against hope, but already knowing, really:

Good old Ellie.

I left it to Ellie to persuade the cleaning lady that truth, justice, and the American way required her to look straight at Peter Christie and lie like a rug, should the occasion arise. I didn't care what she said to him as long as she got into his house, found his phone book, and brought it to us. We could figure out later how to get it back to him without him noticing.

If we ended up caring. Next I called Clarissa, told her what else I needed.

She was waiting for her mother-in-law to arrive to care for Thomas so she could leave for Portland. But she would make the calls, pull a favor or two from old buddies in Augusta, and have the result faxed to me. I got the sense she was grateful for the favor I was asking: it was something for her to do.

"Jacobia, Victor told me what you and Wade . . . thank you."

The CPR, she meant. "You're welcome. I only hope it did some good."

"Victor said it did. He said that without it . . ."

She stopped, began again. "Victor said that you really know how to kick butt in an emergency."

"Really." It was clearly a direct quote and yet so unexpected, I decided she was mistaken. But this was no time to quiz her. We hung up and an hour later the result of my request came out of my fax machine.

I tore the first page off, waiting for the next sheet. Instead, the paper stopped and the machine emitted three beeps, signaling that it was finished.

Which, actually, was what I'd already begun suspecting. But I still looked at the fax paper again, staring as if I expected more words to appear on it.

They didn't. I'd given Mickey Jean's name to Clarissa and asked her to do what she could on finding information about her, apologizing for the lack of other data to narrow the search.

"Jake, she isn't a missing person," Clarissa had replied. "This is easy. They'll just locate her here and backtrack."

But the result of a comprehensive, professional electronic search of Mickey Jean's background—

—or that of any current Maine resident, last name Bunting, white female, f. initial M., m. initial J. (also M. only, J. only, neither, reverse, and for good measure, Last Name Only)—

—consisted of two words:

Not Found.

• • •

I drove this time, Ellie riding shotgun. Turning at the snow-choked rut leading up to the cabin, I hit the horn. I kept leaning on it all the way in.

Ellie didn't comment on my conversion to Indy 500 driver, or the way the car horn ravaged the immaculate silence.

I was mad. Scared, too. And I wanted this woman, whoever she was, to know I was coming.

At the house, Skip and Rascal did their ferocious-guard-dogs act with snarling enthusiasm; I brushed them aside, hammered on the cabin door. The dogs subsided as they saw I wasn't intimidated by their empty threats. She opened it.

"Who are you?" Behind her in the room the printer to her computer was humming out some pages of something; I couldn't see what.

"Get out." She said it calmly. "I have nothing to say to you or anyone."

"Mickey Jean Bunting sure doesn't. She doesn't exist. No driver's license, no credit history, no bank account. No electronic footprint whatsoever. And that, in this day and age, is a sheer impossibility."

She didn't flinch. "It's none of your business. Get out of here, now, or I'll—"

"What? You'll shoot us?" I leaned in toward her. "There was no loan to Merle Carmody. Merle was blackmailing you. You only told us that in case he kept some record, something you'd have to explain."

Behind her: *two* cups on the table. Two chairs by the stove. Ellie came onto the porch. "Old blue pickup truck out behind the cabin," she reported mildly.

"Ben didn't kill the math teacher, did he?" I asked the woman standing before me. This time, she did flinch. "He just wanted it to look that way. And so did she. Enough, I mean, so everyone would believe she was dead."

Mad as I was, I couldn't help admiring the gall it had taken. The nerve, for Ben especially; he'd risked being accused of her murder. They must have set it up very carefully: moving the money, building her a new identity.

Rather, not building one. The money was the obstacle. People can vanish if they're strong enough to leave everything behind. But money—

I glanced around at the snowy clearing. Across it were the prints of every foot that had stepped here since the storm of a few days ago.

And money is like boots in the snow: it leaves tracks.

It always leaves tracks. "Ben helped you disappear. Helped you set up here. He's here now somewhere, isn't he? Waiting for us to go. Because he doesn't live in town with his sister, Melinda. Ben lives here, with you."

While I'd glanced away, the rifle had appeared. She held it in an easy, one-handed grip. But her expression was anything but relaxed. It was the look of an animal hunted to its den. Now it would fight.

"Bet you didn't tell anyone you were coming," she said. Her voice sounded tired, and I felt a moment of pity for her.

But only a moment, replaced by fear I tried not to show. "You had to disappear. Because of the stalking, probably. And you thought you had done it. I don't think anyone's ever even seen you in town, have they?" I sure hadn't. Ellie, either; if she had she'd have said so. "But Merle spotted you in Duddy's and recognized you somehow. Bad luck for you."

"All I would have to do," Mickey Jean went on thoughtfully, as if I hadn't spoken, "all I'd have to do is get rid of your car. Push it," she added, "into the lake."

The stalking she'd complained about to the Lewiston police must have been terrible, I realized. You couldn't look the way she did otherwise: haggard and grim. As if rather than go back to that, she'd have turned the rifle on herself.

"Now Merle's dead," I persisted. "Kenty Dalrymple, too. But how did you set Faye Anne up? Make her forget, or say she did? That's what I can't figure out."

"If you believe you can prove I've done anything, you should tell the police," she said evenly. "But the fact is, you *can't* prove anything—"

She raised the rifle past me, fired it. The side mirror of my car exploded into shining fragments. "And you don't know anything," she finished. "Nothing at all."

"But Bob Arnold's alive," I insisted, hoping to shake her. "Whatever he saw out there last night, you didn't stop Bob from telling everyone about it. When he gets out of surgery and wakes up, he's going to—"

"What are you talking about?"

Her tone stopped me. That, and the look on her face. Because just a minute ago I'd thought I did know: what and why, if not the details behind it all.

Now, suddenly, I was just a woman with a foolish theory, standing in a remote, silent clearing in the middle of a Maine winter, a gun in my face. Because Mickey Jean was the missing college math professor, all right, and Ben Devine lived here with her. But about last night her confusion was sincere: until I mentioned it she'd had no clue anything had happened to Bob Arnold.

And she was right about something else, I realized as I went back to the car. Something I should have remembered from my high-flying days in the city:

Facts are one thing. Truth is another. I'd gathered some of the former and surmised a whole lot more.

But of the latter I still had nothing.

•   •   •   •

"It doesn't mean she didn't kill Merle, or that Ben didn't," Ellie said as we reached town. "It just means she didn't know somebody attacked Bob. Ben could've done it without telling her."

"Maybe." But Ben Devine had trusted the woman called Mickey Jean Bunting enough to put his life in her hands; I had to assume the plan for her disappearance out of Lewiston had included her showing up again, if he had ended up charged with killing her. So why do anything without letting her in on it, now?

"Tim Rutherford told me the state cops are treating it like a simple break-and-enter that Bob interrupted," Ellie said. "They think Bob surprised someone, and maybe made them panic."

It was a reasonable assumption if you believed none of what had been going on was part of a pattern, which they did because Faye Anne was in custody and Kenty's death had looked natural. Not that we had a lot of crime-for-profit around here, but there'd been more since hard drugs invaded the county.

Which reminded me: "What happened at Duddy's? Tim say anything about that?" Bob had been headed there, before his detour around town last night to make sure all was quiet.

Ellie shook her head. "Don't know. I suppose everything went on as planned. I doubt they'd stop a drug raid just because one Eastport cop didn't show up." She frowned. "How can she be trading stocks, or whatever she's doing for money on that computer of hers, if she has no identity?"

"Ben didn't lose *his* identity. If she's trading, she's probably doing it in his account. After all, no one was stalking *him*."

Pulling into my driveway, I spotted the pieces of that newly repaired cellar window lying broken against the old stone foundation, gleaming on the snow. Nearby, a length of aluminum downspout told the tale: gust of wind, blown-off downspout, smashed glass.

"Oh, blast." Ellie grabbed the mail out of the box on the porch as we went in. Monday looked up from her dog bed in the kitchen, settled glumly again.

Sam wasn't home; Wade, either. Grimly, I found another length of aluminum gutter and a glass piece in the cellar. The glass cutter and rivet gun were in the hall cabinet.

"And she's right, I can't prove she's done anything wrong here, or that Ben has," I fumed as I laid the piece of glass on the kitchen table and prepared to deal with it; otherwise, the skunk that had exited voluntarily would be back, too.

Cellar windows break so often around here—blown branches, stray softballs, a stone caught up and thrown randomly by a lawnmower—that I have made a cardboard template for cutting out new glass pieces for them. Now I positioned the template on the glass and etched a line along it with the glass cutter, then used a metal straightedge to make the cut. Tapping the glass broke the piece away cleanly.

"When's she coming?" I asked, examining the rivet gun.

What I wanted was a wrecking ball. "When's who coming?" Ellie asked, glancing through the envelopes from the mailbox.

A rivet gun is among the simplest tools to load and operate, but I don't do it every day. I squeezed the handle. A flattened rivet should have popped out.

The handle jammed. "Peter's *cleaning* lady, when's she *coming*?"

Because *something* hooked everything together: Merle's murder, his blackmail of Mickey Jean, the attack on Bob Arnold, and the fact that it had happened out at Melinda's place. And Melinda, who'd tried to give Ben an alibi, was not only Ben's sister, she was also Peter Christie's new girlfriend. It was at once too much information, and not enough.

I squeezed the handle on the rivet gun again, to no avail. "Because when she *does* come she *might* tell us something that—"

Ellie tossed a brown manila envelope on the table, not taking her eyes from the pages she had removed from it. "She's been here."

"What?" I waved the crippled tool. "Why didn't you say so?"

Suddenly that mental hardware store list of mine looked so long, I could've looped it into a hangman's noose and slung it over a rafter, and . . . But just then Sam came in, looking preoccupied, took the rivet gun from my hand. "Sam," I began impatiently, "why don't you let me—"

"Be right back," he replied, putting down a small cardboard box.

"Ellie, what did she—"

"Wow," she said, turning another page as Sam returned with a tiny screwdriver. The rivet gun fell apart, into two halves. From its innards, a small piece of shiny metal dropped.

"I think a piece of rivet got stuck in there," my son diagnosed as he put the tool back together and handed it to me.

"Thank you. Ellie, *please* tell me what's got you so—"

Riveted, I was about to say, but of course I didn't. I wasn't even sure how she'd gotten Peter's cleaning woman to cooperate, and so *fast*.

But she had. And as it turned out, Peter Christie—computer *and* copying machine repairman *extraordinaire*—was even more ego-bound than Victor. He didn't only keep phone numbers of his conquests. He kept . . .

"Paydirt," Ellie said.

• • • •

"**I can't believe** this."

In two hours we'd gone through five years of Peter's romantic life, boiled down to a scrapbook so detailed that you could've turned it into an X-rated movie just by flipping the pages.

"Seems like our boy isn't exactly a master of the gentle breakup," I said. "Funny, he's had plenty of practice." I washed my hands at the kitchen sink.

"That's because Peter was never the one doing the breaking," Ellie said. "They all dumped him, every one of them. And did he ever get mad or what!"

The photocopied pages weren't as clear as the originals must have been but they were clear enough. And their contents were what had kept the cleaning lady working at that copier, I realized. It had started as a favor for Ellie, reluctantly done. But you could practically smell the outrage that had kept our secret-agent household worker going strong.

Snapshots, obviously taken surreptitiously: through windows. Some with a grainy, telephoto quality to them. Records of intimate trophies stolen from the laundry rooms of women's apartment houses. Transcripts of phone conversations, pieces of filched mail.

Our Peter had been busy, victimizing women who'd had the nerve to reject his attentions. Not that he'd always gotten away with it but he apparently regarded that as worth remembering, too:

Three typed records of criminal complaints had scrapbook pages of their own. All in southern California, by women whom he'd dated, for stalking-related offenses. And all dropped by the complainants. "Three women," Ellie said as she turned the photocopied pages again. "And Faye Anne said—"

"Right, she was dropping him, too. I'm surprised there aren't pages here about her."

"Maybe he just didn't have time. Or maybe—"

I was thinking the same: maybe we'd been on the wrong track with Ben and Mickey Jean. Maybe they had nothing to do with any of this; instead, maybe this time Peter had upped the ante in the how-dare-you-reject-me department:

"This kind of thing fits right in with somebody following us and peeking in your window," Ellie said.

Sam had gone upstairs, taking a grateful Monday with him, leaving the cardboard box he'd brought home on the kitchen table. I squeezed the rivet gun handle and a properly mashed rivet popped out.

"But Mickey Jean Bunting complaining to the cops that she was stalked, too," I told Ellie, "*doesn't* really fit in." From the pages, there was no evidence Peter had ever been in Lewiston. "Also, Mickey Jean doesn't fit the sweet-young-thing profile. The others were young?"

Ellie nodded. "Their birth dates are on the complaint sheets."

I tried the rivet gun again: mash, pop.

Another perfect rivet. Satisfied, I began searching for the tin of glazing compound, which is goo that you use to stick a window pane into a window sash, and located it in one of the kitchen drawers under the shoe polish.

"Also, leaving aside the question of how he'd have set Faye Anne up, he's not a butcher," I said. "Ben Devine is. You don't just whack the pieces of a carcass apart, you know. It takes knowledge of anatomy to cut something up without just mangling everything."

Or to cut someone up. The instructions on the glazing compound tin said don't use it outdoors in freezing weather. But since coming to Eastport I'd developed a damn-the-torpedoes attitude toward instructions, or at least toward those that didn't mention any explosions.

These didn't. From the hall cabinet, I got out the final tool for my cellar window repair project: a blowtorch. "Oh, Lord," Ellie said, seeing it.

Sam returned, spied the box he'd forgotten, then spied me. "Mom," he said firmly, attempting to take the torch.

I didn't let him. "I'll warm the metal window frame with the glass already in it. That'll warm the glass. Add glazing compound, and—"

"Right," Sam said. "But before you do that, I'll call the fire department and the insurance company. Don't you remember what's around that window frame on the inside?"

He put the blowtorch back in the cabinet and shut the door hard. "Wood. Old, dry, extremely *flammable*," he emphasized, "wood."

"Hmph. You never let me have any fun. How am I going to—"

"Jake," Ellie interrupted. "I think we should call these women."

"Fine. If they still live there, if they're home, if they'll talk to you . . ."

But she was already in the phone alcove, pushing the phone buttons for the number listed on the first complaint sheet. Suddenly I noticed again the box Sam had left on the table. "What's in there?"

He turned from the open refrigerator, a cloud passing over his face. "Uh, just something I want to show Dad."

I waited, but he didn't say what. "A guy thing, huh?"

Sam looked guiltily apologetic, but said no more.

Just what I needed, half the men in the family conspiring against me, and Ellie wasn't listening to me, either. Grumpily I took the rivet gun out to work on the gutter: freezing my feet, pinching my fingers twice and wasting a dozen rivets before I got it right.

"There, damn it," I told the repaired downspout, whose lowest length now curved out neatly over the snow. Which was when I noticed that the snow beneath it was at least a foot deep. When it melted, the new downspout would be dangling in thin air, a foot off the ground.

"Guess that's why God invented hacksaws," said Victor.

I jumped. "Criminy, can't you wear a bell around your neck, or something?"

Then I saw the look on his face. "What's wrong? Is he . . ."

No news had been good news: Bob Arnold was hanging on, or someone would have called. But now . . .

Victor shook his head. "Nothing yet."

I looked once more at my botched downspout repair, turned my back on it. Maybe in spring I would put a tiny rain barrel underneath it.

"Is that what you came over here to tell me? 'Nothing yet'?"

"No." He nudged snow with the toe of one shoe. "Jacobia, I really need help. I want you to talk to Joy for me. Tell her I've got marriage potential."

I nearly laughed out loud. "Right. Potential for disaster."

The pink insulation material George had stuffed around the earlier cellar-window repair fell backwards out of it; Sam's face showed down there briefly. Doing something; I couldn't see what.

"Where are they in the surgery?"

Bob Arnold's, I meant. I didn't want to talk about Victor's love life anymore. Reprising his romantic history was like re-hashing a bad car accident; discussing his future was even worse, like planning a head-on collision.

"They got him off the bypass an hour ago. He's not good right now. But that doesn't mean much. It's the next twenty-four hours . . ." Victor spread his hands apart. "I won't lie to you. Anything can still happen."

Yes, you will, I thought. You'll lie to me. Just not now when it might make me feel a little better. He was always doing this: bopping in with his needs or his junk.

He looked out across the yard where the snow of days

earlier was melting, slushy and grey. "I know what you think of me, you know," he said.

Wow, there was an insight. I'd done everything but put it up on billboards.

"But has it ever occurred to you that I might change?"

"Nope." I gathered the glass pieces from the broken cellar window and turned toward the house with them.

"Just not with you."

"What?" I swung around at him. The sky was the pale, watery blue of a skim of ice, clouds scudding across it dark as bruises. Warmth in the air off the water made the afternoon smell falsely of spring.

A line of red blood crossed my palm; I'd cut myself. "What are you saying, Victor? That I wasn't *woman* enough for you?"

"No, damn it. That's not what I said. You always do that, make it about yourself."

"Oh, you're one to talk. Jesus, you're so goddamned self-centered you could suck yourself inside out." I stalked toward the house.

"Wait."

Something in his voice made me do it. But I kept my back turned. "Say what you've got to say and beat it, okay? I'm in no mood."

"What I meant was, I'm sorry."

A pulse in my fingertip pumped red drops onto the snow.

"I can't change the way I acted," Victor said, "when we were married. But I'm sorry. And you're happy with Wade, now. So maybe it was for the best. Please, Jacobia. Joy's perfect for me. She doesn't take an ounce of—"

"Crap," I finished harshly.

"Right." A small, self-aware laugh. Sam came out onto the porch.

"It's not what you think," Victor went on, "I didn't do anything to make her angry. It's Willetta, she's so furious at men. All men. Like Joy said, she's had a bad breakup with somebody around here. I don't know who."

Really, I thought suddenly, and wasn't that interesting? I wondered why it hadn't occurred to me before, as Victor went on:

"And now that she's around all the time, living there . . ."

"She's got Joy in a bad mood, too," I concluded.

I knew the scene: bitterness like poison gas making everyone feel sickened. Making everyone's errors and missteps look like fatal flaws.

The way I was doing now. Oh, what the hell. "Did you really say I know how to kick butt in an emergency?"

Victor hesitated. Then: "Yeah. I did. Bob was lucky you were around. Not many victims survive CPR outside the hospital setting."

Sam was still out there, waiting. "Hey, Dad," he began.

"All right," I told Victor. "I'll try. I'm not promising anything."

Sam went inside, having given up on waiting for his father. "Come in a minute," I told Victor, "your son needs to talk to you about something."

Ellie was just getting off the phone; meanwhile a yelp from the front parlor, followed by dog toenails on the hall stairs, told me that something had scared the dog all the way up them. "Sam, get Monday down here again, will you, please?" I called.

"The women," Ellie said to me. "In California, the ones Peter had been dating."

Sam looked at his father, at me, and at the box still on the kitchen table. "Look in there," he told his father, then went to fetch Monday who was probably cowering in the attic.

"What about them?" I asked Ellie. "And what are they all doing at home in the middle of the day?" Three hours earlier, in California.

"One works nights. One's an aspiring actress. One's a secretary with a regular day job, but she has a bad cold."

Victor pulled a chair out, sat and began examining the contents of the cardboard box.

"So? What's so amazing about these women?"

Ellie looked over her glasses at me, then pushed them back up on her nose with a little frown. "Each one says the complaint she made against Peter was a mistake. He's a fine man, wouldn't hurt a fly."

"Uh-huh. And when you mentioned that this paragon of virtue was now living an entire continent away, what was their reaction?"

"Two sounded relieved. One started to cry. All three said they'd prefer not to be contacted again."

Victor was pulling things out of the box: smaller boxes, mostly, and a few small items swathed in bubble wrap. Sam, I gathered, had already looked at all of them, then wrapped them again.

I heard Sam luring Monday down the stairs, inveigling her with biscuits and promises of safe passage past the dreaded parlor. "What did you put in the cellar window?" I asked as he snapped the dog's leash on.

"A heating pad," he replied, zipping his jacket. "If you leave it there a while it'll warm up the metal frame, and the glass. Safer than the blowtorch," he added with an anxious glance at his father.

Then they went out, and when they were gone I stalked into the parlor. There stood the chair the dog seemed so afraid of, harmless as always, with a bit of stuffing-fluff on the carpet near it.

Ellie followed me. "So either these women are so forgiving, they don't want to tarnish his reputation here in his new home or—"

"They didn't know he had a new home until you told them," I said distractedly. When had the chair started shedding those stuffing bits? And how? No visible tear or worn place accounted for them.

"Right," Ellie said. "*Which* means . . ."

"Help me tip this chair over, will you?"

Outside the front window Monday romped cheerfully, pink tongue lolling. Meanwhile, here inside we had leaks of chair innards, a dog who went around looking as if she'd seen a ghost, and . . .

"Oof." We got the chair over.

"Look at that," Ellie said. A ragged hole in the chair's underside showed a loop of spring. Beyond that more stuffing had been pulled and packed as if by tiny hands, to form the lining of what looked like some small animal's nest.

As if to confirm this, the animal in question poked his head out, whiskers quivering: a mouse.

"Yeeks!" Ellie said, letting go of the chair.

Me, too. Baring his teeth, the mouse let out an irritated squeak and launched himself, streaking for the hall.

The chair hit the floor. I sank into it. Ellie sat down on the carpet in one smooth, graceful motion; she is as flexible as a Slinky toy and mostly intrepid about animals. But she dislikes mice. A lot.

Probably at the moment *our* mouse was already having a restorative snack from the bait in that trap down cellar. Next he would start chewing on the edges of the wooden spoons in the kitchen drawer. What would come after that doesn't really bear describing. But it wouldn't be sanitary.

"So," I said when I'd caught my breath. "You were saying?"

"They're scared of Peter." Ellie waved the photocopied complaint sheets. "I think each of these women in California, after she filed a complaint against him, found out what happens when you call the cops to complain about Peter Christie."

The back door opened; moments later Monday padded

cautiously in. Not sensing mouse vibes, she sat beside Ellie with no hesitation.

"And none of them plans to let it ever happen again," I said with a nod toward the papers Ellie held. "I wish I'd asked Bob Arnold if Faye Anne had complained to him."

Ellie shook her head. "She didn't. Wouldn't have. You know her. I got the sense she felt it was her fault, somehow."

"Yeah, right." A burst of annoyance at the passive Faye Anne hit me, no matter what anyone had done to make her that way. "If she'd stuck up for herself even a little bit . . ."

None of this would be happening, I'd nearly said. Only that wasn't true. It's so easy to blame the victim, but it's not that simple.

It just isn't. "If Peter's got some pathology that makes him *need* to be obsessing about someone, it would account for him being with Melinda the minute they arrested Faye Anne, right away, and for Melinda having Bob's number on the speed dial. And her comment about him being too serious."

"That's a quick switch to a new target, though, even for a creep like Peter. Faye Anne had barely been gone for a day when I found Bob's number at Melinda's. So unless he was bothering both of them at the same time . . ."

She thought about it. "And I had the idea Melinda had been *with* Peter, when Bob was attacked. She was dressed up, you said."

"As if she'd been out on a date, right. But we don't *know* she was with him."

Something was bothering me. Two things, actually. What Victor had said about Willetta Abrams. And . . .

The mouse had been *inside* the chair.

"Ellie. Why'd Kenty say she was *in* the Carmody house that night?"

Victor appeared in the doorway. "You should look at this."

Ellie rose up from the floor in the same graceful, no-hands way she'd sunk down onto it. "People like Kenty do tend to . . ."

Victor looked astonished, which was unusual. He likes people to think he is so worldly and sophisticated, nothing can astonish him.

". . . embroider," Ellie finished, as I followed Victor out to the kitchen. "When they're spreading any gossip it might as well be *good* gossip, you know?"

But she didn't sound certain. Me, either. "I don't know. She made a big point of wanting me to know it. But she *didn't* want to talk to newspeople, because . . ."

Ellie looked at me. "They'd check her story, wouldn't they? Or at least pick out shaky spots, not just accept it as gospel. And someone like Kenty who'd been in the business herself might be more aware than most: that if she did talk to them they might manage to trip her up."

"*And* she'd have known that if they caught her at the wrong time, she might not be quite mentally johnny-on-the-spot. Not well medicated enough, I mean, or maybe *too* well."

I thought some more. "What if Kenty never went to the Carmodys', but she wanted me to think—and to *tell* people—that she did? Saying she'd been inside might make it more believable, she could have thought. One thing I do know, she was most emphatic on the part about *not* seeing anything unusual."

"But really she had?" Ellie frowned pickily. It remained a good motive for Kenty's death, her being a witness to something a killer didn't want broadcast. But it still didn't quite wash; I kept remembering those superthick glasses.

Sam waved at the cardboard box on the kitchen table. "I can't keep this stuff. Dad says it's . . ."

Ellie saw that Sam wanted privacy, and instantly made herself scarce.

". . . narcotics," Victor finished Sam's sentence for him. "And amphetamines. Needles and syringes, a crude dilution chart, some bottles of sterile saline."

The collection included alcohol wipes: a hilarious nod, if you weren't personally involved, to the preservation of the user's health.

"Just possession of some of these is a major felony. Opiate painkillers. Rohypnol . . . that's the date-rape drug." Victor made a face. "You don't even want them in the house."

"I ordered them," Sam said to me. "Tommy and I did it together, for our Internet project. The Web site where we found it said it was an organic mood-moderation kit, herbs and whatnot. You know, holistic medicine."

With the money Sam had borrowed from Wade . . . I just stared. "Sam," I managed finally, "how much did you pay for this stuff?"

He named a ridiculously low figure, which was when I got it: the package was of nearly free samples.

Somebody was weirdly wired, all right; later, the price would go up. Sooner or later, whoever it was would get shut down, too—sooner, now that Victor knew about it—but not before doing a lot of damage. And of course there was no return address on the mailing carton.

Sam raised his digital camera, snapped a picture of the items for his project, since a live show-and-tell of this material could get him years in the slammer.

"Criminy," I said, "is there any place you *can't* get stuff to screw your head up, nowadays?"

"No," Sam replied authoritatively, "there isn't."

"I'll take it over to the clinic," Victor said, "and call the Maine DEA. Don't worry," he told Sam. "You won't be in difficulty over it."

Victor can be very effective when he wants to be. And reassuring; this I suppose is because of his experience as a neurosurgeon, talking to people so calmly just before he starts taking apart their heads.

I followed him to the door. "You're sure Sam will be okay?"

Because the thing is, I lied about him having been in a little trouble. Back in the city, Sam was the kind of kid who would sniff a vial of live Ebola virus if he thought it would get him high. He stole things; he shot up, snorted, and smoked things. And even though all that seemed a whole life and a world away, I didn't quite trust the notion that his juvenile record was sealed. And . . .

"I'll tell them I ordered this stuff on Sam's computer," Victor replied. "That I was curious about it. So yes, I'm sure."

"Oh. Victor, that's . . ."

Good of you, I was about to say. But then of course he went on to spoil it. "Don't forget, you promised to talk to Joy for me."

Quid pro quo, clearly. God forbid he might simply do a fatherly deed, no pay required. So I said nothing as he picked his way over the ice floe formerly known as my front sidewalk.

Ice-melting crystals, my mental list recited automatically; pickaxe, dynamite. Closing the door, I turned back to Sam.

"Listen. I'm sorry, Sam. But I need to ask."

His face flattened. "What? If I shot up some of that stuff? Got up to my old tricks? Yeah, sure," he went on, sounding disgusted. "I get high every morning, Mom. Sit there putting my head together with a few sticks of *primo* reefer, just like the old days."

Which was exactly what I was scared of: the old days. But then he relented, coming over to drape an arm around me. "Mom. If it makes you feel any better, there's a meeting at the college on Wednesday nights. I've been going pretty regular, all semester."

"What kind of . . . oh. You mean Narcotics Anonymous?"

He'd quit cold turkey without any meetings when we first came here. "No, it's AA," he answered. "But it's a program. I figured, school and all, new pressures."

Oh, terrific. But his face was now untroubled. "Hey, I'm not too proud for a safety net. Besides," he added with a grin that was pure Sam, "it's a way to meet girls who won't throw up all over the car."

I swatted at him, quelling the impulse to fling my arms around him. No doubt by now the dratted mouse was snuggled up in the heating pad, chewing on its cord. "Sam, run down cellar and unplug that pad, will you? It's a good idea—"

His face brightened, reminding me to put praise on my mental list more often, too. That he wasn't using drugs was an achievement so huge that I tended not to see it; like a mountain viewed in extreme close-up.

But my son climbed it every day. "I'm not going to be working on the window this afternoon," I finished, pulling my coat on. "I want to ask Melinda where she was before Bob was attacked," I added to Ellie as she returned. "Ask her myself."

Somehow Ellie always knows: when to go, when to come back. "Me, too," she agreed. "And I want to see her face when she answers."

Hat, boots, scarf. Outside, a breeze made the naked branches shiver, hinting at weather; a storm was forecast to come up out of the Gulf of Maine, narrowly missing us before veering off over Nova Scotia.

We traversed the front walk to the car; sand, ice pick, plaster leg cast, my mental list recited mercilessly. "You think she'll say? Melinda, I mean?" Ellie asked as we drove down Water Street.

Out on the bay a barge loaded with fish food trundled

through the grey waves toward the salmon pens. "Maybe. If she's got nothing to hide. She might also shed some new light on Peter Christie. Because it sounds to me like Mister Sensitive has got a real dark side." A familiar profile caught my eye, as if summoned by my thought. "Look, it's him right now."

He was on his way into the flower shop, carrying Melinda's string shopping bag. A wine bottle poked from the bag's top, and through its mesh I saw what looked like foil-wrapped cheese, French bread, and a box of fancy chocolate.

I slowed the car. He came back out, still too intent on his errand to notice us, a bunch of red carnations in his hand. "Looks like Peter's going courting," Ellie observed.

"This must be the carrot side of his carrot-and-stick approach," I agreed as he got into his car, not seeming to notice us.

Minutes later we passed the ferry landing, wooden row houses overlooking it, and the remains of what at the turn of the century was Eastport's gas plant. All that remained now was a massive brick chimney, swathes of round-shouldered red bricks all around it like pools of dark blood. Across the water the snowy hills of New Brunswick were thin white brushstrokes.

"If she's alone . . ." Ellie began. Then: "Hey. Why are you turning here?"

Melinda's lay straight ahead but I took the left up Clark Street instead. Along one side, a cluster of mobile homes strung with enough Christmas lights to illuminate Times Square huddled around a snowy yard crammed with work trucks, their beds full of toolboxes, ladders, and rubber weather garb. Lobster traps heaped on wooden pallets formed a ragged fence between each mobile home and the next.

"Detour," I announced. We passed Hillside Cemetery

and came over the hill, looking south toward the inlet of Passamaquoddy Bay and the bridge that spanned it to Canada.

"Oh," Ellie said comprehendingly. "If he's at Melinda's we can talk to them together."

"And with a few slugs of that wine in them, to loosen them up," I agreed. "Let's give them half an hour. Meanwhile, I have a favor to do for Victor." I let my voice express how eager I felt, as I explained it.

No reply. Ellie believed Victor might make good bait if the fish were very hungry. Otherwise . . .

"I said I'd talk to Joy," I told her. "So I will. I don't have to try to persuade her of anything." Such as for instance that Victor was anything other than trouble. "Besides, she's a smart woman. You saw that. So it's not like it would work, anyway."

The gold rays of early sunset angled from behind clouds mounting threateningly from the south and the west. A left off Route 190 took us out the old Toll Bridge Road, to a warren of short, interlocking streets: Quoddy Village.

Still no comment from Ellie. "Half an hour, tops, we'll be back in town," I promised. In the gathering dusk we passed a rusting water tower, a barrackslike building that was once a Navy administration center, and a burnt-out house lot with plumbing pipes jutting up out of its concrete pad.

"Ellie?" I glanced sideways. She looked worried.

"Did you bring your cell phone?" she asked. "To find out if . . ."

I handed it to her. "To check in about Bob Arnold?"

"Uh-huh." She tried it. "Jake, it's not working."

Drat; dead battery, probably. But we weren't going very far. "Remind me to charge it when we get home, please. But we can call from Joy's and see if there's news, if you want."

She nodded thoughtfully as we passed houses set on quarter-acre lots, the car barely crawling until Ellie spotted a brighter set of yard lights than the rest, and the sign for Joy's beauty parlor: THE BEAUTY PART.

Much brighter. Joy's place was a double-wide mobile home with a slant-roofed, sheet-metal side addition, a long, plowed driveway, and utility sheds, all looking well maintained. There was a little shed for trash bins, a larger one that probably held yard equipment, and some foundation plantings. Each had a neat, securely tied winter jacket of burlap.

Two vehicles stood in the drive: a new Dodge van with the dealer sticker still in the window, and a little white Toyota. "Huh," Ellie said, blinking in surprise from the glare as we pulled our own car in.

Because it wasn't just porch lights. Yard lamps, walkway illumination, a floodlight over the cars, and a pair of security lamps were all connected, apparently, to motion detectors. They snapped on one after another as we approached the deck made of pressure-treated lumber, swept clean of snow.

A face appeared at the window. Another trio of bulbs blazed on, at either side of the door and above it.

"Good thing George fixed that generator," Ellie murmured as we climbed the wooden steps.

"Yeah." I knocked. Inside, women's voices: Joy and Willetta.

"Are they trying to attract someone? Or keep someone away?"

A series of locks clicked open. As I listened to them, my errand for Victor got steadily more interesting. Not that I thought it had anything to do with Merle Carmody's murder.

Still, I couldn't shake the impression that the whole place was lit up like the tarmac around an airport terminal.

Or like a prison yard.

Chapter 9

Really, it was too bad; up until this moment I'd harbored a secret hope for Joy Abrams and Victor. But stepping into the mobile home Joy shared with Willetta, I realized the futility of trying to convince Joy that her relationship with my ex-husband had a future.

Outdoors, her place was a pristine winter paradise; I got the sense that if even a single snowflake were misaligned, Joy would be out there carefully replacing it atop a snowdrift.

And the inside was the same. Joy glanced past us toward the yard lights. "He sent you here? Victor, to talk to me?"

"Well, yes," I admitted, knowing now that it was hopeless.

Smells of soapsuds and scouring powder hung in the air, and Joy herself was perfectly dressed and made-up as if prepared for a camera. She didn't seem to be expecting company and the shop looked closed, yet she even had her eyelashes on, L'Air du Temps wafting sweetly from her. And whether or not she'd articulated it clearly to herself or only felt it, a woman in so much control of her person and her home wouldn't put up with being controlled by Victor. Or with his efforts to do so. Back when I was married to him,

Mr. Don't-Move-A-Muscle-Without-My-Say-So used to choose my shoes for me, always buying them a size too small.

She led us in, sat us down at a small table in the tiny eating area. A countertop with double sink and cooking surface, both gleaming, divided it from a plushly carpeted living room, plenty big enough for two people.

But not for three. And still I spotted not a single thing out of place; in fact, there weren't really any things to speak of other than the neat, unremarkable furniture: no magazines, no old newspapers, not even a potted plant, and of course no messy woodstove.

"Look," Joy said, spreading her hands. Her apricot nails precisely matched the color of her elaborately done hair. "It's not so much that I don't *want* to go on seeing Victor."

Honestly, you'd have thought Joy and Willetta just sat here in the evenings, motionless with their hands in their laps; it was almost eerie. I glanced out at the snow spreading blue-white under the yard lights, shadows deepening as dusk thickened into early evening. The windowsill smelled of ammonia glass-cleaner.

"Go on, Joy, tell her," a peevish voice broke in. "Your kid sister has moved in on you, and she's ruining your life."

Willetta appeared. Wan and aggrieved looking, with lank hair and a spotty complexion, she was the *before* to Joy's carefully tended *after*.

"Now, honey, that's not it at all," Joy began placatingly.

Willetta sat down uninvited at the tiny table. Four was a crowd but she didn't seem to care. "He's such a jerk. Which my big sister would ignore if I weren't around. But," she finished smugly, "I am."

Yeah, and aren't you a little ray of sunshine in everyone's life? I thought, eyeing her bitten nails and chapped lips.

"He's a selfish son of a bitch, a liar, and a con artist," she went on, sounding gratified. "I can tell."

Well, I couldn't argue with any of that. But somehow hearing her say it made me want to, even though those shoes Victor used to choose always had four-inch heels and pinched unbearably.

"You know, Willetta," I began, intending to point out that some people balanced their flaws with competence in other areas: for instance, the ability to eradicate sneaky brain tumors. As far as I could tell, her only balance was between a bad attitude and a lousy disposition.

But: "I'm not going to let what happened to me happen to my sister," she declared before I could get the words out.

Joy's eyes apologized over the red formica of the little table. "Since our dad died, Willetta and I only have each other," she said by way of explanation. "We do get protective of one another, sometimes."

"But I *do* all the protection," Willetta muttered resentfully.

"Your dad was from around here?" I asked. I gazed out at the yard lights again. Ellie nodded, listening.

"Uh-huh. Pembroke," Willetta said flatly. "In the woods."

Pembroke was the first town after you got off the causeway and onto the mainland.

"Our father was a Maine guide." Joy seemed to remember this with pleasure. "Fishing and hunting. We used to spend all our time in the woods with him."

Sullen nod from Willetta. Possibly she hadn't been such a big fan of the outdoor life.

"But when he died," Joy went on, "we felt we had to go along with his last wish, not stay out there in the sticks." She looked up at me. "Not because we were girls. Dad taught us everything after Mom died, just as if he'd had sons. We could've stayed. But the woods is a hard place to make a living."

"And," Willetta contributed sourly, "rich men who want Maine guides don't like hiring women to take them on hunting and fishing trips."

I could imagine. My old clients would never admit it but half the attraction of such a trip, to them, was pretending to be just like the guy who was taking them on it: emphasis on *guy*.

"So first Willetta worked while I went to school," Joy said, "and then I started . . ."

"Come and see the rest of the place," Willetta interrupted abruptly. "You don't need our boring life history."

Although to tell the truth the rest of the place was boring, too, once you got used to cleanliness so intense Victor could have done brain surgery in it. There were two tiny bedrooms, a surprisingly large bath with shelves holding every beauty product ever invented—Joy's hair color, I noted with interest, was called Sunrise Serenade—and another room which Joy apparently used as an office space for the beauty shop, located in the add-on building.

No holiday decorations anywhere. Too messy, I guessed. And Willetta's room was a surprise. I'd expected chaos, but in this regard she apparently took after her sister: bed neatly made, a wicker hamper, louver-door closet. Nothing unusual, except . . .

Ellie stared past me at walls covered with framed displays of paper matchbooks. Bowling alleys, steak houses, beer bars, and sandwich shops: hundreds of matchbooks, many quite old.

"I started collecting them when I was a kid," Willetta said with the first indication of cheerfulness that I'd seen in her. "When I get interested in a thing, I just stick with it. And for me, this was it."

"I guess so," I replied bemusedly. So *many* of them. Then a particular one caught my eye: white, with red lettering. DUDDY'S BAR, ROUTE 214, MEDDYBEMPS. "Kind of a rough joint, isn't it?"

"My friend," Joy had said, *"was out there . . ."*

I guessed I knew which friend she'd been talking about, now: Willetta. Or both of them.

Willetta shrugged. "I'd go with my boyfriend, and afterwards I'd go alone. After our big breakup. I was a wreck, for a while."

It didn't seem to me that any very extensive repair work had been done: a who-cares? attitude toward personal grooming, a sour mood, and a seemingly universal sense of suspicion for any man who came within ten miles were definitely Willetta's main traits. But then she surprised me again.

"It wasn't fair, what I said back in the kitchen," she said. "When we were younger, Joy always took care of me and never once complained about it. I shouldn't have . . . hey."

Her pale-lashed eyes flickered suspiciously as something outside her window caught her attention. Her shoulders tensed sharply and I heard her sudden intake of breath, as if she were about to cry out. I peered past her.

But it was only a cat. Another light went on, this one on a neighboring porch; the animal streaked toward it. The light went out again.

Willetta's shoulders relaxed. "Pretty elaborate illumination you've got," I remarked casually.

"Yeah," she snapped. She hadn't liked my seeing her anxiety.

"Come on," she added curtly, waving me out of the small, neat room where she slept.

If she slept. Pinched face, bony shoulder blades jutting beneath her sweater, sharp eyes . . . I had the sudden feeling that maybe she hung from the rail in her tiny closet like a little white bat.

". . . I've had times when I needed help and didn't get it," Ellie was saying to Joy, out in the little kitchen. Explaining, I gathered, why she was interested in helping Faye Anne. "And other times, I did. Someone helped me for no reason.

And I know which times I'm in favor of, is all," she finished determinedly.

Just then the phone rang. Joy jumped a foot, and I felt Willetta's reflexive, startled movement behind me. The two of them were as nervous as caged animals.

"I don't go to Duddy's anymore, though," Willetta said, trying to pick up our conversation where we'd left off, to sound halfway normal. But she was watching intently as Joy answered the phone, pulled a book from the shelf beneath it, and began writing down what I gathered was a beauty-shop appointment.

Suddenly I put it together with the notion I'd had when Victor mentioned Willetta breaking up with some local guy: the yard lit up like an airport, their jumpiness. "Willetta. The guy you broke up with. That you went to the bar with. It didn't happen to be Peter Christie?"

"Yeah," she admitted. "He liked Duddy's. Liked feeling that he was slumming it, being around those tougher guys. You know," she added, "the kind I mean."

Sure I did. Never mind that despite the rough atmosphere in the place, most of Duddy's regulars were just plain fellows having a beer. Or that most of them worked harder in a day than Peter ever would in his life. His little heart would be thrilled, I felt sure, at the sight of the few with the too-bright eyes and the vials of illegal prescription painkillers in their pockets.

Her next remark seemed to confirm this. "Peter's the kind of guy who likes to drive through a poor neighborhood," she said.

A whiff of permanent-wave lotion wafted through the half-open door that I guessed led out to Joy's shop. Glancing through it, I caught my breath at the sight of a bald, white head silhouetted in the backlit window. But when I looked again it was only a hairdresser's wig stand, for propping a hairpiece while it was combed and styled.

"Gives him a charge, thinking about how much better off he is," Willetta was saying.

A wig stand. I didn't imagine Joy got much of that sort of work. But I supposed she had to be prepared for anything; over the years Wade had collected old tools for working on guns he never expected to see, either, not wanting to have to turn down paying jobs for lack of equipment.

Joy, I guessed, would be the same. "Even though," Willetta added, "when you come right down to it, Peter's not *that* much better off, is he?"

The old car he drove, the tiny house on Prince Street: Peter wasn't going to be showing up in *Forbes* anytime soon, that was for sure. And his own relative poverty was yet another reason for him to relish any measly power he could have over other people: women, for instance.

"But I didn't tell anybody I'd been seeing him," Willetta said abruptly. "Joy didn't, either." Her eyes narrowed. "So how did you know?"

"Call it intuition." A rush of anger against Peter Christie moved me down the mobile home's narrow hallway, toward Ellie and Joy.

"That little rat is doing it to her, too," I told Ellie, angling my head back at Willetta. "She broke up with him, now he's stalking *her*."

Ellie looked thoughtful, putting it together: their nervousness, all the lights. But neither sister wanted to talk about it. As we prepared to go I told them that if Peter gave either of them any more trouble they should call the cops. The women in California had quit complaining too soon, I thought; if faced with official opposition I felt sure Peter would back off.

Still, there was another possibility and I had to mention it. "Two people have died and one's been attacked," I told them. "There is no real evidence against Peter."

"But?" Joy asked, while Willetta's face went still.

"But under the circumstances I think you're wise. It's worth being extra careful," I said smoothly, and they seemed to accept this. Finally, I tried raising the topic of Victor again.

At the mention of his name Willetta went back to her room and shut the door. Slammed it, actually, and cranked up the kind of loud music that would have sounded right at home in Duddy's.

"I'm sorry," Joy replied when I asked what I should tell Victor. "Maybe when she calms down. Right now, though, she's just really upset. I don't like leaving her alone, and having Victor here isn't very . . ."

"Conducive," I finished for her. "To romance, or anything else."

The glare of the yard lights turned her apricot-colored hair purplish. "Right." She closed the door.

Music blaring from inside followed us all the way out to the car. "That was useless," I told Ellie, pulling back onto Route 190. "And," it hit me suddenly, "we forgot to call about Bob Arnold."

"I didn't forget." Ellie's voice was thoughtful.

"What, then?"

"Willetta looks awful," she said, seeming to change the subject.

Icy fog thickened the twilight, making the road surface slick and treacherous. "Can you blame her? First she gets her heart broken, then she's terrorized by that son of a bitch. Not to say she isn't a fairly sizable pain in the neck herself, but—"

"She's a pharmacy technician, isn't she? At the hospital."

"Yes." We came into town. "Although the job doesn't entail anything really technical, I gather. She delivers medications to the nursing stations. But what does that . . . Oh."

"A pharmacy technician who hangs out at Duddy's

where pharmacy is a sideline." Her voice remained even. "An unofficial, unsanctioned, but still well-known—"

"Ellie, a hospital pharmacy has better security than Fort Knox." I turned onto Key Street. Peter Christie had looked laden with at least an evening's worth of fancy foodstuffs and I wanted to charge that cell phone before I forgot it, again. "So if you're thinking maybe she pilfered medications to sell out there, or something . . ."

"I'm not. It's just an interesting coincidence, that's all."

She didn't sound as if she thought it was a coincidence. But I knew better than to press her into rushing her thought process. Ellie's mind is like one of those machines they use to polish gemstones. You put in raw material, it rattles around in there, and later out comes something perfect, smooth, and correct.

The difference is that when Ellie does it she doesn't make noise. Or want you to, either, so I didn't as the two of us went into my old house.

Then I made noise.

Victor was in my kitchen, engaged in three activities so uncharacteristic of him, I knew something was up. First, he was making coffee; ordinarily, he feels it should appear before him as if by magic. Also, he was smiling.

And humming a tune. All bad signs. "Victor, what is this—"

"I straightened out the problem with Sam's package." He pushed the button on the coffee machine; it began burbling, a musical sound that didn't quite cover the *other* sound, emanating from near my ankle.

"What we still need to know," Ellie said, "is *why* Faye Anne—"

"Doesn't remember," I finished, not wanting to look down. But I did when it started nuzzling, its purring as loud as the engine on one of those fishing boats in the harbor. *"Victor . . ."*

Because junk was one thing, but this was beyond junk.

Way beyond. "If we explain that—" Ellie said.

It was a cross-eyed, apple-headed Siamese cat with a kink in its tail, extra toes on its paws, and a smile on its face. A *settled* smile, like it was planning to stay.

"—we've got a shot," Ellie finished. "Because whoever arranged *that* has to be the one who—"

"It's for the mouse," Victor said innocently, gesturing at the animal. "Sam says you have one."

Victor had been trying to get rid of this feline since the moment it had showed up at his house uninvited three months earlier. He claimed it followed him around with a look in its eye.

Which I understood; you live with Victor long enough, you'll have a look in your eye, too: a look that says you're about to run screaming into the night.

"Victor, just because *you* don't want a cat doesn't mean *I* want a . . ."

Monday put her head into the room. Cat? her look said. And then: Cat!!!

What followed put all thoughts of homicide out of my mind, except of course for thoughts of murdering my ex-husband. "So did you talk to her yet?" he demanded as Monday circled the dining-room table for the hundredth time.

The cat had already timed to the millisecond how long it took the dog to complete a trip, so as to stay out of reach while maintaining the highest possible levels of canine frenzy.

"Yes." I reported the result.

Victor looked crestfallen for a moment. But then: "Well, will you try again?"

I ignored this. "Victor, I don't *want* . . ."

Cat food or dishes, I listed mentally; cat toys or cat litter. Or—at a particularly loud thump-and-tumble from the front hall—animal tranquilizers. Then came sudden silence, even more unnerving than the sounds of mayhem. I looked at Ellie, returning from the phone alcove.

"Bob's the same," she reported, peering around. "No change in his condition." Which wasn't good. "What made them stop?"

We tiptoed into the parlor where due to the completeness of the silence that had fallen, I expected animal corpses. Instead, Monday and the cat sat shoulder to shoulder. The two of them were staring at the parlor chair like cops staking out a hideout.

Slowly the dog lay down on the carpet in front of the chair, crossing her paws and gazing fixedly at the target premises. After a moment the cat followed suit, gazing likewise. "Oh," Ellie said. "That's kind of cute."

"Sure," I replied sourly. "And pretty soon, the mouse'll be curled up with them. We can start a cartoon show." I paused.

But it had to be said. "Ellie, has it occurred to you that we might not be able to do it? Help Faye Anne?"

Wade came in and headed upstairs; the shower went on. From the music coming out of his room I knew Sam was at home, too. Pretty soon it would be time to start dinner.

"Yes," Ellie said with a heavy sigh, "it has."

It had been in the air all afternoon: the growing sense that whatever was eluding us might stay elusive.

"Why'd you come here?" she asked suddenly. "To Eastport, I mean. Pick up and move here, start a new life . . . why'd you do it?"

But she didn't wait for a reply. "For a geographic cure, that's why. To start all over, to be a new person in a new place. And so Sam could. But I can't. Oh, I could have a life somewhere else, I suppose. But it wouldn't be *my* life."

I understood: The respect of the women whose husbands

had been on that boat was no accident; Ellie had earned it. By, among other things, not quitting when the going got tough.

But if she did quit, she'd have to live with that, too. For Ellie there would be no geographic cure; she was an Eastport girl born and bred, and what she did here counted.

"Nothing we've learned proves much," I said slowly. "Seems like just about everyone hated Merle and in the suggesting-an-alternative-suspect department it's as bad as if no one did."

Which, I didn't have to tell her, was the department we'd gotten to. Because actually proving someone other than Faye Anne had killed Merle was starting to look hopeless. Still:

"Jake, what you told Joy and Willetta was absolutely true," Ellie replied. "It's not just Merle, it's Kenty and Bob, too. We know they're part of this. And who knows who else will be, before it's over?"

She looked down at the dog and cat. "At least when *those* two go on a rampage, everyone knows it's happening."

A burst of sleet rattled the parlor windows, subsided. "And now," my friend finished discouragedly, "the weather's getting lousy, besides. But listen, you've done enough, you don't have to . . ."

The day after I moved into the house on Key Street, the van not yet arrived and the old place feeling so empty I thought Sam and I might drown in it, Ellie showed up with a plate of cookies. Ribbon in her hair, pale green eyes like a pair of searchlights, their gaze from behind her glasses so penetrating I'd felt as if my X ray was being taken.

And as the enormity of what I'd done—an antique house! on an *island!* in *Maine!*—began sinking in, I'd felt also that I was being thrown a life ring by someone who knew how.

"Look," I suggested, "there's still time to get out to Melinda's before it starts really blowing."

The heavy weather, forecast to veer out over Nova Scotia, wouldn't be much. But it would be enough to make us want to stay indoors, later.

She brightened. "Just talk to her? Once more? Because . . ."

I nodded. This was the other thing that had been in the air: our shared sense that the attack on Bob Arnold had been a kind of climax, like a burst of energy in an electrical storm.

But the relative calm that came after didn't mean the storm was over. Only that it was gathering its forces for another, more violent onslaught. A second sleet shower clattered like pebbles against the window.

"Let's get it over with," I said, not expecting any result.

Oh, would it were so.

"Can't you see she knows nothing about this?" Peter demanded, a glass of red wine in one hand and a lobster puff in the other.

It struck me that his little house on Prince Street offered none of the luxuries of Melinda's well-furnished abode. Here, the blazing gas fireplace, thick rugs, plushly cushioned sofas, and plenty of food and drink made the winter outside seem far away.

I ignored his bullying tone. "Listen, Melinda, this is serious." I stood over her, not caring if I seemed bullying, too. "Three different women from California have as good as told us they're scared to death of Peter. Before he left to come here, they'd all complained to the cops about him."

Melinda said nothing while Peter backpedaled a moment, long enough for me to see his surprise that I knew this. But he recovered swiftly:

"Did they tell you they all knew each other? That I'd

dated one of them and after I broke up with her, in retaliation she got two more of her friends to complain, too?"

"Oh, really?" I turned to him, letting him see that I didn't believe him for an instant. "Any particular reason she decided to make it a stalking complaint? Or was that just out of the blue?"

He flushed, swallowed some wine.

"Pretty serious charge," I went on, deciding that since this was probably our last run at him, it was going to be a good one. "But three different young women got it into their heads to make it against you, even though they could be in serious trouble if it turned out to be false."

Melinda's new computer stood on the desk in a corner. "And now," I went on, "all three are denying anything happened at all. I don't suppose you've got anything to do with that, either? You're such a computer buff, I imagine you could do a lot with, say, a barrage of e-mail to one or all of them?"

His brief startled look said I was on the money again. Peter was good-looking, personable, and skilled enough with computers to make at least a modest living—and a welcome for himself at least at first—wherever he went. But he had a screw loose and the more he lied to me, the more I seemed to hear it rattling around up there, in his handsome head.

"Come on, Melinda, talk to us," I urged. "We don't think you chopped Merle in pieces, *or* attacked Bob Arnold. Bob caught someone who wasn't supposed to be here. Whoever it was, panicked. We're sure you had nothing to do with it."

This wasn't quite true. But if she felt confident that I didn't suspect her of anything, she might be likelier to confide, too.

"Damn it, she doesn't *know* anything," Peter repeated. "Why are you badgering her, when I *told* you . . ."

Clearly, when Peter *told* you something, you were meant

to listen up. That I hadn't was just frustrating the living hell out of him.

And he was annoying the living hell out of me. "Don't raise your voice to me, you slick little son of a bitch."

At this, he actually tried puffing his chest out. "Oh, yeah. You and your nosy friend, here—"

He waved what was meant to be a contemptuous hand at Ellie, but the lobster puff sort of blunted the effect.

"—are just a couple of small-town busybodies, that's all."

Well, that put the frosting on it. While he was popping the lobster puff into his mouth, I gathered up my attitude-adjustment ammunition. He swallowed; I fired.

"Tax audit," I declared, and watched his throat move as the lobster puff went halfway down and stuck.

"Self-employed, aren't you, Peter? Lots of opportunities for all kinds of fudging, especially if you get paid in cash. Did you know," I added, "that for a couple of years I worked on contract for the IRS?"

He gulped more wine, watching me carefully over the rim of the glass, now. I'd hit a nerve.

"I've still got friends, there," I went on. "Ones who could take every tax return you've ever filed apart so fast, you'd be hearing the cell door slam before you ever even knew what hit you."

I stepped nearer to him. "So unless you've always, *always* declared every cent of your income, and *never* padded a single one of your expenses by so much as a dime, you should shut up."

He gulped again, signaling his agreement with this suggestion. I turned, privately congratulating myself on my newfound skill as a liar; I've had a lot of jobs, but the IRS doesn't outsource snoop work.

"Now, damn it," I began to Melinda, "let's discuss the silly idea of your not knowing anything about anything that's gone on. And—"

But there I stopped, as a new voice came from behind me.

"She does." A familiar voice; it sounded at least as fed up as I felt.

Ben Devine stood there, tall, bearded, and blue-jeaned, with a gaze like a cutting torch. "She knows. But she's a good sister. And she promised not to tell."

His glance raked Peter Christie, who seemed to shrink farther into himself under Devine's scorn. More there, I thought, than a brother disapproving of his sister's romantic choice.

If indeed that was what Peter was, and not something darker.

Melinda spoke up quaveringly. "Ben, you don't have to—"

His look instantly silenced her. It wasn't a harsh look, but a commanding one. I saw them suddenly as two sides of the same coin: Melinda shifting with every breeze of event or emotion, Ben unwavering. A man who would do a job and finish it, however unpleasant. A meat cutter, who knew how to take apart a moose or a deer. Or a man. The air was electric with invisible lines of force and emotion as Ben spoke again.

Quietly: "Yes, I do have to tell, Melinda. These two aren't ever going to leave you alone, if I don't."

He turned to us. "I helped Mickey Jean vanish. She had no family to worry about her and her only choice, if she wanted to live, was to seem to have died."

"Because she was being stalked," I said.

Ben nodded, staring at Peter with a look of such contempt, you'd have thought Ben might put his foot out and crush Peter under the toe of his big boot.

I gathered Ben hadn't known about Peter's hobby of watching women who'd scorned him: watching, and sometimes doing more. Not until Ellie and I brought the news to Melinda.

Peter opened his mouth again. "Who'd stalk her?" he wanted to know. "She's just an overweight old—"

Ben silenced him with a look that should have made him burst into flames. "You think only pretty young girls get stalked? You've led a sheltered life." But it wouldn't be so sheltered, henceforth, his tone suggested.

"Ex-student," Ben Devine confirmed to me. "Bright but disturbed. Angry over a bad grade. After that it was a fast downhill spiral until Mickey Jean feared for her life. So when the police weren't able to help us, we made a plan."

"It wasn't as if they had a choice," Melinda put in with a loyal glance at her brother. "They'd moved, unlisted their phone number. But a college teacher is a pretty visible person. Their apartment had been trashed, there were fires. Pets were killed."

I looked at Ben with new understanding. It sounded bad enough, but experiencing it would have been horrific. And attacks like that . . . well, you didn't have to be a math genius to figure out what the next step would be. Someone had been escalating the violence.

"Wasn't the stalker suspected when Mickey Jean vanished?" Ellie wanted to know.

Ben shook his head. For all his previous ferocity, he was gentle in telling his story, as if in shedding secrecy he was dropping other protective armor, too.

"We made sure our tormentor had an alibi. The idea was to escape, start over, not destroy someone else in the process."

Which they could have, probably, if they'd wanted to. A few drops of Mickey Jean's blood, hairs from the stalker's hairbrush—with a history of harassment and the unexplained absence of the stalking victim, a little would have gone a long way.

But they hadn't. I wondered if under the same circumstances I would be so merciful. "What about the money?" I asked. "I can see constructing a new identity, but how did you manage her not having *any* identity?"

He chuckled grimly, then confirmed my earlier theory: "But *I* had an identity. And we never changed that. We banked on the idea that the fixation was on Mickey, not me. And so far, that's been true. But you're right, the money was the hardest part."

"But you wouldn't want to leave it behind if you could help it. So what did she buy?"

Appreciation flashed in his eyes, that I'd gotten it so quickly. But it was easy, really. Money leaves footprints but objects don't, or they don't have to. Valuable objects like precious metals, say. Or gems.

And Ben had been in Africa and Belgium. "Diamonds!" I exclaimed, answering my own question. "You have . . . interesting friends?"

He nodded again. It would work fine, especially if your "friends" had agreed to buy the diamonds back from you, whenever necessary. Bingo: a source of cash.

Ellie spoke up, getting us back to the question before us, again: "How'd Merle find out?"

Because it wouldn't be enough just to catch a glimpse of Mickey Jean in a bar; not without knowing something in advance, or suspecting.

Ben answered: "I'm not sure how Merle caught on originally. But he was the kind of guy always had a handle on people's secrets. Just like he found out about that land with the tree on it."

Melinda's lips tightened resentfully. "And if Merle thought he had something on you, he'd keep after it until he was sure of it. Then try to use it," she said.

"Yeah," Ben agreed. "So first I had that dust-up with him over the meat. Butchering it for people, the weekend-warrior-type hunters who can't do their own. But I never meant to cut in on his turf."

He didn't seem to intend the pun, or even notice it. "But right off, I was on his you-know-what list, on account of that. He was just watching for me to put a foot wrong."

A new thought, still too uncertain for me to articulate clearly even to myself, was forming.

"And then we made the mistake, just that once, of Mickey Jean and me going into that bar, Duddy's, and he spotted her," Ben was saying.

"And he must've put it together," Peter interjected importantly, apparently believing that with a villain like Merle Carmody to talk about, his own bad deeds might fade conveniently.

"How would you like a nice fat lip to go with that fat head of yours?" Ben asked.

Peter scowled, but quieted. I'd been trying to think of what *his* motive for killing Merle might be; that he'd been protecting Faye Anne was nonsense, of course. But now it was obvious: when a woman broke up with him, Peter made trouble for her.

And if the ongoing fear of those women in California was any clue, he was clever at it. And it could be a *lot* of trouble.

"Anyway, once he was mad at me, Merle had made himself a project of finding out all about me," Ben continued. "That I'd been a suspect in Lewiston wasn't hard for him to learn. Then he caught just that one sight of Mickey Jean in the bar, put it together. The next day he was out there at her place, demanding money."

That was Merle, all right: not real smart, but a master of low cunning when there was a chance it might pay off.

Which was bad enough. But if Merle knew their secret, they could not be sure it wouldn't get around to everyone in Eastport, sooner or later. Then their troubles would begin all over again.

"I didn't kill him," Ben said baldly.

His face said he knew how weak that sounded under the circumstances. Even Melinda must have worried that maybe he had; thus the unsuccessful alibi she'd concocted for him.

And for herself. "You know," I said, "I think I will have a glass of that wine."

Playing for time; the inside of my head felt as if a tornado was whirling around in there. So *many* people had good reasons for wishing Merle dead. Even Melinda: she wanted the old maple tree standing, while Merle wanted it cut. Now with Peter hovering over her like some knight in tarnished armor, she sniffed quietly to make sure we all understood how deeply upsetting this was to a sensitive person like herself.

"We'll have a picnic," Peter was murmuring to her. "A winter picnic, to take your mind off all this. It'll cheer you up."

Melinda flinched at his touch, didn't reply at once. But then: "Well, all right. We could go to the beach by the old factory. It's sheltered and there are some flat rocks to sit on. And . . ."

She mustered a little burst of the old, drama-queen blither. "It's *atmospheric*," she finished, fluttering her hands. "I don't care if it's cold, I *never* mind that. I just *adore* it."

Yeah, right. She would probably do it, though, just to keep the jerk happy. I got the sense she'd tumbled to the fact that keeping Peter happy might be important to her peace of mind, and possibly to her health and welfare.

"Or," I said when Ellie and I got back outside again, "she's such a ding-a-ling, she could just be going along with it because it sounds romantic. After all, she just *adores* the cold," I cooed sarcastically.

Wind gusts buffeted the car, fishing boats in the harbor straining at their lines as we made our way through town. "But maybe Melinda's not the one we should be thinking about," Ellie suggested.

"What do you mean?" A burst of wet snow hit the windshield.

"I mean Mickey Jean's the one who is in trouble."

I stopped the car in front of the swinging wooden sign over the door of Wadsworth's hardware store. From the window, a miniature glass lighthouse strobed the sidewalk.

"You're right. She's still the one with the most to lose, besides Faye Anne. But why would *she* be at Melinda's and attack Bob Arnold, there?"

"I'm not saying she was. Or that she did." Ellie watched a couple of seagulls battle the wind in the arc lights over the pier. "I'm saying, who's been protecting her? Who cares enough to give up his career, even, and go into hiding with her?"

Ben Devine, of course. Ben, who had attacked another man merely over a remark about Melinda.

"Ben's acting open and honest right now," Ellie went on, "but the fact is, we have no idea who's really telling the truth and who isn't."

"And he would tell as much of it as he could," I agreed, "so if we found it out later we wouldn't wonder why he *hadn't.*"

She nodded energetically. "And even though Peter's a louse . . ."

"And I trust Melinda about as far as I can throw her one-handed . . ." I put in.

"If it is Ben you know what they'll do, don't you?" Ellie finished. "Him and Mickey Jean, maybe even any minute?"

"Same as before," I agreed. A huge wave slammed the dock as I made the U-turn to head back out of town. "They'll run."

Chapter **10**

An eighteen-wheeler blew by us, spewing a slurry of slush mixed with road sand onto the windshield. I hit the wipers and let my breath out as the glass cleared, peered through the darkness that seemed to be coagulating around us: fog, mist, spatters of wet sleet, and every so often yet another huge, highballing behemoth.

"We aren't going to confront them out there, are we? Or her?" Ellie asked.

She seemed a little taken aback by my sudden eagerness. But if it *was* Ben, and he and Mickey Jean split before we knew it for sure, Faye Anne was done for.

"Of course not. We're going to get the plate number of that car of hers. His, too, if he shows up. And we'll see if she's making any preparations to head out, if we can—packing up the dog gear, closing up the cabin—and find out anything else that we're able to, without being seen." I squinted ahead. "Then we'll come right back. Forty-five minutes, tops, because . . ."

Another wave of sandy slush hit the windshield. "I don't care where that storm veered to," I finished, "it's not fit out here for man nor beast."

Headlights in the rearview said we weren't the only idiots

driving in it; still, what with the big trucks roaring toward the loading docks at the port, I had a vision of myself lying dead in an icy ditch, the mark of the bulldog hood ornament stamped into my chest. Not until we made it across Route 1 and onto South Meadow Road did I realize that the car behind us was actually following us.

"Ellie." I couldn't see anything about the car except that it was still there.

"I know. Take the right fork coming up, and put your foot on it." The road she directed us to was unmarked, narrow, and curving; I'd never been on it before. But Ellie knew every lane and alley in Washington County, so I obeyed.

The visibility here on the mainland was no better than on the island: closing in on zero. We passed small houses, widely spaced; then nothing but trees and thick, tangled brush growing close to the road. The other car stayed behind us, headlights sullen yellow in the murk.

"What's ahead?" I asked, pushing the gas as hard as I dared.

"Straightaway," Ellie replied. "Couple of miles of it. If he doesn't know that, we could lose him; he won't want to go as fast. And I know a place to turn that he'll never spot, if we can get far enough ahead."

So I did it: hands on the wheel, heart in my throat, foot on the floorboard, and God bless whatever road crew had been out that night, spreading sand. "Whoa . . ."

She'd said it was straight. She *hadn't* said it was hilly. We flew up over a rise and for an instant went totally airborne.

Thump. "Here," she said. "Turn hard, and cut the engine."

The interesting sensation of flying through the air was followed by the even more fascinating feeling of hitting the brakes and noticing that the car didn't slow in the slightest.

"Turn," Ellie suggested quietly again, "the goddamn steering wheel, Jake."

The other car's headlights were just now showing again in the rearview, like pale eyes intent on finding us in the thick, freezing fog. Something about them made me feel cold in the pit of my stomach; the fact, for instance, that they were there at all. People don't follow you, in Eastport. They don't menace you.

They just don't. But now on a night so lousy that only the truck drivers were out doing anything whatsoever, somebody was. And that opened a worm-can full of unpleasant possibilities, including the notion that we had made somebody really, really mad.

Someone who had already killed two people and tried very hard to kill a third. All these thoughts went by in an instant as the car's rear end skewed wildly sideways on the icy pavement, until we were turned ninety degrees, aiming—miraculously—in the direction Ellie pointed.

Which meant that for the moment whoever was behind us probably couldn't see us. I tromped the gas pedal as hard as I could one more despairing time, knowing it was probably going to land us smack in a frozen snowbank. But if I didn't, the chase car wouldn't have to chase us much farther; crossways in the road as we were, in another few seconds it was going to come upon us and broadside us.

We shot forward, spewing sand, which was bad enough, but then the muffler scraped horrendously over something much higher and harder than I should have been trying to clear at that speed.

Or any speed, but it was too late. We left the muffler and, it felt like, half the transmission as the car continued barreling between half-visible trees. I braced myself for the halt we were inevitably going to come to: tree stump, old fence post, or chunk of granite. The possibilities for what we could hit were seemingly endless, and as far as I could tell, also endlessly unpleasant.

But we didn't come to any halt at all until Ellie reached

out and shut off the ignition. Then everything went off all at once, including the power brakes and steering, and there was a silence.

Into which, slowly like a being materializing malevolently out of the fog, a car appeared in the rearview mirror on the road we had departed.

The beams of its headlights were solid yellow bars in the mist. A spark of radium-green from the dashboard of the vehicle flashed briefly as it passed. Then it was gone.

"Could you tell who it was?" Ellie whispered.

I shook my head. "Too dark and thick out there."

Then we just sat for what seemed like forever, while the cold seeped through the floorboards and our breaths fogged the windows. Fat clots of snow fell from the trees onto the car roof with soft wet sounds like the tentative patting of cold, searching hands.

"What is this, anyway?" I asked Ellie. "Someone's long driveway, or a firebreak, or what?"

She shook her head. "Camp road. Summer places on the lake, half a mile or so that way." She wiped condensation from the window with her sleeve. "I hope he didn't see our tire marks."

Awful thought: see the tire marks, realize what they were, and come back. "But there are enough of these little cuts into the woods," she went on, "that this one would look like any other if he didn't see us turn. What we climbed over was mostly ice. Plowed snow, melted and frozen again."

So no tracks right near the road: the silver lining to an absent exhaust system. But . . . I turned the ignition key.

"Um, Ellie?"

No reaction. From the ignition, that is.

"Something happened. To the engine."

In the darkness, snow clumps kept falling onto the hood. I turned the key a few more times, hoping for a miracle.

No dice. When I was a kid, as a last resort you could sit

on the fender and pour gasoline from a cup into the carbu-retor.

Not anymore. Also, no gas. And no paper cup.

"Well, I guess we're going to have to . . ."

Light and sound exploded behind us as another vehicle flew over the ice bank we'd cleared and accelerated at us, en-gine roaring. It snarled to within inches of our rear bumper, slammed to a halt.

A door banged. Boots crunched through snow and ice. A shape came to my side of the car and a face, flat with fury, peered in.

"Get in the truck, you damned little fools," Ben Devine snarled.

Ten minutes later, lights from Mickey Jean Bunting's cabin fell onto the dissolving snow and turned the sur-rounding forest ghostly with rising fog. Mickey Jean's old Honda dripped fresh slush, just outside the cabin door.

Ben snapped the ignition off, slammed the truck door hard, and stalked toward the porch, leaving us to get out on our own.

"This is *not* a good idea," I whispered urgently to Ellie as we made our way through the slush. Somewhere, Skip and Rascal were going nuts trying to get out at us.

Devine had refused to take us back to town. I had a feel-ing maybe it was because he'd already dug graves for us, here.

And his mood wasn't improving. By the time we got in-side he and Mickey Jean were in the midst of a furious argu-ment.

"I don't care. I'm tired of running," Mickey Jean de-clared. "It makes me sick, having to hide out like some kind of criminal. We have got to *do* something about it this time. We've got to *finish* what we . . ."

She stopped as she turned and caught sight of us. Ruggedly garbed in checked flannel shirt, boots, and jeans, she reminded me again of Paul Bunyan. Her boots dripped slush; she'd just come in from somewhere. In her hand was some kind of a glossy brochure or magazine. Ben took it from her, tossed it into the stove before I could see much of it.

"Finish what you started," I said. "You don't by any chance mean Merle Carmody's murder, do you?"

Because it was crunch time. The car was dead and I had a feeling we would be, too, soon, unless I gave these two some food for thought. "Ellie and I have been talking it over with Timmy Rutherford," I lied.

Fluently, I hoped. "Merle was blackmailing you," I told Mickey Jean, "but the money wasn't your big problem, was it?"

I waved around the warm, well-furnished room. "The biggest trouble was, if Merle knew, pretty soon everyone would. You can't keep that kind of a secret forever, in Eastport."

The rifle wasn't racked, which meant it was out here somewhere, and probably loaded. But there was coffee in the pot, a clean cup on the counter. I helped myself, hoping like hell that it was harder to shoot someone who was enjoying your hospitality, even if uninvited.

And I kept talking. "But like you said, you can't keep running."

The coffee was fresh and strong. I poured some for Ellie, handed it to her. Her eyes said "what the hell are you doing?" but she sipped it obediently.

"*And* like you said, you had to do something about it."

My plan was that one or the other of them would answer. My plan was, we would remember what they said. With that, Ellie and I could go to Faye Anne's lawyer, Geoffrey

Claiborn, maybe give him enough reasonable doubt to at least start raising a stink.

My plan didn't work. When I turned back to Mickey Jean she was already coming at me, arms outstretched. Before I could even set the cup down she was shoving me, a two-handed straight-arm into my chest that sent me staggering back.

Darn, thought the small part of my mind that wasn't occupied with trying to stay upright. "Or," I began in what I hoped was a conciliatory tone, "it could be that this is all just a big misunderstanding, and—"

Something made me stop. Maybe it was the rifle that had appeared as if by magic in Mickey Jean's meaty grip. I was glad the woodstove was only a small parlor model, because the look on Mickey Jean's face made me flash on the story of Hansel and Gretel.

But then a little frown creased her forehead. "You didn't, did you?" Turning to Ben: "After we saw him, you didn't go back and . . . ?"

"Saw him when?" Ellie inquired gently.

She could do this: full of sympathy. And when she wanted to, she used it like a scalpel, cutting to the heart of the matter. No blood.

But there was pain. "The night he died," Mickey Jean said, responding to Ellie's tone, her own voice raw with remembered anger, "we decided to offer Merle some money. More, I mean, than he asked for, one lump sum."

"Don't," Ben warned, but Mickey Jean ignored him. "But never any more money. Take it or leave it, we told him."

"And he said?"

"He was drunk. There in his house alone, drinking himself stupid as usual," she replied scathingly. "To think I could be ruined again by that sack of idiot blood and guts—"

She stopped, hearing the way that she had put it. "He refused to take the money. Said he knew what I thought of him, and how did I like it? Him having his dirty thumb on a high muckety-muck like me."

She laughed, not pleasantly. "He actually said that. 'High muckety-muck.' "

"And then?" Ellie had a way of listening that made her easy to talk to, like dropping pebbles into a pool. But underneath her stillness there was action going on, I could tell.

"Then I talked," Ben Devine replied. "I told him I was going to kill him if he harmed Mickey Jean in any way. Word or deed."

"Ben, you didn't say anything about Melinda? Or hurt Merle, to help her, too? I mean," I went on, "there you had him. Full of booze, not in the best shape to defend himself. And he was threatening both the women you love."

Mickey Jean Bunting wasn't the standard female love object. She wasn't pretty, slender, or charming. She didn't dress nicely, or possess feminine wiles. Independent as a hog on ice, as one of my uncles used to say about me. And Ben loved her; that much, if nothing else, was perfectly clear.

"He was an ignorant drunk," he said, "a wife-beating stumblebum who wrecked things and hurt people for the pure mean pleasure of it. But I didn't kill Merle."

Another thought occurred to him. "Who do you think made that call about me?" he demanded.

"I'd been wondering about that," I admitted. "I thought maybe it was you. To make me *think* that someone else was behind all this."

He snorted derisively. "Yeah, I'd point a finger at myself. I sit around all day planning ways to be devious."

Which clearly he didn't; there was nothing subtle about him, any more than there was about Mickey Jean. But there wasn't anything subtle about that knife he carried, either.

And no one knew we were here. "We should . . ."

Call home, I was about to say. But Devine was talking

again. "*He's* the sly one. Peter. I've tried to tell Melinda, persuade her she ought to get rid of him. But she won't."

"Or can't," Mickey Jean said; I glanced at her. Something in her attitude had changed; now her look was meaningful. Warning.

Go, it telegraphed to me. Because she knew about Ben's temper, or for some other reason? It was possible, I supposed, that Mickey Jean hadn't known what he'd done but now had begun figuring it out.

One thing I did know: he was getting madder by the minute. Ellie glanced at me: *Outta here.*

You bet, I thought back at her. But there was no way; Ben was between us and the door.

"Peter's so *sweet,*" Ben sneered in bitter parody of Melinda. "Manipulative bastard. But maybe it's just as well she doesn't dump him. Faye Anne Carmody did, and look what happened to *her.*"

He fingered the leather clasp that snapped over the wrapped hilt of the Randall knife. The blade was tempered steel, possibly saw-toothed. And he was a lit fuse. Even Mickey Jean was eyeing him carefully, now.

"Ben," she began, but he cut her off.

"If you two had just left it alone," he said. "But you had to *help.*"

At that Ellie spoke up firmly: "Faye Anne was my friend. We wanted to help her, just the way you wanted to help Mickey Jean."

She took a deep breath. "There's nothing wrong with that, and I'm not going to stand here and let you tell me there was." Saying this she stuck out her chin and looked about as powerfully effective as a leaf in a nor'easter.

But it stopped him: grudging admiration in his eyes, that he didn't scare her. Or that she wouldn't give him the satisfaction of showing it.

"Ellie," I said cautioningly.

No good. "Maybe," she went on, not dropping her gaze, "you killed Merle to keep him quiet *and* solve Melinda's problems with him. Then you threatened Faye Anne with that knife."

Oh, how I wished she hadn't mentioned the knife. It was the last thing I wanted him thinking about.

But Ellie wouldn't quit. "Maybe you told Faye Anne you'd kill her the same way you killed Merle, if she didn't keep her mouth shut. You thought you'd got rid of a possible witness with Kenty Dalrymple. And if you ran into Bob Arnold out at Melinda's place, and he'd seen something he shouldn't . . . well, now he's out of the picture, too. Or you hope he is, maybe."

Another deep breath. "But now you're worried. What else do we know? And who else might we tell? We could get Mickey Jean in more trouble than Merle could, now. And you know it."

Putting her under suspicion as an accomplice, Ellie meant. She might as well have thrown nitroglycerine through the door of that parlor stove. Ben's face went white as he lunged at Ellie, his big fist raised.

"Ben!" Mickey Jean cried.

His move cleared the path to the door. I scrambled, snagging Ellie's coat collar, and we were out, the dogs still going crazy back in the darkness behind the cabin.

"Why did you *say* that to him?" We stumbled in the slush toward what I hoped was the snow-filled way out to the road. What we would do there I had no idea. Freeze to death, probably. But it was better than being carved up by that Randall knife.

"He was already mad. I didn't think he'd kill us in front of her, though. And I wanted to hear his answer," Ellie replied as calmly as she could while nearly going tail-down on a patch of ice. Cold droplets splattered my face: half rain, half sleet.

I glanced back. No one. Yet. But while we were inside, fog had thickened and the temperature had dropped mercilessly. Overhead, branches clattered hollowly together, gleaming in the faint light from the cabin as the wind rose.

"Maybe Mickey Jean will call someone to come get us," Ellie said.

More rain, each droplet stinging frigidly. Soon they would coat everything, freezing on each surface, jacketing it in lethal ice. The power line running from the road to the cabin was already heavy with it, creaking as it swung overhead.

"What are you talking about?" I pulled out the cell phone.

"Oh," Ellie said delightedly. "I thought you'd . . ."

"Forgotten it? Not in a million years. And it has a backup battery," I added, proud of this; those well-prepared fishermen with their fancy safety equipment had nothing on *me*. "So I didn't have to . . ."

Wait for it to charge, I would have finished. But just then something swung suddenly past me with a hot, sizzling crackle. There was an explosive, lightning-bolt crash, and the pale reflections on the iced surfaces around us winked out as all the lights in the cabin behind us went dark.

The power line: down. "Jesus," I breathed. "Where is it?"

"I don't know. Wait . . ."

A thin beam of light appeared; Ellie, God bless her, had brought along a pocket flashlight. "There."

The downed line lay behind us, on the ice. Harmless looking now, but . . .

Suddenly I realized I had dropped the cell phone, too.

Somewhere in the darkness; I bent to search for it.

"No," Ellie said urgently, "we need to be away from here, the water on the ground will conduct . . ."

Electricity; lots of it. "Go, go, *go!*"

A hundred yards down the snow-filled rut, punching

through with each step: "I don't get it. Good way to get rid of us, but how'd he bring a power line down on us?"

"Jacobia. Look around you. Listen to what's happening. Don't you get it?"

I listened. While I listened, tiny, cold objects pelted my face. Overhead, the clattering sound intensified to loud clacking as the wind rose higher. And all the while, rain: cold rain.

Freezing rain. My feet were soaked; my jacket weighed a ton, its collar stiff and prickly.

Frozen. We were having an ice storm.

"Keep walking." Ellie's voice came from the darkness in front of me. "I don't think we'd better go back, no matter what."

She was right: that live electrical wire. And the phone in the cabin had been one of those nifty cordless jobs: no power, no voice connection. So even if Ben had a change of heart (unlikely) or Mickey Jean did it in spite of him (more possible, but I wasn't banking on that, either), no one was on the phone calling help for us.

Or giving us any. Ben and Mickey Jean couldn't get out to us any more than we could get back in: the wire on the ground had trapped them on one side of it, us on the other.

"Ellie. We're in a situation, here."

Now I was squinting, trying to keep ice pellets from penetrating my eyes. With them came enough cold liquid rain to coat everything and glaze it instantly. After that each new layer of water froze onto the ice beneath; in the morning this would all be a glittering fairyland.

Right now, though, it was a death trap.

"A sand truck will come along," Ellie gasped, slogging through knee-deep snow. Her feet still broke through with each step; mine, too. We were fighting our way; between exhaustion and hypothermia it was a toss-up which one would get us.

If another section of power line didn't come down and zap us. As if in answer to my thought, a loud *crack!* followed by a popping sound and another brilliant flash of sick, greenish-yellow light came from behind us.

The weight of the accumulating ice was taking down one section of line after another. Another crash, this time from the woods, as an old branch gave up its grip on a tree that had held it for a hundred or so years. On its way down it took dozens of smaller, ice-coated branches. The sound of breaking glass seemed an odd, tinkling accompaniment as twiglets snapped and shattered.

"If we can make it to the road," Ellie insisted.

I didn't contradict her. I didn't have the heart to, much less the lung power. Every breath of air was like a frozen fist slugging my chest. The cold was seeping up my leg bones, weighting them with a deep, frigid agony that sooner or later was going to stop them.

Would I be found lying down, or frozen standing up, sheeted in ice? Only an hour or so ago we'd been at Joy Abrams' place, looking out at those hideous yard lamps. I'd have killed to be within sight of them, now, and I was dying of thirst, too.

But when I put my tongue out, all I could catch were needle-like ice pellets. They felt dry as grains of rice.

Water was all around, puddled on the frozen snow. I could drink some if I could just get down to it, and then I could . . .

"No! Jacobia, you'll never get back up again, your stuff is too heavy, don't do it. Look, we're almost to the . . ."

Road. Ellie's face bobbed like a balloon. Distantly the thought occurred to me that this was hypothermia; I was losing all my judgment.

A stab of fear pierced me. "Okay."

My tongue felt thick. Soaked through and frozen, and too slow. Too slow for what?

No matter. One foot. The other.

We emerged onto the road that felt pebbled with frozen rain atop a coating of sand. Ice pellets fell with a sound like gravel pouring from a dump truck.

There we stopped. My eyes had adjusted to the darkness: the road a dark grey ribbon, remnants of snow here and there like heaps of dirty white rags, and the woods. Dark and endless, or as good as endless for our purposes.

"Jake," Ellie said quietly.

"We're done for, aren't we?"

"No, Jake." Her tone became insistent. *"Look."*

I followed the slow, heavy gesture of her right arm, aiming at a dark shape, silent and motionless by the road.

A *big* dark shape. It was a car. "Oh, my God."

I moved toward it. If the keys were in it, if we could get the damned thing started . . .

Even if not, maybe we could get inside, out of the icy rain. There might be a blanket, a tarp, *something*. The headlights went on, the sudden glare blinding me, making me stagger back.

Scaring me, too. "Who is it?" I shouted. "Who's there?"

Ice bits fell thickly through the cones of pale yellow projected from the lights. Rain steamed on the hood, billowing up in clouds that obscured the windshield.

Sitting here, I realized, with the engine running. Someone rolled a window down. A face peered out. "Who is that?" a voice called.

My ears felt frozen all the way into the center of my head; the voice came through like someone talking underwater, unrecognizable. I moved toward it—worriedly, but it was our only hope—then stopped as Ellie said my name.

"Jake?" she said again. Puzzled-sounding this time. As if, having come this far, she didn't understand why she had stopped.

But I did understand: she was twenty pounds lighter

than I was and four inches taller. And hypothermia is a function of time, temperature, and body mass.

No exceptions; it was why the men had contests to see who could get into the survival suits fastest.

"Ellie." She'd been wet and freezing for half an hour; her lips in the headlights' glare were indigo against the ghostly white of her face. Her eyelashes had frozen together into clear, tear-shaped lozenges; her teeth were chattering so hard she could barely speak.

The bad part, though, was her level of consciousness. As I reached her, her knees went out from under her; I caught her in arms that felt like blunt lumps, and went down with her onto the frozen road.

The ice bit my kneecaps with that numb kind of pain that means you've really injured yourself and can't quite feel it. But a pair of skinned knees was the least of my worries, now.

". . . okay," she whispered, trying to smile. Then her eyes rolled back whitely and all at once she was dead weight.

"Hey! You, whoever you are, get out here, help me with . . ?"

The car door opened. A person got out. Small, slender.

Like Ellie, in fact. But not half-dead of cold.

Alive and carrying a gun: a small, grey-metal pistol glinted in the headlights.

Behind the weapon Willetta Abrams.

She put the gun away once she saw who we were and helped me get Ellie into the car, into the backseat where I started pulling off her wet, frozen clothing. Chilled didn't even begin to describe her condition; I was terrified for her.

Slenderness may be a good thing for fashion. But for survival, more meat on the bones is better. "Crank the heat," I ordered as Willetta put the car in gear.

A couple of protesting rumble-*thump*s backfired from under the chassis but the engine settled as the vehicle's systems cleared from having been sitting there, idling. "We need to go to the hospital in Calais," I told her.

"You got it." Willetta was a good, assertive driver, unfazed by the ice on South Meadow Road and speedier when we got to Route 1, which was freshly sanded. Also, she was carrying emergency stuff, including a blanket; I remembered Joy saying their father had been a Maine guide and thanked my stars.

"Hey," Ellie muttered, her eyelids fluttering.

"Hang in there, kid." Her flesh felt rubbery.

She tried to sit up. "I want . . ."

"Right, but you need to get checked over."

I'd heard a story once about fishermen dumped into the bay by a combination of bad weather and bad luck. They floated in lifejackets in the icy water until a rescue boat found them. On board, they revived, gratefully swallowing the hot coffee the rescue crew offered.

Whereupon—and this is a true story—they all dropped dead. The shock of a hot drink on their chilled systems killed the fishermen outright; by the time it got to shore, the rescue boat was carrying a dozen corpses.

Willetta glanced in the rearview. "Not much farther, now." She snapped the radio on to WQDY, the Calais–St. Stephen station.

"*. . . guess that storm took a wild turn, folks, and we've got a lot of unexpected ice out there, so the authorities are asking you to stay home, sit tight, wait it out a little longer until city crews can . . .*"

She snapped it off again. No one else was on the road. "What were you doing out there?" I asked her. "And why are you carrying a gun?"

"Sorry I scared you. After you left Joy's, I—"

"Oh," Ellie murmured, huddled into the blanket. "So *cold*."

"—I wanted to tell you the rest of it. About Peter. I went to your house but you were just leaving, so—"

"So you followed us to Melinda's, and then out here in an *ice storm?*"

She shook her head impatiently. "I didn't want to see Peter, and his car was at Melinda's, so I didn't go in there. I thought I'd see you at your house, again, but you made that U-turn. And it wasn't an ice storm. Not right away. I was as surprised by it as you."

So it had been Willetta all along, following us. "Once I realized you must have turned off, I went back but by then you were getting into Ben's truck. So I followed, and waited for both of you to come back out again. I guess I could've just gone home at that point, but I don't trust Ben," she added, frowning.

Right. Me, neither. "And I can understand why you wouldn't want to encounter Peter," I conceded.

"Peter," Willetta pronounced, "is a psychotic bastard."

"Yeah," I agreed, "he is kind of unusual, isn't he?"

"Turn around," Ellie said. Her voice was stronger. "I don't need to go to any . . ."

Willetta laughed harshly. "*Unusual?* That's a nice word for what he is. Peter *drugged* me. He drugged me and he . . . *did* things to me. Awful things. I don't even remember them, but I know it's true. Because . . ."

Oh, for God's sake, of course: drugs.

Willetta found her voice. "It's why I wanted to tell you without Joy listening. Or anyone else . . . Peter took *pictures* of me."

She glanced in the mirror again. "I've *seen* them. I just hope no one else has. That's why no one ever says a word against him, you know. Because he has always got something to hurt you with. You think he has gone for good, that he's forgotten you . . ."

"So that's why the gun, and the lights at your place?"

She nodded. "He'd hang around, hide in the dark waiting for me until I went out to go to work for the night. Joy doesn't know I have the gun, but I *need* it in case he . . ."

"Turn *around*," Ellie said. "Are you both deaf? George is going to be frantic, and Wade, too, we've got to go home . . ."

". . . before he comes back," Willetta finished. "Hey, it's stopping."

The ice, she meant. As we drove, the crispy-sounding road surface beneath the tires became slush, then liquid water. The rain was all liquid, now, cast aside by the wipers in spraying gouts.

"Melinda's supposed to be seeing him tonight," Ellie said. She'd given up on making us turn around.

To my surprise, Willetta nodded. "That stupid picnic at the old gas plant on the beach, probably. Those two are *both* nuts."

I just adore *the cold* . . . "How do you know about that?"

She shrugged, eyes on the road. "He's been planning it for a while. And he calls me, too. Like I said, you don't get away from Peter. He calls and brags how wonderful life is without me. Never mind it was me who dumped him. And—"

She glanced at me. "Anyway, you don't dump Peter. You just don't."

Or maybe Ellie hadn't given up. Maybe she'd just thought of something important enough to *make* us go back.

"This ice storm," she pointed out, "wasn't in the forecast."

A mental picture of them flashed in my mind: Peter and Melinda as I'd last seen them, discussing their planned outing. I remembered something else, too, suddenly: Melinda telling me she was going to have to do something about Peter.

"Willetta. Find a place for another U-turn."

Melinda would do something, all right. She would go on that damned picnic. And then—tonight: so long, sayonara, don't let the screen door boot you in the backside on your way out, Peter.

Willetta looked startled, but scanned the side of the road obediently.

"Jake," Ellie said, "first he threatens people, women, so badly they won't talk about him, even a whole continent away."

Willetta made a three-point turn, heading us south. Big orange town trucks and emergency electric-company vans had begun hitting the highway in force, their yellow rooftop beacons strobing the darkness.

"Next he does his number on Willetta," I agreed. "And that's the answer: why Faye Anne doesn't remember. She stuck with her decision not to see him anymore. So for revenge—"

"He drugged her with whatever he used on Willetta," Ellie said. "Killed Merle and set Faye Anne up so it would look like she did it."

"Maybe," I cautioned. Ellie's color had improved remarkably. "We still don't know that for sure. Twenty minutes ago, we were sure that *Ben* had . . ."

Willetta made the turn onto Route 190 and sped toward the causeway. "But it doesn't matter. From Faye Anne's point of view, two suspects—besides her, I mean—are *much* better than one."

"Oh. Okay." Ellie sat back, satisfied. Her voice was stronger, too.

On the east side of the causeway the ice was gone but there were cars in the ditch and wires down, no lights in any houses anywhere. The storm had hit the island hard.

"Well, I know what I think," Willetta said emphatically. "Bob Arnold caught *Peter* at Melinda's, lurking around.

Maybe Bob suspected him already, and said something that let Peter know it. So Peter attacked him."

"What did Mickey Jean mean, then," Ellie asked, "when she told Ben they had to finish what they'd started?"

But to that we had no answer. Ellie began digging through the box of emergency stuff Willetta carried. Flares, a small shovel, a bag of small things: matches, flashlight, batteries.

Finally: "Here," she said, sounding satisfied.

Like a good guide, trained by a father who'd taught her to be prepared for any emergency, Willetta carried a set of dry clothes. Old and mismatched, too short in the legs and sleeves but plenty warm.

"No," I said when she offered me some of them; her brief collapse had scared me badly. And I guess I must have sounded serious enough not to argue with; as swiftly as she could in the cramped backseat of the car, she began pulling them on.

When she was finished she looked ready to stand out in a garden, to scare crows. She was warm and dry, though, and a pair of old boots underneath the seat fit her well enough, too, for the moment. And by now I thought a cup of hot coffee probably wouldn't kill her, so I was satisfied.

For the moment. "Wade *is* going to be worried," I said. "And mad."

"He'll cheer up when he sees you're okay," Willetta said. We were on Clark Street, taking the back way into town.

Toward Melinda's. I saw lights, suddenly. "The generator. It must be working."

"Of course it's working. George fixed it." Ellie peered out. "I don't get it, though. There aren't any lights at—"

Melinda's house: everything on the way to it was lit up, streetlamps shedding yellow cones through the rain subsiding to mist. Christmas decorations on houses shone merrily: laughing Santas and packs of elves frolicked everywhere.

But Melinda's compound gaped like a black hole. We went up the driveway to the house, dark and deserted looking. "Let's go home," Willetta suggested nervously.

"No. Maybe we should knock, see if . . ."

"No one's here." Ellie's voice was definite. "I think we'd better look for her. Let's try the beach."

Willetta looked more doubtful. "You should go home, anyway," she said, meaning Ellie. "Take a hot shower and make sure you're really all right. We don't know they're even together, not for sure. And besides . . ."

"And besides, you don't want to confront Peter Christie on the beach in the dark," I guessed.

No streetlights illuminated the shore by the old gas plant, and the sound of the water rushing beneath the old, crumbling wharf blocked out other sounds.

"Right," Willetta admitted with a show of embarrassment. But I understood: down there at night, you could feel a million miles away from anyone and anything.

Away from help. "Let's just look," Ellie said persuasively. "It's on our way back to Jake's. And if they're not there, we *will* go home, call Tim Rutherford and ask him if he's seen them."

"And if they *are* there, we'll call him, too," I added, no more anxious to provoke anything with Peter than Willetta was, alone in the dark.

Willetta drove down Water Street, turned on Clark Street toward the bay, and stopped where the road ended above the steep slope down to the edge of the bluff. The glow of the streetlights turned the wave tops the color of gleaming pewter, a hundred yards out, but close to shore the massive legs of the old wharf staggered darkly into them, unlit.

It was high tide; only a narrow stretch of gravel and round-shouldered old bricks showed at the waterline.

"Let's go," Willetta said anxiously.

"Wait." Ellie peered down. "What's that, a footprint?"

The remnants of slush here were grey and rotten looking. She snapped on her little flashlight. "It is."

Willetta looked impatient. "Anyone could have made that . . ."

"No, they couldn't. It's been raining and sleeting. Someone made this footprint not very long ago. And there's . . ."

Another one: blurred but distinguishable, the toe-mark aimed at the shore. I peered at the old wharf, pitch-darkness beneath it, deep water moving against the massive old pilings.

High up under them, deeper pockets of darkness yawned. Big iron spikes for the plant workers from the old days to climb were barely visible against the water beyond. The footprints seemed to emerge from the heaving waves.

In summer, birds nested in the sheltered cubbies of the wharf ruins. Feral cats scrambled up to the support formed by the crossing of beams, planks, and the old wharf pilings, to have their litters there. At low tide, skunks and foxes prowled the beach, eating mussels and urchins, waiting for the eggs, newborn kittens, and baby birds that fell occasionally into their jaws.

But now it was winter: nothing, no one. "The tide was lower," Ellie said. "Half an hour ago, maybe, someone was under the wharf. They walked back on the beach that's covered with water, now. And here, they angled up toward the street."

"But only one set of . . ."

Footprints, I'd been about to say, but the sudden pair of headlights shining straight into my eyes interrupted me. Then the lights cut off and Peter Christie slammed from his car, ran down onto the beach toward us. "Is she here?"

Sounding alarmed. "I went home to get ready for our outing," he added. "I was supposed to go back and pick her up but she's not home, her lights are off . . ."

He spotted Willetta. "What are *you* doing here?"

"I guess I should just drop off the face of the earth," she spat furiously. "Well, let me tell you, you're not going to get away so—"

"Never mind that." I stepped between them. "Peter, you were meant to pick up Melinda at her house? When?"

"An hour ago, we were going to do it right after you two left." He spread his hands helplessly. "We were going to come down here, we thought it would be wild out, but fun. We had no idea the storm would get so bad."

Something about that old wharf made me uneasy. The masses of water moving lazily beneath it: so deep, now.

And something else. A reflection? Halfway to the end of the old structure . . . I squeezed my eyes shut, looked again.

Nothing. "Then I went back to her place, still no one home, walked around it calling for her," Peter complained. "Pounded on the doors. All the drapes are open, and I had a flashlight, so I could see in. In case," he added defensively, "she was there, hurt or something. Then I went home, figuring she'd have called. But she hadn't."

The wind was falling, drifting billows of fog now just sitting, barely moving on the waves. From under the wharf came the faint slop-drip of water draining as the tide ebbed.

"You did something to her," Willetta snarled. "Why'd you come down here? Because you saw Ellie's flashlight, and you thought we might figure out *what* you've done, isn't that right?"

My eyes had adjusted to the darkness, so that everything was in shades of grey.

"The way you did something to Merle," Willetta rushed on. "Killed him to get Faye Anne in trouble. You drugged her, didn't you? The same way you drugged me. So she wouldn't remember, or be able to *tell* anyone *what you did* . . ."

His mouth fell open. "Is *that* what you're telling people? That I— It's not true!"

"Oh, yeah? That's what *you* say. But when they find those drugs in your house, that you used on me *and* Faye Anne, *then* we'll see who people believe. You still have them, I'll bet, and the police are going to *find* them. And then . . ."

She stalked away from him as a shout came from above: "What the hell's going on down there?"

It was Ben Devine, scrambling down the steep slope onto the beach with Mickey Jean behind. He strode up, slammed his hands into Peter's chest.

"Where is she, you little son of a . . ."

"*I don't know!* God damn it, get your hands off . . ."

Great; a testosterone-spewing contest. Just what we needed. "Shut up, both of you," I snapped. "Ben, how did *you* know to come here? Just took a sudden notion to visit the beach, did you?"

His bulk towered above me. But the question took him aback. "She . . . she *said* they were coming here. You heard her. For that goddamned little *picnic* the two of them cooked up together." He swung back to Peter. "I swear, if anything's happened to her I'll take you in the woods and feed your eyes to the crows."

"But I *didn't* . . ."

Mickey Jean came up to me. "We tried to call her once Ben got the generator running, make sure she was okay."

Oh, for pete's sake, of course they would have a generator. The two of them were set up for anything short of Armageddon. Which Peter and Ben looked just about ready to have between them; the shouting was escalating.

"But there was no answer," Mickey Jean said. "The power company had turned off the electricity on account of that downed line, but even then we couldn't get the truck out; half a tree fell on it." She took a deep breath. "But my Honda was okay. So we came in to make sure she was all right. Or Ben did, anyway. He feels he owes it to her, to take care of her."

"Right, Melinda's good at making people feel they owe her," I said. Because it had suddenly occurred to me, why we were here on a beach in the freezing darkness, fighting and worrying:

For Melinda, who despite all our fears was probably sitting somewhere nice and warm, now, drinking wine and thinking up lots of reasons to criticize us.

But Mickey Jean looked surprised. "You don't know? Why he feels that way? But no, of course you wouldn't . . ."

"What?" I turned at her tone. Willetta had climbed the slope again, looking down at Peter and Ben, still arguing.

"Ben wasn't always a strong guy," Mickey said. "Kidney failure, it hit him out of the blue. Three times a week dialysis, until . . ."

"Oh," I said, suddenly understanding Ben's devotion.

"Melinda stepped in," Mickey Jean said. "She found out what he needed, and over his protests she gave Ben a kidney."

Which, in a funny backwards way, sounded just like Melinda. The big, dramatic gesture from the drama queen. But then I caught myself; it was more than that, way more. The one thing she really could have bragged about, only she hadn't; suddenly I had another picture of the drama queen, entirely.

Frivolous, maybe; even foolish. On the surface. Underneath was someone who delivered when push came to shove. And kept quiet about it.

Discouragement washed over me. So many possibilities weaving together in interlocking patterns of deceit. And in the center of them something missing, something I kept looking for, not knowing anything except that when I saw it, I would know it.

But by then it might be too late. "She's not here now," I

began, turning to head back up the slope toward the car. Ben and Peter went on shouting. "I guess we'd better go somewhere, call Tim after all."

And see Wade, let him know I wasn't dead in a ditch. It was time to go home and face the music.

"Come on, Ellie," I said. The men were pushing one another again, Willetta taking verbal potshots from the darkness on the slope above—her voice barely audible in the noise of wind and waves—Mickey Jean down on the beach, still trying to separate them without success.

Peter took a roundhouse swing at Ben Devine, who replied with a clip to the side of Peter's head that sent him staggering, ankle-deep in the frigid water; if there'd been any beer bottles handy they'd have been breaking them over each other's heads. Shouting and cursing . . .

"What a mess." I trudged upward, the sand dragging at my feet. "I don't think we've done a darned bit of good, tonight."

God, but I was tired. Mostly, though, I was thinking about going home and facing Wade. All the energy seemed to be leaking out of me; a slick stone made me stumble.

"Wait." Ellie's voice pierced the shouting and the sound of the waves.

"What?" I turned, peering to where she aimed a finger.

She'd taken off her glasses, and without them my face was no more than a pinkish blur to her, her own hands rounded blobs. But at a distance . . .

"There," she said. "At the end of the wharf, on the water. See it? Something . . ."

Once she'd pointed it out, I did see it: floating. A bit of driftwood or a gleaming rag of rockweed; even a dead harbor seal could look that way in the moving water. But it wasn't any of those, because none of them had—the thing turned sluggishly in the waves—*fringes*.

"It's a scarf," Ellie said. "Drifting."

I was already running. It was a scarf, all right, but it wasn't drifting. Tide going out, currents swirling, but now I could see that it hung by a piling, snagged, its fringes turning like the rag-ends of seaweed anchored to the rocks.

As if it, like the waving rockweed, were firmly attached.

Tied there. I plunged into the water, my legs hammered by mallets of cold. Ben saw me, uttered an oath, dove in behind me.

"I'm calling for help!" Mickey yelled down from where her car was parked, as Ben surfaced, bellowing, and dove again.

Peter was in the water, too, cringing at it but striding on. Ben came up a third time, the Randall knife unsheathed, its blade a glinting horror in the murk under the wharf pilings.

Down again. Gasping with the cold, I watched the water where he had gone under, Peter still struggling toward the spot, but Ben didn't reappear. In the distance a siren began wailing, coming closer.

I couldn't feel my legs; as they started to go from under me Ellie grabbed me and pulled me in. "You can't do anything," she said. "You don't swim well enough to go under the—"

"Hey!" The Eastport squad car slid to a halt above us, Tim Rutherford at a run almost before the car's wheels had stopped turning. The headlights lit up the whole beach, the wharf's underside, and the water with Peter Christie slogging out of it.

No Ben. No anyone. "Tim," I said, my teeth chattering, "we think maybe Melinda's down there . . ."

Ben surfaced, something in his arms. "Ambulance!" he shouted at us, nearly falling, struggling onto the shore.

Another vehicle pulled in: Wade's truck, George Valentine in the passenger seat. The two of them sprinted down, faces anxious.

"Ellie?" George shouted. Then he spotted her, his shoulders sagging with relief. "Tim called us, said you were here . . ."

Wade grabbed me, peered into my face. "Damn you, don't you ever do this to me again."

I fell against him and as his arms went around me I could feel the anger go out of him; not that I wasn't going to get a brisk talking-to, later. But now all I could think about was that he had found me.

"Oh, I'm sorry," I whispered. "So sorry, you must have been so worried."

"Christ." His arms tightened. "I swear, Jacobia." Then both of us realized what it was that Ben had been carrying over the rocks. Melinda . . .

Motionless. Peter and Ben began working over her while Tim ran for the squad car and the radio in it. Willetta ran with him.

Peter knelt on the rocks beside the body; Ben, too. Around its sodden middle was her scarf and a length of nylon rope. And the tide had fallen enough now so I could see where it had been tied before Ben's knife cut it.

In my mind's eye, I saw how it had happened: Melinda lying unconscious on the beach. The rope tied halfway up the piling. As the tide came in, she would drown. Or if she woke . . .

The hideous cleverness of it made me gasp. If she woke, she would have to climb the piling, using the spikes, to reach the rope and try to free herself. But by that time she wouldn't be able to undo the knots, because her fingers would be numb with the devastating cold. So she would cling up there until the water reached her or until she lost consciousness, and fell.

Knowing that she was dying. Screaming, probably, for as long as her voice lasted. No one to hear her.

"Dear God," Ellie murmured. "It was a torture-killing."

"She was under a long time?" George asked quietly.

"We don't know. Last we saw her was a couple of hours ago," I said.

"But that nylon line is long." Ellie pointed at the pilings. "If you climbed, you could stay above water a while. And the way the wharf's built, there are air pockets up under there."

Her hope infected me: those birds' nests, and the feral cats . . . "She's right. And as the water rose, maybe you could push your face up into . . ."

Wade's voice broke in flatly. "It would work till you passed out from the cold, and fell in anyway."

Ben and Peter kept on: chest compressions and respirations. "You getting a pulse with that?" Ben managed.

With the chest compressions, he meant; he knew what he was doing. I did, too. So I knew neither one could have faked the effort without the other noticing. Peter had looked legitimately frantic when he arrived, and Melinda was Ben's sister; he owed his life to her. Yet one of them, I thought, must have been lying.

Lying to us all along. "Yeah," Peter replied, pausing to place his fingers on Melinda's neck. They resumed.

But with no result, and as I watched I remembered also what Victor had said about CPR administered outside of a hospital: how few people survive it.

The ambulance screamed up. "Bring a tank," Wade called to the two fellows getting out. Of oxygen, he meant, and they did, scrambling down with a small green cylinder and a mask to go with it.

Wade and George went to get the stretcher for them, for the transport to the hospital. But I had a bad feeling. "It's been too long." My eyes prickled with tears. The whole long night, all the frights and surprises, all come to this:

A motionless woman, cold on the beach, with a half-dozen people now working urgently—and, I believed, uselessly—to save her life.

"He did it," Willetta repeated bitterly, coming up to me. "He drugged her. That's how he got her there in the first place."

"One . . . two . . . *three*," the ambulance fellows said, lifting Melinda onto the stretcher.

"You wait," Willetta went on. "There'll be drugs in her system, and if they search his house—let's see if he lets them do *that*—I bet they'll find them there, too. I know they will. You just wait."

I was still wearing wet clothes and my legs felt as if tiny teeth were biting into them. The guys with the stretcher had gotten nearly to the ambulance doors.

"I've got to get dry stuff on," I began, and then it happened: from the stretcher came a banshee shriek as Melinda's body jerked half-upright.

The motion surprised the paramedics, throwing them off-balance; the wheeled gurney teetered and bounced back down to the rocky beach, miraculously not overturning. But that wasn't the real miracle.

Melinda's eyes opened. "You!" she wailed, her arm moving unsteadily as she tried to point. But she was shaking too hard from the cold and all that she had been through.

"You," she repeated, her voice gargly with inhaled water and with the effects of who knew what else: a botched drug overdose?

Well, Melinda knew, actually, and for a moment it seemed she would say. Her finger aimed uncertainly at one and then another of us, frozen on the beach.

Meanwhile the frazzled ambulance guys were trying to untangle and refasten the stretcher's fallen chest strap. To do so, they were having to cut the half-frozen sweater off Melinda's body and suddenly they succeeded, exposing what lay beneath the sodden fabric.

Whereupon one mystery, at least, was solved:

The mystery of how Melinda had survived, not just now

but all this winter, prancing around as if it were the middle of May. From beneath the sweater shone a slick, bright-orange skin with a glinting metal zip front.

No one had known her secret; not us, and certainly not her attempted killer. But now . . .

It was an orange neoprene bodysuit.

Her voice trilled in memory: *I just* adore *the cold* . . .

"You!" Melinda cried, pointing around wildly. "You . . . you *ruined my scarf!*"

Chapter 11

We looked at each other. Which one of us was she accusing?

"Melinda," I began. But it was too late.

Her hands clenched convulsively; her eyes rolled up.

"Go!" Ben snarled at the ambulance fellows.

They went.

"Fine," Peter Christie said tightly half an hour later.

It was not what I, had I been an attorney, would have advised. But Willetta kept nagging at him, accusing him, and finally he turned to Timmy Rutherford.

"Go look right now. I give you permission. Here's the key."

To his own house, he meant. Ben and Mickey Jean had gone home to get Ben some dry clothes, and then to the hospital; the rest of us were in my kitchen: drinking hot coffee and trying to get ourselves back to normal.

Which under the circumstances wasn't going to happen soon, but hope springs eternal. I swallowed more of the warming liquid, waiting for it to penetrate the cold, hard lump at the center of my chest.

But it wouldn't.

"What are you waiting for?" Willetta demanded. "I *told* you what happened. He drugged her and tried to kill her."

Maybe so, but he wasn't acting as if he had. I wished desperately that Willetta would go home.

She wasn't going to, though: not until she got what she wanted. "So go *look*," she insisted. "You'll see."

"You have my permission. I want this talk stopped," Peter told Tim Rutherford for the third time. "Please do it now."

Tim was tall, dark haired, and well over twenty years old, a good boy but hardly experienced at police work. Wearing his blue officer's uniform with cuffs, radio, and sidearm clipped to his utility belt, he looked like a kid who'd gotten the whole kit and kaboodle as an early Christmas present.

"Tim . . ." I began as he touched a fresh bruise on his cheek. Bob Arnold wouldn't like this, and I was sure Clarissa would disapprove even more strongly. "Tim, you should get advice. And a search warrant, just to keep it all on the up-and-up." A young officer, verbal permission, emotional circumstances . . . "If only to cover yourself," I finished, not adding the other part: anything wrong with a search could screw up evidence it uncovered.

"No!" Willetta objected. "That'll give him time to get rid of it, waiting for all that."

"Come on." Peter headed for the door. "Tim, you come with me. I'm going to stand there—doing nothing, saying nothing," he added with a hard look at Willetta, "while you come and find all these deadly drugs I'm supposed to be hiding."

Tim was in over his head and he knew it. This kind of thing was not his department when Bob was around.

But Bob wasn't around. He was on a respirator, fighting for his life. No one was yet saying aloud that it was over, but . . .

Tim sighed. "Okay, I'm going to go and check out his

place. For all I know," he added disgustedly, "somebody's hidin' over there, waitin' for *him*."

At this, Peter looked vindicated.

"Then I've got a whole slew of paperwork to do," Tim went on. "A lot of people to talk to—state cops, district attorney, I don't know what-all. But I guess I will find out what-all, and I am going to do it, whatever it is, and when I am finished I expect all of you to be available, if I have any questions. Understand?"

We all nodded solemnly.

"All right, then," Tim said: over his head, indeed, but he was swimming capably, and he would reach dry land if he had anything to do with it.

"So that's it," Ellie said when Tim and Peter had gone. George poured another cup of coffee; Wade ate some fruit-cake, wincing as he bit into a piece of candied citron. "All this, and still we don't know any more than we did when we started."

On Monday's dog bed, the dog and cat lay curled together, asleep. But at some sound I couldn't hear Monday sat up suddenly and gazed around the kitchen suspiciously before settling again.

The cat didn't budge. So much for its mousing abilities. Being Victor's animal, it probably hired other cats to catch mice for it.

"And," I added to Willetta, "I wouldn't get my hopes up for the results of this house-searching expedition Tim Rutherford has gone on. Guys holding contraband don't usually invite cops inside to search for it, in my admittedly limited experience."

"You'll see," Willetta repeated stubbornly. "It'll be there."

Then we all just sort of stewed in our misery for a while. I called Portland to see how Bob was doing now, and he was still critical. Then I called the Calais hospital about Melinda, and she was critical, too.

One bout of consciousness, apparently, did not a recovery make. It would be touch and go for Melinda, the nurse in the ICU informed me gently, for at least a few hours, maybe more.

Which did not cheer me, or Ellie, either. All our choices, which had seemed so reasonable at the time, had gotten us *here*.

Maybe, I thought with a sinking heart, I should just go down in the basement with the mouse. "I'll see you tomorrow," Ellie told me reluctantly, joining George in the hall.

But as I opened the door and switched on the porch light Tim Rutherford was getting out of his car. He came to the steps and looked up at us, framed in the light.

Holding a plastic bag. In it: small glass vials, glassine packets. A half-dozen syringes with needles capped in pastel plastic. Some bottles of capsules. Peering through the darkness I spotted Peter in the squad car's backseat. He was in custody.

"I told you so," Willetta breathed, gratified. "Didn't I? Didn't I tell you?"

"Shut up, Willetta," Wade said. "Tim, what's the story?"

Tim shrugged. "Well, he let me in. I looked around. Didn't find anything. 'Course I couldn't do a real search, every nook and cranny."

Yet here the stuff was. . . . "So I asked myself where would I hide something," Tim went on, "not particularly thinking anyone was going to look? But still wanting it out of sight?" He lifted the bag. "In the freezer. Down at the bottom of a bowl of ice cubes." In the squad car, Peter Christie gazed straight ahead. "Miss Abrams," Tim told us, "was right."

"Did you find any photographs of me?" Willetta demanded.

The ones she claimed Peter had taken of her, drugged. "No, ma'am," Tim replied. "Nothing like that."

The photographs hadn't been among the things Peter's cleaning lady had turned over to us, either. Maybe he hid his current activities better than evidence of his historical ones. Willetta seemed to think so:

"You will," she predicted grimly. "And I'd better not hear about anyone *else* seeing them, you got that?"

"Yes, ma'am," he gulped startledly.

She glanced at her wristwatch. "Hell, it's nearly time for the night shift. I've got to get to work or I'll be out of a job on top of everything else." She stalked to her own car, got in, and roared away, the little vehicle backfiring down the street.

I took Tim aside as her taillights vanished around the corner. "Listen, did the Duddy's raid ever happen? And if it did . . . why now, particularly? Any reason?"

He looked surprised. "Oh, yeah. Some woman phoned in an anonymous tip on the state hotline. How'd you think I got this?" He touched his cheek. "I got there late on account of what happened to Bob, but they saved some for me. Gave us a battle, some of those guys. Should've seen the stuff they had there. But it happened, all right. And now him," Tim added in disgust, glancing back at his squad car. "Never rains but it pours."

"That's that, then," George said when Tim had gone. Victim saved, culprit nabbed, back to our regular programming. But:

"I don't think so," Ellie said. She took George's arm, went down the steps with him. "Real peace might be a ways off, yet."

"Not for me," I retorted. "I'm going to sleep. And I plan to stay that way for at least twelve hours."

Which was a lovely plan, and worked out about as well as all such plans do.

•　　•　　•

"**All right, now,**" I began very soon after I finally got upstairs. I was going over my mental list. My *other* mental list.

Flannel nightgown, chenille bed jacket, thick cotton socks, cup of hot milk: check.

Husband no longer quite so rippingly angry: check.

Scraped knees bandaged, brandy in the hot milk—plenty of brandy, actually: double check.

Wade shoved a pillow behind him and opened his copy of *Working Waterfront,* patting my leg absently. "Warm enough?"

"After what I've been through I may never be warm enough again," I told him. All my bones still felt like iced steel rods; I had the socks on not so much because they helped, but so my feet wouldn't freeze poor Wade to death. "C'mere, dog."

Monday hopped gratefully onto the bed and settled between us, taking up way too much room as usual but radiating toasty heat. I wondered fleetingly where the cat was as I edged toward Wade, with the dog in what would have been my lap and my head on Wade's shoulder. "Mmm."

"There you go," Wade agreed, and turned a page. Sam was in bed, too, and the cat had probably chosen the top of the refrigerator for a perch. Monday began snoring. God rest ye merry gentlemen. And women.

Only I couldn't. "Wade. Remember how Monday got so upset about that mouse, when we didn't even know it was there?"

"Mm-hmm. Smelled it, probably."

"That's what I thought, too. It must still smell like mouse to her, though, in that parlor. Wouldn't you expect?"

He curved his big arm around my shoulders, still reading. "Guess so."

"But she's not freaked out anymore. I think . . ."

From the kitchen came the *thump!* of the cat's feet hitting the floor. Monday's ears pricked up, even in her sleep.

"And have you ever known a dog to be scared of a *smell?*" I went on. "I haven't. I'm wondering if what bothered her was that she *heard* it."

Wade put his newspaper down patiently and turned to me. "So?"

"So what I still can't figure out is Kenty Dalrymple. She said she went over to the Carmody house after Faye Anne got home and that everything was fine."

"And that is important because . . . ?"

"Because she was lying. I don't think she went over to Faye Anne's at all, so why say she did? *And* she never mentioned seeing me and Ellie with Peter, the night we found the diary at Faye Anne's. Or Ben and Mickey Jean, though they've admitted they were at the Carmody house, the night of Merle's murder."

Wade considered. "Kenty was a talker. Always had something to say. And usually what she said got said a few more times all over town," he recalled.

"Exactly. So what if I'm right and she didn't see anything *or* go anywhere. What if she said it all only because she was hoping that I would repeat it. Told me she'd actually been at Faye Anne's, trying to make it all the more convincing. *Hoping* that it would get around, so *somebody* . . ."

". . . wouldn't figure Kenty for a threat?"

"Right." I shot up in bed. "It didn't work, of course. Only an inveterate gossip like poor Kenty could dream that it would. She didn't see anything, couldn't have, because of her bad eyes. And I never even told that silly story to anyone but Ellie. But someone didn't know all that. Besides, the important thing was, *they'd* seen *her.*"

Wade smoothed Monday's ears, his newspaper forgotten. "Or why kill her?"

"Yes. Someone believed Kenty was a witness. But then why did that someone go on to kill Merle at all? Because if *you* were seen going in, would *you* proceed to commit murder?"

"No. That wouldn't make sense."

"*So* it must've been someone coming out." By now my head was starting to ache, but I couldn't quit. "So maybe Peter lied. He didn't just drop Faye Anne off that night. He went into the house with her, came out alone, and that's when he saw Kenty. If he didn't know her, he wouldn't have known she couldn't see him."

"To set Faye Anne up, Peter used drugs?" Wade theorized. "Bought them on the Internet, just the way Sam and Tommy did, maybe? Or at Duddy's? Although I guess it doesn't matter where he got them, only that he had them."

I thought some more. "And he planted the wine bottles to cover the drugs part. Locked the inside doors because he thought it was what Faye Anne would do. To make it look as if she'd been the only one there. That left him no other way out but the front door. Which put him in line with Kenty's front windows."

"Later he followed you and Ellie," Wade took up the theory again, "spied on you to keep up on what you might know, meanwhile stalking Willetta all the time. Bob catches him doing the same to Melinda, sneaking around her place. Surprises him, and Peter attacks him."

"Then *Melinda* tries to dump him, again he loses what little control he's got left, and he tries to kill her, too."

Wade frowned. "I guess it fits. If you're a wacko."

"Peter is," I said. "But there's still one more thing: it was late. So what made Kenty go to the window in the first place?"

Then I remembered something else. "Wade. Has anybody said whose it was? That thing Bob got hit with? The small hatchet . . ."

"Nope. Figured it was Melinda's. Though it was kind of

rough for a gardening tool, specially one of hers. She goes in more for fancy, high-end catalog merchandise."

"You're right. No crummy tools in her garden shed." That little hand axe with its shabby plastic handle and nicked blade would've gone to the trashman.

Wade picked up his newspaper again. "A night's sleep might do a lot to clear up all these . . ."

Questions. Suddenly they were swarming around me. If the hatchet wasn't Melinda's, that meant someone had brought it with them. Brought it for a reason. But . . .

Monday jerked up, hopped off the bed, and scurried down the stairs. *Wuff*, she said, and I heard the cat speak in reply.

Which was when I knew what had drawn Kenty Dalrymple to her window.

"Ellie, Kenty didn't see anything. She *heard*."

If a pin dropped in Eastport . . .

"That's what came first, made her look out her window?"

And what doomed her. "Right. Which was *when* she saw . . ."

As usual, Ellie was right with me. Or one step ahead.

". . . Someone leaving. Someone who'd been waiting, who knew or guessed Peter Christie would be with Faye Anne. But who *didn't* know Kenty couldn't see well enough to recognize him. Or her."

"Had to be," I agreed. "And that hand axe. Ellie, it's a firewood tool. Splitting kindling, that kind of thing. For a stove."

"I'm putting my clothes on," she said, "as we speak. Have you called the hospital yet?"

"Oh, Lord. No. I'll do it, now. Pick me up?"

"Ten minutes." She hung up.

"What's going on?" Sam appeared, rubbing his eyes. Wade was right behind him, already dressed.

"No time," I said, hurriedly dialing the hospital number.

In the ICU, I got the night-shift nurse. Melinda, he said, had been heavily sedated; no change in her condition anticipated until at least morning. Ben had gone home to get some sleep, leaving Mickey Jean to sit with Melinda until the onset of the day shift when things could be expected to start happening.

I had a strong feeling things might start happening before then. But I didn't want Mickey Jean getting the same notion. If she did, she might do something to make them happen even sooner. So I said nothing to the nurse.

"Get rid of Merle," I told Ellie fifteen minutes later as she drove us all up Route 1 as fast as she could. "Eliminate Kenty. And do in her rival for Ben's affections? Because Ben *is* devoted to Melinda, with good reason. More devoted, maybe, than Mickey Jean could stand. She just didn't count on Bob Arnold. But she adapted," I added. "She turned the axe she'd brought to use on Melinda on Bob, when he showed up unexpectedly."

"If he hadn't, she'd have killed Melinda right then?" Sam asked, jammed into the backseat with George and me.

"Possibly." Ellie slowed for a big tree branch downed by the storm. "And Peter Christie, with his habit of stalking women, was the perfect fall guy."

George harrumphed. "Pretty desperate measures, though. What makes you so sure it's her, anyway?"

I leaned past Sam to look at him. "The hand axe. It wasn't one of Melinda's tools, which means the killer brought it to use. And of everyone involved—who hasn't been attacked themselves, anyway—only Mickey Jean burns wood for heat. But we've been so focused on Ben, and then on Peter, that . . ."

Ellie pulled into the hospital driveway, its black macadam

slick and gleaming under the widely spaced sodium lights. At this hour a few cars stood near the employees' door of the low yellow-brick structure. I spotted Willetta's little white Toyota among them, and Mickey Jean's old Honda, mud-and-sand-streaked like the rest.

A passing orderly saw us and came to the glass front doors to let us in. The lobby desk was deserted, presided over by an artificial tabletop Christmas tree hung with miniature Santas. We hurried to the ICU waiting area.

No Mickey Jean. "Excuse me—"

The ICU was a large, dimly lit ward room with six curtained-off beds. At the far end of it, another door to the corridor outside was topped by a glowing EXIT sign. The curtains around the occupied beds were mostly drawn, the volume on the beeping of the cardiac monitors muted. The nurse at the desk looked up at us, a small frown creasing her brow. It was definitely not visiting hours.

"Sorry about this, but we need to see Mickey Jean Bunting. She's with Melinda Devine?"

The nurse's face cleared. "Oh, yes. Melinda is doing much better. Mickey Jean's in there now, I think."

"What're *you* doing here?" Mickey Jean's rough voice fractured the hush.

"Shh, keep it down." I glanced at the nurse, whose glance was a warning: *Quiet!*

"What *you're* doing is my big question. Or maybe what you're going to do the first chance you get to try it," I told Mickey Jean.

Her look flattened. "What are you—"

"Talking about?" I finished impatiently for her. From the corner of my eye I could see Wade and George out in the visitors' waiting area, magazines and other light reading material on the low table between them.

"You wanted Merle dead," I continued. "Maybe you

framed Faye Anne for his murder, but now that it looks as if Peter is a better target for the blame, that's all right, isn't it?"

She gaped at me as I led her away from Melinda's cubicle. If by some chance Melinda could hear anything, she didn't need to hear this. The nurse was on the telephone, one eye on us.

"You've been out to Duddy's," I went on. "You might know some of the men who also used to go there. Some of them are pretty tough characters. You could have bought the drugs that gave Faye Anne amnesia, later planted them in Peter's house to incriminate him, while Ben and the rest of us were at Melinda's earlier."

"You," Ellie chimed in, "could have sneaked in and scared Kenty Dalrymple to death, because you thought she saw you coming out of the Carmodys' *after* you and Ben were there the first time. She probably heard Ben's truck backfiring, or your old Honda."

I took over. "A hand axe was used on Bob Arnold. Like the one *you* would use for your woodstove."

She waved the glossy magazine she was holding, opened her mouth to speak. But I got in before her. "You tied Melinda to the piling. Maybe she'd figured out who really killed Merle Carmody: not her brother, Ben, as she'd first feared, but you. And you got back to your place just before we arrived, earlier tonight. Where were you?"

Again she tried to answer. "I was looking for Ben. He was so mad over what I've been planning, I didn't know what he might—"

"What plan?" I interrupted. Then I saw what the magazine she held really was: not a magazine at all.

It was a glossy brochure extolling the benefits of plastic surgery. Sam had said Tommy Pockets got one, too, and now I recalled the shiny pages Ben Devine had thrown into the woodstove out at Mickey Jean's cabin.

Once upon a time, doctors and lawyers didn't advertise.

But no more; this advertisement, I supposed, came from the stack of reading material in the ICU waiting area. And Tommy wasn't the only one who'd picked up ideas from its pages, I suspected. Suddenly I knew what she had done: gotten rid of Merle, then decided to change what he'd recognized, so no one else ever would: "You were going to change your *face*?"

"What else can I do?" she asked, looking helpless. "Ben was absolutely furious at the idea. But I go out in public one single time, and . . ."

The far door to the ICU clicked shut but I didn't bother to look. Instead I stared at Mickey Jean, realizing irrelevantly that although I'd read her old name in the reports the Portland *Herald* writer had sent me, I didn't remember it.

"Rose," she said softly, as if hearing my thought. "My name was Rose." A laugh, or a harsh sob: "Isn't that a hoot?"

"Mom?" Sam interrupted urgently.

"Just a second," I replied, not turning.

The nurse went into a utility area adjacent to the desk and began setting doses of medication out onto labeled trays. "Do you mind if I sit while you sling accusations?" Mickey Jean asked me.

I waved her at a chair away from the cubicles. "But Ben doesn't know, does he? What you did, or how far you've gone. What you've *already* done to try to keep your secret."

My voice rose as I thought of Clarissa sitting near Bob now. Waiting; praying, probably.

"Because of *you* . . ." I began angrily.

"Mom? You'd better come, there's someone . . ."

"Sam, just a minute, can't you see I'm very— Oh, God."

He'd pulled the curtain back. In the cubicle, surrounded by wires and tubes, IV poles and monitor screens, a motionless form lay peacefully under a blanket.

Too motionless. Too peaceful. Unlike the look on the face of the person at the head of Melinda's hospital bed.

Caught in the act.

It was Joy Abrams.

As the curtain around Melinda's hospital bed slid back all the way, Joy pulled a hypodermic needle from the IV bag hanging above. Melinda's heart rate, counted by glowing green numerals on the monitor screen, began dropping: 90, 80.

An alarm *thweeped* urgently. "Don't move," Joy said. She held the hypodermic up. "Or I'll put the rest of it straight into her heart."

It wouldn't make much difference if those numbers kept on dropping. How much of it had she already gotten into the IV?

"Joy," I began, as it finally all fell together: the outdoorsman's daughter, skilled at outdoor tasks: hunting, fishing. The gun and the knife. Later she and her sister had gone off to school, fulfilling their father's wish.

Far from the woods. But in all Joy's travels, I realized now—the bar where she had been a dancer was in Lewiston, near the school where Mickey Jean had acquired a persistent stalker—she hadn't lost one of the Maine hunter's primary skills: butchering the slain animal.

Her father would have known. And . . . *he taught us everything,* she'd said. What happened next seemed to occur in slow motion. Joy's fist came down, needle glinting.

Then a concussive bang and a bloom of red on Joy's shoulder. Her hand opening, eyes widening in shock and pain. The syringe clattering to the floor.

"Someone told her. Told Joy that Melinda was here," I said through the ringing in my ears as Joy began falling.

Her hair caught in the mechanism used to raise and

lower the bed. She went on falling but the hair stayed, a glorious apricot-blond mass of curls perfectly arranged . . .

Too perfectly: a wig. Beneath it, straggly white-blond hair like her sister Willetta's. Those eyelashes, I realized, and all her many cosmetics: part of the plan. Even the bottle of hair color in her bathroom had been an element of it, placed there to make sure the impression she wanted to make remained consistent, even to a casual visitor.

You'd never know it was the same woman, Ellie had said when Joy and Willetta first came to dinner. Now that evening seemed so long ago.

"Oh, my God," Mickey Jean breathed, at my shoulder. "It's her."

Feeling, movement, sound all came back to me. Turning, I saw who Mickey Jean meant: not Joy but Willetta, seized by George and Wade as a security guard belatedly burst in.

The gun was in her hand. Gently, Wade took it from her. "I'm sorry," Willetta said.

"But," Mickey Jean squinted puzzledly at Joy, "she looks so *different.*"

"I tried," Willetta said desperately. "Oh, I tried so *hard.*"

"You followed us. You thought we might have begun to suspect her," I said. "You tried to get us away from the beach, and never let Mickey Jean get a look at you. Bob Arnold's not really expected to wake up, or you'd be in Portland, now, doing something to make sure he didn't. But you knew that if Melinda survived, she'd say who had attacked her: Joy."

Joy, whose job required her to meet people, unlike Willetta who worked at night in a hospital, where almost everyone she saw was asleep. So Joy had to be unrecognizable, because hers was the greater risk of being seen by the wrong person.

". . . more security," the ICU nurse snapped into the phone, "stat."

Willetta couldn't meet Mickey Jean, either, of course. But for her it was much easier, making sure she didn't.

Until now. "You never went out to Duddy's at all, did you?" Ellie asked her. "Joy went, brought you the matchbook from the bar where the bad guys congregated. It was always Joy who'd done things like that."

Risky things, even dangerous ones. Willetta nodded brokenly. "I couldn't turn her in to the police, I just *couldn't*. Back when we were kids, she always took care of me."

So Willetta had stayed in the background, scuttled around in darkness trying to protect her flamboyant sister, to save her from herself. But admiring her secretly, too, probably.

The way we all secretly admire people doing dangerous things, living on the precipice. "Merle deserved it," Willetta added bitterly.

Until somewhere along the way they go over the edge and we get pulled over with them if we're not careful. If we're foolish or unlucky.

Or just very young. I opened my mouth to say something to Willetta, then stopped, struck by the realization that the blood smell that had haunted me since I'd found Merle Carmody was gone.

Vanished as if it had never been there at all. "But Joy got worse, kept doing more, I couldn't *stop* her," Willetta insisted pathetically.

"You let her in, though," I replied, brutally. "The hospital doors are locked at night." We'd had to be buzzed in. And in a small hospital like this one you didn't just stroll in through the emergency room, unnoticed. "You must have opened one, told her where Melinda was."

Yet in the end she hadn't been able to let Joy do it. Until this, it had all been things that Willetta had heard of, not ones she had been obliged to witness herself.

But Joy in the *act* of murder: that, even Willetta had had

to do something about. The ICU nurse looked up from where she knelt trying to stanch Joy's shoulder wound with a wad of dressings. "I think," she said, "you might have stopped her, now."

The medical team swarmed over Melinda, some barking orders, others following them. The monitor numbers rose as another crew surged in, lifted Joy, sped a gurney from the cubicle, and raced away down the corridor.

Later, the Calais police showed up and took Willetta.

And then it was over.

Sort of.

Chapter 12

"J oy went to Lewiston because Willetta was there in school," I said two hours later to the group assembled in my parlor.

Tim Rutherford had arrived, looking as if he felt he'd chosen the wrong profession. I disagreed and made a mental note to say so to him, sometime soon. Meanwhile under the influence of friends and fresh coffee, he was rallying.

"We know that," Victor said impatiently to me. "But then what?"

His shock was being replaced by indignation, as he began to realize he'd been used merely as a source of news: it wasn't until Ellie and I started looking into the matter of Merle's death that Victor had actually become a serious item on Joy's social calendar.

"Then Willetta flunked out of Mickey Jean's freshman econ class," Sam said, repeating what Mickey Jean had told us at the hospital and sounding as if it were an event that he could well understand.

Me, too. Economics is a demanding subject. It requires, among other things, a certain amount of bonehead stubbornness. This, I must humbly assume, is why I ended up being halfway decent at it.

Willetta hadn't been. And she'd complained to Joy: Mickey Jean was tough. Not only on Willetta. But that wasn't the way Joy had taken it.

"So Joy went to see Mickey Jean at the college," Ellie said.

Wade put his hand on my shoulder, steadyingly. I'd never seen a person shot at close range before. "And when that didn't work—"

Mickey Jean hadn't been a bit swayed by Joy's special brand of persuasion: promises of harm. "Push came to shove," George said simply.

George wore bibbed overalls, a tattered red sweatshirt, and work boots. Ellie took his hand. "Then Mickey Jean vanished and Joy came here, not knowing that of all possible places, Ben and Mickey Jean had chosen to come here, also."

"Because Melinda was here," I agreed. "Willetta followed Joy to try keeping Joy under some control, worrying about what new obsession Joy might develop. She even moved in with Joy, finally." But none of it had worked.

The phone rang. It was past two in the morning. We looked at one another. There was no reason for a phone to be ringing unless it was about Bob Arnold.

"I'll get it," Victor said, and went.

"Joy got the drugs out at Duddy's," Tim Rutherford said, wanting, I supposed, to break the silence. "That's why the state fellows were in town early. Not for murder, but to get ready for the raid on the bar."

"She probably phoned in the tip, too, right after that," I agreed. "Hoped whoever sold her the contraband would be arrested, not be around here to talk about a certain customer: herself."

I was still seeing the look in Joy's eyes as she realized who had shot her. "She told us about the government guys being here a day early just to put us off balance. A little joke on us, among the others she played."

But not a funny one. Victor's voice came from the phone alcove. All I could see now was Clarissa's face, and little Thomas'. And Bob's: full of good will, despite all the bad things he'd seen in his career as a Maine cop.

"Yeah, Joy gave it all up in the recovery room," Tim said. Her wound, it turned out, had looked awful but had been fairly superficial.

"I didn't ask her anything," he added hastily. "She was full of sedatives. But she told them she wanted to see me and when I walked in, she just started talking. On account of being doped up, I guess. Told me the whole bit, right from the git-go." He sighed.

"She'd drugged Merle, gave him a story about how they were both on the same side, then she put it in his booze. Once he was looped: wham."

"And later she drugged Faye Anne and arranged the scene to make it look as if Faye Anne killed him?" I asked.

Tim nodded. "Merle was already dead when Faye Anne got home. She walked in, Joy grabbed her and told her she'd slit her throat if she didn't drink what was in the glass."

He shook his head unhappily. "See, Joy had spotted Ben in town when she first got here, realized where he and Mickey Jean must've vanished to: Eastport. The coincidence convinced Joy that her campaign against Mickey Jean was still righteous."

Ellie leaned forward. "But just as Joy was about to *resume* her campaign, she learned that *Merle* knew about Mickey Jean, too, and was blackmailing her over it? Because there had to be a reason for killing Merle in the first place."

Tim agreed: "Yep. Joy was keeping tabs on who went in and out of Mickey Jean's place in the woods. And that's where she made her mistake: she guessed the reason for Merle's visits, then she went to Merle and suggested maybe they should join forces."

Sam frowned. "So what?"

"So," Ellie explained patiently, "Merle was not exactly a team player. By then he had Mickey Jean figured for his private gravy train. He didn't want anybody else along for the ride."

Mickey Jean had been taking a chance, going into Duddy's. Lots of people there; she couldn't be *sure* no one would know her. *I go out just that once . . .*

But she couldn't have known how disastrous it would be. "Mickey Jean never saw Willetta or Joy, before? I mean since they came to Eastport?" Wade objected.

Ellie just shrugged. "No one ever saw Mickey Jean except for Merle, other than that once in the bar. Why should she see anyone else? Besides, Willetta was careful, and Joy wouldn't be recognized; even I wouldn't have. But then Merle threatened to *tell* Ben and Mickey Jean that Joy had found them, didn't he? It'd be just like him."

"You got it," Tim confirmed. "I guess old Merle finally just chose the wrong woman to try to bully."

We all pondered that in silence for a moment.

"Joy called here," I said, "to try to put suspicion on Ben, once she realized Ellie and I might clear Faye Anne, her first choice for a scapegoat. It was Joy's face at my window, too."

That was why the eyes and mouth had stood out so distinctly: her makeup. "Partly to spy on us but the plastic sheets prevented that. Partly to intimidate me. Which worked pretty well."

"Not well at all," Ellie contradicted loyally.

I turned to her. "You suspected one or both of them early on, didn't you? It was why you didn't want to use their phone to call and inquire about Bob, out at Quoddy Village."

She nodded. "I didn't want to give those two any more information than they already had about anything, was all. I mean, I do like cleanliness but *their* place . . . and no Christmas decorations? *None?*"

Her face said what she thought of that. "Besides," she added, "you tell me: who wears false eyelashes at home? And that new van of hers just put the frosting on it."

"Huh? What about the van?" It had been in the hospital lot with the other visitors' cars, of course, but in a fresh coating of road slush from the storm, it had looked like all the others, too.

"But then," Ellie was saying, "Ben Devine started looking so suspicious to us. And after that, Peter."

"Right, he was the further complication," I said, forgetting the new van for the moment. "Our old pal Peter, who had the poor judgment to victimize Willetta, incurring the wrath of the most protective big sister in history."

The hand axe, of course, hadn't belonged to Mickey Jean. It was from the kit of survival gear in Willetta's Toyota.

"Joy put drugs in Peter's house to incriminate him," Tim told us. "Willetta might've made up that story about photographs and being drugged, to back Joy up. Or," he added, "maybe not. Even if Peter wasn't our killer, he's still a nasty piece of work."

"And that—planting the drugs—put Melinda in the bull's-eye," Ellie concluded. "She went to Peter's to break their date on account of the changing weather, caught Joy in his house or coming out."

No picnic, then. But she had decided to break up with him. So she went to break the date in person *and* break the bad news: two birds with one stone.

Tim nodded, confirming what Ellie had said. "And the other night, Joy was at Melinda's—not for the first time, I guess—casing the place to see what mischief she could get up to because of Melinda's connection to Ben. Then Bob turned up there. That's why Bob's phone number was on Melinda's speed dial—because she'd told Bob she'd had a prowler. And Joy couldn't have Bob catching her at Melinda's, because she had no business being there."

"I still don't get why Faye Anne didn't remember Joy doing it," Sam offered troubledly.

Victor replied from the doorway. He hadn't been at the hospital for the main event, but he'd been there for the aftermath, checking on the man who'd run afoul of the debarking machine. "She will, eventually. But I gather she'd had a couple of drinks that night with Peter Christie. That, plus a big dose of the drug and the shock of the event itself, probably gave her some retroactive short-term memory deficit."

"But Joy couldn't have known that," I objected.

"No. So I think she was also counting on something else." He pressed his fingertips together, still absorbing his own disappointment. "I suspect that when Joy talks about that evening again, she'll add one more detail: that she wasn't groomed in her usual careful, elaborate manner. And . . ."

He looked at me. "Without the hairdo, Joy looks an awful lot like her sister, don't you think? Not in size or general build, but at first glance. If you only," he finished, "got a brief glimpse."

And even more so, probably, without the makeup. The awful implication was all too clear. ". . . *she always took care of me* . . ."

But not if push came to shove. Willetta didn't know that Joy's dark obsession had gone far beyond its original purpose: punishing a teacher for Willetta's bad grade. I wondered if Joy even recalled now, what that original purpose had been. Because if her plan didn't work, if Faye Anne Carmody did remember what happened that night, Joy had added a last, madly self-preserving twist.

Faye Anne would have described Willetta.

"Wow!" Sam said. "That Joy, she thought of everything."

Or almost everything. And it all would have worked,

except for a few things that didn't fall her way. Suddenly I felt a warm burst of affection for that orange survival suit. But my mood of upbeat optimism didn't last long.

"Who was on the phone?" I asked Victor, torn between wanting more bad news held off and wanting it over with. But for once . . .

"Bob Arnold went back to surgery," he answered. "They found a bleeder and tied it off, looks like that's turned things around. He's awake and off the ventilator, grousing about everything."

A noisy cheer went up. "So I think he might be out of the woods," Victor added, as we all hugged one another. "Melinda, too. I called, they say she's stabilized, looks good. No long-term effects from the stuff Joy shot into her."

He puffed himself up a bit, readying to deliver a medical lecture. "One good thing about drowning in cold salt water: it's not over till it's over. Chills all the body systems," he added to George. "Keeps your gears from chewing themselves up."

He seemed to believe that if he described the human body in this elementary way, even a simple downeast rustic like George might understand.

"Right," said George, who as a volunteer fireman had been on rescues so hair-raising, they'd have curled Victor's toes. "And the salt water doesn't screw up the electrolyte balance as much as fresh water does."

Victor blinked. "Ah, correct," he mumbled, and busied himself with getting more coffee.

Ellie came to stand by my chair. "Everyone around here knew Joy and Willetta from the old days. Or thought they did. What they didn't know was that Willetta must have been busy even back then, desperate to keep her big sister out of trouble."

Because having a youth so wild it was the stuff of legend, then becoming a tattooed strip club dancer whose act included a live snake, was not exactly evidence of personal stability. But everyone had been fascinated by these stories, even a little envious, maybe, of a woman with nerve enough to do such things. So no one had taken them seriously for what they were:

Symptoms. Getting worse. I said, "So what Kenty heard was—"

"Nothing," Ellie replied. "Or *almost* nothing. Which was the strange thing, of course, to her."

At last I understood it. The sound of a vehicle starting up with *no* backfire at all: a brand new van, purring like a well-creamed kitten.

Like the one I'd heard out at Melinda's the night Bob was attacked. Kenty would have wondered whose it was, so she could gossip about it, later. That was why she'd looked: in hopes that she *might* be able to see something.

And as she did, Joy Abrams had looked, too.

"Poor Kenty," Ellie murmured. But my mention of the dead woman had lighted a beacon of purpose in my friend's green eyes. "Jake, I don't suppose you'd like to have a collection of African violets?" she asked, as if this idea were only just now occurring to her.

It wasn't. "They're going," she added with quiet urgency, "to the dump, otherwise. I asked the garden club people first, but they all had the same verdict about African violets."

It was mine, too, about this particular species. "Fattish and hairy," I said. "And persnickety. I don't think I—"

But then I stopped. Ellie held up a small potted plant. "This one is called Nancy's Mustard Gold."

From the clay pot grew a dark green specimen only six inches across. Its leaves, plump and juicy-looking, were ovals whirled in dark maroon. A blossom was opening on it: sunshine yellow.

"Oh," I said, feeling my heart captured. "It's—"

"Yes, well," Ellie said, satisfied. "I'll bring the rest over to you tomorrow, and you can decide where to set up the plant trays and fluorescents, where to store the plant food and the soil testers and the watering jug and the potting soil."

Just what I needed: more hardware. The Fein "Multi-master" box still stood in the back hallway, reproaching me with all the polishing, sanding, and cutting it could do if only I would put it to work. Which I resolved to do, first thing in the morning . . .

"Oh, and books about African violets, lots of them, you'll want those, and the videos about them, of course," Ellie added happily.

Of course. I got up and put my arms around her, careful not to crush the sprig of holly she had found somewhere and pinned to her scarlet sweater.

"Merry Christmas," I told her.

"You, too," she whispered back. "And Jake . . . thank you."

Soon afterwards Tim Rutherford had departed, George and Wade were finishing their plans to go down to the dock together in the morning and work on the tugboat, and Sam had excused himself to begin reconstructing his Internet project.

Victor pulled his coat on while Ellie tugged the purple-tasseled hat over her red hair.

"Jacobia," he said. "Tell Sam's friend Tommy I've found someone to pin his ears back for him, will you? He'll do it as a professional courtesy to me. No charge."

"Why, Victor," I said, surprised, "that's very . . ."

Nice of you, I would have finished. But then being Victor of course he had to go on and spoil it. "You know, if that kid could wiggle those things, I'll bet he could fly."

I shut the door firmly on him. "So," Wade said when everyone had gone, the porch lights were out, and we were alone.

"So," I replied, feeling renewed contrition. "Wade, I do solemnly promise that I will never, ever—"

"—fail to maintain safety equipment properly," he finished ominously. "Jacobia, if I'd done that you'd carve out my giblets and roast them for supper."

He was under the impression that I'd forgotten to refresh the battery in the cell phone, and I'd decided not to tell him what had really happened. After all, it had only been a *near* electrocution . . .

Or anyway, I wouldn't tell him right now. But the thought of giblets was not a welcome one and he must have seen it.

"Oh, all right," he said, relenting. Then:

"Listen, I put that salt fish kettle out in the snow."

I'd wondered why I didn't smell cat food anymore. He looked embarrassed. "I think maybe my aunt helped my uncle with it. The recipe, I mean. I ate a bite." He grimaced.

"You poor thing." Food from the old days could be a comfort, I knew. Sometimes even I hankered for a taste of squirrel.

Just a wee taste. "Tell you what, we'll try it again," I said. "But we'll ask Ellie how. I'll bet she knows. Okay?"

He brightened. "Okay. And . . . what the hell, I might as well tell you the other thing. The sawmill's down for a few months, without it there won't be extra ships. Not enough cargo for 'em."

So the harbor-piloting business was going to be down, as well. Which meant even worse than *less* extra cash, for Wade . . .

"I meant to get us rings," he said. Wedding rings; diamonds like the ones I had wanted.

Naturally he'd known. "We'll do it someday," I told him. "It doesn't matter . . ." But just then came a knock on our back door.

It was Ben Devine. "Mickey Jean's still up at the hospital

with Melinda," he said. "But we both wanted to say we appreciate your help. All of you."

"She's not furious with me?" I asked.

He shook his head, pulling a small manila envelope from his jacket pocket. "Not a bit. Said to give you these."

"You don't have to pay us," I began, but he wouldn't listen.

"It's not payment. It's a gift. Please," he said, "we'd like for you to have them. Look inside," he invited.

So I did, shaking the envelope's contents carefully out onto the palm of my hand: four glittering stones.

Diamonds; Ellie must have told him. "Ben, we can't . . ."

"You people didn't just help us out, see. You showed us we've got friends. Ones we can trust. And that," Ben finished, "is worth more'n diamonds. To us."

I glanced a question at Wade. He nodded.

"Thank you," I told Ben. "They're beautiful."

They were, too: at least a carat apiece and bright white.

"Mickey Jean figured you could get a pair of matching rings for 'em, maybe, two stones apiece."

"If it's all right," I ventured, "I was thinking of earrings, too. For Ellie. One stone each for us, a pair for her?"

She would love them. And the whole thing had been her idea, really: helping Faye Anne.

And it *was* Christmas. Wade nodded, and after a moment Ben did, also. "All right, then. I gotta go. Oh, and . . ." He looked embarrassed. "Timmy Rutherford mentioned to me that you guys, and the cops, too, found some cigarette ashes by Melinda's shed. And look, I promised Mickey I'd quit smoking. But I didn't, really."

I had a sudden mental picture of him in La Sardina, puffing away as if it were a rare opportunity. "Used to sneak a smoke by the shed," he said. "But no more. So if you could maybe . . ."

I made a zipping-my-lip gesture. "You got it."

"Great." He turned toward the door again. But then he turned back, his face crinkling into a grin he tried mightily to repress.

"That . . . that *suit!*" he burst out.

Bright, tight neoprene rubber: Melinda had looked like a neon-orange water animal in it. I tried suppressing a giggle and failed utterly. " . . . just *adore* the cold . . ."

"Maybe she'll wear it in the parade next Fourth of July," Wade speculated, chuckling.

"Right," Ben guffawed. "I'll try to talk her into it." Then, grinning as if the weight of the world were off his shoulders, he went out, Wade and I watching as he got into his truck.

"Wade. What do you suppose did it?"

"Made Joy get that way?" He draped an arm around me. "Don't know. But if I had to guess I'd say maybe she felt guilty about something from back when. Something she *didn't* protect Willetta from, maybe?"

"Maybe." Two motherless girls in the woods, men coming in and out on a regular basis. We would never know, probably. But:

"Trying to make up for it," I mused aloud, thinking again of how murder divides everything into *before* and *after*.

They never found my father's body after the explosion. Later I was told that the blast was so powerful, no portion survived. But now, as Ben's old truck started up with a ba-*rump!* of backfire, I wondered if there was another reason, a *before* I had never suspected. Ben drove off and I closed the door on the question.

For now.

"One last thing," Wade said as I came back into the kitchen. "I know you want to save on fuel. However . . ."

He strode to the windows and pulled off the milky sheets of plastic. "Sorry. But can we please spring for the double layers of clear plastic out here? This is just too damn *ugly*."

Suddenly I could see through the windows, out and up into the pitilessly clear night sky full of icy stars.

But when I moved, the reflection of the lights here in the house shone back at me. Warm air coming up off the hot radiators smelled of balsam from the tree Wade had brought in so we could decorate it, tomorrow. And . . . my hands felt clean.

"You're right. It's better," I told Wade.

Much better: later in the darkness of the big old barnlike kitchen, with the moon shining in through the tall bare windows and glazing the pointed fir trees outside with a rime of winter silver, I gave one of those diamonds to Wade and he gave one to me. It was a magic moment—

Until the kitchen light snapped on, Sam sloped out to raid the refrigerator, the dog engaged the cat in a marathon around the table, and a mouse streaked merrily across the floor, pausing only to shoot me a mousy grin and—I swear— a tiny, upraised mouse-middle-finger.

Whereupon I was ready to command Sam to forget the late-night snack, put a stop to the dog-cat hostilities, and trap the mouse or at least make it very, *very* sorry for that outrageous gesture. But Wade stepped in front of me, leading me gently into the darkness of the hall.

Abruptly the chaos in the old house receded, leaving only the interested twinkle in Wade's eye, more precious than any gems.

"How about if we let this old world turn without us for a while?" he suggested softly. "We're still practically newlyweds, aren't we? The diamonds just make it official."

"I think," I said, moving in waltz-step with him, "that's a fine idea. But . . . Sam's home, you know."

Wade's arm snugged around my waist as we climbed the stairs together. "Silence," he predicted, "is golden."

All was calm.

All was bright.

ABOUT THE AUTHOR

SARAH GRAVES lives with her husband in Eastport, Maine, in the 1823 Federal-style house that helped inspire her books. She is the author of four previous *Home Repair Is Homicide* mysteries—*The Dead Cat Bounce*, *Triple Witch*, *Wicked Fix*, and *Repair to Her Grave*—and is currently at work on the sixth, *Unhinged*.

Visit Eastport, Maine, on the Web at www.nemaine.com/eastportcc—*or visit in person!*

For more information:
Eastport Chamber of Commerce
P.O. Box 254
Eastport, Maine 04631
Phone 207-853-4644

If you enjoyed Sarah Graves'
WRECK THE HALLS, you won't
want to miss any of the exciting books
in her *Home Repair Is Homicide*
mystery series. Look for
THE DEAD CAT BOUNCE,
TRIPLE WITCH, WICKED FIX,
and REPAIR TO HER GRAVE
at your favorite bookseller's.

And turn the page for a tantalizing
preview of the next *Home Repair Is
Homicide* mystery, UNHINGED,
coming soon in hardcover from
Bantam Books.

UNHINGED

A *Home Repair Is Homicide* mystery by
SARAH GRAVES

Harriet Hollingsworth was the kind of person who called 911 the minute she spotted a teenager ambling down the street, since as she said there was no sense waiting for them to get up to their nasty tricks. Each week Harriet wrote to the *Quoddy Tides,* Eastport's local newspaper, a list of the sordid misdeeds she suspected all the rest of us of committing, and when she wasn't doing that she was at her window with binoculars, spying out more.

Snoopy, spiteful, and a suspected poisoner of neighborhood cats, Harriet was confidently believed by her neighbors to be too mean to die, until the morning one of them spotted her boot buckle glinting up out of his compost heap like the wink of an evil eye.

The boot had a sock in it but the sock had no foot in it and despite a diligent search (one wag remarking that if Harriet was buried somewhere, the grass over her grave would die in the shape of a witch on a broomstick) she remained missing.

"Isn't that just like Harriet?" my friend Ellie White demanded about three weeks later, squinting up into the spring sunshine.

We were outside my house in Eastport, on Moose Island, in downeast Maine. "Stir up as much fuss and bother as she could," Ellie went on, "but not give an ounce of satisfaction in the end."

Thinking at the time that it *was* the end, of course. We both did.

At the time. My house is a white clapboard 1823 Federal with three full floors plus an attic, forty-eight big old double-hung windows with forest-green wooden shutters, three chimneys (one for each pair of fireplaces), and a two-story ell.

From my perch on a ladder propped against the porch roof I looked down at Ellie, who wore a purple tank top like a vest over a yellow turtleneck with red frogs embroidered on it. Blue jeans faded to the color of cornflowers and rubber beach shoes trimmed with rubber daisies completed her outfit.

"Running out on her bills, not a word to anyone," she added darkly.

In Maine, stiffing creditors is not only bad form. It's also a shortsighted way of trying to escape your money troubles, since anywhere you go in the whole state you are bound to run into your creditors' cousins, hot to collect and burning to make an example out of you. That was why Ellie thought Harriet must've scarpered to Vermont or New Hampshire, leaving the boot as misdirection and her own old house already in foreclosure.

From my ladder-perch I glimpsed it peeking forlornly through the maples, two streets away: a huge Victorian shambles shedding chunks of rotted trim and peeled-off paint curls onto an unkempt lawn. Just the sight of its advancing decrepitude gave me a pang. I'd started the morning optimistically, but fixing a few gutters was shaping up to be more difficult than I'd expected.

"Harriet," Ellie declared, "was never the sharpest tool in the toolbox, and this stunt of hers just proves it."

"Mmm," I said distractedly. "I wish this ladder was taller."

Shakily I tried steadying myself, straining to reach a

metal strap securing a gutter downspout. Over the winter the downspouts had blown loose so their upper ends aimed gaily off in nonwater-collecting directions. But the straps were still firmly fastened to the house with big aluminum roofing nails.

I couldn't fix the gutters without taking the straps off, and I couldn't get the straps off. They were out of my reach even when, balancing precariously on tiptoe, I swatted at them with the claw hammer. Meanwhile down off the coast of the Carolinas a storm sat spinning over warmer water, sucking up energy.

"Ellie, run in and get me the crowbar, will you, please?"

Days from now, maybe a week, the storm would make its way here, sneakily gathering steam. When it arrived it would hit hard.

Ellie let go of the ladder's legs and went into the house. This I thought indicated a truly touching degree of confidence in me, because I am the kind of person who can trip while walking on a linoleum floor. I sometimes think it would simplify life if I got up every morning, climbed a ladder, and fell off, just to get it over with.

And sure enough, right on schedule as the screen door swung shut, the ladder's feet began slipping on the spring-green grass. I should mention it was also *wet* grass, since in Maine we really only have three seasons: mud time, Fourth of July, and pretty good snowmobiling.

"Ow," I said a moment later when I'd landed hard and managed to spit out a mouthful of grass and the mud. Then I just lay there while my nervous system rebooted and ran damage checks. Arms and legs movable: okay. Not much blood: likewise reassuring. I could remember all the curse words I knew and proved it by reciting them aloud.

A robin cocked his bright eye suspiciously at me, apparently thinking I'd tried muscling in on his worm-harvesting operation. I probed between my molars with my tongue, hoping the robin was incorrect, and he was, and the molars were all there, too.

So I felt better, sort of. Then Ellie came back out with the crowbar and saw me on the ground.

"Jake, are you all right?"

"Fabulous." The downspout lay beside me. Apparently I'd flailed at it with the hammer as I was falling and hooked it on my way down.

Ellie's expression changed from alarm to the beginnings of relief. I do so enjoy having a friend who doesn't panic when the going gets bumpy. Although I suspected there was liniment in my future, and definitely aspirin.

"Oof," I said, getting up. My knees were skinned, and so were my elbows. My face had the numb feeling that means it will hurt later, and there was a funny little click in my shoulder that I'd never heard before. But across the street two dapper old gentlemen on a stroll had paused to observe me avidly, and I feel that pride goeth before *and* after the fall, like parentheses.

"Hi," I called, waving the hammer in weak parody of having descended so fast on purpose. The sounds emanating from my body reminded me of a band consisting of a washtub bass, soup spoons, and a kazoo.

Some were the popping noises of tendons snapping back into their proper positions. But others—the loudest, weirdest ones—were from inside my ears.

The men moved on, no doubt muttering about the fool woman who didn't know enough to stay down off a ladder. That was how I felt about her, too, at the moment: ouch.

In the kitchen, Ellie applied first aid consisting of soapy washcloths, clean dry towels, and twenty-year-old Scotch. A couple of Band-Aids completed the repair job, which only made me look a little like Frankenstein's monster.

"Yeeks. All I need now is a pair of steel bolts screwed into my skull." The split in my lip was particularly decorative and there was a purplish bruise coming up on my cheek-bone.

"Yes," Ellie said crisply, putting the first-aid things back into the kitchen drawer. "And you're lucky you *don't* need bolts."

Responding to her tone my black Labrador retriever, Monday, hurried in from the parlor, ears pricked and brown eyes alert for any unhappiness she might abolish with swipes of her wet tongue.

"You could have killed yourself falling off that ladder, you know," Ellie admonished me. "I *wish* you'd let me—"

Wriggling anxiously, Monday threw a body-block against my hip, which wasn't quite broken. Monday believes you can heal almost anything by applying a dog to it, and—mostly—I think so, too.

But next came Cat Dancing, a big apple-headed Siamese with crossed eyes and a satanic expression. "Ellie, I'm fine," I said, trying to sound believable. "I don't need a doctor."

Except maybe a witch doctor if Cat Dancing kept staring at me that way. She was named by my son Sam for reasons I can't fathom, as the only dance that feline ever does will be on my grave. She wouldn't care if I died on the spot as long as my body didn't block the cabinet where we keep cat food. We'd gotten her from my ex-husband Victor, who lives down the street and is also reliable in the driving-me-crazy department.

"Right," Ellie agreed. "Why, you're just a picture of health." *Pick-tcha*: the downeast Maine pronunciation.

When Ellie's Maine twang gets emphatic it's a bad time for me to try persuading her of anything. Fortunately, just then her favorite living creature in the world padded into my kitchen.

"Prill!" Ellie's expression instantly softened as she bent to embrace the newcomer.

A ferocious-looking Doberman pinscher, Prill sported a set of choppers that would have felt right at home in the jawbone of a great white shark. But the snarl on her kisser was really only a sweet, goofy grin. Prill was an earnest if bumbling guardian of balls, bones, dishrags, slippers, hairbrushes, and cats.

Especially cats. Squirming from Ellie's hug, Prill spied Cat Dancing and greeted the little sourpuss by closing her jaws very gently around Cat's head. Then she just stood there wagging her stubby tail while the hair on Cat's back stiffened in outrage and her crossed eyes bugged helplessly.

"Aw," I said. "Isn't that cute?"

Cat emitted a moan keenly calculated to warm the heart of a person who has just pushed the cat off the kitchen table for the millionth, billionth time, and that was about how many times I'd done just that Cat's first week here.

"Prill," Ellie said in gentle admonishment. Days earlier she and I had found the big dog alone and tagless on the town pier, gamely trying to steal a few mackerel heads from the seagulls. No owner had yet claimed her, and I doubted now if anyone would.

Cat's moan rose to an atonal yowl as Sam came in with his dive gear over his shoulder, wearing his new wristwatch which read out in military time. It was, my son had informed me happily, the way the Coast Guard did it. In love with all things watery, this summer he'd signed up for an advanced diving-operations seminar so risky sounding, I disliked thinking about it.

But if he was going to be in and on the water for a living, as seemed inevitable, I guessed as much supervised practice as possible was only prudent. Now he dropped his gear beside the buckets of polyurethane and tins of varnish remover I'd put out a few days earlier. Besides the gutters, I was also refinishing the hall floor that spring.

"Wow, where'd you get that big shiner?" Sam asked with the half-worried, half-admiring interest of a young man who thinks his mother might have been in a recent fistfight. At nineteen, he had his father's dark hair, hazel eyes, and the ravishing grin—also his dad's—of a born heartbreaker.

"Oh, no." I rushed back to the mirror, finding to my dismay that Sam's assessment was correct. An ominous red stain was circling my right eye; soon my face would be wearing two of my least favorite human skin colors: purple and green.

And *speaking* of green . . .

A bolt of fright struck me. "Ellie, come and hold my eyelid out, please, and look under it. I think when I landed I shoved a contact lens halfway into my brain."

One blue eye, one green; oh, blast and damnation. But just as I was really about to panic, Sam's girlfriend Maggie arrived with a tiny disk of green plastic poised on her index finger.

"Did you lose this?" Maggie was a big red-cheeked girl with clear olive skin, liquid brown eyes, and dark, wavy hair that she wore in a thick, glossy braid down her plaid-shirted back.

"I spotted it on the sidewalk," she added. It was Maggie who'd bought Sam the military wristwatch, shopping for it on-line via her computer.

Then she saw me. "Jacobia, what *happened*?"

Well, at least the lens wasn't halfway to my brain. "I was testing Newton's law. The demonstration got away from me." I popped the other lens out. Suddenly I was blue-eyed again. Both eyes. "I'm okay, though, thanks."

Actually parts of me were hurting quite intensely but if I said so, Ellie would insist on taking me to the clinic where Victor was on duty. And rather than submit to my ex-husband's critical speculations on how my injuries had happened, I'd have gone outside and fallen off that ladder all over again.

"I guess I can't be in your eye-color experiment, though," I said. Like Sam, in the fall Maggie would be a sophomore at the University of Maine. "I don't think I should put the lens back in right away," I explained.

The experiment, for a psychology-class project, was to see how long it takes a person to get used to a new eye color. If my own reaction was any indication, the answer was *never*. It was astonishing how jarring the past week had been, seeing a green-eyed alien with my face looking out of the mirror at me.

Disappointment flashed in Maggie's glance, at once replaced by concern. "Oh, I don't care about that silly experiment," she declared.

But she did. She had designed it, proposed it, and with some difficulty gotten it approved, to get credits while staying in Eastport—where Sam was, not coincidentally—for the whole summer. It wasn't easy getting people with normal sight to wear the lenses, either. I was among the six she'd persuaded, the minimum for the project. "It's you I'm worried about," she added.

The girl was going to make someone a wonderful daughter-in-law someday. But it wouldn't be me if Sam didn't hurry up and get his act together. Other mothers fret if their kids get romantically involved too fast, but my son's idea of a proper courtship verged on the glacial.

Luckily in addition to her other sterling qualities Maggie was patient. "You should put something on it," she said. "A cold cloth or some ice."

"That," Ellie interjected acidly, "would mean she'd have to sit still. And you're allergic to that, aren't you, dear?"

Dee-yah. Catching the renewed threat of a clinic visit, I sat down and accepted the ministrations she offered: aspirin, a cloth with cracked ice in it. If I didn't, she might hogtie me and *haul* me to Victor's clinic. She could do it, too; Ellie looks as delicate as a fairy-tale princess but her spine is of tempered steel.

Also, I'd begun noticing that something about Newton's law had hit me in a major way. Sunshine slanting through the tall bare windows of the big old barnlike kitchen wavered at me, and the maple wainscoting's orangey glow was shimmering weirdly.

"Oh," I heard myself say. "Psychedelic."

"Jake?" Ellie said in alarm, reaching for me.

Then I was on the floor, Prill's cold nose snuffling in my ear while Monday nudged my shoulder insistently. Faces peered: Sam, Maggie. And Ellie, her red hair a backlit halo, green eyes gazing frightenedly at me and even the freckles on her nose gone pale.

"Okay, now," I began firmly, but it came out a croak.

". . . call the hospital?" Sam asked urgently.

"Lift your feet up," Maggie advised.

So I did, and felt much better as blood rushed back downhill to my brain again. Newton's law apparently had advantages, although if my brain planned depending on gravity for all of its blood supply, I was still in serious trouble.

Which was how things stood when my husband, Wade Sorenson, walked in. Tall and square-jawed, built like a stevedore, with brush-cut blond hair and grey eyes, he surveyed the scene with an air of calm competence that I found hugely refreshing under the circumstances. And while Sam asked again if he should phone the hospital and Maggie insisted I put my feet up higher and Ellie was all for summoning an ambulance right that instant, Wade said:

"Hey. How're you doing?"

He doesn't freak out, he doesn't screw up; he's the only man in the world into whose arms I would trustingly fall backwards.

Or forwards, for that matter. Crouching, he assessed me, smelling as always of fresh cold air, lime shaving soap, and lanolin hand cream. He'd already noticed that I was breathing and had a blood pressure. The dogs backed off and sat.

"Your pupils are equal," he commented mildly. Meaning that I likely did not have the kind of brain damage that would kill me. Or not right now, anyway.

Victor would have scoffed at the notion of Wade assessing anything medically, but guys who work on boats learn how to eyeball injuries pretty accurately, reluctant to forfeit a day's pay for anything but the probably-fatal. And as Eastport's harbor pilot, guiding freighters safely through the watery maze of downeast Maine's many treacherous navigation hazards, Wade works on boats pretty much the way mountain goats work on mountains.

Eager to lose my invalid status, I sat up. Not a good move. "Hey, hey," Wade cautioned as the room whirled madly. "Take it slow."

"Okay," I said grudgingly. That Newton guy was beginning to be a real pain in my tailpipe. But I was *not* lying down again.

Ellie was just waiting to bushwhack me into the clinic, Sam resembled a six-year-old who wanted his mommy, and Maggie—

Well, Maggie looked solid and unruffled as usual, for which I was grateful since I had an idea I'd be needing her, later.

For one thing I'd planned a special dinner in honor of the tenant who'd moved into my guest room that morning, an aspiring music-video producer filming his first effort here in Eastport.

For another, somewhere between the ladder and the ground I'd had an important epiphany. Harriet Hollingsworth wasn't just missing.

She was dead. And she'd probably been murdered.

"She had no car, no money. No family as far as anyone knows. So how did Harriet drop off the earth without a trace?" I asked a little while later, sitting on the edge of the examining table at the Eastport Health Clinic.

The clinic windows looked out over a tulip bed whose frilly blooms swayed together in the breeze like dancers in a chorus line. Across the street, a row of white cottages sported postage-stamp lawns, picket fences, and American flags. Beyond gleamed Passamaquoddy Bay, blue and tranquil in the spring sunshine, the distant hills of New Brunswick mounding hazily on the horizon.

"Well?" I persisted as Victor shone a penlight into my eye. "Where'd Harriet go? And how?"

The clinic smelled reassuringly of rubbing alcohol and floor wax. But years of marriage to a medical professional had given me a horror of being at the business end of the medical profession. Ellie had brought me here while Wade finished the gutters, knowing that otherwise I'd go right back up the ladder again; if you let any element of old-house fix-up beat you for an instant, the house will get the upper hand in everything. And although I wasn't graceful or sure-footed I was stubborn; so far, this had been enough to keep my old home from collapsing around me.

Victor snapped the penlight off. He'd tested all the things he could think of that might show I was *non compos mentis,* which was what he thought anyway. When I came here from New York and bought the house he'd had a world-class hissy fit, saying that it showed my personality was disintegrating and besides, if I moved so far from Manhattan, how would he see Sam?

I'd said that (a) at least I had a personality, (b) if mine was disintegrating it was under the hammer blows he had inflicted upon it while we were married, and (c) as it was, he hadn't seen Sam for over a year.

That shut him up for a while. But not much later he'd moved to Eastport, too, and established his medical clinic.

"Normal," he pronounced now, sounding disappointed.

"A person needs money to run," I reminded Ellie, "even when money trouble is why they are running in the first place."

"She scavenged, though," Ellie countered. "Cans, return-able bottles. Over time, Harriet could have gotten bus fare to Bangor from that."

"Then what?" I objected. "Start a new life? Harriet was barely managing to hang on to the old one. And what about all that blood at her house?"

"Nobody reliable ever saw any blood," Ellie retorted.

After her boot was found, a story went around that a lot of blood had been seen on the top step of Harriet's porch. By whom and when was a matter of wild speculation, and when I'd gone to see for myself it hadn't been there, so I'd discounted the rumor. But now . . .

"Ahem," Victor said pointedly. He had dark hair with a few threads of grey in it, hazel eyes, and a long jaw clenched in a grim expression. Partly this was his normal look while ferreting out illness and coming up with ways to knock its socks off.

Also, though, it meant I was not regarding him with sufficient awe. "Could you," he requested irritably, "pay just a little more attention to the situation at hand?"

Reluctantly I focused on him. This took some doing, a fact I'd failed to mention when asked about symptoms; blurry vision, I understood, could mean Something Bad. But I was determined not to become a patient if I could help it, and I *had* just taken out the contact lenses . . .

"You might have a mild concussion," he pronounced at last.

"That's all?" Ellie questioned. "She seems quite shaken up."

She was complicating my exit strategy: find the nearest door and scram through it, lickety-split. I rolled my eyes at her to get her to pipe down; the room lurched, spinning a quarter turn.

"The simplest possible explanation is usually correct," Victor intoned. " 'Shaken up,' is as good a description as any."

"So I can go?" I slid hastily off the examining table. If it meant getting out of here right now, I'd have hopped off a cliff.

Which, it turned out, was just exactly what getting off that table felt like. Somewhere were my shoes, making contact with the tiled floor. They seemed far away and not entirely reliable as if connected to my body by long, loose rubber bands.

Feets don't fail me now, I thought earnestly. If I had to, I would take floor-contact on faith.

The way, once upon a time, I'd taken Victor. "Someone would remember if Harriet took the bus," I told Ellie.

Victor frowned. He feels everyone should keep silent until he finishes giving *his* opinions. And as he will finish giving *his* opinions a day or so after his funeral, mostly I ignore him.

But now we were in the land of traumatic head injury, where Victor is king and all he surveys is his to command. He'd gotten reeducated for country doctoring, but back in the city Victor was the one you went to after all the other brain surgeons turned pale and began trembling at the very sight of you.

So this time I listened. "Twenty-four hours of bed rest," he decreed. "Watch for headache, disorientation, and grogginess."

Breathing the same air as Victor made me groggy. We'd had a peace treaty for a while, but now Sam was away at college most of the time and without him to run interference for us, Victor and I were about as compatible as flies and flyswatters. And guess what end of that charming analogy I tended to end up on.

"Great," I said glumly. It wasn't enough that I looked like I'd gone nine rounds with a prizefighter. My X rays were clear but my face was a disaster area, and the click in my shoulder had gone silent, probably on account of the swelling.

But I *couldn't* lie down. I had *things* to do: dinner guests.

And Harriet's murder. First, I had to convince Ellie that it had happened. I had a pretty clear idea of how to do that, too; Harriet hadn't owned much, but she had possessed *one* thing . . .

"Well, maybe not actual bed rest," Victor allowed. "But if you won't take it easy," he added sternly, "I'll admit you to the hospital for forty-eight hours of observation."

An odd look came into his eye, and I realized he could make good on this threat if he came up with dire enough reasons. Wade might believe Victor, if he sounded sincere; Ellie, too.

And Victor was good at sincere. "I will," I vowed, "take it easy. Um, and is it okay to put the contact lenses back in?"

Because if I could, Maggie's project might get saved. Victor looked put-upon.

"Oh, I suppose," he replied waspishly. "It looks bad but the orbital processes were spared, the swelling's minimal, not *in* the eye at all, and you have no signs of neurological dysfunction."

Never mind if your face looks like road kill; if you can follow his moving finger with your eyes and touch your nose with your own, you're good to go. "But why in heaven's name are you participating in amateur-hour science?" he wanted to know.

"Thank you, Victor," I cut him off. It's yet another of his talents, making me feel like a rebellious child.

Leaving Ellie to settle up at the business desk I made for the exit before he could decide to prescribe a clear liquid diet. Maybe I'd learn later that I'd knocked an essential screw loose and it needed replacing right away, before my brains fell out.

But I doubted it. And I doubted even more that the gleam in his eye had been benevolent, when he realized that if only for an instant there, he'd had me in his power.

Again.

So I was getting the hell out of Dodge.

My name is Jacobia Tiptree and once upon a time I was a hot-shot New York financial expert, a greenback-guru with offices so plush you could lose a small child in the depth of the broadloom on the floor of my consulting area. I was the one rich folks came to for help on the most (to them) important topics in the world:

(A) Getting wealthier, and

(B) Getting even wealthier than that.

Everything was about money. Fallen in love? Break out the prenuptial agreements. Somebody died? The family is frantic not with grief for the dearly departed but because the old skinflint stashed his loot in an unbreakable charitable remainder trust.

Loot being the operative term; most of my clients were so crooked their limousines should've flown the Jolly Roger. But I didn't care, mostly on account of having started out with no loot whatsoever, myself. Until I was a teenager my idea of the lush life was glass in the windows, shoes that fit, and not too much woodsmoke from the cracks in the stove chimney, so I could read.

At fifteen I ran from the relatives who were raising me, trusting in my wits and a benevolent universe to pave my path, which is why it was lucky I turned out to have a few wits about me. Getting through Penn Station I had the sense I'd have been safer in a war zone; men sidled up to me, crooking their fingers, weaving and crooning. In my pale shiny face and hick clothes, lugging a cheap suitcase and in possession of the enormous sum of twenty dollars, I must've looked just like all the other fresh young chickens, ready for plucking.

Fortunately, however, all my cousins had been boys. Something about me must have said I knew precisely where to aim my kneecap, and the nasty men skedaddled. Before I knew it (well, a couple of weeks after I hopped off the Greyhound, actually) I was living in a tenement near Times Square where I'd found the best job a girl from my background could imagine: waitress in a Greek diner.

My feet were swollen, my hair stank of fryer grease, and in the first couple of days I learned thirty new ways to buzz off a lurking creep-o. Meager wages and no tips; Ari's Dineraunt wasn't a tipping kind of place, except on the horses. But it was all-you-could-eat and most of the other girls didn't enjoy the food. Too foreign, they said, turning up their well-nourished noses.

Which left more for me. Short ribs and stuffed grape

leaves, moussaka and lamb stew; ordinarily the owner was tighter with a dime than a wino with a pint of Night Train, but for some reason Ari Kazantzakis thought it was funny to watch me shoving baklava into my mouth.

Maybe it was because he had enough family memories of real hunger to know it when he saw it. Ari had a photo of Ellis Island behind the counter, and one of the Statue of Liberty in his fake-wood-paneled office. The tenement where I lived was just like the one his parents had moved into when they got here. Or exactly the one.

Whatever. Anyway, one day Ari's accountant didn't show up and the next day they found him floating in the East River, full of bullet holes. Suddenly it wasn't all sweet-meats and balalaikas at the Dineraunt anymore. More like hand-wringing and sobbing violins until I said I was good at math and that when I wasn't slinging hash I was taking accounting courses. By then I'd gotten a high school equivalency and talked my way into night school.

I'd figured it was the only way I would ever get near real money, which was true but not in the way I'd expected. Two days later I was carrying a black bag, the one the accountant had been expected to pick up and deliver. That was how I got to know the men at the social club, several of whom later became my clients.

They thought it was hilarious, a skinny-legged girl with big eyes and a hillbilly accent running numbers money. But they didn't think it was so funny a few weeks later, when every other runner in the city got nabbed in an organized crime crackdown.

All but me. Like I said, I'd had boy cousins, and if there was anything I was good at besides math, it was evasive action. A few years later when I'd finished school, gotten married, begun solo money management, and had a baby, one of the guys from the social club came to my office.

He wore an Armani suit, a Bahamas tan, and Peruggi shoes. The diamond in his pinky ring was so big you could have used it to anchor a yacht. His expression was troubled;

they always were on people with money woes. And this guy's familiar hound-dog face was the saddest that I had ever encountered. But when he saw me behind my big oak desk, he started to laugh.

Me, too. All the way to the bank.

And there you have it: my own personal journey from rags to riches. Victor's another story, not such a pleasant one; first came the hideous coincidence of our having the same uncommon last name. At the time, I regarded this happenstance as serendipity. And I'll admit I was still full of bliss when our son Sam appeared. But soon enough began the late-night calls from lovelorn student nurses whom I informed, at first gently and later I suppose somewhat cruelly, that the object of their affections was married and had a child. And in the end I got fed up with the city, too.

I'd thrived in it but when Sam hit twelve it began devouring him: drugs. Bad companions. And our divorce half killed him. So I chucked it all and bought an old house that needed everything, on Moose Island seven miles off the coast of downeast Maine.

It's quiet: church socials and baked-bean suppers, concerts in the band shell on the library lawn when the weather is warm. There's the Fourth of July in summer, a Salmon Festival in fall, and high school basketball during the school year, of course.

But that's it. Not much happens in Eastport.

Unless you count the occasional mysterious bloody murder.